THE EMPTY QUARTER

Harry St. John Bridger Philby (1885–1960) was one of the most dedicated and respected of British desert explorers. As chief of the British political mission to central Arabia from 1917 to 1918, he carried out extensive exploration in many fields, and was the first European to visit the southern provinces of Najd. But his main goal, inspired by his love for Arabia, was to cross the Rub' al Khali desert, known as the 'Empty Quarter', the most savage and impenetrable desert of southern Arabia.

It was not until 1932 that he could fulfil his dream. With the patronage and assistance of King Abdul Aziz idn Sa'ud, the King of Arabia, Philby was finally given permission to make his epic journey. He kept records of all he saw and accomplished throughout the expedition—from catalogues of plant and insect life to documentation on obscure desert tribes—and, on his return, presented the mass of material he had accumulated to King Abdul Aziz. *The Empty Quarter* is the distillation of those unique records, combining a passion for Arabia and her people with critical analysis. The collection of documents was ultimately bequeathed by the King to the British Museum.

First published in 1933, *The Empty Quarter* is reprinted for the first time in paperback, and includes the author's original appendices and introduction. St. Philby also wrote several other books about desert exploration, including *The Heart of Arabia*, *Arabia of the Wahhabis* and *Forty Years in the Wilderness*.

On Sledge and Horseback to Outcast Siberian Lepers
by Kate Marsden
Introduction by Eric Newby

With an Eye to the Future by Osbert Lancaster
Introduction by Richard Boston

Earls of Creation by James Lees-Milne

The Rule of Taste by John Steegman

Ghastly Good Taste by John Betjeman

Nollekens and his Times by J. T. Smith

Adventures of a Wanderer by Sydney Walter Powell
Introduction by Geoffrey Powell

Isles of Illusion by Asterisk
Introduction by Gavin Young

George, Memoirs of a Gentleman's Gentleman
by Nina Slingsby Smith

Italian Hours by Henry James
Introduction by Tamara Follini

Revolt in the Desert by T. E. Lawrence

Mayhew's London Underworld
Edited and introduced by Peter Quennell

The cover illustration is taken from the collection of paintings at the
Mathaf Gallery, 24 Motcomb Street, London SW1.

To my
WIFE and MOTHER
who bore the brunt of my long travail
through anxious years
I dedicate this record of my wanderings
in the
EMPTY QUARTER.

Inn' al harimu atyab ma 'andina hast—for verily
women are the best of all that we possess.

From the sayings of FALIH ABU JA'SHA.

THE
EMPTY QUARTER

being a description of the
Great South Desert of Arabia
known as Rub' al Khali

H. ST. JOHN B. PHILBY

Century
London Melbourne Auckland Johannesburg

First published by Constable & Co. Ltd

© Century Hutchinson 1986

All rights reserved

This edition first published in 1986 by Century,
an imprint of Century Hutchinson Ltd,
Brookmount House, 62–65 Chandos Place, London, WC2B 4NW

Century Hutchinson Publishing Group (Australia) Pty Ltd
PO Box 496, 16–22 Church Street, Hawthorn, Melbourne, Victoria 3122

Century Hutchinson Group (NZ) Ltd
PO Box 40–086, 32–34 View Road, Glenfield, Auckland 10

Century Hutchinson Group (SA) Pty Ltd
PO Box 337, Berglvei 2012, South Africa

ISBN 0 7126 1282 3

Printed in Great Britain by
Richard Clay (The Chaucer Press) Ltd,
Bungay, Suffolk

FOREWORD

MUCH of this volume was prepared in the rough as I wandered from day to day amid the sands of the Great Desert. But expert examination of the material of all kinds brought back by me from the Empty Quarter has inevitably necessitated the recasting of the whole work, which, as it now appears, is wholly the product—under pressure of modern publishing conditions—of ' holiday ' months in a remote corner of Wales. For such faults and repetitions as may yet remain after careful pruning of proofs I can only crave the reader's indulgence. And to those who have assisted me in the preparation of this record of a land which for long years I have regarded as the chief goal of my ambitions, I tender my grateful and cordial thanks.

Apart from the successful accomplishment of a task conceived and attempted—which is reward enough in itself,—the modern explorer is more fortunate than his predecessors in finding a host of eager and expert minds ready against his return to pounce upon his often haphazard collections and to separate the grain from the chaff through the sieve of their knowledge and experience. The critical appreciation of such as these—their simmering enthusiasm over a new bug or beast, to say nothing of a meteorite crater !—is sweeter than the plaudits of a mob. And Arabia is still so little known to the world at large that it flatters the labours of any reasonably inquisitive visitor.

At the end of my own work I have placed, in a series of appendices, the reports or results emanating from the study of my material by numerous experts in the various subjects. The work of each is duly acknowledged there and in other pages. I need not here, therefore, weary the reader at the outset with a catalogue of names, but I would invite him (or her) to study the appendices with diligence if he (or she) would have a proper understanding of the mysterious Empty Quarter of Arabia—in detail as well as in the mass.

To Dr. L. J. Spencer and his colleagues of the British Museum, who have provided some of the appendices ; to others who have placed at my disposal material used both in the appendices and in my own text ; and to Dr. C. Tate Regan and the authorities of the British Museum generally : my cordial acknowledgments and best thanks are especially due. It is gratifying to me to think that all the material collected by me during this expedition has been presented to the British Museum by His Majesty King 'Abdul 'Āziz ibn Sa'ud, the King of Arabia, to whom I had the honour of making it over on my return from the desert and to whose princely patronage and assistance I owe all that I have been able to achieve in the Empty Quarter.

For the map which accompanies this volume and for the computation of all my instrumental records ; for much other assistance and for the encouragement and appreciation which no explorer, outgoing or returning, seeks in vain : my gratitude goes out to the Royal Geographical Society. Where all or many have helped it is perhaps invidious to mention names, but Admiral Sir William Goodenough and Mr. A. R. Hinks have been too kind and helpful to be omitted from my catalogue of benefactors, while Mr. A. R. Reeves and Mr. H. F. Milne have rendered me services too important to be forgotten.

To several others, whose names are duly mentioned in the appropriate places, my thanks are due for suggestions on many topics, on whose discussion I could not have ventured without their aid. If I do not detail their names here it is not for want of gratitude, but I must leave them individually for specific mention in later pages while thanking them generally in the person of my old chief, Major-General Sir Percy Z. Cox, who has done me the honour of reading through my proofs and making some suggestions for the improvement of my work.

And, finally, I owe a special debt of thanks to my wife, who enabled me to complete the text of this volume within a reasonable time by undertaking the whole of the labour involved in typing its pages from my scribbled manuscript sheets.

H. St J. B. PHILBY.

MECCA, *November*, 1932.

CONTENTS

APPENDICES

INTRODUCTION

WHEN all is said and done, the Empty Quarter would seem to be far from justifying the lurid colours in which it has been painted by some European travellers, and in which it is always painted by the Arabs of settled tracts who have never been within view of it, though the crossing of it is an adventure not to be lightly undertaken by the uninitiated.[1]

For fifteen years my life has been dominated by a single idea, a single ambition—rather perhaps a single obsession. Faithfully, fanatically and relentlessly through all those years I have stalked the quarry which now, in these pages, lies before the reader—dissected, belabelled and described. I have not, perhaps, accomplished all that I planned to do, but I have done enough to set my soul at rest, released from its long bondage. Nor, again, have I been alone, or even first, in the field. The honours of priority have gone to another that outwent me in the race ; and Bertram Thomas deservedly wears the laurels of a pioneer. I have but gleaned where he reaped, though perchance it was no mere coincidence that we had laboured together—*Arcades ambo*—in the same vineyard of Ammon before he went to Omman. As the Arab poet sang of old :

'Twas I that learn'd him in the archer's art ;
At me, his hand grown strong, he launched his dart.

My own inspiration came from one of the great masters of Arabian lore. It was on January 6th, 1918—just after my first crossing of the Arabian peninsula from the Persian Gulf to the Red Sea—that I first met the late Dr. D. G. Hogarth. He was disguised as a mere Commander of the Royal Navy, while I wore the flowing robes of an Arab Shaikh. Our meeting was in the spacious mess-room of the British politico-military Mission at Jidda, in which were merged the British Consulate and Agency destined, in due course and for reasons at that moment unforseeable and unthinkable, to be transformed into a Legation. I was a stranger within the gate, the envoy of a ' hostile ' camp, a

[1] *The Heart of Arabia*, vol. ii, p. 217.

voice crying in the wilderness—a new and unknown chal-
lenger in the breathless tourney of Arabian exploration.
Yet none had crossed Arabia before me except one—Captain
G. F. Sadlier, my predecessor by a hundred years.

Dr. Hogarth, on the other hand, was the right-hand man
of the British Government in all matters of Arabian import.
Director of the wartime Arab Bureau at Cairo, he was *the*
acknowledged and pre-eminent authority on Arabian affairs.
And as far back as 1904 he had, under the title of *The Penetration of Arabia*, published an exhaustive and inspiring sum-
mary of all that had been done in the field of Arabian exploration from the days of Nearchus and Aelius Gallus up
to the beginning of the twentieth century. The gaps he had
noted in our knowledge of Arabia were still for the most part
gaps after the lapse of fourteen years. And one of them was
perhaps the largest blank on the map of the earth outside
the Polar regions. He was content to contemplate its vast
silence without encouraging rash adventurers to their doom.
The ends of science could be served as well in other ways.
If oxygen could surmount the summit of Everest, the aeroplane or even the motor car would surely expose the emptiness of the Empty Quarter in all good time. But he would
perhaps scarcely have credited a forecast that within fourteen years more the Rub' al Khali would have yielded up
its secrets—not once, but twice—to ordinary travellers
equipped with no means of locomotion that has not been
at the service of explorers since the beginning of time. Yet
no one desired more intensely to know the exact nature of
that great emptiness, and the suppressed twinkle of his
cautious cynicism was more than a spur of inspiration. More
than anything I regret that he himself had passed beyond
the veil before the veil was drawn from an earthly mystery of
whose significance he would have been the ideal interpreter.

From pleasant weeks of closest contact with Dr. Hogarth
at Jidda and in Egypt I passed that year back into Arabia
and down into its southern depths round the great Wadi
of the Dawasir, whence I had to turn back regretfully on
June 6th, 1918, having ' to rest content with what had been
achieved and the hope of satisfying some day the insatiable

craving within me to penetrate the recesses of that Empty Quarter, whose northern boundary I had now skirted along its whole length from east to west, from the Hasa to the Wadi.' [1]

I had then unveiled a part of the unknown south, but only enough to whet my appetite for more. From my companions —and particularly from one Jabir ibn Faraj of the great Murra tribe—I had heard of mysterious ruins in the heart of the further sands and of a great block of iron as large as a camel. And through their spectacles I had had a glimpse of the Empty Quarter. But that was all, and I knew that an opportunity for further investigation of those mysteries would not soon recur—if ever. ' I hope some day,' I wrote, ' that another more fortunate than I may be able to test the veracity of my informers.' [2] That hope at least was partly fulfilled in the exploits of Major Cheesman (1924) and Mr. Thomas (1931), and I could scarcely expect that between them they might have left me anything to do when my own turn should come in due course.

Meanwhile, though unsuccessful, I had not been idle. The vicissitudes of life and work had carried me this way and that, and very nearly carried me out of Arabia for ever, but the magnet held the needle. And to Arabia I went back in the autumn of 1924 to try a throw with fate. To that effort and its consequences I sacrificed everything—the security of an orthodox career and the rest of it. But I did it without regrets.

During the summer of that same year Dr. Hogarth had been elected President of the Royal Geographical Society and I had become a member of its council. The coincidence of our association in a common task seemed to me the best of omens for the enterprise which had so long monopolised my dreams. The unveiling of the Rub' al Khali in his first year of office by one whom he had himself, though unwittingly, inspired to the effort would be a fitting memorial to the presiding genius of Arabian exploration. And to that end I bent my best endeavours.

But not alone. Alone I could have done nothing for want

[1] *The Heart of Arabia*, vol. ii, p. 216.   [2] *Ibid*. p. 222.

of funds. And it so happened that at that time my friend, Mrs. Rosita Forbes, the heroine of an arduous journey through the Libyan Desert to the then almost unknown,[1] though now notorious, oasis of Kufra, had bethought herself of the Empty Quarter in her search for new worlds to conquer. We joined forces and concerted our plans together, while it was she that secured the necessary financial backing for the joint enterprise.

By the autumn everything was ready except Arabia itself, which was rocking to the music of a revolution. Without warning the pent-up fires of Wahhabi Najd had burst forth in a mighty eruption along the borders of the Sharifian kingdom. The massacre at Taif had shocked the world in September, and a month later Mecca, deserted by its king, surrendered peacefully to the fanatics. It seemed but a matter of days to the fall of Jidda and Madina, while, with Ibn Sa'ud dominating all that mattered of Arabia, the omens seemed propitious enough for the prosecution of our plans. Only a measure of secrecy was necessary in the circumstances lest those plans should be divined and frustrated by sympathetic and well-meaning British officials.

Bahrain was the agreed rendezvous, and I set out alone about the middle of October. On the train carrying me across France I met Dr. Hogarth, who may have fathomed the purpose of my journey but kept his counsel. I saw him but little thereafter, for he was soon struck down by the malady which carried him in the end to his grave. And I never knew what he thought of my futile endeavour, if he ever knew its objective. Meanwhile at Marseilles, having already in London secured a ticket and berth to Bandar 'Abbas, I had boarded a vessel of name more than auspicious—S.S. *Registan*, ' the land of sand ! '

At Suez, on hearing the latest news from Arabia, I changed my plans, and a few days later I landed at Jidda as the guest of His Majesty King 'Ali, who had succeeded to the remnants of his father's throne on the latter's abdication and hasty departure. For a moment it seemed that peace might be restored on reasonable terms. But the die was cast other-

[1] It had previously been visited only by Gerhard Rohlfs in 1879.

wise by the folly of the defenders, and the arrival of Ibn Sa'ud himself at Mecca early in December was the signal for the investment of Jidda. It scarcely seemed that the place could hold out a fortnight with its ill-officered, ill-fed, ill-armed army of mercenaries drawn from the unemployed rabble of Syria and Palestine by the illusory prospect of pay.

From my point of view time was precious, though I could still afford to wait some weeks for the developments which might forward my immediate objective. But Fate proved churlish, and Jidda struck me down with its foul dysentery. As soon as I could move, I fled away to meet my colleague at Aden ; and Rosita Forbes, nothing daunted by the collapse of our plans, set forth to explore Abyssinia while I returned home—a sick and disappointed man. My first attempt on the Empty Quarter had ended in futility.

For seven years I had laboured in vain as Jacob of old for Rachel. In place of the Rub' al Khali I had found a home by the green waters of the Red Sea—to toil other seven years for the bride of my constant desire. And the great peace of Islam slowly and surely descended upon me, enveloped me, who had known no peace before, in the austere mantle of Wahhabi philosophy which, tilting at the iniquities of the ungodly, had imposed a peace ' that passeth all understanding ' upon a country which since the beginning of time had known no peace but that of death and desolation.

Mecca became my home to remain so, *inshallah*, to the end of my days ; and I was admitted to the privilege of daily intimacy with the Great King, who had been my hero since the first days of our easy friendship—than whom indeed I know no man more worthy to be called great. During thirty years he has done for Arabia what none has been able to do during thirty centuries. *Si monumentum quaeris, respice* ! But this is not the place to speak of the achievements of Ibn Sa'ud.

My homage and faithful allegiance he has ever had—the tribute of my admiration. But now I lay at his feet another tribute—of thanks and heartfelt gratitude. In December, 1930, I accompanied the royal cavalcade into Arabia, even to Riyadh ; and there the king, knowing all too well the secret longing of my soul, raised my hopes to the zenith with talk of an expedition to the Empty Quarter. He was minded to examine the uttermost recesses of his far-flung empire ; and in me he had a convenient instrument for the mapping and scientific investigation necessary for the vindication of his claim to rule the restless sands. I knew that Bertram Thomas had left Masqat and landed at Dhufar for a final effort on the virgin waste. I had no doubt that he would succeed and I was impatient to be off. The necessary preparations went forward in consultation with 'Abdullah ibn Jiluwi, governor of the Hasa. And early in January, 1931, my hopes were dashed to the ground by the advice tendered by him to his sovereign. He was engaged in certain projects for the extension of his administrative influence along the southern borderlands and did not want to be saddled with responsibility for an expedition of a somewhat different kind. A year's delay would not be of serious moment. So they all thought except myself. Thomas was already at Shanna, and on January 16th, when we left Riyadh on the return journey to Mecca, he was already half-way across the sands. A month later he was through with it, though it was not till March 6th that I knew the full bitterness of my own disappointment. He had won the race, and it only remained for me to finish the course.

My plans remained unchanged for the following winter. The king's word stood, and in November I was back again at Riyadh. But the weeks passed by with never a word from the king to suggest that he was even thinking of the Empty Quarter. Daily in the royal train I hunted bustard and gazelles in the desert round the Wahhabi capital, while each night Jupiter, consorting with the Lion, mocked my impatience with its solemn query. To be or not to be ? That was the daily question as I woke each morn to the call of prayer.

The strain of possessing myself in patience till the word of fate should be spoken had become almost unbearable when, one evening about the middle of December, we were sitting in the parlour of the palace. Vague talk there was of an European tour for the Prince Faisal. Would it not be pleasant, suggested one of the great officers of the court, to accompany His Highness thither and, perchance, to visit your own folk again ? It is, forsooth, long since you last saw your own country. It is not of Europe, I replied, that I am thinking these days. No, said the king, and his words nearly took my breath away, but we will send Philby to the Empty Quarter ? Would you go thither ? Would I not indeed ? Then, he continued, there is no harm in your going. May God requite you with weal! I replied. Pleasanter words I have not heard these many months.

So there was an end to the long tension. We spoke for a day or two of necessary matters connected with the proposed expedition, and then came the day for which I had waited so long. I am minded, said the king, to go down to the Hasa before long—perhaps in a fortnight or a little later. You could go down with me and start from there. But if you would go earlier, there is no harm in your starting to-morrow. I ride forth then to Khafs for the shooting. You may come to the first night's camp and thence go down in your car to the Hasa. I will give you letters to Ibn Jiluwi, and he will arrange everything as you wish. Would you then go to-morrow or wait till you can go with me ? If there is no harm in it, I replied, I would go even to-morrow. Good ! said the king, so be it.

On the evening of Christmas Day I arrived at Hufuf to spend, as it proved, exactly a fortnight in the Hasa. Ibn Jiluwi sent forth his messengers east and west and south and north to summon the necessary array, while his son, Sa'ud, took over all responsibility for the commissariat arrange-ments. Meanwhile I explored the great oasis from end to end, visiting the northern palm-groves of 'Uyun and mapping the whole district, whose gardens I ransacked for their lovely butterflies and other insect denizens.

The old year passed into the new, and my impatience grew as the days followed each other without outward and visible sign of progress in the necessary preparations. A strange and ominous silence seemed to have descended upon the pro-ceedings of Ibn Jiluwi, and my friends eyed me askance as a fool seeking perdition. The suspense again became horrible, and I sought to soothe my nerves with a visit to 'Uqair on the sea-coast. Thus on January 4th, after a strenuous journey by car across the heavy dunes of the coastal sand-belt, I had the satisfaction of completing my second crossing of Arabia. And on my return to Hufuf next day I found myself on the very threshold of the Promised Land!

PART I

JAFURA AND JABRIN

CHAPTER I

THE CURTAIN RISES

MY nerves had been stretched so long and mercilessly on the rack of prevarication and disappointment that my brain reacted but sluggishly to the shock that awaited me on our return from 'Uqair. A messenger came from Ibn Jiluwi. The Amir salutes you, he said, the camels and men are ready for you, and you may start when you will. It was good news, indeed, but I was far from ready. I had grown accustomed to delay, but never thought that I myself should be responsible for it. Now there was not a minute to lose as there were rumours that the King would be coming to Hufuf almost immediately. His arrival and presence would inevitably divert attention from the business of launching my expedition. But the fact remained that I was not ready. Some of my indispensable gear was, indeed, marooned with my car in the deep soft sand of the heavy dune country within a mile of 'Uqair. I had gone thither with one of the Qusaibi brothers to meet another of them expected from Bahrain. I had thus completed my second crossing of the Arabian peninsula—this time by motor car—from sea to sea. I had been glad of the opportunity of examining and measuring up the ruin-field which I cannot but believe to be the site of the ancient sea-port of Gerrha. And not the least pleasing experience of my short sojourn had been a meeting with my host of 1917, the governor of 'Uqair, 'Abdul Rahman ibn Khairallah. You have grown thin, he said to me, but praise be to God, that has guided you into the right way. He had grown old and grey and very mellow. We talked pleasantly of old times, sipping coffee and tea. And what, I asked, of Ibn Suwailim, who was governor of Qatif in those days ? He died a few years ago, he replied, God have mercy on him !

His son, Muhammad, succeeded him but was transferred elsewhere—it is two years ago now—and Ibn Thunaian was sent to Qatif in his stead. By God! I would that I might be transferred from here, but the service of the King is my only desire. God is bounteous. His words struck a strange chord of memory. Fifteen years ago in this very same parlour he had uttered the selfsame words. I reminded him of the coincidence. Yes, he replied, I am still here after all these years, during which I have never left the place but for an occasional visit to the Hasa and last year, when the King permitted me to go to Mecca for the pilgrimage—praise be to God. Why, all these years I have never even been to Bahrain. What a contrast, I thought, between his tranquil life in the tenure of a virtual sinecure and the storm-tossed years that had been my lot since our last meeting !

Next day I had plunged my car into a veritable crevasse of soft sand and had to leave my luggage to be recovered later on, while I made a rough journey over the billowing dunes of that sand-ocean on the running-board of another car already overloaded with the household paraphernalia, including the wife, children and several female attendants, of the Hufuf doctor.

That was January 5th. It was imperative to recover my cameras and other stuff from the derelict car, but there were no cars likely to be going in that direction. There was nothing for it but to send my servant, an ineffective, purblind youth of Riyadh called 'Abdul Latif—I had decided to dispense with his services, which would have been useless to me on a serious journey,—by camel to fetch the gear and bring it direct to some suitable rendezvous in the desert. That would be better than delaying my own start, and Sa'ud, the eldest son of Ibn Jiluwi, to whom had been consigned the task of arranging the commissariat and other practical details of my expedition, proved more than helpful. A rendezvous was duly arranged and 'Abdul Latif —whom I had rather unwisely paid all his dues—went off with a guide to fetch my stuff to Bir al Nabit, a desert well which we should be visiting. To anticipate the course of events, the guide kept the tryst faithfully—and profitably for himself—with my valued

possessions in his saddle-bags, but he came alone. 'Abdul
Latif, sorely tempted by the prospect of seeing something of
the great world, had taken ship from 'Uqair to view the
wonders and women of Bahrain with the proceeds of his
service to me up to date. I saw him no more.

With Sa'ud I agreed that the men and camels allotted to
the great adventure should proceed the following day (January 6th) to the wells of Dulaiqiya and there await my
arrival by car on the morrow. So all was well. I was left to
work up to a programme that was satisfactorily precise, and
I had had the good fortune—thanks to Ibrahim ibn Mu'am-
mar, an old friend from the wonderful days of 1918—to find
an excellent substitute for 'Abdul Latif in Sa'd ibn 'Uthman,
a native of the dour township of Majma'a in Sudair, a cockney
youth of semi-servile origin—for his mother had been his
father's slave—with some experience of travel in foreign
parts. He had seen Bombay and Basra and, in the service
of Ibrahim, he had gone through the campaign against Faisal
al Duwish and had taken part in the historic scenes that had
attended the meeting of King Ibn Sa'ud and King Faisal on
board the ships of His Britannic Majesty in the Persian Gulf
in February, 1930. He was, therefore, no ordinary serving
man. He had an active, well-seasoned brain and he had
ambitions. He regarded me as a god-sent stepping-stone to
the realisation of some of the latter—roughly speaking he
regarded wealth and a plurality of wives as a desirable foundation for ultimate bliss—and I reciprocated his flattering
impression of my possibilities by regarding him as a potential
superman.

Sa'dan—to give him forthwith the pet-name by which he
was generally known—did his best to create a favourable
first impression. With the privity of his former employer he
ransacked the Government stores for everything that might
conduce to my comfort and his own—money, clothes, soap,
biscuits, sweetmeats, Eau de Cologne and what not ! By the
evening of January 6th the eight wooden kerosene-cases,
fitted with hinged lids and padlocks, in which I had decided
to carry all my paraphernalia, were ready packed with the
strangest assortment of things necessary and unnecessary.

But it was something that they were packed and ready, and that was largely due to him. He was certainly efficient and enjoyed the bustle and importance of his new rôle, but when he talked of the Empty Quarter there was a tremor in his voice and his spirits sank leadenly to the region of his soles. It was long since he had last seen his wife, whom he had left with their little son at Mecca when he had accompanied Ibrahim on an important mission connected with the crown-lands in the Hasa. Would he ever see her again ? His courage ebbed and flowed in turns—but the die was cast.

Meanwhile, in the intervals of packing and preparation, I paid a visit to the new mobile wireless station in the great fortress of Ibrahim Pasha to check my half-chronometer watches by the time-signal from distant Mogadicio [1]; and called on 'Abdullah ibn Jiluwi to take formal leave of him. With him I found the appointed leader and deputy-leader of my expedition. In the presence of the three of us the governor of the Hasa wrote out the drafts of certain letters which might be of use to us in the desert. While a secretary was preparing fair copies thereof on the typewriter for his signature he turned to those to whom he was about to commit me for better or for worse until we should come again to the haunts of civilised men. He had doubtless discussed everything with them in detail already. His present speech was therefore little more than a formality enacted for my benefit, but it was characteristically impressive. Look you, he said, addressing Zayid al Munakhkhas, a man of the Bani Hajir tribe but more than half town-bred and a myrmidon of long standing in the governor's service, look you, this man is dear to the King and dear to us all ; see that you have a care of him. See that he wants for nothing within your power to provide. You will take him to Jafura, even to Salwa and Sikak and Anbak until you come to Jabrin. In all things serve him as you would serve me. Thence you will go to Maqainama, and beyond that is beyond my ken. He speaks of Wabar. You will take him thither—you have guides with you who know the desert in those parts. You will take him

[1] More properly Mukdishu in Italian Somaliland.

to the Hadhramaut if you can find the people to whom I have
addressed these letters—Saif ibn Tannaf and Ibn Kalut, I
forget his name, and others. See that you avoid danger, but
take him whither he would go. For his life you answer with
yours. Forget not that. And when you are come thither
your return is across the desert, even the Empty Quarter, to
Wadi Dawasir. Your companions are already gone out to
Dulaiqiya. You yourselves will ride with this man to-morrow
in the motors. So in the keeping of God, but see that you do
all my bidding, and more. As he ended two men strode into
the audience-chamber, messengers from the King. They
smiled knowingly, sympathetically at me. They were
Ibrahim ibn Jumai'a and Sa'd al Yumaini, who had con-
ducted me down to Wadi Dawasir in 1918. A good omen!
I thought as I rose to bid the governor farewell, kissing him
on the forehead and grasping the hand that had thus launched
us on the great adventure of my dreams.

We went out from the presence and, making a tryst for
the morrow, parted. Everything was ready. Before lying
down to sleep I skinned a Gerbil captured at 'Uqair. It was
my last night under a roof and my slumbers were disturbed
by vague nightmare visions of ill-skinned rats and refractory
theodolites.

I awoke at chilly dawn. Nobody else seemed to be up, but
very soon messengers began to pester me at ten-minute
intervals, bidding me in the governor's name to make haste.
The cars allotted to myself, my companions and my baggage
were wanted to carry others as soon as possible to the King's
camp in Wadi Faruq. The final details of my packing did
not take long, and then there was breakfast to get through.
The necessary bounties had then to be distributed among
those who had served me during my sojourn at Hufuf, while
my boxes were being carried out to the lorry. At 9 a.m. a
small party of friends had assembled around the cars to bid
us farewell, rather dismally and forebodingly. They scarcely
expected to see us again, but that was no business of theirs.
They soon passed out of sight as we rounded a corner of the
narrow main street of the Kut.

It was a cold, raw morning; and a low fog hung over the

cheerful palm-groves as we passed through the dark arch of
the 'Victory Gate,' by which Ibn Sa'ud had entered Hufuf
in triumph after the surrender of the Turkish garrison in
1913. We skirted the city walls and swung out into the
desert and the mist, which limited our vision to about 200
yards and blotted out the landmarks of the world we knew
as we passed through the veil into the unknown. I felt as a
bird must feel when released from its cage, a little awed and
bewildered but happy. The heavy shackles of years had
fallen from my soul. The grim bogey that had haunted me
for so long now beckoned me into the Promised Land. The
great adventure had begun.

Mechanically I noted the mileage of the few recognisable
points on our route—the great fort of Khizam, the Thulai-
thiya garden in which the Qusaibi family had installed a
pumping machine without much success, and some derelict
wells whose naked superstructures loomed through the surrounding gloom like great gibbets. Behind us in the town I
pictured the busy market scene of the Suq al Khamis, which I
had attended the previous Thursday wondering how long I
was yet to be detained amid the unessential pleasures of Hasa
civilisation. Sa'dan, shivering with cold and fright, cowered
silently in the back seat between Zayid and 'Abdullah ibn
Ma'addi, while I sat in front with the driver. The car raced
along over the bare limestone plain, undulating and lightly
covered with sand, until, crossing the gravel patch of Hidba
Talla'iya, we passed into the desert tract of Al Ghuwaiba,
a sandy expanse lightly dusted with grit and dotted with
Shinan[1] bushes, each set on a typical tuffet of sand. The
driver pointed out a car-track diverging from ours in the
direction of the Jabal Arba' hillocks, usually a conspicuous
feature of the scene but now invisible. In their highly
eroded cliffs are numerous caves much frequented by the
governor of the Hasa and his friends during their excursions
after gazelle and bustard. The meandering car-tracks of
such expeditions told of many an exciting chase in the sandy
wilderness which becomes, however, impracticable for

[1] For the identity of all plants mentioned in the text see Appendix.

motoring beyond the line of the *Sabkha*[1] channel which we
were to cross during the afternoon.

Suddenly a mud wall appeared out of the mist in front of
us with a few palms. We had covered the 10 miles to
Dulaiqiya, and it would be long indeed before any of us again
rode in a motor car. We came to a halt and dismounted. A
dozen figures surged out of the fog to greet us and unload the
lorry. They had been cowering for warmth over a camp fire
in front of a double-poled tent. Another tent, single-poled,
circular and spacious—to say nothing of quite an attractive
scheme of mural decoration—stood a little apart, destined for
myself. A cauldron was set upon a second fire to give us in due
course our first meal of plain boiled rice liberally mixed with
the clarified butter called *Samn*.[2] Meanwhile I went through
the rather solemn business of being introduced to the companions of my coming wanderings. Sa'dan I had known for
a week or so. Zayid and Ibn Ma'addi, who, besides being
deputy-leader, was also the chaplain of the party, I had met
the previous afternoon. The rest I had never seen or heard of
before. It was perhaps better so. We started all round
without prejudices or preconceived notions. Some of them
shook me warmly by the hand, others saluted me with the
kiss of peace. They looked rough enough and tough enough for
anything, but at the moment they were all miserably cold. The
temperature in the open at mid-day, when the sun was trying
feebly to show himself through the mist, was only 50° Fahr.

We sat down thirteen round the great dish of rice to cement
the bond of our new fellowship ; and the occasion was, I
think, of sufficient importance to justify a catalogue of my
companions, whose very names will ever evoke in my mind
memories of the pains and pleasures of what I need not hesi-
tate to describe as the greatest and pleasantest experience of
all my life.

Zayid ibn Munakhkhas was, as already stated, our leader.

'Abdullah ibn Ma'addi, deputy leader and chaplain, was
of the Bani 'Amr section of Subai', but, like Zayid, mainly
town-bred and hailing from the oasis of Ranya.

[1] Saline flat or valley.
[2] The *Ghi* of India, but generally made from sheep's milk.

The great Murra tribe of the Great South Desert was strongly represented by four members, namely :

'Ali ibn Salih ibn Jahman of the Ghafran section, chief guide ;
Muhammad ibn Humaiyid, of the same section, guide ;
Salim ibn Suwailim of the Dimnan section, guide ;
Suwid ibn Hadi al Azma of the same section, guide.

The 'Ajman tribe had three representatives :

Hasan Khurr al Dhib, of Ibn Jim'a's section ;
Falih abu Ja'sha, of the 'Arqa section ;
Farraj, cousin of Falih and of the same section.

The non-tribal elements were represented by the following :

Sa'd ibn Ibrahim al Washmi of Dhruma, who had special charge of my camel, saddlery, etc ;
'Abdul Rahman ibn Khuraibish, also of Dhruma, in charge of the coffee-making ;
Zaid ibn Hubaish, the cook ;
'Abdul 'Aziz ibn Musainid, in charge of the transport animals ;
And Sa'dan, my personal attendant already sufficiently introduced.

Such was the party I joined at the rendezvous, a party of fifteen including myself. Two of them were otherwise engaged when lunch was served to the remaining thirteen, while I ascertained that we were to pick up four other persons during our passage of the Jafura desert to complete our personnel of nineteen. To round off the catalogue I will set forth their names in this place, namely :

Humaid ibn Amhaj of the Manasir tribe (Al bu Rahma group) ;
Salih ibn 'Aziz, also of the Manasir (Al bu Mandhar group) ;
'Ali ibn Salih (?) of the Buhaih section of Murra ;
And Muhammad ibn Rashid, also of the Buhaih.

Our complete party had thus a satisfactory representation of the three important desert tribes : the Murra (no fewer than six), the Manasir (two) and the 'Ajman (three) ; but I could not help feeling some disappointment at the absence of any representative of the southern tribes, such as the Sa'ar, Manahil, Rashid and other sections of Ahl Kathir. There had been none of these about in the Hasa at the time, and we could only hope that we might later on be able to recruit suitable individuals from some of them in the southern sands with the help of Ibn Jiluwi's letters. Zayid and Ibn Ma'addi represented the town-bred element with tribal affinities, while the rest of the party were townees pure and simple with more or less specific functions.

So much for the human element of our expedition. We had 32 camels, all females except one gelding and all of various strains of the famous *'Umaniya* breed whose relationship to camel-kind in general is comparable to that of the Najd race among horses. Our animals were all bred to the sands, of the type known as *Ramliyat*,[1] as opposed to those of the steppe, which are too heavily bred for work in the eternal sands. Three of them were milch animals,[2] one of which was allotted by Ibn Jiluwi's personal orders to my exclusive use. In money value the beasts ranged down from the princely sum of 500 dollars (about L25) to some 150 or 200. Such prices are considered high in Arabia at the present time though during the War they ranged a good deal higher. Doubtless in Egypt and the Sudan better prices are obtainable for first-class riding camels.

We seemed to have a prodigious amount of stores, for we were provisioned on the assumption of a three months' journey, and in fact there was precious little left of anything when we re-entered the civilised world after two and a half months in the desert. Dates and rice formed the bulk of our commissariat (with two special skins of the best *Khalas* dates of the Hasa intended by the governor for my own use), while coffee, tea, sugar and butter with accessories such as cardamum, cinnamon, onions, salt, pepper, etc., had not been forgotten. In fact the only serious omission, which I realised too late, was that of flour. Of that we had none for two and a half months—and often we longed for it. There is nothing

[1] From *Raml*, meaning sand.

[2] Called *Mish* (plural *Misuh*)—i.e., milch-camels without their calves; the term *Khalfa* is used of such animals when their calves are in attendance.

more satisfying than a lump of coarse bread cooked in the ashes and kneaded with dates or sugar and butter to make the mess they call *Hunaini*. Eternal rice seasoned with butter is apt to pall, especially when served up for the pre-dawn meal of the *Ramdhan* fast. It is true that, thanks to Sa'dan, I had a dozen tins of biscuits for my own use, but sweet biscuits do not fill the place of plain bread and I found it quite hard to empty the tins rapidly enough to serve as receptacles for the insects, fossils, and other things which I collected as we went along.

An optimist had come out with my companions the previous day in the hope of palming off on me at a good profit to himself a hawk which had apparently been given to him by its previous dissatisfied owner. I imagined at first that the man was a member of our party and was prepared to accommodate myself to the circumstances, but Sa'dan soon discovered the bird's antecedents and, as Zayid declined to vouch for its ability to do what is required of professional hawks, I excused myself from making the purchase in time for the disappointed salesman to get a ride back to Hufuf in the returning lorry. I noticed by our camp fire a simple but ingenious specimen of a bird-trap,[1] but it was apparently left behind through somebody's forgetfulness and we remained without any means of catching the small birds of the desert. I was ultimately able to secure a specimen of such a trap at Bisha, but then it was too late to be of any practical use, though I took advantage of the incident at Dulaiqiya to explain to my companions my passion for collecting birds, mammals and other creatures and my readiness to reward any assistance I received from them in that direction.

Over our first meal and the coffee that followed it we established a friendly and cordial atmosphere, and I was gratified to find that my companions did not seriously resent my firm opposition to their suggestion that it would be better in the circumstances to defer our start till the morrow. They would have preferred to spend the afternoon warming themselves over the fire, but we clearly could not afford to waste time gratuitously. Besides, with the King now arrived

---

[1] Called *Fakh*.

at Hufuf, I had every reason to want to place ourselves beyond the reach of recall. So we set to work, striking the tents, packing my cases into the stout fibre saddle-bags[1] of Hasa manufacture, and arranging the loads.

While my companions were loading up I strolled about examining the little plantation—a single stoutly-built grange of clay in a walled palm-grove of a couple of acres with a well. A small patch of millet stubble occupied some of the walled space, and some little fields of young wheat lay outside. The plantation seemed to be untenanted at the moment, its owner being a man named Ibn Wutaid of Dawasir origin. As a last contact with the civilisation we were leaving it was an uninspiring little spot and the climatic conditions were horrible in the extreme. A cold, dull wind of moderate force blew over the bleak scene from the north-west, and our horizon was a wall of grey, damp mist through which every now and then came a faint reminder that the sun was somewhere beyond it. We could scarcely hope to make much progress during what remained of the afternoon, but we could make a start and that would at least enable us to get our marching routine going. I thought, too, with satisfaction, that a short ride would be a wise beginning for muscles long unaccustomed to camel-riding. I had not ridden since the pilgrimage of the preceding April, when I had not been severely tested, while previous to that I had not done any serious camel riding since my journey from Rabigh to Wadi Fatima and back in 1925.

At 1.30 p.m. we made a start and the dim ghosts of the Dulaiqiya palms soon disappeared into the mist behind us. Almost immediately we passed the abandoned mud-grange of Qasr Qarradi in the midst of a sandy waste sprinkled here and there with scatters of pebbles, among which I noticed a good deal of whitish quartzite. A run-away camel necessitated a short halt to recapture it and adjust its load. Many of the beasts seemed indeed to be very heavily loaded, though those carrying my own paraphernalia got off very

[1] These *Mahasin* (sing. *Mahsan*), or *Khasaïf* (sing. *Khasifa*), are ingeniously made of palm-fibre woven round a skeleton of ropes, and the amount of wear and tear they stand is astonishing.

lightly in comparison with the kitchen and commissariat animals. My own mount was a huge beast with a veritable mountain of a hump, and I seemed to tower high above all my companions. Also I did not find Al Bahraniya—for that was her name in allusion to the fact that she had come from Bahrain, a present from Shaikh Hamad to Ibn Jiluwi— particularly comfortable. For all her length of stride she marched sluggishly and planted her feet rather heavily on the ground.

We now entered a tract of low sand-ridges profusely covered with shrubs of *Shinan*, from whose burned ash they produce a soap reputed to be excellent for laundry purposes. The kindred *Harm* plant, apparently of more succulent structure, also produces a soap, though of inferior quality and injurious to clothing. In the midst of this undulating area we came to and halted at Qasr Dhuwaiban, a derelict fort-like building suggesting human occupation at some period in the distant past when there was water in wells or springs for the purposes of agriculture. A profusion of tamarisk bushes in the neighbourhood left, indeed, little doubt that we were in the sand-choked bed of some old line of drainage, and the discovery of a dry well-pit confirmed the impression. The building, now in a ruinous condition, appears to have con- sisted of a two-storeyed fort about 40 paces square with an open courtyard about 25 paces square adjoining it on the east side, the axis of the whole lying roughly east and west. Among the ruins we found fragments of common pottery, glass bangles and the like, apparently similar to what we were to find later at Jabrin and the remnants found by Major R. E. Cheesman at Salwa in 1921. What the age of such relics may be it would be difficult to say and I shall have occasion to discuss the matter more fully in connection with Jabrin, but the feature that interested me most was the slabs and fragments of a highly fossiliferous and somewhat brittle rock, which the builders of the fort seem to have used freely to reinforce their mud brickwork. As far as I know such rock has never been found in the Hasa area, and it would seem that the stuff must have been brought from the cliffs along the coast at a considerable distance from this spot. Similar material is certainly to be found in the fort at Salwa but not at Jabrin, and would seem to be of Miocene age. If Dhuwaiban is a relic of the Carmathian occupation of the tenth century A.D. or thereabouts, it is now, as we saw by their signs, the abode of wolves and owls and hyenas. Man has abandoned the unequal struggle with the desert sand.

Almost immediately after resuming our march we entered the broad channel of a *Sabkha*, a band of salt-impregnated mud about 500 yards across, which divides the Ghuwaiba plain from the soft undulating sandy downs of the Mutaiwi district. The head of the saline channel is said to be at the wells of Khuwaira, whence it runs, roughly northward on a winding course, to the neighbourhood of Jisha and Taraf on the eastern confines of the great Hasa oasis. When I had passed through those parts on my way to and from 'Uqair there was a considerable lake or marsh to the south of the route.

I now noticed that Zayid, who professed to know all this country intimately, was diverging from the direct route to the wells of Mutaiwi which I had expressed a desire to see. He had indeed changed his mind with the idea of getting to a desirable camping spot without delay, and I considered it expedient to remonstrate very gently with him against any change of plans without consultation. He declared that he was not aware of my desire to see the altogether uninteresting wells, but without a word changed course again towards them. At the same time he sent the baggage animals straight on to an agreed camping place while we followed the right bank of the *Sabkha* channel for half an hour until we came to Mutaiwi, two small water-pits, two feet in diameter at the mouth and ten feet deep to the water level. The mouth of each pit was protected by a structure of woodwork and wattle, and round the wells is a wide circle of bare ground liberally covered with the droppings of sheep. Khuwaira, half an hour's ride due south from Mutaiwi, also has two similar wells.

The afternoon being now sufficiently advanced, we drew water—pleasantly warm it seemed in contrast with the chill air—for the requisite ablutions and lined up on the far from

clean precincts of the wells for the first prayer of our journey.
When travelling, the five prayers of the normal day are
telescoped into three. The dawn prayer is taken alone and
in full as usual, while the noon and afternoon prayers are
halved and said together—each preceded by a separate call—
and at sunset the usual prayer, said in full, is followed at once
after a separate call by the halved evening service. It is a
very simple and practical arrangement reflecting the common-
sense of the founder of Islam and his appreciation of the
difficulties inherent in a community which normally spends
a greater part of its time in travel.

We passed out of the dung-circle of the wells into the low,
firm sand-downs to the eastward, having on our right hand
about a mile away a low ridge of rock. I noted a large proportion of black pebbles in the gravel sprinkled about this
area, in which there were some scattered *Harm* bushes, each
with a comet-like trail of sand extending some four or five
feet to leeward—*i.e.*, to the south-south-east, the wind during
these days having been from the diametrically opposite
quarter. About 4.30 p.m. we entered a rolling dune country
which Zayid vaguely named to me as Hamarir[1] al Thuwair.
He was obviously very much out to please, very friendly and
conversational, but his voice was half way between a bark
and a squeak and his manner too sanctimonious and precious.
Also he had an annoying habit of trying to monopolise my
attention, butting in in an explanatory and entirely helpful
sort of way whenever I tried to get on to conversational terms
with the wary and undemonstrative *Badu* of the party.
However, thought I, there was plenty of time to change all
such habits and I had no mind to go too fast for the time
being, although I did privately register the opinion that Zayid
was not up to the standard of some guides I had known in the
past. It was, therefore, unfortunate that he appeared to be
the only guide available for the first few days.

A voice hailed us from over the rolling waves to our left,
and we were soon in camp in a tract of dunes called Al
Mutrib to find that the tents had been pitched and tea made

---

[1] Plural of *Hamrur*, a name applied to pink *Nafud*-like sands. The word
Nafud does not seem to be used much in this south country.

ready. The cold was now intense and my limbs seemed to have been stretched on the rack though we had ridden less than 10 miles. The camp-fire was a welcome sight indeed and I went to warm myself by it before visiting my tent. Unwisely, and until driven off by weeping eyes, I chose the warmer and smokier side of the fire, whose fuel was of pungent *Shinan* faggots. Stiff and cold, I would have been better advised to tramp about a bit to give my blood a chance of circulating. I chose the fire instead and my new friends plied me with cups of hot sweetened camel's milk after I had drained the last of a pot of tea. Suddenly a feeling of unease came over me. I lay back against a friendly saddle to shake off what appeared to be a stupid fit of biliousness or chill—all to no purpose. I rose rather unsteadily to go to my tent and my companions helped me down the slope to its door, seeing that I was not well. And there I went out in a dead faint, from which I came to apparently after about four minutes of lifelessness. According to Sa'dan, my face went yellow, and they thought I was finished ; but, on coming to, I had a perfectly lucid idea of all that had happened and bundled myself into bed without delay, piling every available rug and blanket over me and taking two aspirin tabloids to encourage perspiration. In spite of the coarse wool and leather boots[1] I was wearing I felt astonishingly cold in my feet, but that passed off when I had removed the boots and settled down to the generous warmth of blankets in a tent which kept off the cold wind. I soon began to feel well enough to wonder at such an occurrence at the very outset of a journey which presupposed complete fitness in the adventurer. I began to wonder, and could not help remembering that eighteen months before, during a hot July afternoon at Jidda, I had had a sudden and devastating reminder of the frailty of human life. Was this another—another warning from the Infinite to hasten the completion of my worldly tasks ? I wondered, and sank into the caressing arms of sleep. And the morning and the evening were the first day.

[1] These *Zarabil* (sing. *Zarbul*) are made in the Hasa for the Badawin and are more like snow-boots than anything else.

B

CHAPTER II

NORTHERN JAFURA

THE voice of 'Ali Jahman, calling to the dawn prayer, awoke
me at 6 a.m. No trace remained of the evening's indisposition, and I rose from my bed refreshed as a giant to run his
course. It was an auspicious day, the eighth of January, the
anniversary of Ibn Sa'ud's public acclamation as King of the
Hijaz in the great mosque of Mecca in 1926—a pleasant date
in my calendar, and surely a propitious one for the first full
day's march of our great adventure. It was also, officially,
the last day of the month of *Sha'ban* and the new moon, if
seen that night, would usher in the great fast of *Ramdhan* on
the morrow. There was no sign of the last fragment of the
waning satellite in the dark sky of the false dawn, but there
was a heavy ground mist overlying the desert and visibility
was very poor.

I bundled out of the tent, barefooted, to range myself with
the rest of my companions behind Ibn Ma'addi, who led the
prayer. The sand under foot was intolerably cold and I
noticed that most of the men wore their 'snow-boots'. The
Wahhabi code is astonishingly reasonable in such matters,
and I have seen sandals on the feet of worshippers on the
painful gravel-strewn floors of the Riyadh mosques as well as
in the steppe desert. One prays barefooted unless there is
good reason for doing otherwise and each man answers only
to his own conscience in the matter. Inevitably some laxity
is produced by such latitude, but the main object of the code
is to secure or enforce regularity of prayer by removing all
obstacles thereto.

It was too cold to think of marching yet awhile, and we foregathered round the camp-fire to warm ourselves with tea,
coffee and hot milk. It would be time enough to start when

18

the sun had infused some of his warmth into the chilly world
around us. I reclined against a skin containing, as I thought,
salt or sugar. It was a skin of water frozen hard, for they
had laid the water bags round about the fire to thaw them !
My thermometer, placed outside the tent, recorded 27° Fahr.
—five degrees of frost. To think of such things in Arabia,
proverbial for its fierce heat ! Yet for the past month or
more, at Riyadh and in the desert and at Hufuf, there had
been frost and ice at frequent intervals. It was one of the
coldest winters in the memory of living men, and it was certainly my first experience and knowledge of temperatures
actually below freezing-point in Najd. No wonder that the
sand had seemed like ice under foot, burning my soles as with
red-hot needles !

Our camp lay in a hollow surrounded by dunes, and the
mist, a good deal lighter than on the previous day, allowed a
fairly clear view for several miles around. But the scene was
utterly featureless except for the low hillock of Thuwair, to
which we should come early in the day's march. The sea was
said to lie to our eastward a good day's journey by express
camel.

The transport animals having preceded us by 10 minutes,
we started off at 9 a.m. after a good warm breakfast of boiled
rice. In less than an hour, marching over low sandy downs
succeeded by a vast flat plain of light gravel, we came to the
group of low parallel ridges that constitute Thuwair. Two
hillocks, some distance apart, rise substantially higher than
the general level of the ridges and, sending the baggage train
ahead, a small party of us ascended one of them to enjoy such
view as might be afforded by its summit. According to my
companions the palm-groves of Hasa can easily be seen from
here on a fine day, but we saw nothing but mist. The Thuwair
tract extends some three miles east and west with sand all
round, the short ridges being echeloned one behind another.
Its surface, lightly covered with sand and profusely strewn
with hard white pellets of the disintegrated parent rock,
seemed to be whitish sandstone,[1] weathering to a pale pinkish
hue. Whether it is a normal marine sedimentary formation

[1] For geological and petrological details see Appendix.

or of aeolian origin cannot perhaps be determined with any
certainty, but the absence of fossils from all this vast tract,
including the Summan and the Hasa district, is quite remarkable.   Geologically the eastern desert would seem to
overlie the Cretaceous protruding from the 'Arma uplands,
the intermediate Eocene and the Miocene of the Jiban
depressions.

A chilly wind made our short sojourn on the Thuwair
eminence, barely 100 feet above the general level of the desert,
exceedingly unpleasant, and we were glad enough to descend
from our perch and resume the march. My companions had
perhaps begun to wonder what manner of man this was that
sought every possible occasion of discomfort to satisfy a
profitless curiosity. After all, there was nothing to see, so
why go out of one's way to look for it ? In all this country
and, in fact, as far southward as Anbak no rain had yet
fallen this season and the desert bore a very parched aspect
with scanty dry tufts of the familiar *Arfaj* and *Thamam* and a
reedy grass, new to me, called *Andab*. During the previous
afternoon's march one of my companions had brought me a
flowered shaft of the obscene desert fungus known as
Dhanun. It had been half eaten by a fox, but cannot be
eaten by man. Its cousin, more obscene in appearance,
because more naked, the *Tarthuth* or ' Desert Penis ', of
which also they brought me a specimen soon after leaving
Thuwair, is however edible by human beings, a salutary
purge.

What with the cold and the sluggish gait of my enormous
steed—and nothing is more tiring than continual goading of
a lazy camel with one's heel applied to the base of the neck
and shoulder—I found the initial stiffness resulting from the
first day's short ride getting worse as the march progressed.
Once or twice my saddle had to be adjusted, for the prodigious
hump of Al Bahraniya defied all the efforts of Sa'd the groom
to saddle her comfortably or effectively. Nevertheless we
did a good day's march in spite of a determined but unsuccessful effort on the part of Zayid to curtail it before we
entered the great dune tract of Al Mughammidha which was
so utterly bare of vegetation that, once entered, there could

be no question of halting until we had passed out of it on the further side. Slowly but surely I began to take stock of my companions, as they too of me. Zayid kept himself at all times conspicuously in the limelight, and the rest for the moment seemed to maintain a discreet reserve, especially the Badawin elements, among whom 'Ali Jahman stood out in a class by himself—a strange, mysterious, brooding creature of fine physique and strikingly handsome Semitic features. His closer acquaintance would obviously be well worth cultivating, and I was attracted by his apparent aloofness. I knew of course that he was to be our chief guide as soon as we came to the serious business of the expedition. He was, moreover, a cousin of Hamad ibn Sultan ibn Hadi who had served Bertram Thomas in a similar capacity the year before. And in his early days he had served some sort of apprenticeship in the *Ikhwan* movement, though he was too wedded to the life of the desert to go as far as taking up residence in any of the colonies of the brotherhood. He had however acquired a certain degree of proficiency in the scriptures, while a voice of unusual charm would have assured him of success in the rôle of parish priest had not the lure of the sands kept him free of such shackles. As I afterwards came to know, he had the Semitic avarice in more than full measure, gnawing mercilessly at his soul.

Beyond the Thuwair tract the country gradually developed into a vast flattish, sandy wilderness with slight undulations and occasional small patches of gravel. Afar off to the left appeared a long line of lofty sand-billows. It was so cold that animal life seemed totally in abeyance, and the only living creature we saw during the morning was a raven. The sand in the depressions and on exposed slopes was much rippled and ridged by the wind, while the lines of dunes seemed to be uniformly oriented with their long axis lying east and west. The smooth, rounded sides of the dunes lay northward, while the characteristic sharp escarpments of their crests faced southwards over a hollow, semi-circular or shaped like a horseshoe. Within such hollows and at the base of the dunes there was generally a light scatter of gravel or an exposure of the bed-rock forming the foundation of all

this tract. As we advanced eastward and south-eastward
the horseshoe formation tended to disappear in favour of
ridges of oval shape with the sand uniformly disposed at an
easy gradient all round them. The lie of the sands suggested
a prevalent north wind, and it was certainly a very bleak
north wind that blew chilly upon us as we marched.

Just before noon we entered a tract called 'Araif after
passing over a series of low sand-ridges. It was a vast sand-
plain without any kind of feature, but heavily furrowed with
wind and fairly well covered with dry vegetation. Just
before reaching the spot selected for a short mid-day halt we
noticed that we were being pursued by two men, and my
heart sank at the thought that they were perhaps messengers
sent by the King to recall us. They proved to be Fahad ibn
'Isa and Jabir, myrmidons of Ibn Jiluwi, who had come out
on our trail with some business papers from the Minister
of Finance, which should have been dealt with before my
departure but had been overlooked in the turmoil preceding
the King's arrival. His Majesty, they told us, had duly
arrived an hour or two after we had left and apparently
intended to spend a good part of the month of *Ramdhan* at
Hufuf. At any rate he had sent forth messengers to search
out the daughter of Ibn Nuqaidan, one of the leading Murra
chiefs, that he might wed and be comfortable during his
sojourn. As the papers sent out to me required more consideration than I could spare for them during our halt we
took Fahad and his companion along with us to our evening's
camp.

The ridges of the Thuwair tract may be regarded as the
northern limit towards Hasa of the great Jafura desert, which
is itself a northward-thrusting promontory of the Rub' al
Khali. The 'Araif tract is thus well within the borders of
Jafura, and our south-eastward course during the afternoon
carried us over a featureless sandy waste, in which one low
ridge was named to me by Zayid as 'Arq al Adhir, so-called
from the abundance in it of the pleasantly green *Adhir* plant
which, at any rate in northern Najd, is spurned by camels,
and generally regarded as poisonous to them. I was therefore astonished to see my camel stretch forth her long neck

towards the stuff and crop great mouthfuls of it with apparent satisfaction. It seems that the *'Umaniya* camels are bred to eat the plant and suffer no ill effects. Another plant that now began to be a prominent feature in the scene—to continue with us for practically the rest of our wanderings—was the *Abal*, growing to the tree-like stature of 5 or 6 feet with trunks of substantial girth, which provide excellent fuel. Its roots are often 20 feet or more in length and seemed to spread out horizontally over the sands.

Half way through the afternoon we entered the bare dune-tract of Al Mughammida, forming apparently part of the great band of similar character which had gradually been converging on our route from the left and which extends eastward to and along the sea coast. The name of this tract suggests limitation on the traveller's outlook, and we meandered blindly among the dunes, generally of the typical horseshoe pattern, seeking a way through the maze. As we advanced the undulations became more and more imposing, our course being dictated by the contours of the hummocks which often ran together in parallel groups. At times we had to descend steep slopes, our camels lurching heavily down to my growing discomfort as my stiffness increased. 'Ali's sharp eyes soon picked up the tracks of a party of five camels that had passed this way as recently as the previous evening, doubtless a party of Murra folk returning to their grazing cattle in the further sands. The riders had done a good deal of walking to ease their beasts in the heavy going, and one of them was a girl—ay, said 'Ali, and a virgin, and may be beautiful as are often the girls of our people. We were to see those same tracks again and again on the morrow, though we never saw their makers, until finally they diverged from our route and we regretfully abandoned the pursuit of the fair one, whose light and jaunty tread had distinguished her trail from that of a matron. Why! said 'Ali, we Murra, if we know a camel, can with complete certitude identify the tracks of its off-spring though we may never have seen it.

A broad band of dung-pellets in the midst of generations of obliterated or all-but-obliterated camel-tracks pointed the way to the watering of Bir al Nabit, whose exact position in the otherwise featureless ocean of bare, rolling dunes is further marked by two low pyramids of sand. At least so they appeared as viewed from the west though they merged mysteriously in the general welter of undistinguishable billows as we drew near. These two peaks are known as Niqyan al Bir. We came to the well itself about 4 p.m., lying at the very foot of a steep sand-slope which seems to threaten it with extinction. There was formerly, indeed, a second well not far off to the north, which now lies buried deep under a great dune. These wells were sunk by and form the pivot of the wanderings of the Nabit section of Murra. The existing shaft is nine fathoms deep to water, the upper portion to a depth of some ten feet being cleared through loose sand and lined with a structure of wood and wattle to prevent its falling in. The remainder of the shaft is sunk through a reddish sandstone, and the water is brackish. The well-mouth is a rough square of three feet each way.

A pair of ravens withdrew warily to the safe summit of a neighbouring dune on our approach, while a Bifasciated Lark, bolder but less intelligent, fell to my gun, my companions being quite astonished at my shooting it on the wing. They prefer sitting shots to husband their ammunition.

Our baggage animals now being a long way behind, we could not draw water from the well and contented ourselves with the substitute sand-ablutions to prepare ourselves for the belated afternoon prayer. We then continued our march through the same maze of dunes and hollows, seeking as easy a passage as possible in the circumstances. At length we came to the end of the tedious dune-tract and struck out over a gently undulating sand-plain to the exposed rock-ridge of Kharza, where we halted to camp for the night. A similar ridge, called Manifa, lay at a considerable distance to the north, but all else around us was an unrelieved monotony of sand.

I was glad enough to dismount, and strolled about to ease my racked muscles. It is quite extraordinary how camel-riding calls into play nerves and sinews which seem to lie idle in all other occupations whatsoever. I was mentally and physically radiant with well-being, though I behaved absurdly like an octogenarian in all that concerned rising from and sitting down on the ground. But it was all good training, I thought, for the serious business of months of desert-wandering before us, and I congratulated myself on the brilliant idea of prefacing the attack on the Empty Quarter with a preliminary canter of exploration in the Jafura desert. By the time we should arrive at Jabrin I would be hardened or acclimatised, while, if I proved unfit, we would still be near enough to civilisation to turn back. So for the time being I lowered myself gingerly to a sitting position and unashamedly sought the assistance of my companions' sympathetic shoulders and arms in rising to my feet. As for mounting Al Bahraniya during these early days of stiffness, I simply did not attempt it without an army of assistants.

The Kharza ridge, rising to a height of some 40 or 50 feet above the surrounding plain, is no more than an exposure of the undulating bedrock forming the desert floor under the sands. It was about half a mile in length lying north-east and south-west, apparently of sandstone in two shades of dirty pink with a whitish layer on the surface, which was profusely strewn with pebbles of curious shapes weathered out of the friable, ever-disintegrating rock. Most noticeable and very plentiful were flat copper-coloured discs resembling pennies scattered on the ground. The plain, unlike the Mughammidha tract behind us, was fairly well covered with rather parched vegetation and the camels found plenty to eat, while the *Abal* bushes provided us with all the fuel we wanted.

Just before reaching the dunes round Bir al Nabit we had encountered another of Ibn Jiluwi's men, Nasir, who had gone with 'Abdul Latif to rescue my belongings from the derelict car which had in due course been brought in safely to 'Uqair. My servant having decided to go off to Bahrain, Nasir had struck out alone for Bir al Nabit and, not finding there any record of our passage, had wandered slowly along in the direction of the Hasa in the hope of meeting us. I was glad to have my possessions back again in my keeping, and it was pleasant enough to have the society of the three

extra men over our evening meal. We also had other
visitors, for 'Ali Jahman had gone off before we dismounted
at Kharza to scour the surrounding country for Badawin
encampments with the idea of buying a sheep for our dinner.
He had only encountered a single family of the Shaiba subsection of the Ghafran, his own group, but they had no
animals worth purchasing. They had, however, scented the
prospect of dinner and during the evening an old man and
two lads came over to our camp to share our rice. That they
did with a gusto suggesting that they had not had a square
meal for some time.

At sunset all eyes were riveted on the darkening western
sky in search of the moon's young crescent, but our seeking
was in vain and we turned to our dinner with the knowledge
that we had been granted a day's respite from the fast. The
official calendar, in the preparation of which I had played a
modest part with the assistance of the Nautical Almanac, had
allowed only 29 days for *Sha'ban*, but the opening and ultimate breaking of the fast are inexorably dependent on the
sighting of the moon, failing which the maximum tale of
thirty days must be allowed to each month concerned. So
Sha'ban had automatically lengthened out to 30 days, and we
thought optimistically that, by the general law of compensation, we should only have to face 29 days of fasting.

On the whole the day had passed off well enough and we
had covered 20 miles. The proceedings had only been marred
by a slight altercation arising out of an unauthorised adjust-
ment of our loading arrangements. I had insisted on my
boxes, full of instruments, bottles and other easily damage-
able articles, being carried in a vertical position, but found
that during the march they had been carelessly piled up,
three to a camel instead of two, to facilitate a redistribution
of the heavier loads of the commissariat animals. The
intention had been laudable enough, but it was essential that
everyone should understand that my possessions should not
be exposed to any risk of damage ; and my objection was
received in a reasonable enough spirit of accommodation,
though I felt that a vague undercurrent of irritation had been
left behind by the incident. Fahad was indeed suborned to

lecture me on the urgency of lightening all burdens as far as possible, and was rather taken aback at my simple suggestion that the proper course in such circumstances was not to jeopardise my delicate paraphernalia but to hire extra camels from the Badawin to lighten the burdens of the other carriers. The trouble in such cases always arises from the fact that the Arab accommodates himself but slowly to any needful modification of a routine developed by generations of carrying. He simply does not understand that a load is not just a load. The stranger's point of view is apt to be regarded as unreasonable, but there could be no yielding on the point and my companions shuddered at my suggestion that, if some lightening of loads was really necessary, we could send back the tents by the three men who would be going back to Hufuf on the morrow.

The maximum temperature of the day had been only 59°, and next morning, with a recorded minimum of one degree below freezing-point, our water skins were again frozen hard. The desert air had a knife-sharp edge, and we cowered over the fire again until the sun had tempered it somewhat. The three men returning to civilisation were first off the mark, and it was past 9 a.m. when we said good-bye to our aged Marri visitor and his sons to launch out again over the rolling sand-field past the Kharza ridge. Afar off on our right appeared the long low coast of another rocky ridge called Khartam, but in general the landscape was a featureless waste with occasional bare patches of the pinkish bed-rock until, in due course, we came to a line of higher dunes of soft sand.

On the way we passed between scattered groups of the camels of the Buhaih section, grazing on the dry grasses[1] and *Abal* bushes of the plain. We exchanged greetings with a girl of the Zaqiba subsection who appeared to be in sole charge of the pasturing herds, though her father's tent was doubtless not far off in some sheltering hollow. A lonely life it is, indeed, of the herding nomads, though no longer in Ibn Sa'ud's broad dominions a life of constant fear as it was in former days. Yet hunger is the rule of the desert with little

---

[1] *Thamam* and *Sabat.*

but butter and milk to stay its pangs. And in the winter it is cold. The girl shivered under the folds of her ragged mantle as she told us what she knew of the dispositions of the various families and subsections of her group.

The sun gradually filtered through the mist and the morning warmed up under the influence of a mild southerly breeze which had taken the place of the chill northern blasts. For the first time since leaving the Hasa we began to feel alive as we plodded on over the changeless scene. 'Ali Jahman, riding a great whitish beast which was held to be the best in all our party, rode far ahead with Zayid, on his dark brown *Dara'iya*[1] camel, in attendance, gossiping about his experiences on a recent tax-collecting expedition to the southeastern districts along the frontier of Oman, from which he had only returned at the beginning of *Sha'ban*. In those parts, he declared, he had often seen and shot the wild ass which frequents the valley country of Ash'ab al Ghaf under Jabal Hafit. And the women of the Manasir are passing fair. If God wills, he said, I would go thither again next year and perhaps Shaikh 'Abdullah will go with us to see that country, which is better than this desert. Everywhere you will see palm-groves and villages and rich pastures. It is a fair land and the folk are hospitable, but there is a girl among them I would wed. I was interested to hear from him that Ibn Sa'ud's influence is felt to-day in all the Dhahira country, as they call the tract westward of the Oman massif, including, of course, Buraimi, a Wahhabi centre of long standing, and apparently even 'Ibri. These tax-collecting expeditions scarcely, perhaps, do more than pay the expenses involved in equipping and sending them out, but they do tend to spread the gospel of Wahhabi peace and Arabian unity. Slowly but surely the ripples of stable government broaden outwards from the centre, and the Manasir may be counted to-day as subjects of Ibn Sa'ud, who asks little of them but the acceptance of his sovereignty and the maintenance of the public peace. Zayid had obvious limitations in the capacity of guide and a full quiver of quaint and slightly irritating mannerisms, but he was a born story-teller, with a strange,

[1] So-called because bred by the Duru' tribe of the Oman border.

dry, staccato style, and never tired of inflicting himself on some member of the party. His fund of conversation was inexhaustible, and he showed a curious resentment at any attempt on my part to draw on the funds of the others.

Both Zayid and 'Ali rode in the fashion of Oman, now squatting and now kneeling on the neat, light saddle, known as *Haulani* and set well back towards the camel's rump with only the small wooden vices of the frame gripping the hump fore and aft. Their riding was entirely by balance, and it seemed to me that the southern saddle was a great improvement on the ponderous structure of Najd. It was lighter and more compact, but it reduced the storage capacity of the saddle-bags, which in Oman are made smaller to fit across the narrow rump, providing a seat for the rider actually on and between the flaps. The rifle is fitted at the trail under a bag instead of being slung, as in Najd, from the rear pole of the saddle-frame. For my purposes the capacious *Najdi* saddle-bags were more useful, but at this stage I was suffering agonies from the rough paces and sluggish gait of Al Bahran-iya. My joints ached again and I was as stiff as could be. Yet the beast had been especially selected for my riding by Ibn Jiluwi himself, an expert in all that pertained to camel-mastery. The trouble was that the animal had been too long at the pastures, and had grown a hump which looked better than it felt. In other hands she would probably have performed very differently, and the opinion gradually matured among my companions that I should be transferred, at any rate temporarily, to another animal. It was not, however, till the fifth day of the march that I exchanged mounts with Sa'dan with astonishingly satisfactory results due, perhaps, in part to the fact that my stiffness had then worn off—quite suddenly as it generally does. Later, when I resumed riding Al Bahraniya, I experienced no further discomfort though her walk was never anything but sluggish and it was always irksome egging her on. Only once afterwards did I exchange her for another animal for a few hours when we found it necessary to speed up our progress, while for the final desert crossing Zayid took her and I rode Na'riya, the great white brute now forging ahead under 'Ali Jahman.

It was at the trot that Al Bahraniya showed her true merits,
her paces being perfect, though in desert travel such as ours
there is little or no trotting. I rode her, however, during the
pilgrimage and could have found nothing more charming.

What are you two talking about, I asked of Zayid and 'Ali
riding up to them on one occasion, that you ride so far ahead,
forgetting us all—perhaps secrets that you would not have
me hear ? No, laughed 'Ali, just gossiping, talking of journeys, raids and women. That is the way with us *Badu*, we
wear away time and distance with our talk. I had noticed a
few stray locusts as we rode and asked them if they had seen
any swarms. 'Ali had seen them in large numbers during
three days about the beginning of *Sha'ban* in the Habl district
about 'Araira, whither he had gone with the governor of the
Hasa on a bustard-shooting expedition. I had myself seen
an immense flight of the insects in the 'Arma uplands about
the same time while similarly engaged with the King, and
the great cars charging through them in pursuit of bustard
must have slain tens of thousands. The mangled corpses
decorated the radiators, while insects in flight hurtled against
our heads and faces like rifle-bullets. Zayid had also seen
swarms at Sikak at the same time when returning by that
way from his Oman expedition. The swarm seen by myself
had appeared to be moving south, but it missed the Hasa
by some dispensation of Providence and does not seem
to have done any damage to crops within the borders of
Arabia.

We halted for an hour about noon in the plain of Marbakh[1]
al Sa'qa for coffee, and I made the most of the mist-filtered
sunshine to wander about in search of insects among the
scanty gravel-patches amid the sands. My whole bag consisted of a single desert Mantid. Otherwise there was not a
sign of life anywhere though I noticed the trails of larks
running in and out among the bushes seeking their food.
Little mounds of sand lay to the south-east of the bushes,
while in the open the surface was ruffled into surf-like crests
breaking in the same direction from the long smooth waves

[1] The term is generally applied to flat or slightly undulating desert
pasture-lands.

behind them. Higher dunes lay far out to the north-east in
a patch called 'Atshan, while another group south of it was
Hidab with the wells of Bahath a mile or more eastward of it
in a broad patch of gravel, which was shortly to traverse our
path, forming a break in the continuity of the Jafura sands.
The gravel tract is known as Al Ghafa and extends southward
to a line of sand-ridges, in which at some distance we saw a
party of graziers with their camels. Suddenly the cry went
up : Look, plenty of fuel, bushes everywhere and pasture !
That was the signal to halt, dismount and camp for the night
not far from a large and prominent barrow of sand known as
Zubara Mahmid, the sand-ridges in our neighbourhood marking the resumption of Jafura after the gravel strip. The
country seemed to be better favoured in the matter of
vegetation than anything we had already seen, but our luck
was out so far as meat was concerned. The Buhaih herdsmen we had observed came over to our camp with a brace
of very thin sheep for which they demanded ten dollars. To
my surprise Zayid, who thought they were worth no more
than five, stood out resolutely against more than seven dollars
being offered and the bargain fell through. Meanwhile the
young crescent of the new moon was spotted high up in the
sky—obviously a second-night moon—and we hailed the
advent of *Ramdhan*. The fast is, of course, not an obligation
of the traveller, but we had all agreed to keep it during our
journey, as do the Badawin in their normal wanderings.
Our kitchen, after we had disposed of the usual rice dinner in
company with our visitors, was therefore in a bustle all night
adjusting itself to the new situation, which postulated a substantial meal—a sort of morning supper—between 4 and 5
a.m. before the dawn call to prayer, after which there might
be neither eating nor drinking until the usual breakfast at
sunset. Smoking and sexual intercourse are similarly pro-
hibited during the daylight hours, but these particular hard-
ships were in our circumstances little more than formalities—
our party including at the moment only one smoker, Farraj
the 'Arqani, as I had forsworn tobacco temporarily since
leaving my home at Mecca nearly two months before and
maintained the taboo till my return thither in April. Sa'dan

had also proclaimed his intention of giving up the habit by leaving all his smoking apparatus behind at Hufuf.

Zaid and Ibn Musainid rose nobly—almost too nobly indeed—to the occasion, for it was barely 4 a.m. when I was aroused from my slumbers by the announcement of supper, a large dish of plain boiled rice, for which that first morning I found myself with little appetite. The change of moon had brought a remarkable change in the weather. Instead of the frosts of the first days, the day dawned dull and cloudy with a touch of mild sultriness in the air, but the sun failed of his duty and by noon it seemed to be colder than at dawn with a fresh blustering south-west wind to stir up the sand about us. After supper the camp composed itself again for slumber which was in due course interrupted by the call to prayer— and again they slumbered. But whether it was these disturbances of our normal régime or the satisfactory change in the temperature or some other reason, everybody seemed to be astir at 7 a.m. and it was I that delayed our start by insisting on packing away the specimens of rock, insects, etc., collected during the previous day's march. I felt that I would have to develop a routine suitable to the new conditions, and celebrated the beginning of *Ramdhan* by forgetting to wind my watches, which had, of course, run down when I next looked at them at our evening camp. That was a most disastrous lapse, for which I have never forgiven myself though it proved not altogether irreparable as I shall explain later.

It was 8 a.m. when we started out on what was to prove a good day's march of exceptional interest. I thought comfortingly that the *Ramdhan* penance would obviate unnecessary halts by the way, but we had marched little more than two hours when my chilly companions clamoured for a halt to warm themselves by a fire. I told them they could please themselves but that I should not be sitting over a fire in the event of a stoppage. So we continued for another hour before halting to let our transport get well on in advance.

At starting the long line of the high Mashura dunes, an eastward promontory of Jafura, was visible afar off across our path beyond the gently undulating wilderness, in which many groups of grazing Badawin were settled down to enjoy

the favourable pastures. Most of the morning indeed we
seemed to be within hail of camels or human beings, and it
was here that at last we parted company with the tracks of
the pretty girl and her small party, which we had first encountered near Bir al Nabit. They had gone off to the left
doubtless to seek out their tents and cattle. On the right lay
an encampment of a small group of the Manasir and in the
same direction we saw at a distance the tents of the folk who
had visited us during the night, one group of seven tents
and another of three or four a little apart. A little further
on we were accosted by a small party of the Rashid subsection (of Buhaih), who came hieing across the sands from
their tents with a charming white *Saluqi* hound in attendance. They say that, of all the Arabian tribes, the Murra
and Manasir breed the best hunting dogs and we had agreed
among ourselves to annex one if we could to keep the pot
going with hares in collaboration with my 12-bore gun and
the rifles of my companions.

Very beautiful is the meeting of Arabs in the desert, with
their greetings of each other—very formal, very long-drawn-
out and repetitive, for every member of each party exchanges
the same friendly enquiries and assurances with each member
of the other, until all have greeted all, and they part or
proceed to any business that may be in hand. Peace be
upon you ! And on you be peace ! How is your state, oh
Salih ? In peace ; how are you, oh 'Ali ? In peace ! May
God give you health ! May God improve your condition !
How are you ? In peace ! And then follows the abrupt
transition to business with : What is your news ? In most
cases, of course, parties meeting thus casually in the desert
contain mutual acquaintances, while a man like 'Ali Jahman
would be well-known, at least by repute, to everyone. He
himself claimed to know personally the heads of every family
of the Murra and to have a fairly large acquaintance among
the rest, especially in his own clan, the Ghafran. Zayid too
appeared to be fairly well-known to the groups we met and
was, of course, a person of some consequence. I was beginning to find that he improved on acquaintance and certainly
appeared to have the best intentions towards myself, but I

C

could not bring myself to play up to his manifest policy of making a corner in my attention and favours and he was beginning to be jealous and suspicious of 'Ali, with whom I was beginning to make satisfactory headway now that the instinctive caution of his desert-bred soul had begun to thaw in the give-and-take of daily association with me.

Major Cheesman[1] has suggested that the Murra converse with each other in a dialect which is not intelligible to other Arabs, but I found nothing in my experiences to justify such a conclusion. On the contrary their speech is not only unquestionably Arabic but a particularly beautiful, almost classical, Arabic at that. In many ways it reminded me strongly of the language of the Hijaz mountain districts round Taïf, the language of the Quraish and Bani Sufyan, who share with the Murra the characteristic softening of the J sound to Y and the labiation of the peculiarly Arabic sound called *Dhad*, the *DH* of our transliteration. I have heard the Bani Sufyan refer to the capital of Najd as Riyal, while the Murra pronounce Haral for Haradh, but I shall have to revert to this subject in connection with the Manasir whose acquaintance I was yet to make. According to 'Ali Jahman, and as one would expect, every tribe has its *Lughwa* or dialectical mannerisms, but the language they all speak—the Murra, Manasir, 'Awamir, Bani Kathir, Sa'ar, etc.—is Arabic and they appear to have nothing in the nature of a true dialect or *Ratna*. Even the Harasis, he declared, speak and understand ordinary Arabic, but not the Mahra who have a dialect which is not intelligible to other Arabs. I can only speak of my own experience of the true Arab tribes, and, without trespassing on the more controversial aspects of the question, I would hazard the conclusion that the dialects of the south, inevitably exposed to corrupting influences from overseas and from the ancient neighbouring civilisations of the Yaman and the Hadhramaut, represent a linguistic hotch-potch of generally Semitic character rather than the remnants of pure aboriginal tongues of non-Semitic origin. But the matter is evidently one that merits the closest study, and it is satisfactory to know that Mr. Bertram Thomas is

[1] *In Unknown Arabia*, p. 225.

engaged on such a study of the linguistic and other material which has led him to views in conflict with the conclusion I have here stated somewhat summarily. As regards the Murra, however, it seems to me that Major Cheesman's suggestion must be dismissed as untenable. He did not himself profess to be an Arabic scholar, and his difficulty in understanding his Murra acquaintances may safely be attributed to the fact that the Badawin of Arabia have not attuned their conversational ideas to the prosaic standards of the modern world. They still think and speak in poetical terms, in proof of which I may quote a sentence from the conversation of the Marri, Muhammad ibn Humaiyid, on the very march whose incidents I am recording : There came life (*i.e.* rain), said he, in the autumn but the cold has burned it (*i.e.* the herbage) up. In the realm of thought the Arabian nomad—and to some extent also the Arabian townsman—is poles apart from the sophisticated product of Western systems of education, and the influence of religion on conversation is as clearly marked in the Arabia of to-day as it was in the England of the Puritans.

It was at this stage of our march that we collected two more recruits for our expedition from the camp of the Rashid subsection, to which Zayid and 'Ali had turned aside to engage their services. The new men, Muhammad ibn Rashid and 'Ali al Buhaihi, increased our total Marri strength to six and were specifically engaged as herdsmen to watch over our beasts at the pastures. They would ride any available camel, generally perched on the top of baggage, and no specific payment was stipulated for. They would just take their chance of my bounty like the rest and, in so doing, they did relatively better for themselves than some of their more distinguished fellows. But they worked hard and the lad Muhammad, in particular, was to prove a great asset to our expedition.

Our route lay over typical Marbakh country—a flattish, sandy tract with a profusion of dried-up grasses and some scattered bushes. A diversion was created by the appearance of a pair of vultures,[1] at which Ibn Humaiyid had an un-

---

[1] *Nasr.*

successful shot after some elaborate manœuvring, while
'Ali Jahman, his close relative, stoutly refused to try his
prowess on such creatures. The Oryx-hunter, he said by way
of explanation, does not go after such carrion. But it trans-
pired later that, in the days when he had studied religion
seriously, his teacher had discouraged the shooting of the
unclean bird. 'Ali had once progressed sufficiently in his
studies to be able to read, but he had never got to the stage of
writing, and now he had even forgotten the art of reading,
having no time for study. Nevertheless he ever and anon
betrayed a strange intellectual curiosity—uncommon among
the Badawin and even among the oasis-dwellers of Arabia—
and he was intrigued by my vigorous pursuit of what he
imagined to be the sciences. He felt instinctively that I
would not waste my time collecting insects and pebbles if
there was nothing to be got out of them. He just wondered
what it was.

In due course the sand gave way to a vast expanse of light
gravel dotted with bushes of *Rimdh* and *'Arrad*. The dune-
line of Jafura circled round on our right at a distance of a
mile or two to recross our path ahead in the Mashura promontory. And here and there broad strips of light sand lay
across the gravel plain. We passed another nomad encampment and I was surprised to see a Painted Lady butterfly
flutter away before us in the breeze from a pile of camel-dung
in an abandoned camping site. It was the first butterfly seen
since we had left the Hasa, and one of a very small number
seen during these months of wandering. Tracks of bustard
were observed quite frequently, but only once during these
early days did we have a distinct glimpse of the bird itself,
which has now grown very timid of man's presence and is being
rapidly thrust back into the more inaccessible parts of the
desert by the new habit of hunting them with motor cars. Ibn
Jiluwi, like the King himself, decimates them at the rate of
50 or 60 a day in his shooting expeditions, and one wonders
how long the bird, presumably a migrant visitor to Arabia,
where it breeds, will take to develop an aversion for those
parts of the country where cars can overtake their rapid
flight. Another seasonal migrant, the Cream-coloured

Courser,[1] was seen fairly often but was by no means as plentiful as I have found it in other parts of the country. The Gazelle we never saw in the sands of the Great Desert between Hufuf and Sulaiyil, but a more astonishing absentee was, perhaps, the sand-grouse, which is plentiful in the Hasa but was not seen again until we got to Sulaiyil.

As we marched thus over the plain of alternating sand and gravel they pointed out the direction of the wells of Qaraïn, about two hours' ride away in the midst of the Jafura dunes —two dead pits now buried by the sand and a single well with brackish water at eight fathoms.[2] A pair of Coursers vacated a clump of bushes, which we had marked down for a short mid-day halt. I wandered about in search of Mantids while the rest of the party sat over a welcome fire. Every little patch of gravel seemed to have its colony of the strange creatures, and I wondered if they ever exchanged visits over the barriers of sand that separated one colony from another. Seldom does one find them actually on the sand, where they would be comparatively conspicuous objects, but it struck me as strange that they betrayed their presence so often by movement when they would have been quite invisible in their native gravel patches if they had kept still. As often as not my attention was attracted, even when I was on camel-back, by their peculiar, rapid movements in the gravel, after which they lay stock-still, allowing me all the time I needed to get out a pill-box for their capture. That is a simple matter provided one rivets one's eyes on the spot where they lie— otherwise one might as well search a haystack for a needle. What these creatures eat I am unable to say but doubtless their main function in life is to provide meals for the larks and other birds, whose neat trails are to be seen everywhere on the tell-tale sand.

The wind had increased somewhat when we resumed our march, spreading an unpleasant veil of sand over the face of the earth, but, fortunately, such conditions proved to be temporary and the rest of the afternoon, though far from

[1] *Daraja* or *Darjalan.*
[2] The Badawin fathom would seem to average about five feet six inches, as I found by frequent testing.

bright, was by no means disagreeable. In the midst of the
desolation we passed a very old man resting on the sand by
the side of a scare-crow or dummy[1] such as sleeping shepherds
use to keep their flocks from straying. But nowhere in the
neighbourhood could we see any sign of the old man's
flock, though in the distance we saw a haze of dark shapes
which may have been bushes or sheep. The ancient of days
proved to be a man of some note in his now distant prime,
Muhammad ibn Luhaim, renowned among the warlike
Murra for his prowess in battle. Now in his dotage he was of
no more account but to herd sheep for a pittance ; and some
day, perhaps before very long, he would lie down on the
sands to die. Then the desert, which still kept him just alive,
would cover him with its mantle. We learned from him the
whereabouts of certain Manasir elements, whose Shaikhs
were to join our party if we could find them. They lay, he
said, somewhere amid the sand ridges of Al Khaiyala ; and
thither in search of them we sped Farraj and Ibn Humaiyid
with instructions to rejoin us on the morrow at our evening
camp.

A little further on we entered the dune-tract of Mashura,
which we traversed by a winding and almost continuous
causeway of gravel with the high billows of typical *Nafud* on
either hand. Long wisps of sand streamed like banners in the
wind from the peaks and crests of the dunes, while the plentiful bushes of the lower levels harboured a considerable colony
of locusts, mostly rose-coloured but with an occasional yellow
individual. It was certainly interesting to find such an
apparently isolated colony, for the whole desert had yielded
but few specimens, and those far between. So far as I could
ascertain they did not appear to be breeding and 'Ali was of
opinion that they would not do so until they had had time to
grow fat on the spring vegetation which would be due a
month or so hence. The Badawin have a whole mass of un-
scientific lore on the subject of locusts, which are reputed to
come into being out of the nostrils of fishes. They call them
Tihami after the coastal plain of the Red Sea whither they
first come from across the water and where, as also inland

[1] Called *Khaiyul*.

wherever they may descend after their long flight, they breed
to produce the dreaded hoppers which do so much harm to
any young crops in the line of their ordered march. In turn
the hoppers take flight as mature insects, creating havoc
wherever they go and providing the Arab with a welcome
addition to his diet when they have fattened on his crops
and pastures. The survivors disappear no one knows how
or whither, and the Arabs believe that they breed no more.
There is perhaps more fancy than fact in some of this lore,
which possibly serves, however, to record the bare observed
facts of locust visitations to Arabia.

The passage of the Mashura sands presented no difficulty
and we emerged on another gravel plain, steering towards a
gap between two further groups of dunes known as Taiyib
Ism and Qalalit. The outer line of Mashura seemed to run
down southward to the limit of our vision, the individual
dunes being also oriented with their horseshoe-shaped hollows
facing southward. Afar off to the left was said to lie the
watering of Khariqat al 'Ashaiyir, and I noticed in this area
that the sand-trails lay both to north and south of the little
bushes that dotted the plain. Whether this indicated a permanent balance between the prevailing winds or, as seemed
more probable, a transition from the earlier north wind to the
south wind now blowing, I cannot say. We passed between
the dune groups already mentioned on to an immense flat
plain of gravel which reminded me strongly of the great
Rakba plain along the eastern flank of the Hijaz mountains.

Zayid and 'Ali seemed a little vague about the nomenclature of these parts, and it was only by the irritating process of continual questioning and sifting their often inconsistent and contradictory answers that I was able in the end
to piece together the topography of the region. The sands of
these outlying dunes appeared to form the boundary of the
Jafura desert on this side, while the gravel plain represented
a transition from it to the coastal region which could not now
be far off though the horizon ahead of us was far from indicating either any dramatic change of scenery or the vicinity
of the wells of Ba'aij, which had been suggested as a suitable
spot for the evening's camp. We were, however, no longer in

any need of guiding, for the desert was scored with numerous meandering camel-paths which led us in a south-easterly direction, presumably towards the wells. For all his lack of topographical knowledge Zayid had led us on a true course over a vast area of almost featureless desert, and I felt that he deserved at least some credit for such an achievement. Under his guidance I had explored some 70 miles of a previously uncharted wilderness, and it was not his fault that the resulting map should be so bare and naked. Jafura is a limb of desolation, a dismal, unattractive wilderness, whose western fringe Major Cheesman had skirted on his way from Hufuf to Jabrin in 1924, while I had now struck diagonally across its northern arm to come out on its eastern frontier. Later I should cross its southern section in a south-westerly direction to Jabrin, and we should have a fair idea of its general character.

Suddenly the flat gravel plain began to sway and dip to an abrupt transformation of rocky depressions outlined by ridges and headlands. We had left Jafura behind us and stood on the brink of the Jiban. And beyond them out of sight lay the blue waters of the Persian Gulf.

CHAPTER III

THE ESTUARIES OF JIBAN

THE desert plain runs out flat and uncompromisingly to the fringe of a chasm, whose intricate outline of low cliffs has evidently been fashioned by the sea in ancient times. We paused a moment on the brink to survey the scene, a broad valley or bay trending eastward between rock-slopes which descended easily to the level of the depression in a series of low steps. It was as if the desert had thrust out two arms to embrace the hollow, while from the surface of each arm rose great wharts of rock, to a height of perhaps 200 feet or more. The mouth of the depression evidently debouches on the coast of the Bahrain Gulf, but the sea was hidden from us by the headlands at the further end, the most impressive of which was named to me as Ri' al Hamda.[1] It is said to mark the point at which the main Hasa-Qatar route, the Darb al Sa'i or postal road as they call it, traverses the valley to follow the sea-coast.

What is the name of this valley ? I asked of 'Ali. It has no name, he replied, it is one of the Jiban, but it has no name, God knows. That sort of answer had been all very well in the featureless desert behind us, but I could not bring myself to believe that a feature as striking as this great cliff-bound bay could really be nameless. 'Ali might indeed be ignorant of it, but I expressed myself very strongly on the subject of Zayid's remissness in not finding for me a competent guide among the numerous Badawin we had encountered in Jafura. It was difficult to be patient and long-suffering under such provocation, and there was an exchange of angry words, sharp and short and followed by the resumption of our march, now southward, along the fringe of the cliffs in sullen silence.

[1] Or Mahdar Hamda.

41

As we rode, a small and select deputation of my companions
accosted me to make peace. Look you, they said, 'Ali is not
to blame, he was only shy to pronounce the name of this
place in your presence, out of respect for you. Its name we
all know—a foul name, for they call it Jaub al Hirr.[1] 'Tis but
the fashion of the Badawin, they give rude names to everything, for they have no shame. I found it difficult to be or
pretend to be shocked, and I laughed aloud at their delicacy.
It was certainly a pretty trait in an unexpected quarter.

By the time we had skirted the cliffs of the western extremity of the valley not-to-be-named and struck out across a
promontory of the gravel desert which separates it from the
neighbouring depression of Jaub al Ba'aij the painful incident
had been consigned to oblivion. Up to this time indeed the
conversation of my companions had been astonishingly free
of the broader forms of obscenity, perhaps out of deference to
myself, but in due course such restraints would be thrown to
the winds and there would be free speech among them on all
things, pleasant and unpleasant. Where sex is concerned the
speech of the Arabs is coarse and naked rather than indecent
while, at any rate among the Badawin, the commonest theme
of conversation is, so far as my experience goes, not sex but
food. That is perhaps natural in a hungry land, where the sex-
reflex is simple and without complications though voracious.

Having stopped on the gravel plain for the afternoon
prayer, we came almost immediately to the edge of the cliff
that skirts the northern side of the great estuary-like depression of Jaub al Ba'aij. Here I called a halt for a leisurely
examination of the scene, but we sent on the main body with
the baggage to select a site for our camp and to pitch the
tents and prepare our dinner. The cliffs on which we stood,
some 30 or 40 feet in height, descend abruptly to the valley-
bottom in which, about half a mile apart, lie the two groups
of wells known collectively as Ba'aij. The valley rises southward and by an easy gradient to low sandy downs extending
to the further cliff, whose extremity to the north-east is
marked by the headland of Khashm al Ba'aij. This feature
lay south-east of our position, and between these two points

[1] *Hirr = Pudenda mulieris.*

the cliffs ran south-west to unite at no great distance in a narrow bay forming the landward head of the depression. From this head the estuary—that seems the most appropriate term to use in connection with these Jiban depressions—splays out delta-wise towards the sea in a north-easterly direction, the prominent headland of Ri' al Hamda forming the seaward extremity of the northern cliff as it does of the southern fringe of Jaub al Hirr.[1] The true channel of the estuary runs north-eastward along the northern cliff to the vast salt-flats that extend to the waters of the Gulf of Bahrain, while on the southern side of the valley a series of broad rock-steps, liberally covered with dunes and ridges of sand, descends towards the salt-flats from the Ba'aij headland. Salwa lay about NNE. of our point of observation though its palms and the sea were invisible to us in the afternoon haze. And here and there on the flanks of the channel strangely eroded stacks[2] of rock stood out as evidence of the progressive denudation and weathering of the cliffs, of which doubtless they once formed part. One of these fragments, known as Naslat al Tarad or ' the rock of the battle,' preserves the memory of a famous tribal encounter of some 30 or 35 years ago when 'Ali Jahman was a child. It was fought between the Murra, who were in possession of the wells, and the 'Ajman, who entered the depression at, and launched their attack from, this rock. The battle was stubbornly waged throughout the day and in the end victory rested with the home tribe, the Murra, who had as many as 50 casualties to mourn, while the losses of the defeated 'Ajman were very much heavier. That was in the good old days when cavalry still counted in Arab warfare, but now the modern rifle has deleted the horse from such affrays, while the thirty years' peace of Ibn Sa'ud has all but eliminated war from the normal programme of the tribes. Gone are the days of horse-breeding among the warlike Murra, for now, as like as not, if any man have a mare worth having she will inevitably drift into the stables of Ibn Jiluwi, as fine a judge of horse and camel flesh as lives to-day in Arabia, and a tiger, they

---

[1] The word *Jaub* (plur. *Jiban*) signifies a depression.
[2] Such isolated rocks are called *Nasla*.

say, for virgins for all his three-score years. The governor of the Hasa is indeed become a legend in Arabia already in his life-time—and many the tales told of him as once were told, truly or otherwise, of the greatest of the Caliphs of Baghdad.

With 'Ali I descended on foot to the western group of wells, of which only one—Bir al Tawil or ' the deep well,' as it is called—has survived the vicissitudes of time. The depth to water in the underlying sandstone is only two fathoms, and the pit is lined with a wattle frame to prevent the collapse of the soft alluvial soil through which it is dug. Strongly it reeked of the staling of camels, which filled the air with a noisome stench. In the close neighbourhood are other wells, whose positions 'Ali pointed out to me, of this ' deep group,' but they were all dead.

The second group of water-holes, where the camels awaited us, was only half a mile distant and differed from the first in being shallower, for which reason they bear the name of Bir al Qusaiyir or ' the shallow well.' In the two pits of this group the water is, or was, only one fathom from the surface, but both were so completely buried in the sand that they would have been quite unrecognisable as water-holes but for the circle of camel-dung that invested them with its familiar halo.

As we rode hence towards our tents a Stone Curlew [1] was seen among the bushes in the sand and 'Ali went off in unsuccessful pursuit. The sun was very near its setting as we reached camp, and I realised with some surprise that throughout this first day of fasting, during which we had marched some 24 miles, I had experienced not the slightest inconvenience. Not for a moment had I felt even hungry or thirsty, but 'Ali confessed to a slight headache as the result of long abstinence from coffee and some of the others showed manifest signs of distress. The call to prayer was a signal for our gathering round the camp-fire, where a dish of dates was set ready for the breaking of the fast. Coffee was then served round and we lined up for the prayer about a quarter of an hour after sunset. An hour later our frugal dinner of

[1] *Karwan.*

rice was served and meanwhile I had become aware of the tragedy which had befallen my watches. Fortunately we were within easy reach of Salwa, whose position had been astronomically determined by Major Cheesman in 1921, and in due course we would be visiting Jabrin, where I would again have the advantage of his work in 1924. Our plans contemplated proceeding from our present camp direct to Anbak, but it was clearly imperative now that I should visit Salwa to redeem my unfortunate lapse and my companions were not averse to an easy day on the morrow. It was agreed therefore that the main body should make a short march to Abu Arzila, the next ' estuary ' southward, while I should go down with a small party to Salwa to shoot the sun. We could then work round to Abu Arzila by way of the rumoured ruins of Sikak, and the unfortunate accident proved indeed to be a blessing in disguise. Without it I should have missed the exploration of a very interesting area which was to provide me with an important clue for the solving of the problem of the Jiban estuaries.

By now after four days of riding I had reached a climax of stiffness and physical discomfort though in all other respects I felt exceedingly fit in spite of the fasting and the short hours of sleep allowed by my multifarious preoccupations— the daily or nightly writing up of notes, the packing or labelling of specimens collected, and the like. It was humiliating and annoying to be such a cripple, unable to rise without assistance, and it was generally agreed that I should have a respite from Al Bahraniya. In consequence of this decision I rode Sa'dan's camel on the following day and, when we got into camp after a long outing and a round trip of some 26 miles, I found to my joy and relief that every vestige of my crippling stiffness had disappeared—never to return. It had thus taken me five days to acclimatise myself to camel-riding, which henceforth became an unmixed pleasure. Perhaps with another mount than Bahraniya I should have achieved this result more rapidly, for my new steed, smaller, lighter and more compact, never gave me a moment of discomfort, though I was sore and stiff enough in all conscience when I was helped on to her saddle that morning.

The cliffs of the great estuary towered magnificently over the low mist in the young light of dawn as the camels were driven off to the well for their first drink since leaving Dulaiqiya. It was but four days since then—and cool days to boot—and most of the animals spurned the potation offered them. Seven or eight days without water constitute no hardship for camels under such conditions, and they can manage as many as ten in full marching order provided that there be reasonable grazing available on their route. In our case the pastures had been rather poor, and here among the sands round our camp the *Ghadha* bushes were all miserably brown and dried up by the prevailing drought. The late summer rains had indeed paid a fleeting visit to this country south of the Hasa, but there had not been sufficient precipitation to make the desert blossom. And it was not till two days later that we were to see the first scanty signs of really fresh herbage in the uplands beyond Judairat, where we encountered the faint flush of green that precedes the spreading of spring's welcome carpet over the parched desert.

At 8-30 a.m. I started off with my small party on a north-easterly bearing, following the contours of the ground to avoid the higher ridges of sand. Afar off the sea burst upon our view as we topped the first rise, from which we now descended easily from step to step of the high ground on the southern bank of the estuary. The surface was of a friable sandstone weathered in places to queer mushroom shapes and dolmen-like formations. The distant palms of Salwa came into view with the blue sea on one side and the conspicuous flat-topped hillock of Qarn Abu Waïl beyond Sikak on the other. The scenery was both impressive and interesting after the dreary monotony of Jafura, and it was still a little puzzling for I had not yet been able to assimilate the true significance of the Jiban formation. Yet slowly enlightenment grew upon me and, as I looked upon the cliffs of the valley and the great expanse of salt-flats that stretched out before and below us, I could not resist the conclusion that the broken, sinuous line of the former encircled an ancient estuary, while the latter could not but be an old floor of the sea, from which the waters had receded to their present line

on either side of the Qatar promontory. That was surely
once an island as Bahrain is to-day, for the salt plain (in
parts actually lower than sea-level) runs right across its base
from sea to sea. From the third shelf of rock we descended
to a salt strip on a higher level than the main flats below
and perhaps, therefore, betraying a part of the old estuary
floor. From that we passed through a further barrier of rock
down to the main salt-flat, an immense plain that sounded
crisp and hollow under our camels' feet. Here my aneroid
showed the same reading as it recorded later on at the edge
of the sea at Salwa five miles distant. The whole of this vast
plain would seem therefore to be at sea-level more or less—
either a part of the original floor of the sea itself or a lagoon
separated therefrom by some sand-barrier like that of Khisat
al Salwa to which we soon came.

The flanks of the estuary here fall back right and left into
the far distance and there were only the sand tracts to inter-
rupt the great flat. The sand was of a dazzling white and
profusely covered with the green *Shinan* and the darker
Suwwad, which somehow seemed to create an impression of
noisomeness. In the midst of the sands lay the depression of
Khisat al Salwa containing numerous shallow waterholes of
unhealthy aspect with slightly brackish but drinkable
water, at a depth of two fathoms. Such wells can be easily
scrabbled up out of the sand anywhere in the hollow. I saw
three of them lined with wattles to prevent the falling in of
the sand, but the rest were open pits, most of them half
choked by their fallen debris. In spite of its name there
did not seem to be a single dwarf-palm[1] in this locality, which
must not be confused with Salwa proper further on. Major
Cheesman's plan[2] makes it clear that he did not visit this
spot and the ruined castle he investigated was that of Salwa
itself.

Beyond the sandhills we entered a firm, flat, grit-covered
plain with scanty *Shinan* bushes and quickened our pace to a
cheerful trot. We soon re-entered the *Sabkha* or salt-flat, over
whose firm, smooth surface a single camel path led us in
single file towards the palms of Salwa. As we went they

---

[1] *Khis, Khisa.*   [2] *In Unknown Arabia*, p. 33.

pointed out to me the track of a solitary Ford car which, after the pilgrimage of 1931, had made the stupendous journey from Mecca to Abu Dhabi on the Pirate Coast of the Persian Gulf under the guidance of a man of the Manasir tribe. The car had struck across the peninsula to 'Uqair and thence followed the coast to its destination. It was certainly a great performance, which deserves to be rescued from oblivion, though I was unable to ascertain how long the journey had taken. By such feats of pioneering a network of practicable motor roads is being slowly but surely spread over the face of the Arabian desert, which until a decade ago had never known any means of transportation other than the camel.

Similar paths to that on which we rode were seen now to be converging from numerous points beyond the salt-flats towards the ' harbour ' of Salwa, which is no more than a strip of tidal mud on the coast of the long tongue of sea that projects southward from the Gulf of Bahrain into the base of the Qatar peninsula. The harbour, in which rode a dozen or so of *dhows* at anchor, faces the derelict coastal palm-groves of Salwa across the channel perhaps a mile wide, more or less. Our course lay dead on the palms across the flat which, as it approaches the sea, turns to a glistening, salty whiteness. It is profusely strewn with little spiral shells[1] so common in the Hasa and to be found by us in due course at numerous places, in the Empty Quarter and beyond. They crunched deliciously under the soft padding of our camels, which shied nervously as they came to the channel, now narrowed to about 50 yards and crossing our path to a considerable distance beyond. At times the water at this ford is deep enough to necessitate a wide circuit to the southward but we found it barely knee-deep. Yet the camels had to be coaxed, forced or led into the water, and such is the perversity of their race that no sooner had they reached mid-stream than some made vigorous efforts to bathe while others, having refused to drink fresh water at Ba'aij, stretched forth their long necks to take a gulp of the salt liquid as they passed. It is not good for them and the Arabs showed no sympathy for such depravity.

[1] For details regarding shells see Appendix.

In ten minutes, having ridden past the first of the coastal palm-clumps, we drew rein at the second—a miserable grove of neglected stems separated from the sea by a belt of unhealthy-looking reeds and a line of dirty flotsam marking the tidal limit. 'Ali went off stalking a Stone Curlew with my gun while I made all possible haste to get the theodolite into action. The rest, having nothing to do but fast, lay down to sleep till I should be done. A large colony of locusts continued undisturbed their voracious depredations on the fronds of the miserable palmlets, and we added some of them to my collection before resuming our march at noon.

The main oasis of Salwa—a considerable area of scattered and unprosperous groves—lies about a mile back from the coast. Its central feature is a ruined fort in the midst of one of the thicker plantations, while the palms depend for their sustenance on a number of brackish springs with water almost up to the ground-level. A large party of Manasir camels was being watered at the time of our arrival at one of these springs in the courtyard of the fort, and some of our men went off to hobnob with Rashid al 'Abd ibn Mani', a handsome and attractive young shaikhling of the tribe who was on his way from Dauha to the Hasa. Meanwhile I spent a pleasant half-hour examining the ruins and the oasis.

The fort, a square enclosure of 73 paces oriented ENE. and WSW., consisted of a keep or dwelling-room in the SW. corner and an open courtyard, which occupied the remainder of the enclosure and was presumably intended for the accommodation of the owner's camels in times of danger. The crumbled walls were of the same fossiliferous rock as we had seen at Dhuwaiban, and the general lay-out of both places suggested that they belong to the same epoch. I did not trouble to collect pottery or other remains as Major Cheesman had already investigated the ruins very thoroughly in 1921. Nor did I visit another smaller and apparently similar ruin on or near the coast, beyond which lay the waters of the Gulf, resplendent with every shade of green and blue. The palms of Salwa are ownerless and unattended but produce an annual crop of dates to be gathered by any chance comer. What an opportunity, I thought, for some enterprising body of the

D

ever-poor and ever-hungry Badawin to settle here in per-
manence to enjoy and improve the advantages provided by
Nature! Yet evidently there had been something in the
nature of a permanent occupation here in centuries long gone
by. And there must be some explanation of the present
derelict aspect of the place. It is the fever, said Zayid, that
prevents settlement in such places. Everywhere, indeed, as
at Sikak and Anbak and even Jabrin, the *Ikhwan* have made
such attempts but always the fever drives them back to the
desert. The Arabs cannot face it and die off quickly, so the
palms are left untended for God to fertilise and bring to
fruition.

This strange fever of the spring-fed oases of the desert
would be an interesting subject for expert study. The Arabs
have not learned by experience and will not learn from
preaching that modern science can both cure or mitigate the
fever in individuals and eradicate it from its natural haunts.
I saw no signs of mosquitoes either here or elsewhere, and
even in the Hasa they do not seem to be the scourge they are
at Mecca and Jidda. Curiously enough Madina is almost and
Riyadh entirely free from the pest. Perhaps the fever of the
eastern oases is due to some other source than the mosquito,
and perhaps some day the problem will be tackled to add
appreciably to the cultivable area of Arabia.

We resumed our tour of inspection by setting off at a
swinging trot towards the conspicuous landmark of Qarn
Abu Waïl, a flat-topped hillock to the south-east, detached
from the long escarpment of Qalaïl, which forms the westward
face of the Qatar plateau. We rode over the same vast salt-
flat, whose perfect surface was littered with tiny spiral shells
and dotted with clumps of *Suwwad* and *Qataf*, which in a
rougher patch of ground further on gave way to *Shinan* and
Thullaith. We crossed the camel-paths leading to the Sikak
watering and kept straight on across a broad and stormy
strip of astonishingly white sand-waves with dark contrasting
vegetation until we came to the foot of the hillock, just five
miles distant from the Salwa ruins.

Leaving 'Ali and Ibn Ma'addi to guard the camels at its
base—and incidentally to sleep—Zayid and I began the

ascent to the summit about 200 feet above the plain-level.
Abu Waïl, who had given his name to the hill, was, he had
told me as we rode, one of the great ones of ancient Arabia.
He was wont to stable his mare on this (almost inaccessible)
summit and there, to this day presumably—for he himself
had seen it with his own eyes some years since—is to be
found, embedded in the rock, the iron staple to which he used
to tether her. From this description I imagined that the iron
might be a ship's anchor[1] picked up from some wreck on the
coast or perhaps some other relic from a vessel captured by
the pirates of old. The ascent certainly proved none too
easy, and near the summit the steep, eroded crags offered but
little foothold for our clambering or came away in our hands
to leave us precariously poised on the edge of miniature
precipices. But the lower slopes of the hill were full of
interest. A few fossils I had picked up at the base proved to
have slipped down from a thick fossiliferous stratum—perhaps a 100 feet or so—underlying a 50 foot thickness of
unproductive sandstone at the top. I soon had a couple of
haversacks full of these relics of an ancient oyster-bed, which
has proved to be of Miocene age[2] ; and I was gratified at
finding also a single well-fashioned flint implement. My
search for other indications of ancient man was in vain and
it may be that the flint had been dropped here accidentally
by some more recent visitor, for the modern Badawin still
strike lights with flints and would certainly pick up a good
specimen of their ancestors' handiwork to use for the purpose
if they should come across one. Meanwhile Zayid was investi-
gating the lair of a hyena, whose tracks proclaimed that the
animal was still within as there was no sign of its exit. The
sleeping pair below were summoned to his assistance only to
discover that the beast had left his home by a back-door which
Zayid had not discovered.

So we all moved on to the summit, collecting fossils on the
way. On the flat top, some 180 paces long and 50 broad, we
found nothing but a cairn of stones and a hole in the rock
about a foot deep and wide enough to accommodate the base
of a thick mast. It was here, explained Zayid, that he had

---

[1] The word he used was *Dhahal*.   [2] See Appendix.

seen the now non-existent iron and I was left to conjecture
what it might have been and what had become of it. The
flint and fossils—to say nothing of the view from the top—
were however sufficient compensation for all the trouble we
had taken to get here. It was indeed a magnificent, far-
flung, desolate scene that we looked upon from that chilly
wind-swept summit. Leaving my companions at the empty
socket of the missing iron I walked to the further end of the
hill overlooking the oasis of Sikak to take a round of bearings
when, suddenly, silently and without warning, an armed man
appeared before me a few yards off. Peace be upon you ! I
jerked out rather taken aback. And upon you be peace ! he
replied. I saw you not, I explained somewhat unnecessarily
and trying to spirit away the prismatic compass which he
had already doubtless observed, how did you come up that
way ?—it was indeed a sheer precipice behind him—and
whence are you ? Marri or Mansuri ? I hazarded, knowing
that any nomads in the neighbourhood would probably be
from one of those tribes. His reply astonished me. I am of
the *Ikhwan*. I remembered that there was said to be a colony
of the fanatics at Sikak and it lay indeed on the plain below,
visible from where we stood though I had not yet noticed it.
My imagination rapidly pictured the rest of the village
warriors posted round the hill in an unescapable cordon.
Possibly our camels were already in their hands. Yet the
man seemed friendly enough. What are you doing here ? he
continued, hunting perchance ? And who are those with
you ? Be there of the Murra among them ? We are from the
Imam, I replied using the *Ikhwan* title of the Wahhabi King,
and 'Ali Jahman is with us. That seemed to satisfy him and
we moved slowly towards my companions, with whom I left
the man to resume my survey of the scene. He had, I was
afterwards told, evinced some curiosity about myself,
obviously an unusual type of visitor to these parts, and they
had satisfied him with the explanation that I was an engineer
charged with some task of inspection by the King himself and
studying the water problems of the district. Many weeks
later in rather similar circumstances in the vast lava country
of the Buqum I was passed off as a doctor. In Arabia the

white man is the reputed repository of all the sciences—and years ago I had passed for an artillery expert !

Our descent by another route proved to be no easier than the ascent but in due course, loaded with fossils, we reached the bottom and mounted our beasts to visit Sikak, of whose widely scattered palms in a setting of low rolling white sand-hills I had had an excellent view from the summit. In less than half an hour we reached and halted at the first of the many springs of the oasis, a fair-sized pool at ground-level and more than half filled with tall flowering reeds.[1] A few wretched palms grew at its side and all around we could see similar groups of reeds and palms. A little way off on rather higher ground of less marshy character lay the little hamlet[2] of perhaps a score of mud-huts and a hundred souls at most, founded in the early days of the *Ikhwan* revival by Hamad ibn Barjis ibn Hanzab, a sectional Shaikh of the 'Adhba clan of Murra. Unlike many rather similar settlements of this tribe the place was still actively inhabited, though its population spends a good deal of its time out in the desert pastures. The oasis was rather a contemptible specimen of unaided Nature's efforts—for of course the owners leave the palms to fertilise themselves—to contribute to the food-stocks of man, who enjoys the ripened fruits of the groves without toil and has not yet realised that better results could be obtained if only he would do a little of the work he leaves so contentedly to the Almighty.

Besides the reeds and palms the oasis, which lies about 25 feet below sea-level, contains a good deal of tamarisk, but there was little of interest to detain us longer and we resumed our journey after disposing of the afternoon prayers. The rumoured ancient ruins had proved a myth unless they lie buried under the dunes which appear to be encroaching on the oasis from all sides. Finding the saline soil here somewhat slippery owing to the underlying moisture, we struck across the sands and skirted a low rocky ridge which lay on the hither side of the great salt-flat. Recrossing the tracks of the motor car already mentioned we struck out at a trot across the vast salt field, steering SSW. towards the

[1] *Ghaf.*   [2] These *Ikhwan* settlements are generally called *Hijra.*

mouth of the Abu Arzila estuary. Afar off to the south-east appeared the isolated ridges of Mushaikhila and a long series of tent-like cones between them and the mainland. We still had far to go, and the sun was rapidly sinking before us when we reached the sand-ridges which have practically obliterated the bed of this estuary. We had to resume an ordinary walking pace over the gentle switchback, and darkness found us still groping forward without any very clear idea of the position of our camp and with nothing in our saddle-bags to break our day's fast withal. At length we sighted our camp-fire afar off and it was 7 p.m. when we reached the tents to find dinner awaiting us. We had been travelling on and off for eleven hours, but I felt no weariness and spent part of the night initiating Sa'dan into the mysteries of taxidermy on the body of the Stone Curlew we had brought from Salwa.

With our travelling routine now well developed I was beginning to find the time at my disposal too short for the multifarious interests with which, at least in theory, I had saddled myself at starting. I had to do everything myself and found in consequence that everything was falling sadly into arrears. Even my journal was not up to date and I was aware from previous experience that arrears of work accumulated beyond a certain point can never be overtaken. This applied rather pungently to the collection of birds and mammals which had either to be skinned when fresh or thrown away before they became too unpleasant. So far we had met with little to shoot except a few birds, but most of these had had to be thrown away and I had regretfully arrived at the conclusion that, to make time for other things, I must jettison the activities connected with the collection of anything that required skinning. Before doing so, however, I decided, as a forlorn hope, to teach Sa'dan the very little I knew about the art of skinning. So we struggled that night with the Curlew, the blind leading the blind, and after a day or two of similar joint efforts it was he who took on the whole responsibility for preparing the specimens collected during our wanderings. In the end I brought home some seventy or eighty birds and mammals from the Rub' al Khali, and it may fairly be claimed that the collection has been of some use—not perhaps for exhibition but to facilitate the identification[1] of the desert fauna. The insects, fossils, rocks, and other things I dealt with myself, but it was a relief to know that the collection of birds and beasts could go on.

It was with something of a shock that I heard later in the evening that the discarded carcase of the Curlew had been roasted in the ashes of the camp-fire and eaten by my companions. I could only formulate a silent and pious hope that any arsenical soap that had attached itself to the meat during the skinning operation might not prove injurious to human beings, but it was understood from now onwards that all meat, however obtained, should go to the cook-house. I could not bring myself to partake of the meals resulting from this process, though many weeks later hunger triumphed over such squeamishness and I shared, like and like with my companions, in anything that was going.

The estuary of Jaub Abu Arzila differed from the Hirr and Ba'aij depressions in being almost completely filled up with a moraine of sand-dunes fairly well covered with parched *Ghadha* and other vegetation. The fact that it was a valley or depression at all was only apparent from the low rocky ridges on either side, terminating at their eastern extremities in the headlands of Khashm Abu Arzila and Khashm Anbak to north and south respectively. Only at the mouth of the estuary between the two headlands, lying several miles apart, did its true character appear from the narrowing tongue of saline plain that ran up westward for some distance into the sands which otherwise filled the valley. Our camp amidst the latter lay about 200 feet above the salt-flats and was therefore approximately at the same level as the wells of Ba'aij.

The climatic conditions had now undergone a complete change. The bitter cold and frosts of the early days seemed to have gone for good and I found it unnecessary to wear the ' snow-boots ' any longer, except at night and in the early mornings when the sand was still cold underfoot. It was good to be alive these days with all the old stiffness gone and

[1] See Appendix.

a growing consciousness of physical fitness. The air of the desert was marvelous, pleasantly warm by day with light southern breezes bringing up thin wisps of cloud to temper the sun's rays, and mild by night with thick mists and heavy dews at dawn. So thick indeed was the mist next morning on the Abu Arzila downs that our *Ramdhan* routine suffered a serious set-back. We had been summoned as usual to our pre-dawn supper and had actually begun to sup when a strange light, filtering through the fog, warned us that prayer time had stolen upon us unawares, after which there might be neither eating nor drinking. Suwid abruptly interrupted the meal with the call to prayer. The day's fast had begun and with it came the first signs of backsliding among my companions, who had not yet had their coffee and shrank from the long ordeal without that stimulus. After all, said some, we have already offended unwittingly and our fast is vitiated, so we may be travellers[1] to-day. As well, they meant, be hanged for a sheep as a lamb ! Not so, replied the more devout, let them ' travel ' who will for God is merciful, but for those who willed to fast—the definition in fact embraced the whole party—it is not too late. Man's actions are judged by his intentions. Let us pray and eschew the coffee. Put therefore your trust in God. But the devout were in a minority of five—'Ali Jahman, Abu Ja'sha, Ibn Ma'addi, Suwid and myself—against the more numerous backsliders, who gathered round the coffee-fire and loudly denounced the would-be monopolists of piety. At their suggestion—for I had retired to my tent—Sa'dan brought along my usual pot of tea. I told him to take it to the devil and put a curb on his tongue, for he knew his scripture well enough to take advantage of its loopholes when it suited his convenience and had been airing his learning before his admiring fellow-' travellers.' What fools are they, he said to me of some of our companions many days later when we had set out on a long march with no prospect of finding any game in the desert, to ' travel ' to-day when in any case they will go fasting. It is better to ' travel ' when we get a whole day to

---

[1] *Musafirin* used in the technical sense of persons availing themselves of the dispensation from fasting while on a journey.

rest in camp and there is meat to be had. Fortunately the
heavy artillery was on our side, including the chaplain, and
of the five only 'Ali failed to keep the whole thirty days of
the fast without a break, while Suwid went on to do the extra
six days of the voluntary fasting after the feast-day that
ended *Ramdhan*. ' The day of the fog ' thus became a landmark in our wanderings.

On coming to camp from our expedition to Salwa I found
that our party had been reinforced by the arrival of Salih
ibn 'Aziz, a sectional Shaikh of the Al bu Mandhar, one of
three main groups of the Manasir tribe. It was the camels of
this group that we had seen watering at Salwa, having come
up *via* Dauha from their summer-quarters and palm-groves
in the Dhafra district over against Oman. Their chief oasis
settlement has hitherto been shown on our maps as Liwa on
the strength of the pronunciation of the Manasir themselves,
who have a strongly developed tendency to change J into Y
and to labialise the DH and other letters of the Arabic
alphabet. The correct name of the place, as they all agreed
when we discussed the matter, is Al Jiwa.[1]

Salih's brother, who had also come along to see him off on
his long journey, departed to the tents of his own folk in the
morning when, having started off our baggage-train on the
direct route to Anbak, we set out to visit the Abu Arzila
wells, two water-pits of a fathom depth in a circular sandy
depression in the midst of the downs. Here we found about
100 camels of another Manasir group, the Al bu Rahma[2]
whose chief Shaikh is Sa'id ibn Suwit, watering under the
charge of a few herdsmen. Just before reaching the wells,
about two miles from camp, we were joined by two men, who
turned out to be the young shaikhling whom we had met the
previous day at Salwa with a servant in attendance. After
leaving that locality they had enjoyed good sport with their
hawks, and the young man had had the charming civility to
come over, seeking us out in the desert, with his bag of three

[1] Or Al Jua, the interior ; *cf.* Al Batina (inner) and Al Dhahira (outer),
districts E. and W. respectively of the main Oman range ; *cf.* also Kharija
and Dakhila, the ' outer ' and ' inner ' oases of the Libyan desert.

[2] The third group, which we did not encounter at all, is Abal Sha'r, whose
leader is Ghanim ibn Juraib.

bustards as a gift. Very splendid too he looked in a robe of
deep red, which set off so well the swarthy countenance and
aquiline nose inherited from a father, whose birth of a slave
girl had sent him through life with the nickname of Al 'Abd—
' the slave.' Young Rashid was perhaps about seventeen,
though he bore himself like a grown man, speaking with the
easy assurance that comes of the best desert breeding. It
would be long perhaps before he succeeded to the leadership
of his group, for his father still lived in hopes of stepping some
day into the shoes of the grandfather, Rashid ibn Mani', by
common repute the most considerable individual of all the
Manasir. I insisted on young Rashid riding with us to Anbak,
where he spent the night in our camp, and it was interesting
to see the deference paid to him by Salih and Humaid, both
considerably his seniors in years but rendering the tribute of
men to the quality of birth, which ranks so high in the
Semitic mind. I wished that Rashid might have been of our
party, but he declined my invitation with a grave smile and
took his leave of us, delighted with the few pieces of silver
with which I sought to make some return for his courtesy.

From the wells we struck south-east across the valley
towards the high ground of its southern bank which went up
before us in a series of broad shelves to a narrow pebble-
strewn plateau separating the Abu Arzila depression from
the striking estuary of Anbak. On the way we saw coming
towards us from the left two men, one walking and the other
riding. The latter proved to be Farraj who, leaving his companion to fend for himself, trotted up to us to report the
successful accomplishment of the mission entrusted to him by
Zayid the previous day. He had found the man he sought,
who now came toiling through the shrub-covered sand—a
ragged nomad, it seemed, though of fine athletic stature. It
was Humaid ibn Amhaj, a minor shaikh of the Al bu Rahma,
whose arrival completed the party which was to accompany
me on my wanderings. Two teeth protruded horizontally
and rather aggressively from the front of his mouth as the
result of an old encounter with an enemy bullet. Otherwise
his face was attractive enough, long, hollow-cheeked and
intellectual. He had the reputation of being something of a

poet though I was to find his productions somewhat disappointing ; and he proved to be the strong, silent man of the party.
He and Hasan Khurr al Dhib were perhaps the least voluble
but most dependable of them all, suffering my unreasonable-
ness in silence and seeking ever to keep the peace at times of
dissension. Salih was a striking contrast to his kinsman and
will figure more prominently in my story. After the formal
greetings Zayid courteously relinquished his mount to
Humaid, whose camel had been sent to Anbak with the baggage, and himself rode pillion behind Salih. The newcomer
rode on his knees in the Oman fashion, supporting his but-
tocks on the upturned soles of his feet—a strange seat on the
flat saddle but apparently comfortable enough and dependent entirely on balance. But such folk are born on camel-
back and can ride gracefully enough—even their women do
as much—on the bare rump of a saddleless, trotting dromedary. At times they change to a side-saddle position,
dangling one leg with the other tucked under them on the
saddle. And sometimes—the favourite attitude of Zayid and
'Ali—they ride astride, sitting far back behind the hump.
'Ali claimed to be the owner of two herds of some 80 animals
apiece, which at an average value of 200 dollars would make
him worth about L1500 of our money, a considerable capital
judged by the standards of Arabia. The three milch camels
with us had been commandeered from his stock—at least so
he said. If I had great wealth, he confided to me, I would
wive often, but I have only the one wife now, and she but my
second. My first bore me a son, now a youth of seventeen,
and when I divorced her my brother took her to wife. 'Ali
was not himself a Shaikh but of the kinship of one of the
chiefs of the Ghafran, Salih ibn 'Ali Abu Laila of the Zayid
section.

A large herd of the Ghafran camels came breasting up the
slope from the Anbak watering as we went down thither in
the opposite direction. With them strode a woman, red-
smocked, bright-eyed but veiled with the quaint mask of the
nomad females. She stared intently at me and seemed not
to resent my equal interest in herself. 'Ali and Ibn Humaiyid
dallied in the rear to glean the gossip of their kinsfolk newly

come up out of the great sands, but the rest of us passed on till we came to the cliff-girt edge of the valley. Meanwhile Farraj had stalked and missed a pair of eagles[1], which had settled on an eminence not far off.

The estuary was outlined on three sides by cliffs in various stages of picturesque erosion and in some parts completely detached to form isolated knolls or ridges in mid-valley. One of the latter, at some distance to the south-east, is known as Maqarr al Suqur[2]—the hawk's nest—being a well-known breeding-place of the *Saqr* falcon, whose fledgings the Badawin seek out on the almost inaccessible ledges of its cliffs to sell to Ibn Jiluwi and other lovers of this form of sport. Nearer at hand at the bottom of the cliff on which we stood was a large group of low and fantastically weathered rocks which looked like the ruinous remnants of some stricken Sodom or Gomorrah—the origin, possibly, of the vague Badawin story of the otherwise non-existent ancient ruins at Anbak. Out in the bed of /the estuary—where patches of white saline soil alternated with low hummocks and ridges of sand—lay the insignificant oasis of Anbak with its small, abandoned *Ikhwan* village close by to the south-west. And finally far to the east shone the floor of the great white salt-flat, on which debouch both this estuary of Anbak and that of Judairat, separated from each other by a wide band of billowing sand though originally no doubt forming a single bay within the same encircling line of cliffs. Afar off to the south the opposite bank of the double estuary ends in the little black knoll of Al 'Abd, which marks the hither side of a further estuary known as Khaur al 'Abd.

I had now seen enough of these estuaries to establish in my mind the conclusion that the sinuous line of their containing walls—from the nothernmost depression of Jaub al 'Uwaidh to the great Jaub *par excellence* of the south which Mr. Bertram Thomas entered after leaving the well of Bunaiyan

[1] *'Aqab.*

[2] Major Cheesman noted near Salwa a headland named Khashm Skhul, of which my companions professed complete ignorance. It is possible that his guides, having heard of this famous spot near Anbak, applied the name (*Skhul* is obviously nothing but a corruption of *Suqur*) at random to some feature of the coast of the bay at Salwa.

at the northern limit of the true sands of Al Rimal—represents the cliff-outline of an ancient sea. Fossiliferous deposits of Miocene[1] age are exposed in the lower strata of the Anbak and Judairat cliffs, and presumably elsewhere, under a considerable thickness of non-fossiliferous sandstone which appears to extend far back into the eastern desert, though its age and geological character cannot perhaps be determined finally in the present state of our knowledge. The immense salt-flat extending from north of Salwa down to the furthest extremity of Sabkha Matti doubtless represents the floor of the open sea in the days when it penetrated far inland up these estuaries. And I shall have occasion to suggest in a later chapter that the same sea extended in an enormous bay down to the Khiran tract over against Shanna where it washed the flanks of the Eocene mountains of the south and east. In those days the distant oasis of Jabrin also was presumably the upper part of an estuary whose configuration will in due course be discussed. Nothing surely can be of greater interest than an attempt to throw back the veil which hundreds or tens of thousands of years have drawn over the earth as it was when our earliest ancestors knew it or as it was even before the crowning glory of Creation. It is perhaps a bold task for a layman to embark on, but it is well enough if he bring with him to lay at the feet of the professors the material needful for the testing of his fancy's flights.

In this case and at this stage of my journey such material lay, as it were, at my own feet ; for as we descended the stepped slope down to Anbak we marched upon a surface littered with fossil oysters, such as we had already found in the cliffs of Qarn Abu Waïl. My companions chafed at my desire to halt, which would delay their coffee-bibbing. But halt I must, and I begged them to leave me to my work and go forward to pitch the camp. It was decided therefore that those who were fasting and were thus debarred from coffee in any case should remain behind with me, while the rest went on for their refreshment. For four hours under the afternoon sun we laboured, collecting and sorting the fossils about us,

[1] See Appendix.

studying the limestone strata from which they emanated,
mapping and planning and the like. 'Ali and Ibn Ma'addi
joined in the game with a good will, and we started a hare to
see it streak up the steep hillside to safety. At length we too
descended into the valley and marched towards our camp in
the oasis. Of what use are those shells ? asked 'Ali who had
been quick to recognise their marine origin, and what will you
do with them ? Noah's flood provided an easily intelligible
explanation of the presence of sea-shells so far inland. Yes,
by God ! he exclaimed, that is true, for all the earth was
covered by the waters and these things remained behind
when they receded. By God ! it is true indeed. The shells
are of no use, I went on, but it is knowledge I seek which is
better than wealth. I will take them to my country, where
they will put them in treasure-houses[1] for people to see and
study. You see, I too am a tracker like you. When you ride
you read the sands and know what men and women have
passed upon them a month ago or more or less. But when I
see shells like these I understand what was happening a
thousand years ago or more—it was idle of course to talk of
millions—back to the world's creation. You see at once the
tracks of animals and know that a fox or hyena has passed
yesterday or before, but I see the tiniest insects as I ride over
gravel or sand, which you cannot distinguish even when I
point them out. Your eye is trained in one way, mine in
another ; and you are not interested in the things that
interest me. On several occasions already I had indeed had
an amused and astonished ring of spectators, as I reined
back suddenly at sight of a little Mantid in the gravel. With
eyes glued on the motionless creature I had couched my
camel and dismounted to stalk the quarry while they
stood by open-mouthed with amazement at my apparent
insanity, seeing nothing themselves until I showed them the
minute captive in its glass-bottomed pillbox prison. But
gradually they too learned to use their eyes, bringing me
beetles and lizards and other things.

So we came to camp at Anbak late in the afternoon and
they all rejoiced to hear of successful hunting in the sun while

[1] *Mithaf*, the ordinary word for Museum.

they had had coffee and devoured one of Rashid's bustards. The half-dozen palm-groves of the oasis draw their nourishment from as many springs welling up into reedy pools flush with the ground-level, in addition to which there were one or two shallow wells surmounted by the usual tackle for lifting the water. The reeds grew thick and luxuriant to a height of 12 or 15 feet, and their graceful flowering heads against a dark background of palms made a magnificent show where the camels coming to water had not cropped them down to the semblance of ravaged millet-stalks. Tamarisks also struggled with the reeds and palms for existence, and a pair of sparrow-hawks[1] seemed to be having good hunting among the numerous warblers and other small creatures until one of them was itself stalked by Salih and shot at such close range with my gun that its head was almost completely blown off.

I took advantage of the plentiful—and excellent—water to have my first good wash of the journey by the largest of the pools, where the camels had been watered and our skins filled and laid out in rows in readiness for the morrow's march. The water was quite tepid at sunset but earlier in the day my companions had found it deliciously cool. By the time I had finished, dinner was served and very good it was with the meat of a bustard to vary the monotonous rice meals of the past week. I had noticed by the pools a fair number of sheep belonging to the folk of Ibn Nuqaidan, whose tents were scattered about on the sands round the oasis, and I had suggested that it might be a good thing to purchase a few of the animals so as to have meat for a couple of days to infuse a little vigour into us. Zayid, however, declared that the sheep were in poor condition and not worth buying at any price, but some of the others hinted strongly that there was a nice young camel to be had of the Arabs. I replied that such a plethora of meat would only damp their ardour for the chase, whose results—two hares and two curlews—had scarcely vindicated their early boasting. Ah ! wait till we come to the Sands, they said, and you will surely see hares as plentiful as locusts, and we shall eat of the meat of the Oryx to our heart's content. We had seen tracks of foxes and hares,

[1] *Shabbut.*

wolves and hyenas, bustards and other things, but all to no purpose.

It had certainly been something of a disappointment to me that we had found neither ruins nor traces of early man at Anbak,[1] always though rather vaguely spoken of as a locality of some ancient importance. The fossils had however been some compensation for this failure and we found the little spiral shells again in plenty in and about the plantation. Otherwise the place was of little interest except for the fact that it lay a few feet below sea-level. Such a site would scarcely have remained unoccupied in ancient times, but there was in fact no surviving trace of occupation earlier than the founding of the little *Ikhwan* hamlet by one Salim ibn Nuqaidan a dozen or more years ago. Its now derelict mud-hovels lay grouped round a rather larger building of the same type with a spacious open court, which had served as the local mosque.

Next day at dawn there was a light dew upon the ground and clouds in the sky, while a thick white fog lay low upon the valley, rolling slowly down towards the sea. The cliffs and headlands showed up above it, seemingly suspended in mid-air. The atmosphere was as mild as we could wish and the baggage-train was got off to a good start. Just as I was getting ready to mount myself, I was astonished at being accosted by a deputation of two Marri ladies from the neighbouring tents—the wife and a younger relative of a sectional Shaikh named Ibn 'Afair—with a bevy of very lugubrious children clinging timidly about their trailing skirts. Oh Shaikh 'Abdullah ! began the older lady with the bright-eyed girl in active support and the tearful children as chorus, they have taken away our bitch and we have nought but her to bring us meat from the desert, for our men are away, as you know, and only we women are left behind with these children. All along we had desired to secure a *Saluqi* hound if we could to hunt for the pot—and the Museum—and we had on one or two occasions seen animals which had been rejected as unsuitable. The previous evening indeed a dog had been offered to us and refused with thanks,

[1] Incidentally our maps have hitherto wrongly shown the name as Mabaq.

while a very light-coloured bitch, nice looking but very thin
and cold, had been discovered and coveted. At first I thought
that the complaint of the ladies was merely an indirect
method of bringing to my attention the fact that they had
not yet received the gift that custom demanded in such
circumstances ; and Zayid confirmed that conjecture as well
as the ladies' statement that the bitch had gone on with our
baggage-train. I returned therefore to the women rapidly
calculating the number of dollars which might constitute a
suitable counter-present, but they remained steadfast in their
protests that the bitch had been taken without their consent
and that they wanted her back—not her price.[1] The truth
was that Zayid, knowing that I would never have consented
to high-handed action in such a matter, had simply confronted me with a *fait accompli.* I insisted however that the
animal should be returned at once to her owners and refused
to mount until she had been brought back. And as I sat
there the women overwhelmed me with their voluble gratitude, while the children began to whimper with pleasure
through their streaming tears. May God bless you indeed !
Oh Shaikh 'Abdullah, cried the old lady, for in any case you
are welcome to the hound and I had said nought, but these
children, God save them! they were broken-hearted to see her
go and we could not remain silent before their weeping. May
God therefore prolong your life and improve your lot ! So the
matter was settled to my satisfaction and theirs. The incident had been both charming and instructive, and I had
delighted in their language, which was as pure and perfect
Arabic as one could wish to hear. I rode away contented and
never more had any doubt that Arabic is the mother tongue
of the Murra. Zayid growled at the folly of such squeamishness, but 'Ali privately applauded my championship of a just
cause. A firm hand is doubtless needed to curb the unruly
Badawin, but actual tyranny is unnecessary.

We marched south-west up the valley, over alternating
sand and sun-cracked saline clay, until we came to the
' Hawks' Nest,' by the side of which I discovered another
rich deposit of fossils in a detached rock called Mulaiha. The

---

[1] The Arabs do not traffic in dogs, whose price is unlawful money.

E

valley became more sand-ridden as we advanced towards and
followed the cliffs, where they bend round to form a great
promontory of eroded rocks at the junction of Jaub Anbak
with the estuary of Jaub Judairat. Here again we halted to
collect fossils from a fairly thick stratum of dazzling white
limestone sandwiched between an underlying band of
reddish-brown clay and an upper deposit of the fossil-less
pink sandstone which forms the desert floor east of the line
of these estuaries. A pair of ravens were in occupation of
these crags as we approached but did not remain to tempt
Providence; and Farraj, who went off to stalk them, never
got within effective rifle-range.

We now turned north-west towards the head of the
Judairat estuary, dotted with isolated and much-weathered
stacks of rock along the cliff on our right hand, between which
and the opposite ridge the mile-wide valley runs down eastward to the great salt-flat. Our objective was the two wells
of Judairat, of whose position 'Ali retained a vague memory
from a single visit ten or fifteen years before. A slight film of
green covered parts of the valley as the result of the late
summer[1] rains, which had been far from bountiful, while the
autumn rains had failed altogether. A hare was shot here to
celebrate the first showing of spring, and we wandered along
wondering where the wells might be, while far off ascending
the western ridge we saw our baggage animals creeping
slowly towards the plateau. We would soon be passing
out of the Jiban estuaries back into the desert and Jafura.

Look you, said 'Ali suddenly, I am lost. I thought the
wells were here by these rocks, but I see them not. Perhaps
we should have sought them in that patch of bushes we
passed just now; would you now that we go back to seek
them? Almost as he pronounced the words he turned
abruptly to the right and pointed triumphantly to a shallow
saucer in the sands. I thought suspiciously that he was imposing on me. It was difficult to believe that the dip in the
ground had ever been a well. Yet there was camel-dung
about the circumference, though the mouth of the pit was

[1] Called *Sfiri*, perhaps *Asfari* or *Safari*. The autumn rains are called
Wasmi, whence *Mausim*, our monsoon.

entirely concealed by the overlying sand. Yes, he continued, there it is, sure enough, but buried and the second well should be yonder beyond that rock. And there in fact we found the miserable hole in the sand with water in it at a depth of only five feet. It's briny, said 'Ali, like the sea. Men cannot drink of it, but the camels endure it. A string of camels of the Badawin was at that moment slowly passing along the sky-line of the ridge at the head of the valley a mile away. It was a Murra party proceeding to new pastures, almost our last contact with humanity.

From the wells we turned south-west again to cross the valley and, as we climbed up the further ridge, we enjoyed a splendid view of the snowy *Sabkha* at the end of the estuary. It is even like that, said Salih, to the end of Sabkha Matti and that is three days' journey from end to end on the road to our country. In it is neither bush for fuel nor even stones for the necessary cleansing. These we must carry with us when we travel that way and, if you err from the track, there are bogs that may swallow up camel and rider and leave no trace of them, even as happened to one called Matti who disappeared in that tract. We call it, therefore, by his name. Near it also are ruins of the ancients in the district of Majann, which some day I will show you, if God wills.

A great shelving beach of pebbles sloped upwards before us from the crest of the ridge to a vast gravel plateau of the desert similar to that which lies between the Mashura dunes and the northern Jiban. In all that monotonous waste, known vaguely as Hidbat al Hafaïr, two low ridges stood out in contrast with the surrounding flatness, while to our left appeared some slight indication of a cliff-edge encircling the invisible depression of Khaur al 'Abd.[1] Rare bushes of *Markh* and a few tufts of *Shinan* emphasised the appalling nakedness of an ill-favoured landscape. We marched on doggedly until 4 p.m., when we pitched camp for the night in a poor belt of *Shinan* bushes, where the gravel plain was lightly strewn with sand. Our camels were turned out to graze and a pair of ravens circled about them, perching now and then on their backs in search of ticks. I tried to stalk

---

[1] There is a well of briny water in the depression.

one of them with 'Ali piloting me by a devious route, but the birds of the desert are mistrustful of human beings and I had to be content in the end with a distant, unsuccessful shot, after which we saw the visitors no more.

The camels remained out while the moon lasted and, when they came in, 'Ali Jahman found the halter of his beast missing. Quite unconcernedly he took a lantern and, following her tracks in the darkness where she had wandered grazing with more than a score of others, came back triumphantly with his lost property. It seemed simple enough, but behind the simplicity lay generations of experience.

CHAPTER IV

SOUTHERN JAFURA

WE were now between 200 and 300 feet above sea-level but still within range of the coastal humidity. At 5 a.m., when we were roused for supper, it was pitch-dark and the sky cloudless but the ground was sopped with dew and a thick, clammy mist enveloped the whole country. The air was pleasantly mild, however, and the minimum temperature of the night had been as high as 50°. We had now left behind the varied and interesting scenery of the Jiban estuaries, and for the next few days our horizon would be limited by the rolling dunes of Jafura but, before re-entering them, I wanted to see the well of Hafaïr Ibn al Adham of which 'Ali had spoken. We accordingly sent forward the baggage on a direct bearing of SSW., while four of us—'Ali, Ibn Humaiyid, Zayid and myself—struck out more to the right over the gentle swell of the gravel plain dotted here and there with bushes of *Hamdh*.

The cool morning made marching over the featureless scene pleasant enough and we talked, as we went, of Wabar and the Empty Quarter, whose fringe we were so steadily approaching. But 'Ali was decidedly vague about the position of the well we sought and it seemed to me almost incredible that we could succeed in our quest in such circumstances. He had only visited this watering once in his life and that was in the ' day of Sarif ' just about 30 years before, when he had come hither with his father to water the family cattle. And, apart from the dull outline of Jafura which appeared on our left hand extending in a wide shallow arc towards the north and the low ridge already noted, which was now seen to be trending towards its grave at the edge of the sands, there was not a landmark to assist the traveller to

the water. ' There the guide falters, and you cannot blame,'
quoted 'Ali from a poem attributed to the legendary King of
Wabar. Yet as we marched we soon found ourselves in the
midst of unmistakable indications of the propinquity of a
watering—the almost obliterated camel-paths of an almost
forgotten past, meandering apparently aimlessly across the
plain. Suddenly 'Ali's quick eye perceived the strewn dung-
pellets that betrayed the immediate precincts of the well and
in a few moments we had dismounted at the spot we sought.
The well was dead and completely buried, scarcely perceptible indeed except as a shallow dip in the surrounding flatness. Long neglected, deserted and forgotten, the site alone
remained as a pathetic memorial to the enterprise and industry of its author, Ibn al Adham of the Buhaih Murra
whose name it bears. In the now dim past he had dug out the
shaft to a depth of eight fathoms, and the Murra camels had
been watered here for years until a period of neglect—
doubtless also a period of drought which had kept the
grazing herds away—had done its inevitable work of
destruction. Since then no man has had the energy to
reopen the pit.

As we now breasted up towards the conspicuous brown line
of the Jafura dunes, the plain gradually became more sandy
with long trails lying to south-eastward of the scanty *'Arrad*
shrubs. We passed into Jafura at the point where the low
ridge already mentioned plunges into the sands and, as we
stood on the crest of the first wave surveying the scene, it
seemed that at intervals on either side of us the gravel desert
ran into and under the sands in a series of parallel groin-like
dykes. Here and there these ribs lay exposed amid the
sands with a thick covering of pebbles as of some ancient
beach. Elsewhere all was sand, in long monotonous waves or
tumbled dunes or shallow and undulating plains. And it
was all amazingly bare—such vegetation as there was in the
hollows or on exposed patches of gravel or rock at the base
of the dunes being dead or moribund. Animal life was
correspondingly conspicuous by its absence—an occasional
tiny colony of larks, once an eagle poised high above the
desolation in search of game, a single dragonfly and a few

Mantids in the gravel. From time to time we saw the tracks of hares, foxes and other animals but that was the nearest we got to making their acquaintance, and I wondered whether the eagle ever found anything to reward his patient soarings.

Such for the next three days was the scene of our wanderings. About eight miles from the eastern fringe of the sands we came in their midst to the well of Qadha, which was a welcome break in our monotonous proceedings. How 'Ali ever found it without map or compass and, again, only the vague memory of a single visit several years before, I cannot pretend to explain, but he did lead us to it almost in a beeline ; and when we came to it there was nothing to see except a litter of camel-dung half buried in the sand to mark a pit over which the desert had spread an impenetrable veil. The shaft, situated in the cavity of a horse-shoe dune, had been in use as recently as five years ago, since when it had been neglected and allowed to disappear. Its depth to water was five fathoms.

Similar wells in this part of Jafura, and both apparently still in use, are Zibda (a day's journey to south of Qadha) and Sha'la (two days to WSW., and a little north of the line of Wadi Sahba), while in a westerly direction one might strike the Hasa-Jabrin camel-route in two days. Half a day on in the same direction one would, according to 'Ali, come to the wells of Haradh, of whose existence Major Cheesman was for some reason so sceptical that he erased it from the map in which I had, tentatively and on hearsay information, inserted it as a result of my journeys in 1917-18. It is true that I had been mistaken in assuming that this watering and Khin (of which more hereafter) must be in the bed of the Sahba channel and on or near the main Hasa-Jabrin route. But there can no longer be any doubt about the existence of Haradh approximately in the position here indicated— perhaps 10 to 15 miles north-west of the position originally suggested by me—for it lies on the only feasible motor-route between Hasa and Jabrin and incidentally it is on an alternative and longer camel-route with the advantage of water at half-way. It had been visited by several of my present companions either by car or camel. Furthermore this watering

had been used by Ibn Sa'ud in 1900 as his base for the operations that led to his recapture of Riyadh from the usurping
dynasty of Ibn Rashid in the following spring. No motor car
had yet visited Jabrin at the time of Major Cheesman's
journey, and it would seem that, while cars have since
reached Haradh not infrequently in the course of hunting
expeditions, the through trip to Jabrin itself has only been
performed once as a pioneer experiment. Between Haradh[1]
and Jabrin, however, the going is said to be excellent, while
the occurrence of long patches of heavy sand makes the
northern section of the route rather more difficult.

We had thus made a considerable detour for the barren
satisfaction of placing on the map the two waterings of
Hafaïr and Qadha, which had long since been abandoned to
the tender mercies of the sand. Our next objective was to
rejoin the main body and we turned south until from the
crest of a range of dunes we espied the caravan crawling
along in the far distance—a dark streak in the yellowish
immensity of the rolling wilderness. We crossed the tracks
of a wolf and saw occasional traces of bustard, but the most
interesting experience of this first day in the sands was an
object-lesson in the noble art of tracking evoked by the sight
of northward-trending camel-tracks spread out over a wide
front. Look, said 'Ali to Ibn Humaiyid, it is the folk of
Salih ibn 'Ali (a minor chief of the 'Uwair section of Ghafran)
come up from the south. They spoke of his coming soon but
I thought we might find his people yet in the sands. It is
but a day, or perhaps two, since they passed this way.
Doubtless they watered at Zibda. And look, there is So-and-
So and So-and-So—for there were human footprints too and
these people were of his near kinship—and there is Salih
himself, God save him! So they marched on against the
current of the tracks, communing with each other aloud,
exchanging notes on those eloquent prints in the desert
sand. It was months since 'Ali had seen anything of his own

[1] About 1½ days' journey south of Haradh lies an unimportant watering
called Waqar, while a group of rocks and caves known as Qusur ibn 'Ajlan
lies not far from Haradh and a day's journey south of the Hasa-Riyadh
road. Major Cheesman was in error in stating that there is no water
between Zarnuqa, Hasa and Jabrin.—See *In Unknown Arabia*, p. 16.

folk, and he pored affectionately over the signs of their
passing. What news had they, he wondered, of those further
sands whither we would be going, of foes and pastures, of the
Oryx shooting and other things? And now they would be
spending the winter in the north and he would not see them
till his coming again from the Empty Quarter. He sighed at
that prospect with a heavy heart, for there was none in our
company but wished he might be back by the comfortable
camp-fires of his fellows at the pastures. By now they knew
in rough outline the main objectives of our enterprise and
they groaned—some aloud and others silently—at the madness of it all. Homesickness accounted for much of their
distress in these early days, but there was also a gripping fear
at their hearts when mention was made of the Hadhramaut[1]
and the Empty Quarter. And once in these early stages,
when I asked 'Ali in the hearing of others some simple question about the relative positions of Qa'amiyat and Shuwaikila,
he stared at me with quizzical incredulity as if to say : The
man's possessed ! would he have us venture our lives where
no one ventures but to hunt the Oryx. Yet how comes he to
know of these things ? To enlighten his curiosity I showed
him the map of ' the Christian '[2] who had come up, as he
well knew, through the desert only the previous year under
the guidance of his own cousin, Hamad ibn Sultan. But
surely, I added, to put him on his mettle, the map that you
and I will make, oh 'Ali, will be even as good. I will omit
nothing, he replied, that you may write it in your chart. And
we will seek out even Hamad himself that he may make good
my deficiency. Never once—and it stands to his credit—did
he betray the slightest sign of jealousy of the worthy rival,
against whom he was pitted by my challenge. And in the
matter of tracking, in which he was himself obviously a past-

[1] Commonly but without reason believed to mean ' the land of death '.
It is the Hazarmaveth of *Genesis* and its people (sing. *Hadhrami*, plur.
Hadharim) may be referred to the biblical Hadoram, *cf.* the Greek
Χαδραμῖται of Ptolemy.

[2] It was always thus that my companions referred to Mr. Bertram
Thomas. Major Cheesman was ' Salih's companion ', referring to his guide.
Captain Glubb of the 'Iraq borderland was always Abu Hunaik—' the
fellow with the jaw,'—while Colonel H. R. P. Dickson of Kuwait was just
Duxon.

master, he acknowledged that the greatest experts were to be found among the Dimnan group, who had incidentally carried out quite recently a raid on some Dawasir cattle within the Hasa border and had been reported as having watered at Jabrin—a fact that made it desirable for us to walk circumspectly. The raiders had been from that part of the group which remained based on Najran[1] when Suwid and his section seceded some years ago to sojourn in the Hasa. The whole of the waterless desert is accounted to the Dimnan from Maqainama westward, while the Ghafran of the south and the Jabir of Jabrin only spill over spasmodically into its fringes.

So in due course we overhauled the main body and an hour later found a shallow depression to camp in, where there was some scanty vegetation—*Hamdh* and *Abal*—for the camels to browse on. In the midst of it and close to our camp was a patch of gravel out of which rose a low conical hillock[2] of the underlying rock. It was still fairly early in the afternoon when we camped and I spent some time in a fruitless search for insects, while, on returning to the tents, I found one member of the party—Sa'd al Washmi, my groom—completely prostrated with a bout of fever. I had a small store of medicines for such emergencies and treated him with aspirin fairly successfully, but it was some days before the ague left him and meanwhile he managed to convince himself —if no one else—that he at least would never return to his sorrowing family if we proceeded any further into the desert. He was at all times the most lugubrious of individuals with an incurably defeatist attitude towards life. Even when well he went about his business with mournful groans and muttering invocations to the Almighty to grant us a safe return home from all the perils of the unknown. Abu Ja'sha had started out on the expedition with eyes so sore that he was practically blind and seemingly in great pain, which he bore in stoical silence though generally shunning the society of his fellows.

---

[1] About this time a Wahhabi expeditionary force under Khalid ibn Luwai of Khurma and the Qahtan chief, Ibn Shaflut, was on its way to Najran to bring its turbulent folk to book.

[2] Such features are known as *Quwid* or *Qarn* (horn).

He had come to me for help in his affliction and all I could do was to give him boracic lotion to wash his eyes in. With the change in the climatic conditions, however, he now seemed to be rapidly getting better, though he obviously needed expert medical attention if he was to recover the full use of eyes manifestly affected by some serious form of ophthalmic disease. The trouble had doubtless been intensified by the extreme cold and his methods of keeping it at bay either by sitting close up to a blazing, smoky fire or by smothering himself under the blankets or clothing which served to keep him warm in sleep. To sleep with the head completely covered is of course normal in Arabia and they wondered at my exposing my head to the night chill. It is healthier, like that, I would say. No, by God! retorted Abu Ja'sha, for at home on a cold night there is nought better than to get under the warm blankets with your wife, clasping her to your body with both arms round her and to sleep the night through like that. Can you then sleep like that? I asked. Yes, by God! he replied, I can; I always do.

'Ali Jahman had something of a hankering for mild drugs, such as salts (Eno's and Epsom), throat lozenges, quinine, aspirin and the like, and freely indented on my stocks; he now complained of pain and boils on his gums, for which I could think of nothing but a mild solution of iodine and water or zinc ointment as possible methods of treatment. He took some of both and presumably experimented with them but, noticing that he asked for no more though he still complained of the boils, I twitted him with loss of faith in my doctoring. No, he said, it is not that, but we Badawin also have our cures, and this morning before the fast I washed my mouth with the urine of my camel to ease the pain. Yet still I suffer. And he continued to suffer some days longer and I can claim no credit for his eventual recovery, which was probably merely a question of time.

Our *Ramdhan* routine was now well established and we were already quarter way through with the fast. The weather conditions had been cool enough to mitigate the discomfort of thirst and the unattractive monotony of our diet kept hunger at bay. There was indeed only the absence of coffee to

trouble my companions—it was extraordinary how they
hankered fretfully for their wretched tots of the feeble liquor
and degenerated progressively as the warming sun played on
their nerves distraught—while two of them suffered an
additional penance not less acute. Farraj, as I have already
mentioned, was a devotee of tobacco ; and the newcomer,
Salih, was in like case. If you could tell me a cure for that, he
sighed when we were talking of 'Ali's gumboils and the rival
merits of iodine and urine, I would thank you from the bottom
of my heart. The only possible remedy was imposed on them
in due course when their slender supply of tobacco came to
an end. But meanwhile none yearned for sunset more
earnestly than those two and their breaking of the fast was
an impressive rite. There was but a single pipe of common
clay for them to share, turn and turn about ; but their
ingenuity was equal to the occasion and an empty cartridge-
case, pierced through the cap, served as a substitute bowl,
the smoker inhaling the smoke through the tiny orifice held
between his lips. In the morning, an hour or so before the
dawn prayer, we would be roused from sleep for supper, after
which my companions proceeded to imbibe as much coffee as
possible in the time remaining to them while I retired to my
tent and, with a pot of tea by my side, wrote up my journal
or packed the insects and other specimens demanding my
attention. The call to prayer was the signal for beginning the
fast and, after our devotions, my companions composed
themselves to slumber again, while I continued my interrupted labours until they were again checked at, or soon after,
sunrise by preparations for the day's march. I seldom
seemed to get more than four or five hours of sleep during
these days of fasting as I was generally busy with my notes
and other things till midnight, but short hours of slumber
involved no hardship under the healthy conditions of our
out-of-door existence in a climate which was as nearly perfect as possible. I was gloriously conscious of physical well-
being and spiritual contentment as I marched through the
desert and thought fondly of the greatest of deserts beyond it,
the promised land into which I should so soon be entering.

Next morning (January 15th) a brilliant sky greeted me as

I issued from my tent at the supper call. The Southern Cross stood upright and Spica shone from the meridian, while Antares twinkled hazily from the upraised head of the Scorpion in the south-east. A light mist enveloped the camp and there was dew upon the ground, though less than there had been in the coastal tract. We started off at 8 a.m. and I rode with 'Ali and Salih. How far now, think you, I asked, to Jabrin? Three days, replied 'Ali; yes, three days or two days —or two days. God knows. And Salih sought to entertain me with instructive information about his own tribe and country. Our origin, but God is all-knowing, is from the Qahtan, they say, for we reckon Ghuwainim al Zahri as the ancestor of the Manasir and he was of Qahtan; but we are of the Nasara of old, the Christians, whence our name. Surely there is something written of that in the books of the Franks. I agreed that the similarity of names supported the tradition. Several times, he continued, I have seen the consuls at Masqat, for we had a dole prescribed for us formerly from the Sultan's treasury, but now our resort is only to Ibn Sa'ud. Buraimi is of the Manasir—full of the mansions of our Shaikhs who settled there under the Wahhabi government. But we are not of the Wahhabi religion, not Hanbali but Maliki. Yet there is little difference between us, God knows, though we only shorten the prayers when travelling without combining them as do the Wahhabis. We pray the five times each day separately and we stand for prayer with our hands loose at our sides, not joined over our bellies. But that is all the difference. I noticed, however, that Humaid conformed to our practice or Salih's indifferently. Perhaps he thought little of such minor distinctions, for he was a philosopher. Both he and Salih, when performing the formal dry ablutions before prayer, took up a handful of sand to bless with a kiss. You should see our settlements of Dhafra, continued Salih, where you may ride for three days among palm-groves and villages. Before them the gravel plain stretches unbroken to the sea and behind us are the sands—waves and billows like this Jafura but better pastures. I have crossed them to Muqshin, where once we raided the 'Awamir. It is a ten days' journey across the sands, whither we go with our camels. The best of the Manasir camels is of the breed called *'Usaifir*, light-coloured dromedaries as good as any. But of all the *'Umaniya* breeds the very best come from the Duru' and Al bu Shamis tribes. And 'Ali's mount, Na'riya the first of all our beasts, is of the *Dara'iya* race. The folk of Al bu Shamis are not of the Muslimin but of the 'Ibadiya sect and they pray in a strange fashion.

About five miles on from our starting point we came upon bushes of *Hadh*,[1] one of the most characteristic plants of the south, which I thus saw again for the first time on these wanderings. It is evidently of the *Hamdh*[2] family and of salty flavour but it is the staple food of the sand camels. Every now and then we passed by or across patches of gravel, sometimes of considerable extent like great lakes in the sands. But animal life was scarce enough though we did see two hares. It is different in our country, said Salih, where game is plentiful—Oryx and gazelles and the wild ass and foxes, which we of the Manasir eat though the Marri dubs them unlawful. We have the wild-cat too, which they call *Hirra* and we *Atfa'*, and the badger.[3]

A light SW. breeze made things pleasant enough in the early afternoon, but after some six hours continuously in the saddle the men began to clamour for a halt and I had to resist their pressure to make sure of reaching the channel of Wadi Sahba, which lay somewhere ahead of us and where I was anxious to halt for the night in order to determine its position by astronomical observations. They only had the vaguest idea of its distance and I feared that a halt might baulk me of that important objective. My anxiety however proved to be as needless as their irritation, for scarcely an hour had passed when the vegetation suddenly began to show fresher and, almost without realising it, we found ourselves midway across the channel. Here it is, said 'Ali, the Sahba! Look, there is the *Birkan* which we always reckon to find in

---

[1] I had collected specimens in 1918 which were identified as *Salsola* sp. G. Rohlfs figures it under the name *Cornulaca monocantha*, Del. See Appendix.

[2] Both are *Chenopodiaceæ*.

[3] *Dharimban* apparently ' badger ' or possibly the Ratel.

the channel. It grows not further north than this, but it is one of the best herbs of our southern pastures.

There was general rejoicing now that we had reached the spot where they might camp in peace till the next morning, while the camels grazed to their heart's content on the *Birkan*. I was equally satisfied to have all the time that was necessary to investigate the Sahba problem though it required some searching to discover the alignment of the two banks of the channel, which at this point of its course is almost entirely engulfed in the sands. The Sahba is one of the great and long-dead rivers of ancient Arabia, having a total length of more than 500 miles from its head in the flanks of 'Alam in the central highlands of Najd (in Long. 44 E., Lat. 25 N.) to its mouth in the Persian Gulf. Its upper reaches known as Wadi Sirra I had crossed during my journey of 1917, while in the following year I had seen something of two further sections to the eastward known as Sha'ib al Birk and Sha'ib 'Ajaimi. The latter runs down to Yamama in the Kharj province, where I then saw the sand-choked head of the final reach which alone carries the name of Sahba. Major Cheesman had crossed this section about halfway between Yamama and the sea on his journey[1] down to Jabrin and had found it a well-marked channel between low banks, but had not been able to ascertain exactly its ultimate fate. It was not known therefore whether the Wadi came to grief in the Jafura sands or succeeded in pushing its way to the sea, while Mr. Bertram Thomas in his journey of last year did not notice or mention the channel, which he presumably crossed before reaching the palms of Nakhala, though it was probably so shallow there as to be imperceptible in the absence of the necessary knowledge in his guides. In Salih and Humaid, however, I had the good fortune to find natives of those parts who knew the Sahba channel in its lowest reaches, where it runs through the gravel plain of Majann to the sea between the tongues of Sila and Ba'ja. And in its bed, they said, at no great distance southward of Nakhala lies a well called Batha. Thus we now have a good general idea of the whole course of the ' river ' from source to sea.

[1] *In Unknown Arabia*, pp. 237 *et seq.*

At the point where we had pitched our camp there was, as I have said, much sand spread over both the bed and the containing banks of the Wadi, but there was enough of the latter exposed to show that the channel was about a mile in width. The banks on either side scarcely exceeded 20 feet, while considerable sections of the floor were exposed along the north side, where a chain of gravel and pebble patches was broken at intervals by narrow isthmuses of sand or isolated dunes. The direction of the Wadi at this point was almost due west and east, but next day after marching about five miles on a SW. bearing we encountered the channel again in a well-marked gravel strip close on our right lying SW. and NE. It is probable, therefore, that the course of the ' river ' meanders somewhat through what must in its heyday have been very flat country.

Here again there was a slight dew in the morning and a pair of ravens appeared to see us off before prospecting our camp-site for any crumbs that might have fallen from our frugal table. The landscape now flattened out to an extensive sandy plain, gently undulating and frequently interrupted by wide stretches of gravel. Jafura seemed indeed to be petering out, and I imagined that we might be entering the great gravel plain of Saramid mentioned by Major Cheesman. Yet my companions seemed to have no knowledge of any such tract though many of them were perfectly familiar with all the ordinary routes between Hasa and Jabrin. I wondered vaguely how this could be, and dismissed the matter from my mind, when the sight of more high dunes beyond the unusually large gravel tract we were negotiating showed that in fact Jafura was still very much alive and by no means done with.

So we marched over gravel and sand conversing of many things as we went to while away the time. I asked them about the much-fabled ' walking stones,'[1] of which I had heard so much at a safe distance from Jafura but which seemed unaccountably non-existent now that we had actually entered the reputed arena of their activities. Humaid scouted the very idea of such things and evidently did not place any

[1] See Appendix.

reliance on the many tales of them told by professing eye-witnesses ; but Salih came to the rescue with assurances that he himself had seen them in those far-off sands around his wonderful home, where there are according to him pre-historic ruins in which I might still see, if I cared to visit the scene under his guidance, the guns used in the days of the ' Ignorance ' ! Doubtless he may have seen pieces of artillery dating back to Portuguese times, but I was beginning to realise that he preferred colour to truth and I reserved judg-ment on the ' walking stones ' until they could be produced to perform in my presence. The only specimens of such I had myself seen hitherto were two bits of basaltic scoria from the volcanic tract of Harrat al Kishb in western Najd, but these had been duly examined by the authorities of the British Museum and divested of all reasonable claim to the magic qualities imputed to them by the Arabs.

Abu Ja'sha, now more or less recovered from his ophthalmic troubles, was beginning to play a prominent part in the desultory conversations that accompanied our marching. Among his treasured possessions was a pocket compass, on the strength of which he boasted something of a scientific attitude towards life, and he was as delighted as a child one day when, before an admiring audience, his needle was found to point in exactly the same direction as that of my prismatic affair. But his strong subject was sex, and he loved to poke fun at Salih by dilating on Manasir practice in the matter of female circumcision. Take it from me, he said, they let their women come to puberty with clitoris intact and, when a girl is to be married, they make a feast for her circumcision a month or two before the wedding. It is only then that they circumcise them and not at birth as do the other tribes— Qahtan and Murra, Bani Hajir, ay, and 'Ajman. Thus their women grow up more lustful than others, and fine women they are too and that hot! But then they remove everything, making them as smooth as smooth, to cool their ardour with-out reducing their desire. Zayid blushed for his unblushing frankness. Be not angry with him, he urged, it is his way and his tongue masters him but he has a good heart. And if they make a feast for such occasions I asked, do they perform the

F

ceremony publicly as with boys ?   God save you !   No, he
replied, but the girls are dealt with in their tents by women
who know their business, and get a dollar or so for the job.
They are expert with the scissors, the razor and the needle,
which are all used for the operation.   The Dawasir do not
practise female circumcision nor the townsfolk of Najd ; and
some of the northern tribes do, while others do not.

We were now marching over an ever-widening gravel plain
which seemed to undulate very slightly, while beyond it they
pointed out the dunes called Al Qasam, before reaching which
the desert surface sank to a shallow but well-marked depression—more like a valley indeed than the Sahba had
seemed at our crossing of it, though its lowest point was
scarcely more than 20 feet below the banks on either side—
perhaps half a mile apart.   You see this trough, volunteered
Suwid, it is a branch of the Sahba which leaves it in the
Summan about level with or further back than Haradh.   We
call it Surr al Ma'id—the depression of the well-camel—for
once upon a time, they say, a party of men were crossing this
desert with some of their well-cattle, and one of the animals
died in this channel near where it forks off from the Sahba.
Therefore they called it Surr al Ma'id.   My mind jumped to
an obvious inference, for the name solved the mystery of
Major Cheesman's ' Saramid.'   The channel appeared to be
completely blocked by a line of sand about a mile to the west,
while eastward it ran or seemed to run for some three miles to
the sands on that side.   The surface of the bed was of light
gravel with a thin covering of sand, and the upward slope
southward was very gentle.

We now entered a broad belt of dunes as high as anything
we had encountered in all the breadth of Jafura behind us
and I admired the quickness of the Arabs in detecting and
avoiding the spots where the sand was deep and soft.   Occasionally there was no alternative to crossing narrow strips of
such character and it was interesting to see the camels fall
instinctively into single file so that those behind, treading in
the footsteps of their predecessors, might enjoy the advantage of a beaten track.   This belt of dunes, occasionally
interspersed with small patches of gravel and belts of good

vegetation, is known as Al Qasam, that is to say 'the division' between Jafura proper and its westward continuation, of similar though barer character, called Al Haml. In a sense therefore Jafura ends here at the channel of Surr al Ma'id though southward of our line of march it crosses the depression and appears to run on to the edge of the Jaub.

Beyond Al Qasam, nearly 10 miles wide but much interrupted towards its further fringe by extensive gravel patches, we emerged into the gravel plain of Hidbat al Budu'. Our course lay south-west between the southward-trending line of Jafura to our left and the westerly horn of it (Al Haml) on our right. The divergence of these two lines of sand made for the progressive broadening of the plain, over which we marched in grim desperation in the hope either of reaching the great basin of Jabrin before sunset or of finding in the gentle undulations of the plain itself a line of herbage which would make it possible to camp for the night. Both objectives eluded us and it was nearly 5 p.m. when we decided to relinquish the effort and to camp in a shallow drainage-line where there was dead vegetation to serve as fuel but no fodder for the camels. A violent altercation, in which I took no part, ensued among my companions as to whether we should stop or go on to the bitter end. And it was perhaps as well that the Ayes, thinking chiefly of coffee, had it, for we still had very far to go next day and the quality of the desert certainly did not improve.

We had done some 25 miles with practically no break, and the latter part of the march had been made rather disagreeable by a moderate but persistent wind in our faces. Apart from a few lizards found in the gravel my collecting had not prospered and we had seen no hares or other game all day. I had, however, noticed a solitary locust in the Jafura sands and we were to encounter another on the gravel plain next day, while a few brilliantly-coloured scarab beetles had rewarded my exertions at our last camp in Wadi Sahba. What a lifeless, desolate waste it was—and this vast plain was as bad as any part of it, extending some 10 miles across from sand to sand. The Hasa-Jabrin road was said to lie about a day's journey to our westward at this stage, while the first well of the Jabrin basin proved to be 25 miles on and the important watering of Bir 'Aziz in the Jaub itself was said to be about two days' march to south-east of our present camp.   Here and there an isolated sand-dune stood up out of the gravel, across which ran the camel-paths pointing the way from the Jafura pasture-grounds to the Birkan watering, which we should seek on the morrow.

We resumed the march earlier than usual in the morning to come to the water as soon as possible and ambitiously hoping to make Jabrin itself before nightfall.   We had been marching for a quarter of an hour when the sun rose out of a little pool of light on an almost sea-like horizon.   With the sun came quite a thick haze over the distant sands on our left hand, but out on the plain the air was clear and dry.   At times we had glimpses of the sands afar off to the north-west and in front of us where their line curves round to a promontory known as Sula' al Haml.   But most of the time we marched over an unbroken desolation, where the sands had receded for good on both sides.

A brisk breeze from the south-west served to keep us cool and Salih was again to the fore in praise of the greater beauty and charm of his own country.   If you saw it, he said, you would indeed wonder.   It was inhabited of old by Bani Hilal and it was of their guns I spoke yesterday.   The place is called Sirra, and I will conduct you there next year if God wills, but you should bring an engineer with you to see it. Perchance there may be gold there for the hills are all red. Also in Dhafra there are bones and other remains, they say, of a great battle in old times between the Persians and Bani Hilal.   And you shall stay with my people as long as you will ; ay, and I will find you a girl to wed, and one also for Zayid.   But the conversation flagged somewhat.   We were all getting rather tired of this stage of our journey.

Soon after midday, however, the country began to show signs of breaking up in wide shallow saucers with some slight vegetation including the *Dhumran*.   A little further on the undulations became more marked, and yet a little while later the surface shelved down rapidly, but easily, to a vast shallow basin whose hither fringe was guarded by a line of sandy

ridges thickly dotted with bushes. On a small knoll of the
gravel plain we halted to survey the scene, a vague lowland
encircled by insignificant ridges ending in petty headlands
near the watering of Birkan. To the right of it, showing
above an intervening sand-ridge, appeared a small group of
tall palms. And beyond the depression the desert extended,
broken and indistinct, to the southward towards Maqainama.

We hastened on to come at 5 p.m. to the Birkan well at
the edge of Jaub al Budu', and found ourselves thus, after
three days of the desert sands, back among the estuaries of
the ancient sea.

CHAPTER V

JABRIN

' It seems to be an extensive palm tract, now too malarious for
permanent habitation, but visited at the time of date harvest by
Aal Morrah Bedawins, who report that they have seen ruins of
habitations and, after rain, coins lying on the surface of its
soil.'—D. G. HOGARTH.[1]

THE oasis tracts of Hasa and Jabrin are situated nearly 150
miles apart at the base of a broad belt of steppe whose major
and minor divisions, known by various local names, may conveniently be regarded as forming a homogeneous geographical
unit under the general designation of Summan.   This steppe
probably overlies Cretaceous,[2] Eocene and Miocene deposits in
that order from west to east and is separated respectively from
the central plateau of Tuwaiq and the sea by two long sand-
arms thrust out northwards by the Great South Desert.   The
western arm is the famous Dahna, traceable southwards
through the belt of Rumaila into the great welter of sands of
the Empty Quarter beginning with Bani Ma'aridh, to whose
northern frontier indeed the Summan steppe itself runs down
approximately in Latitude 19 N. under the name of Abu Bahr.
The more easterly sandbelt is Jafura, which we had by now
pretty thoroughly explored and which is itself separated
from the sea by a series of estuary-like coastal indentations.
Its southern fringe is similarly cut off from the main body of
the great southern sands by an estuary of considerable length
and importance running up roughly westward from the sea
to the Jabrin basin at the foot of the Summan.   This estuary
is the great Jaub, which is however divided up in local
nomenclature into several sections, the westernmost of which
is the Jabrin basin proper generally known as the Juba.

[1] *The Penetration of Arabia*, 1905, p. 233.

[2] For geological details see Appendix.

Proceeding eastward we come to the section called Jaub al
Budu' whose easterly limit is roughly in the neighbourhood
of Birkan, where we had now arrived. The depression continues hence south-eastward under the name of Jaub (*par
excellence*), wherein lies a whole series of wells including the
important watering of Bir 'Aziz, to the Longitude of
Bunaiyan or thereabouts, whence the estuary splays out into
a bay of irregular outline whose individual indentations
northward and eastward are grouped together as the Jiban,
while each bears a distinctive name. The more northerly
of these minor estuaries we had already visited, while Mr.
Bertram Thomas, when marching from Bunaiyan towards
the Qatar peninsula, traversed the valleys or passed the
mouths of those further south. Subject therefore to further
exploration and more detailed survey of the outline of these
Jiban depressions we would seem to have sufficiently good
grounds for linking the Jabrin basin with the general estuary
system and thus to some extent providing an explanation
both of its existence where it is and of its very peculiar
character.

Of the Jaub proper it is unnecessary here to say much as I
did not see any part of it during my journey. So far as I
could gather, its course at first runs south-east and later
turns north-east past Bunaiyan into the lesser Jiban. In its
bed are numerous wells at fairly wide intervals beginning
with the important watering of Al Qasab about 50 feet deep
and a day's journey south-east from Qaliba which we were to
visit in due course. Between Al Qasab and the not less
important well of Bir 'Aziz, perhaps two days' journey or
rather less south-west of Bunaiyan, are no fewer than eight
waterings.[1] This section of the great estuary is therefore of
considerable importance to the Murra herdsmen pasturing
their camels in the sands on either side and becomes a
favourite line of tribal concentration in seasons of favourable
rain-fall. The depth of the wells appears to decrease progressively eastward, the deepest of them being Qasab itself.

[1] From west to east: Dhumaidan (7 fathoms), Mulaihat al Qibliya,
Mulaihat al Hadriya, Latit, Asal, Huqsha, Hidba and 'Atsa (one day SW.
of Bir 'Aziz).

The depression of Jaub al Budu', as we saw it from the higher ground of the gravel plain northward of it, appeared as a wide long salt-flat extending westward between firm sand-ridges which form a buffer between the low ground and the surrounding escarpment. At its eastern extremity, tucked away in a sharp bend of the sand fringe, lay the single well of Birkan, near which but in a well-wooded hollow of the sands we pitched our camp. It was then 5 p.m., and those concerned with such things got busy with the coffee and supper against sunset—the zero hour of the Arabian day and by conventional usage 6 p.m. by the reckoning of the European population at Jidda. I went down to see the camels watered at the well, whose plentiful and excellent water—it was a spring rather than a well—lay at a depth of only four feet. That done, I wandered about in the veritable coomb of *Tarfa* and *Ghadha* bushes and met Suwid returning from a tour of inspection. Well, I asked, what have you seen ? Are there any Arabs about ? No, he replied, I have been all round back there and saw neither Arabs nor camels, but I did see a ' walking stone '—if you go up there to that bush yonder you will find it yet. I saw its track in the sands and then came to it. I strolled away in the direction he had indicated, and on a steep slope of sand actually saw the pattern of tracks made by what seemed to be a rough nodule of flint. Otherwise the phenomenon was not of great interest as the movement of the stone was quite obviously due to the slipping of the sand under it on the steep slope. Far off we could see the dark headland of Fardat al Khin marking roughly the position of the *Ikhwan* hamlet of Khin and the general direction (approximately west-north-west) of the morrow's march. But I was disappointed to see nothing of the great Jabrin oasis which, according to Major Cheesman's map, should have lain almost due north of Khin. Perhaps, I thought, our guides had managed to bring us to the most southerly point of the basin ; yet it puzzled me to hear that we now had to march west rather than north to get to our destination. Suwid, our expert for this part of the journey, insisted that it was indeed so and scoffed at my ideas of the lie of the land. Who should know Jabrin if I don't ? said he, for I settled here with Hamad ibn Muradhdhaf and his *Ikhwan* for some years and wandered all over the place seeking new springs on which to plant palms. I gave up that life when Hamad died and the fever drove his folk out of the houses they had built. Many of them died and the rest took to the desert, and no more do they live in the village.

The lightest of easterly breezes sped us on our way over the mile-wide salt-flat at 8 a.m. next day. The saline mud of the depression was very rough and dirty with occasional miserable patches of *Tarfa* and dwarf-palms. In half an hour of rather tiresome marching we came to the palms we had seen the previous evening—only four tall, weedy stems surmounted by thick tufts of fronds and fed by a single wellspring of the same depth as that by which we had spent the night. We had sent the baggage-train on by the direct route up the depression to a named rendezvous in the Jabrin oasis itself, in order that we might have all the time we needed to see what there was to be seen in Jaub al Budu'. Their route lay westward through the wells and *Tarfa* scrub of Umm Ithila,[1] while from the palms now reached we struck northwest across the salt-flat to re-enter the bordering sand-ridges over which we switchbacked up hill and down dale, getting good views of our surroundings from each successive crest.

A hare went away from under our feet as we marched through the copious scrub of *Shinan* and *Ghadha*. The salt-flat came round parallel to our course at no great distance on the left with occasional inlets protruding far into the sands. These we crossed or skirted as was most convenient, and in some of them we found the wreckage of small dead clumps of palms which had at some time subsisted on the salty water obviously close up to the surface. In a hollow of the sands close by we came upon a single palm-stem growing by the side of a shallow well, about two feet deep, and then we went by another more extensive bay of the Sabkha with masses of *Halfa* grass, from which the well and the wretched palm-clumps of this neighbourhood derive the name of Bid' al Halfa.

[1] This is the correct name of the locality and not Umm Maithala as shown on Mr. Thomas' map.

The sand-ridges now gave way to a sandy plain extending between the vast salt-flat on our left (our course being now very slightly north of west) and the edge of the steppe desert, which here ran down towards the edge of the depression in a series of well-marked ridges studded with higher buttress-like headlands. At one of these, vaguely labelled Khashm al Khin, we drew rein for a while to enable me to survey the country from its summit some 50 feet above the level of the plain. From here the edge of the steppe could be picked out in such eminences as Al Usba' (a tiny needle of rock at the end of a ridge on the north side of the Juba basin) almost due west ; a group of eroded rocks to north-west called Ghar al Jaul ; and the twin headlands of Fardat al Khin to the north-east. Here and there small isolated rocks rose out of the salt-flat to south and south-west, while the palms of Birkan were visible to the south-eastward. They pointed out also another miserable palm-clump marking the position of Bid' al Nakhla somewhat south of west and the palms of Khin itself due west.

Towards the latter we now directed our course over a plain of alternating sand and light gravel with patches of the exposed white or pinkish sandstone bed-rock. On the way, and with much to do and fuss involving practically every member of the cavalcade, they extricated a charming little Jerboa from its hole in the sand, while on a bare stalk of *Ghadha* I had the pleasure of finding and capturing my first—and, as it turned out, only—specimen of the Leopard Moth discovered by and named after Major Cheesman. My companions stood by and wondered if I had suddenly taken leave of my senses as I dismounted to stalk the quarry, which in fact they did not see until it had fallen still slumbering peacefully into a killing-bottle to be held up to their admiring gaze.

And so we came to Khin, a wretched little hamlet of six mud-huts, of which one was the mosque and another, the largest, the residence of the chief of the little *Ikhwan* colony, along the western base of a low sand-ridge. The huts were arranged in a rough semicircle with four wells in the open space between them and the ridge. Of these one was completely buried by sand, while another encircled by a wall was choked by the trunk of a living palm. The other two wells, dug out of the sandstone rock, had plenty of excellent sweet water at a depth of only four feet. In the largest house, belonging to Rashid ibn Andaila[1] of the Hasana subsection of Buhaih who had founded the colony soon after the birth of that at Jabrin itself, we found the wooden frame of a camel saddle, but that was the only sign of human occupation we saw. The mosque indeed told the full tale of the hamlet's desolation for it was half buried by the all-devouring sand. Its niche of direction was oriented at 253°—a result which was more than creditable to an unknown architect working without compass nearly 600 miles from his objective.[2] Such a sense of true direction is almost incredible in people who have never so much as seen a map.

Yet here I was involved in a violent argument with my own (professional) guides about the direction of a very much nearer locality. Major Cheesman's map placed the well and *Ikhwan* settlement of Jabrin north-north-west of Khin, while Suwid insisted that they were slightly south of west. So we ascended to a point of vantage on the sand-ridge to argue the matter out. What are those palms, I asked, a little beyond the houses ? They have no name, replied Suwid, just the palms of Khin. But, I countered, surely the different groups must have different names. There are three groups I see. They are all just the palms of Khin, he replied stubbornly— they have no other names. Surely, I urged, that lot to the left must be Umm al Nussi and that to its right is Umm al 'Adhwa and the third lot only is Khin. A curious, incredulous light came into his eyes. Who told you that ? he asked. My book and my map, I replied, tell me that—the book of the Englishman who came down to Jabrin with Salih in the year of Ibn Sa'ud's illness—and Salih was of the Jabir ; surely he would know such places. He may have known, he replied, but he may have lied. I bear witness before God that he lied to the Englishman if he told him that was Umm

---

[1] Major Cheesman met him in 1924 and was presented by him with a *Saluqi* hound which subsequently won a prize at a show in London. He calls him Rashid ibn Daleh but the correct name is as given by me here, or perhaps Nudaila.

[2] *i.e.* Mecca.

al Nussi and that Umm al 'Adwa. I know both these places
well enough, for they are not far from my own palms of
Ghubaiya, palms I planted with my own hands. If God
wills, I will show you them that you may know Salih lied.
They are over there (pointing about south-west) and far
away. You cannot see them from here and those palms
yonder are all Khin. Am I a liar then that you do not believe
me ? As for Salih, may God cut off his house ! but he must
be dead by now, for when we left the Hasa he was lying sick
to death in his tent. They said he could not live much
longer—he was dying of consumption, but God is almighty in
all things. Suwid was obviously rattled at my sceptical
attitude, and I did my best to soothe his wounded feelings,
for the truth of the matter would obviously be revealed to me
during the next few days. And, to do him justice, let it be
said at once that he was perfectly right ; while, to do equal
justice to Salih, I cannot do better than quote the words pur-
porting to be his own in Major Cheesman's account : ' Al
Khin is a well close to Jabrin, half a day on a camel to the
east of the palm-tract, and there are a few palms there.'[1]
That is an admirably exact description, and it was clear to
me later that the error in Major Cheesman's map must be
attributed to himself rather than his guide. After quoting
the description given above he added : ' I was able to see
Al Khin later and confirm his account,' while two pages
later[2] he writes : ' We reached the end of the big palm tract
about six miles south of the northern margin. After this
there were merely patches, a few isolated tolls, a mile or two
apart, one of which was Al Khin mentioned above.' In fact
the patches included both Umm al Nussi and Umm al 'Adwa
as shown in his map but not Al Khin which, as Salih had
told him and I saw with my own eyes, lies half a day's
journey east of Jabrin proper and not merely seven or eight
miles south of it. Major Cheesman therefore could not have
seen Al Khin and his remarks about it are apparently based
on some misunderstanding.

From the sand-ridge of Khin I saw the plantation of Umm
Ithila far out on the great salt-flat somewhat east of south,

[1] *In Unknown Arabia*, p. 259.   [2] *Ibid*, pp. 259 and 261.

but the rest of the landscape was much the same as we had seen from the eminence already mentioned, except that we now had a distant view of the Barq al Samr uplands south of the Jabrin basin. So, with judgment still suspended as between Suwid and Major Cheesman, we marched west-south-west and then more south-west on the line indicated by the former. My companions made no secret of their agitation at my hypercritical attitude towards their geographical contributions, but a second Jerboa obligingly appeared to change the trend of their thoughts and a wild chase, greeted by chaotic laughter, ended in the capture of the jinking quarry.

We marched at first over a rough and dirty patch of salt-flat and then in an easy, gently undulating tract of sand and gravel, towards which the steppe desert ran down in a series of low, degenerate, echeloned tongues. Passing by the end of the chalky sandstone ridge of Al Usba', with a hillock called Al Thaniya far to our right and the headland of Khashm Na'aiyim to our right front, we rode on over more undulating sand and gravel to a plain strewn with broken fragments of flint or chert, among which I could detect no sign of ancient artifacts.

From a low hillock in this tract they pointed out to me the two ridges of Jawamir between which the Hasa road runs down into the Jabrin basin, whose vague blur of vegetation lay before us with the setting sun in our faces. There, said 'Ali, are the Mubarrazat (a line of low rocky hummocks) whither the Arabs of Jabrin go to camp, fleeing from the fever. They cannot live in the midst of the palms, where the ague falls upon them that they die. It was ever thus here, but Hamad ibn Muradhdhaf[1] planted his colony at the edge of the palms in the fever-heat of the new religion. He is gone now, God have mercy upon him ! and many of those who settled with him. The rest have fled, leaving their houses empty, to live in the desert, and they come again only in the season to glean the dates, which they tend not at all. They shun the fever as the devil himself.

[1] He was Major Cheesman's host in 1924. The guest returned his hospitality by handing down his surname to posterity in the more picturesque form of Maradvath. *In Unknown Arabia*, p. 247.

Sending the rest ahead while we surveyed the scene, 'Ali
and I dropped down into the wide salt-flat which marked the
beginning of the Juba depression. He led and I followed but
suddenly his camel began to flounder about, knee-deep in a
veritable bog. Warned by such behaviour I slipped to the
ground from my saddle—thereby earning some kudos
from my companions, to whom my exhibition of skill and
agility was duly reported by the approving expert with suitable exaggerations—and, being myself on firm ground, was
able to seize 'Ali's bridle and lead his mount back into safety
without necessitating his own dismounting in the sloshy
quagmire. Look you, said 'Ali, the sun sets. Let us therefore pray now—it will be a long time yet before we can break
our fast. So we prayed together at the edge of the bog, he
reciting the prayer formulae with me at his right side—when
the congregation is not more than three persons, one acts as
Imam and the others stand on either side of, not behind
him. The praying over, 'Ali made a cup of his hands to
catch the urine of his staling dromedary and broke his fast
by rinsing out his mouth in the approved fashion. Then he
produced from a fold of his shirt two cough lozenges which
he had had from me some days before. You take one, he
said, and I will eat the other. So we broke the long day's
fasting and continued our march, walking for a bit to feel
our way cautiously across the morass of salt to the sandhills
beyond. We then mounted and trotted on until the camp-
fire of our companions appeared in the distance as a beacon
to guide us in the dark. Soon after 7 p.m. we arrived at the
camp, pitched as arranged beforehand with our baggage-folk
by the sweet-water wells of Al Mushammara, reputed to be
among the best in the whole basin. One was buried but the
other had water at a depth of only six feet. The Mubarraz
knolls lay close by to the north-west and north in a semicircle
on some high bare ground, while nearer at hand to east and
south lay the scanty palm-groups of Ghuraba and Ma'jaba.
A mile away to the south-west was the patchy plantation of
Nakhl 'Ali ibn Najran, and a low forest-like tract of palms,
tall and small, seemed to extend to the far distance both
north and south. But there was nothing impressive about

the oasis of Jabrin when I saw it by the light of the morning. Only the distant hillocks of Dharbun and Mutrib stood out prominent like watch-towers in the south-east, while the twin Jawamir gloomily guarded the Hasaward approach and the tumbled upland of Summan closed the western horizon like a wall.

A wolf and a fox made an inspection of our camp during the night but got nothing for their pains and left nothing but their tracks. A cold breeze sprang up at dawn but the day broke fine and sunny, while we took our ease to celebrate the completion of the first stage of our journey—the exploration of Jafura and its fringes. These three days (January 19th to 21st) we would devote to a thorough examination of the last outpost of civilisation towards the Great South Desert of the Empty Quarter, on which we would then embark. Meanwhile it was pleasant to think of restful days, good pasturing for the camels, water and food for ourselves and perhaps even human society, though we had so far seen no signs of man. Yet here many centuries ago there was something like civilisation and a well-organised society, though human memory retains little of the past beyond the one romantic fact that the poet Farazdaq was born and lived in Jabrin to sing of the chivalry whose champions are forgotten or merged in legend.

Yet their works live after them in the ruinous remnants of a dozen mansions, solidly though simply built of clay and coarse masonry for protection rather than display, and scattered about the oasis to remind us of a past at least more impressive than the present. And when was that ? Was it in the tenth century of our era or, as Major Cheesman suggests, about 600 years ago ? Or was it in the ' Days of the Ignorance ' before the dawn of Islam ? We know not and cannot say, though we may be certain that the history of Jabrin as a centre of human activity goes back to a very early period in the annals of man, if only we could unearth the necessary material for its reconstruction. Perhaps we should find some corroboration of the vague and seemingly valueless local legend that the original inhabitants of Jabrin were driven forth into the desert by 'Ad ibn Kin'ad himself, the great King of Wabar. That one at least of the old mansions—and perhaps the greatest—was destroyed by fire in some form is rendered certain by the ashes that have given it its name, Umm al Ramad,[1] but we need not follow the modern story-tellers in the highest flights of their fancy which attributes to 'Ad the use of gunpowder for the destruction of the enemy stronghold !

We spent the days of our sojourn at Jabrin in exploring the whole oasis as thoroughly as possible from those very ruins of Umm al Ramad amid the rolling downs of sand on the northern fringe of the oasis, which we made our base of operations. My companions would have preferred to remain on the water at Mushammara but I was anxious to select for my astronomical observations a site as near as possible to Major Cheesman's camp of 1924. The exact site of his work I failed to determine as all our researches failed to discover the 40-foot well of which he speaks,[2] though the single mud-built dwelling of eight years ago was now swollen to the dimensions of a hamlet of six houses, of which the largest was that of the late Hamad ibn Muradhdhaf and another the local mosque. In this village we found two wells with water at three fathoms and palm-timbers framing their mouths. The settlement, now completely deserted after a gallant but losing battle with the fever, lies at a distance of a quarter hour to the south-east of Umm al Ramad in a fold of the sandy downs less than a mile north of the first palms of the oasis—a grove belonging to one Salih ibn Minya and containing a well with water reputed to be the equal of Mushammara in sweetness. Its depth was not more than 10 feet.

The first day we spent in exploring the oasis southward from Mushammara with the result that we did not arrive at the ruins of Qasr Umm al Ramad till after dark. Next morning I found a heavy dew on the ground and on the plentiful vegetation of the downs, while a thick mist descended upon and blotted out the landscape after sunrise. I spent all the morning until considerably past midday in

[1] Meaning ' Mother of ashes ' ; Major Cheesman's Jam Ramad.
[2] *In Unknown Arabia*, p. 260.

exploring and making a plan of the fairly extensive ruins. In them we found all manner of remnants of the past—broken bangles, scattered beads, fragments of pottery and an earthen jar of some size which unfortunately fell to bits as we removed it from its grave of sand and ashes. Major Cheesman does not appear to have visited these ruins, but the material I collected from them has elicited from Miss Gertrude Caton-Thompson—a distinguished authority in such matters—the guarded suggestion that they may date from the twelfth century or earlier. Such a date would perhaps indicate a connection with the Carmathian occupation of the Hasa and the Persian Gulf littoral, but the remains are probably too fragmentary and undistinguished to justify any dogmatic determination of their date.

About a couple of miles south-east of these ruins lies the simpler but better-preserved square building of Qasr Tuwairif,[1] wholly constructed of the local salt-impregnated clay which seems to wear better than its crumbling appearance suggests. It is about 25 yards each way but of no great interest except as a conspicuous landmark just outside the north-eastern fringe of the oasis.

From the palms of Salih ibn Minya southwards to the spring of 'Ain ibn Marshad, with a width of perhaps three miles east and west, extends the richest palm-tract of the oasis. The shallow springs which feed the untended palms—for the experiment of artificial fertilisation, noted by Major Cheesman as having been introduced in 1924 for the first time, has of course been abandoned with the exodus of the colonists—are far too numerous to mention. Some are dead; others are choked by the struggle of reeds and palms to monopolise their pits; while others again are alive and active. On the whole the palms are degenerate, but here and there are groups of well-grown and apparently prosperous trees, while the pleasantest part of this tract, to my eye, was a fairly extensive jungle of the species of acacia called *'Aqul*, whose russet foliage and brown, fruit-like galls made a pleasant contrast with the dark green of the palms and the lighter green shades of the tall reeds. In this neighbourhood too are to be

[1] Major Cheesman has two illustrations of it. *Ibid*, p. 271.

found two ruinous mansions, one of which, the property of
Major Cheesman's guide Salih, lies in the midst of a charming
palm-grove but otherwise presented no feature of interest.
The other, known[1] as Qasr 'Uwaida ibn Adhaiman, stands at
the junction of the two main palm-belts of the northern
section of the oasis—Al Ghubba to eastward belonging to two
prominent men of the Murra, Hamad ibn Nautan and Sa'ud
ibn Qurai', and Ummhat al Fasam to the west owned by
Faisal ibn Muradhdhaf and 'Aïdh ibn 'Uzra of the Jabir
clan—and appears to have formed part of a very much larger
enclosure, whose foundations are clearly visible though
almost flush with the ground.   The surviving walled enclosure consists of an open courtyard with a dead and reed-
choked pool in its midst, while about a quarter of the space
is occupied by a square keep still in a fair state of preservation.

The southern section of the oasis, whose total length from
Qasr Umm al Ramad in the north to the most southerly
well of Hafaïr is about 12 miles in a straight line, is more
sparsely dotted with groves though some of them—for instance that of Harbaqa belonging to one Ibn Juhaiyim of the
Jabir—are as rich and prosperous as any in the northern
sector.   In this area the saline soil is more liable to the characteristic subsidences known as *Sarut* (plural *Sawarit*), of which
I saw two good specimens.   They were only a few feet in
diameter and not deeper than the shallow pools found all
over the oasis at a depth of two or three feet.   In fact these
tiny crevasses seemed to me to be probably due to the collapse
of the surface covering by the evaporation of the underlying
water and the consequent drying up of the salt-impregnated
soil.

Along the western fringe of the oasis, indeed, I came upon
three extensive groups of curious dry saline mounds, which
are known as *Jifdara* (plural *Jifadir*) and which at the time
I imagined to be the result of something like the same process
as is at work to this day to form such subsidences.   Only in
the case of the *Jifadir* it occurred to me that they might
represent the relics of ancient palm-groves killed by the desic-

[1] Named Qasr al Khirba by Major Cheesman. *In Unknown Arabia*,
p. 256.

cation of the sub-soil pools and subsequently rotted to dust by a combination of centuries and salt. Since my return to England, however, Miss Caton-Thompson has told me of her interesting discovery of fossilised springs in the oases along the fringe of the Libyan desert.[1] My mind harked back at once to these *Jifadir* mounds of Jabrin and I would suggest— for what it is worth and in the hope that some future better-qualified visitor may investigate the matter more carefully— that they may possibly be another instance of the same phenomenon of fossilisation.

Another interesting point about these mounds is that, at any rate in two out of the three groups, there are quite distinct traces of typical subterranean aqueducts of the *Kariz* type, with manholes at intervals along their course, such as are found elsewhere in Arabia in association with springs, though in the part of Jabrin concerned there are, as far as I could discover, no extant springs to justify the aqueducts. It seemed to me, however, that this now bare and deserted western strip of the oasis may formerly have been an important, if not the most important, area of cultivation and palmiculture in the oasis. In it at any rate occur the ruins of another mansion, now known as Qasr Salim ibn Jabir, consisting of a 30-foot square keep jutting out from the north-western corner of a considerable rectangular courtyard. The walls of this ruin are still clearly traceable, ·though in parts half buried in sand, to a height of about 10 feet. And a little way beyond it to the south-east I came upon a low knoll on whose summit were some large blocks of the local stone with all the appearance of a fallen dolmen-like structure. Close by it was a similar mound or ridge which may have been formed by Nature but looked to me like the wreck of human handiwork.

To return to the southern section of the oasis I saw at Harbaqa, where the palms are much interspersed with flowering reeds and tamarisk and where incidentally I met a Painted Lady,[2] the ruins of another fort, only 25 feet

---

[1] For a description of such springs see Miss E. W. Gardner's paper in the *Geological Magazine*, vol. lxix, No. 819, September, 1932.

[2] I saw three of these in all during our sojourn at Jabrin but no other butterflies.

square but with a mass of debris in its midst which may perhaps have been a tower or dwelling-room. A second ruin of
similar aspect lay close to it on some higher ground, while
about a mile to the southward was a considerable and interesting group of plantations—all in a state of advanced decrepi-
tude—comprising Umm al 'Adwa and Umm al Nussi with the
raised hump of a subterranean aqueduct between the two.
The former must formerly have covered an area of about
half a square mile to judge by the few surviving palm-stems
and a number of springs, all dead except one. This area has
been much encroached upon by blown sand, from whose
hummocks I had a good view of the surrounding country
between the always prominent Jawamir cliffs and the hog's
back hill of Dharbun in the steppe to the south. Another
prominent hillock to the south-east seen from many points in
the oasis is Mutrib, while the whole of the western horizon is
occupied by the Summan slopes which they call Al Mahadir.[1]
They stand up in the distance like a cliff with occasional
eminences, one group of which is named Al Uthaithiyat, being
likened by the Arabs to the stones they put together to form
a cooking tripod. The upland swings round in the promontory of Barq al Samr to cut off the Jabrin basin on the south
and to form the southern bank of Jaub al Budu'. The bare
folds of this projection are sparsely dotted with acacias,[2]
which at all times provide food for the Badawin camels
when the ordinary pastures fail, while from the upland two
well-marked valleys descend into the Juba tract. The more
southerly of the two is Al Afja, a wide sandy torrent-bed
with a great profusion of typical bushes like *Suwwad* and
Shinan. In its bed is the most southerly spring of Jabrin,
'Ain al Nifl, whose pit is choked with palms and reeds, while
near by are the wells of Hafaïr at the edge of the flint-strewn
steppe. Only one of these wells still lives with somewhat
brackish water at a depth of two fathoms in a white chalky
sandstone soil, but it is here that the Badawin camp for the
rich pastures of Afja on arriving at or departing from Jabrin.

[1] Major Cheesman's ' Umm Hadiya.'

[2] Though the area bears the name of *Samr* (a kind of acacia), its acacia
bushes are of the variety known as *Salam*.

And it was here that we also camped on the night of January
21st to prepare for our departure next morning into the
unknown south. I searched the flint strewn plain for artifacts without success, though here was a mine of material
ready to the hands of the ancients. The fragments would
seem to be the broken up remnants of a flint-bed overlying
the sandstone, which we were to see later *in situ* on the summit of Dharbun.

The northern valley appears to be nameless and runs down
to a group of four wells in a saucer about half a mile wide
called Al Khuruq, somewhat north of the ruins of Qasr Salim
ibn Jabir, to eastward of which lies a remarkable line of
springs—three in a straight line at intervals of 100 paces with
another near by—called Qabaliyat, the property of one
Hadi ibn Shaduk. The Khuruq wells, like those of Hafaïr,
are a favourite resort of Badawin visiting Jabrin, whose
camels find plenty to eat in the *Shinan* of the sandy valley.
A little way up the latter lie two ruined fort-like buildings
about a quarter mile apart called Qasr 'Ali ibn Dahbash, the
most westerly outpost of ancient Jabrin.

The eponymous lord of these mansions, to which we paid a
visit, belongs to the Jabir clan of the Murra, which is regarded
as centring on Jabrin. Among the ruins we found copious
fragments of pottery and broken bangles of the kind found
already so plentifully at Qasr Umm Ramad, while the only
well of the outpost has been buried by the sands which swell
to great waves here on both banks of the Wadi. The first
building was of considerable interest as the arrangement of
the rooms which occupied the interior is clearly traceable
and seems to have been somewhat more elaborate than the
usual court-and-keep type. The roof of course was no more,
and a part of the outer wall opposite the doorway has been
badly breached to a width of several feet—the whole building
being 25 paces long and 20 broad. The northern wall had a
row of what looked like pigeon-holes at about the height
of a man's head—perhaps to support the ceiling beams of
the lower rooms if there were two storeys—with two larger
recesses below them at nearly ground-level. There were
wall-traces of five small rooms along the north and east

sides—four of them only about 5 paces square and the fifth about 15 by 5 paces. Such a building could have been nothing but a frontier guard-post, while the other ruin was clearly intended for a like purpose. It was somewhat larger, however, and consisted of a courtyard occupying the whole enclosure with a two-storeyed keep centrally placed against the western wall. In the upper storey, which dominated a fine view of the surroundings, we found a tiny chamber strewn with the debris of generations of owls' droppings, bones of small mammals and other birds, twigs of their nests and the fluff and feathers of their young. The owl and the lizard alone remain to tenant the haunts of men, who had obviously not disdained to share their romantic life on the fringe of the desert with their spouses.

About a mile from Umm al 'Adwa to the west lay perhaps the most attractive of all the features of Jabrin, the ruined mansion and plantation of Umm al Nussi. In the midst of the latter, between a large, more or less dry marsh bearing a thick forest of reeds and a rather derelict palm-grove with some tamarisk, lay a shallow spring-pool in an open glade strewn with the litter of trampled reeds and grasses. Just outside this riotous scene of decayed luxuriance lay the ruins, perhaps not so extensive as those of Umm Ramad but more elaborate than any other habitation of Jabrin, with bastions at intervals commanding the whole length of the various walls and an inner fort up against the northern wall and a mound in the centre of the great court which was probably a dwelling place—possibly for the women, as we again found broken bangles and beads here. Also in the courtyard there is or was a well of which now nothing remains but its sand-covered site.

With Umm Ramad to the north, Qasr ibn Dahbash and Qasr Salim ibn Jabir along the west side and Umm al Nussi on the south we have a semicircle of forts facing the inner steppe with nothing of the same kind towards the sea. It is perhaps, therefore, a fair inference that the old inhabitants of Jabrin, whoever they may have been, had nothing to fear from the seaward, which probably they had secured against foes with forts such as those of Salwa and Dhuwaiban and possibly also of Majann, of which Salih ibn 'Aziz spoke in tones of admiration as being situated near the mouth of Wadi Sahba.

Therefore, as in later Turkish times, it was against the great tribes of Central Arabia that the folk of Jabrin had to be on their guard, while it seemed to me at the time—though such a supposition is now unnecessary—that the southerly aspect of Umm al Nussi possibly indicated a source of danger in what is now the Great South Desert. Wabar, I thought on the strength of the legend above mentioned, may have been the capital of a rival southern principality or kingdom with Maqainama as its northern outpost. But we were now to proceed in that direction to disprove such a theory.

Enough therefore of the topography of Jabrin. As already stated I did not arrive at our camp over against Umm Ramad until after dark on the day following our arrival in the Juba basin. I was then surprised to hear that we had a visitor in our midst, whose acquaintance I made in due course at our frugal board. Jabir ibn Fasl, a son of Salim of the Jarraba clan, had come up from the south, where he had been summering with various elements of the Ghafran, on receipt of the good news that the Hasa had been blessed with copious rains during the autumn. His entry into the Juba tract had coincided with ours and he had crossed the tracks of our baggage-train in the neighbourhood of Umm Ithila. A glance had told him that we were no ordinary party of grazing Badawin or normal visitors. He had seen that all our camels were of the sand class and he had assumed from our numbers and the fact that we were travelling with more than ordinary *impedimenta* that we constituted a Government force bound for the south on business. His mind could envisage no reasonable business but tax-gathering or war and he had, as a matter of fact, heard from Saif ibn Tannaf the chief of the Manahil that, when he left the Hasa only a few days before ourselves, Ibn Jiluwi had been busy collecting the personnel and superintending the other necessary arrangements for such an expedition.

Saif had come up in December from the borders of Hadhramaut for no other purpose than to make his peace with Ibn Jiluwi, whom he had offended the previous spring by keeping

out of the way of a tax-collecting mission under the leadership of Zayid, which had gone down to gather the tribute due
from the tribes round Shanna. To appease one who was
quite capable of sending a second expedition to make good
the failure of the first, Saif had brought with him a dromedary of excellent pedigree as a gift for Ibn Jiluwi, but the
Governor of the Hasa was for some reason not to be soothed
with gifts or flattery, and the camel had been refused.
Nevertheless Saif had remained in the Hasa in hopes of an
improvement in the situation, and it was just at this moment
that I arrived at Hufuf with the King's letters instructing
Ibn Jiluwi to send me with a suitable escort into the Empty
Quarter. The Governor's enquiries regarding the whereabouts of the necessary personnel alarmed Saif who, jumping
to the conclusion that an expedition was being organised to
punish his tribe for its former recalcitrance, decamped without ceremony to warn the desert of our coming.

The truth of his words was confirmed to Jabir by our
tracks. He had come up from beyond Shanna—he had met
Saif, I think, at Naifa or Ziqirt—with only his wife and two
children and his livestock consisting of some 40 camels. In
the circumstances he had nothing to fear from us, but the
nomad Arab always acts with circumspection. He had
accordingly stowed away his family and property in some
safe retreat and come up alone on our tracks with a *Saluqi*
bitch in attendance to investigate our temper and intentions.
On the way the dog had run down a hare which he had
promptly dry-roasted over a desert fire and eaten to give him
courage for the encounter.

He now sat with us at dinner—a youngish man of keen,
frank visage and the charming courtesy of the desert-born
—and he spoke little, sizing us up as he partook of our hospitality. Over the coffee he thawed somewhat and we talked
of the game prospects in the sands before us. There was little
enough in all conscience. The drought lay unbroken on the
land. He had seen no Oryx or gazelles for weeks or months
—there were hares, to be sure, though few even of them. But
we were welcome to the bitch, a slim, shivering, short-coated
beast of gentle and affectionate temperament, who now makes

her appearance on the stage of our wanderings to remain with us to the end. She shared our simple meal and went off into the darkness with her master to seek out his camp.

The next afternoon, on my return from a tour of inspection, I found Jabir installed with his family in a single booth of the poorest fashion at a stone's throw from our camp. Followed by the bitch—Al Aqfa her name—and two wild-eyed, completely naked children with long, brownish unkempt hair, he came over to us carrying a hare—the result of his day's hunting—and leading a young camel-colt. Peace be upon you, he murmured at me as 'Ali Jahman brought him to my tent, and welcome ! See, Al Aqfa has brought you a hare ; may she bring you many another ! But take it not ill of us desert folk that our hospitality is meagre. Would that we had much to offer you, but you see us as we are. With an understanding glance at 'Ali he glided gracefully out of the tent towards the colt, which, before I could understand what was happening, lay struggling on its side in an expert grip. The next moment its life-blood was gushing forth upon the sands from a wide slit at the base of its throat.

It was late before we dined that night but the meat was tender and good with titbits of hare to flavour the meal. I hope and think that the little family, sitting apart in the dark tent, was not forgotten in the joy of our feasting. Next day I was permitted to photograph the tent with its occupants posed in front of it, but it was a dismal, misty morning and the result of the operation was not very brilliant. I had secreted the princely sum of 20 dollars (about £1) in the folds of my mantle and, as I took my leave of the party, I slipped the silver into the fist of the larger of the naked sons of the house. He ran with it to his mother who invoked charming blessings on my head. And so we parted from our last contact with the world of men to see no more of humanity till 53 days later, when we came up out of the Empty Quarter into the inhabited world at Sulaiyil.

In the keeping of God ! I said to Jabir as we parted, but see that you forget not the box. Deliver it even into the hands of Ibn Jiluwi when you come to the Hasa—there is nought in it but pebbles, yet I value it. Fear not, he replied laughing, I will deliver it if God wills.   In the keeping of God !

So we went our ways—we with the bitch that had hunted for him to hunt for us, and he with my box of stones and fossils.   And we shall see in due course how God kept us all in the days yet to come as we turned our backs on the castle of ashes and fared forth into the great wilderness of the south.

PART II

AL RIMAL

CHAPTER I

MAQAINAMA

This Juba land is all of it water
But there beyond it's the Empty Quarter.

So spoke Suwid. Jabrin lay behind us as we marched over
the flint-sprinkled steppe southward. It was a fine, cool,
crisp morning with a lightly clouded sky, and we had crossed
the Rubicon. Now there could be no looking back, no com-
munication with the world. And I rejoiced at the thought
that at long last I had entered the Rub' al Khali. The same
thought seemed to have a sobering and depressing effect on
my companions, for the sight of Jabir heading for the Hasa
had made them homesick. But perhaps it was their stomachs
rather than their hearts that suffered. During the two preceding days, while I with a few companions wandered about
Jabrin, the rest, or most of them, had taken advantage of the
situation and a larder well stocked with the colt's delicious
flesh to play the ' traveller '. In other words there had again
been backsliding from the fast, whose resumption now with
the resumption of the march had brought back all the empty
discomfort of a first day. As for myself and the few others
who had remained faithful all the time—in some cases with
the sole exception of the ' day of the fog '—we had reached
the thirteenth day of the fast and the ordeal was as nothing.

Our objective was Maqainama and our marching was over
a steppe country vaguely named by Salim, who had now
taken up the torch of guidance from Suwid, as Khushum
Summan. The name, signifying ' noses of the Summan ',
was apt enough, for the steppe ran down across our path from
the main Summan upland in an easterly direction in long
broad strips separated by wide sandy valleys carrying away
the drainage of the whole area into the estuaries of Jaub al

Budu' and the great Jaub, which appeared from occasional points of vantage such as the summit of Dharbun as a broad, dark river of vegetation sweeping through the desert some miles away.

For some reason Salim had been sent ahead with the baggage-train which had started a little before ourselves, and both 'Ali and Suwid professed to be unable to name the various points of interest we passed. I had to protest strongly to Zayid against such treatment and, to add point to my argument, I couched my camel on a suitable eminence of sand and announced my intention of remaining there until a guide was produced. Salim was immediately brought back and given strict injunctions to remain by my side all the time. So we marched again and I found in his uncouth, primitive spirit a charming companion for my curiosity. He was the senior of the whole party in years and had a great experience of the desert behind him but he had two deep regrets. He had lost the keen sight of his prime, and could no longer spot the elusive gazelle in its arid haunts. Nor was he any more the man he had been for women. Ay, by my Lord ! said Falih the 'Arqani who rode with us and a few others discussing these serious matters, he is of the sort we call *Tarbil*,[1] whose member rises not to its work. Is it even so, Salim ? I asked. Abu Ja'sha (Falih) talks in the air, he replied gravely, and his mind is in his stomach or below it. Yet am I not as I was, but God is bountiful. He was as good a trencherman as any of them and that was the consolation of his old-age.

Passing through low gaps in two ridges that form a bridge between the Summan slopes and the somewhat raised promontory of Barq al Samr, we came to the foot of Dharbun and halted to explore its summit on foot. The ridge scarcely exceeds 100 feet in height but its prominence in the landscape from afar off served to emphasise the lowland character of its surroundings. It rose, however, quite sharply from the plain in an imposing cliff of ruddy sandstone which had been scoured out by the desert winds into deep caves protected in front by a disorderly row of fallen boulders. An owl flew

[1] I think the word derives from our ' torpedo ', a word familiar enough to the Arabs during the Great War.

out of a cave objecting to the intrusion of one of our men
and 'Ali went in pursuit, though he failed to get a shot.
Above the sandstone lay a thick whitish layer of limestone
surmounted by slabs and broken fragments of chert or flint—
obviously part of a more extensive bed whose remnants lay
scattered over all this section of the steppe. We found no
flint implements, though many of the smaller fragments
had jagged edges showing that they had been used for
striking lights by modern man.

The view from the summit was extensive but amazingly
monotonous. All the slight ridge features and undulations
apparent on the level had merged now in a flat, featureless
study in brown with the black splash of our baggage animals
seemingly crawling over it in the distance ahead, where also
appeared some small dark hillocks marking the position of
the Qaliba well, our immediate objective. Afar off to the
north we had our last view of the Jabrin basin, a vague,
variegated film of vegetation in which the only distinguishable features were the twin Jawamir ridges and the palms of
Umm al Nussi. Salim pointed out to the south-east a row of
low hills marking the position of Qasab, the eastern-most
of the Jaub waterings, with the long coast of a ridge called
Ghazala over against Birkan.

There was nothing to detain us here and we soon clambered
down the rocky slope to remount our camels, which had been
enjoying the varied vegetation of the sand-patches amid the
steppe. Since April, 1931, there had been no rain in this
part of the desert but the graceful *Ghadha* was already putting on its spring garments of tender green and there was
Dhumran in abundance. That is good for them, said Abu
Ja'sha the coarsest of our wits, for the *Dhumran* is to the
camel even as women are to the Arab. And verily women
are the best of all that we possess. Falih had many virtues in
a soul corroded by the rough life of his kind, and that
struck me as a most profound remark. It came from his
heart. He had a passionate love for his family, and a little
daughter called Ja'sha was the apple of his eye. One
could always reduce him to tenderness by playing on that
memory.

At mid-day, having marched about 12 miles from Hafaïr, we came to Qaliba, a single well of 10 fathoms in a wide bare depression in the midst of sandy downs. On the way we had seen the desert surface streaked with the winding camel-paths converging on the water, while at one side of the basin lay a series of curious dark kopjes of a hard bluish limestone, fragments of which, weathered almost to black, lay strewn about the depression. The well itself had been sunk through a similar formation, which would, therefore, seem to be of considerable depth. It certainly contrasted strangely with the calcareous monotony of the steppe, through which at this point a fairly well-marked valley runs down to and beyond the well.

The sky was of an astonishingly brilliant shade of blue spotted here and there with wisps of white cloud as we resumed our march over a slightly undulating plain of flint and gravel. A warm southern breeze blew in our faces while the hot sun, now straight in front of us, induced a torpor which would have forced us to a halt but for the lucky circumstance that our baggage was some way ahead and rather wide of our course. We gradually overhauled and converged on it, but the afternoon was far advanced by the time we were near enough to observe that the main body had decided to halt in its tracks on a sand-slope richly covered with *Ghadha*.

Shortly before this we had crossed the tracks of a single dromedary carrying two riders, and our experts had disputed among themselves as to the date of its passing, which was in any case sufficiently remote to be a matter of only academic interest. Our hunters, who had started off with the baggage and roamed the desert on either side of its route, brought in three hares, one of them a baby captured alive. We tethered it with string to one of my boxes only to find in the morning that Al Aqfa had enjoyed an unexpected and unintended meal—her tracks betraying her guilt, of which there had, of course, been no eye-witness. The loss was regrettable, but we consoled ourselves with the hope of more captives with better success, while we still had our mascot—a raven wounded, not seriously, and captured alive at Ghubaiya, a small plantation in the Jabrin oasis, which Suwid had proudly displayed to us as his own handiwork. He had planted the palms in a pool belonging to a cousin, and they had been engaged in a dispute as to their respective rights in the resultant harvest. The raven had been the sole occupant of the garden on our arrival and 'Ali had secured it, while I had christened it Suwaiyid, a diminutive form of the name Suwid which itself means ' black '. Unfortunately he only survived a day or two when he died to become a specimen.

Animal life had been disappointing at Jabrin. To the Painted Ladies already mentioned should be added a few moths taken at night and fewer solitary locusts. I had been surprised to see no sign of sandgrouse in a locality apparently so favourable, but we were to see none all through the journey until we came to Sulaiyil. A few small birds there were and some ravens with a hare or two and a few Jerboas, but otherwise there was nothing but tracks. Since leaving Jabrin the latter had become more plentiful, and three hares in one day proved to be as good a bag as could be expected in the droughty desert. Fox, hyena and bustard were among the creatures that had left signs of their passage but we saw none of them, and the nearest we got to one was next day when at Bir ibn Juhaiyim we saw the pug-marks of a hyena quite fresh upon the sands. It had evidently visited the well in the hope of finding water spilled at its side and had retired disappointed on finding the mouth closed.

The pleasantest surprise of this first day, however, was brought in by Humaid who had found the fragments of a complete ostrich egg in the sand. They all agreed that the egg must have been laid and hatched *in situ*, but that was certainly long ago as the ostrich is generally believed to be extinct in these parts. I have never seen one, said 'Ali, but my father, who is now an old man though still able to carry and use a rifle, has shot them in this desert. That may be forty years ago but earlier than my earliest memories. At many places in the desert before us we were to find small fragments of the shell from comparatively recent hatchings, and others, polished by sand and wind, relics of a possibly pre-historic antiquity, for Dr. Lowe of the British Museum has detected among my collection a fragment that he attributes

H

not to the ordinary ostrich but to its remote ancestor the
Psammornis[1]—perhaps the Roc itself of the Arabian saga !
A second shell, shattered but complete, was found later in
the midst of the waterless desert, and who shall say for certain that the great bird does not still survive in the remotest
recesses of the wilderness ? The evidence is probably against
such a chance, and it is only in Northern Arabia that the race
still maintains its precarious struggle against Nature and
man.

The hares provided a welcome addition to the evening's
menu, being cooked for the sunset breakfast in a sort of broth,
into which my companions dipped their dates. Nothing of
such delicacies is wasted and only the unextruded food in the
intestines is squeezed out before the remaining contents of the
stomach are thrown into the pot with the meat. The skins,
of course, went into my collection, but my companions discussed among themselves the meaning of what was nothing
but unaccountable squeamishness on my part. I could touch
neither the flesh nor the offals. Perhaps, said one, he holds
the hare unlawful—as do some tribes of the Arabs. No, said
another, he would leave the meat to us for he sees us ever
hungry. Sa'dan, who reported the conversation, kept the
secret to himself and in the coming weeks I was to overcome
my delicacy at the bidding of hunger.

The clouds prevented any attempt at astronomical work
that evening and, with everyone now fasting and no watering
of camels to be thought of, we got off to a good start soon
after 7 next morning. The air had the crisp coolth of late
autumn in England and the wind, now in the north, made life
pleasant indeed. There is something in the uncontaminated
atmosphere of the desert that makes one actively conscious
of health. Perhaps it is the ozone of which the German
traveller, Gerhard Rohlfs, wrote[2] in the 'seventies : ' In the
open desert in January and February there was an average
ozone content of 7·3 while in the oases about the same time
only 4·9 was observed as the highest average. The desert is

[1] See Appendix.

[2] *Drei Monate in der libyschen Wüsste*, p. 177, as translated by E. C.
Wheeler.

marked off not only from the oases and the Nile Valley through the ozone richness of the air, but it equals (anyhow in winter) the most favourable ozone stations of Europe'. Perhaps it is this that accounts for the ' lure of the desert ', which cannot be cured in him that has once tasted of it.

The sandy floor of this tract soon gave way to gravel, and the baggage animals were sent straight ahead while my small party made a detour to visit the well of 'Uj,[1] which we found about five miles on from our camp in one of the valleys descending from the Summan uplands. We came suddenly upon a basin of dirty, ruffled gypsum about half a mile across, which recalled the *Jifadir* of Jabrin and looked almost like the bleached remains of an ancient settlement, although we found no remains of actual buildings. This impression was, however, enchanced by the discovery of plentiful relics of man similar to those of Jabrin—fragments of household pottery and bangles and rough flints used for fire-lighting. Perhaps the princes of Jabrin had come out here with their families to enjoy the better hunting of those days and had pitched their tents about the single well now completely buried by sand. Salim had not heard of its being actually used by the Badawin these many years, but he had apparently camped on it himself in a bygone age when, so far as he could remember, water was to be found in it at 15 or 16 fathoms. The supply was, however, intermittent and dependent on the seasonal rains, and the modern Badawin have no longer the energy to dig to such depths on a sporting chance. The long drought of recent times has sapped both their vigour and their optimism.

All round the gypseous circle extended in dull monotone a vast featureless gravel plain which was at length succeeded by a pleasant, cheerful tract of sandy downs with a rich covering of *Ghadha*, in which 'Ali stalked and shot a hare. Its colouring of light chestnut struck me as being something different from the specimens we had already secured, and I insisted on its being carried in a leather water-bucket to prevent unnecessary elongation by the ordinary process of

[1] *Cf.* Burton's *Arabian Nights* where reference is made in the tale of 'Abdullah ibn Fazil to a city named 'Aūj.

suspending it head downwards by the hind legs. Unfortunately my solicitude ruined the specimen, which was found on arrival in camp to have been so soaked in a pool of its own exuded blood that the skin was not worth preserving.

A vast bare shingle plain with very dry and scanty scrub succeeded the sands. On it we found the typical camel-paths leading forward to the water, while afar off on the left began to appear a long line of lofty orange dunes—the first of the vast sands of the great desert! About mid-afternoon we came to them or rather to a firm, undulating sandy plain projecting from them towards the Summan; and from here onwards to Maqainama itself we marched, now on one and now on the other, along the sinuous boundary between the sands and the steppe. Here and there we passed by patches of exposed gypsum suggesting that the desert floor—once doubtless the bed of the sea—lay very close beneath the surface of these sands. Salih had a shot at a raven and missed it, while I had better sport among some brightly coloured Scarab beetles winging among or settled on the bushes. At the base of one of the latter I noticed a splash of liquid crimson. It is water, said Salih, the water of dew washing the bark of the bush. It looked to me like a resinous exudation similar to the stuff which, according to Dr. Yahuda, the Israelites of the Exodus called *Man*[1] ' because they knew not what it was '. We call it Manna, but Salih said *Ma'n*, meaning water.

By now we had done a satisfactory day's labour and all thoughts centred on the idea of camping when suddenly we came upon four or five patches of exposed gypsum, in the midst of which lay the well of Bir ibn Juhaiyim. All I saw was a short wooden stake protruding from a shallow saucer of sand. But no sooner were we dismounted and the cooks at work against sunset than 'Ali and some others initiated me into one of the common customs of the great sands. The well was not buried but protected with a covering of wattle and skins over its mouth. There was a sufficient thickness of blown sand over the cover to show what would have hap-

---

[1] Dr. Yahuda interprets this as an Egyptian word meaning ' we do not know ', used currently in the speech of the Hebrews.

pened to the well if left to its fate. And its depth as measured
by me was 80 feet—16 or 17 fathoms according to the Arab
reckoning. Out of curiosity I measured the span between
the finger tips of the outstretched arms of Abu Ja'sha as
typical of the normal in our party. It was exactly 5 feet
6 inches, from which I reckoned that the Arab fathom[1] may
be taken as meaning about five feet. To my intense surprise
the camels, turned out to graze, made straight for the well to
congregate round it patiently while the men opened it up.
And then, as the bucket went down and up to pour out the
liquid into the metal tray which was also our dinner dish, they
fought for the water, drinking greedily though they had been
fully watered only 36 hours before at Hafaïr. Their astonishing thirst had been engendered by the salinity of the bitter[2]
pastures on the way. I commented on the phenomenon as
suggesting that the prospect of long, waterless marches before
us portended trouble with the camels. But wait, replied
'Ali, until they come to the *Abal* and *Hadh* of Al Rimal—it
will be better there and they will go many days without
water, but these bitter herbs make them thirsty.

My companions had wanted to halt short of the well and
there was some grumbling at my insistence on camping
actually on it for the barren delight of making my astronomical observations on the exact spot. Admittedly the pas-
turage near the well was not as good as it had been further
back, but the animals had been cropping *Dhumran*, etc., all day
as they marched, while the morrow's march to Maqainama
would be a very short one and the following day we might
halt, as I would require as much time as possible to study the
geology and antiquities of the place. So we would gain on the
swings what we might have lost on the roundabouts. But
my companions had become querulous and fretful as the
ordeal of fasting and marching ever deeper into the unknown
lengthened out.

The well lay in a short length of valley half obscured by an

[1] *Qama* or *Ba'* ; Humaid's span, however, was 6 feet and 'Abdul Rahman's
5 feet 8½ inches.

[2] Collectively known as *Hamudh* and comprising *Ghadha*, *Dhumran*,
'Arrad, *Shinan* and *Suwwad*.

elbow of the great sands thrust against the flank of Summan
proper now close by. Next morning the sands fell back round
a shoulder of the steppe dotted with low kopjes and ridges of
chalky sandstone overflowing from the uplands. Across this
we started before 8 a.m. until we came to a hillock at its
southern edge from which we looked out on a long wedge-
shaped gravel plain with the sands on the left and the rocky
upland on the right converging towards a distant apex, where
sand and steppe merged in a confused struggle for the
mastery round the well of Maqainama itself. The gravel
corridor was longer than it seemed, scored with camel-paths
leading to the well but otherwise very similar in character to
the gravel patches of Jafura and elsewhere. My imagination
worked apace as we approached the object of my quest, and
my companions had a fleeting attack of nerves at the sight of
some bushes dancing in the distant mirage—for all the world
like mounted men jogging along towards us. The gravel plain
narrowed to a wasp-waist, beyond which it bulged out again
into an oval strip of mixed gravel and sand with dunes on this
side and that, those on the right and ahead actually imping-
ing on and partly burying the border fringe of the Summan.
Within this ring a low ridge rose some 10 or 20 feet out
of the plain with flattened top. 'Ali and Salih trotted forward from my side and dismounted at the foot of the barrow.
We had reached Maqainama !

But what went ye forth for to see ? A well buried in the sand !
Well, well, well ! I thought, involuntarily remembering the
snare of a childish riddle. For eight years I had been
intrigued by a name and a problem. And was this all that
there was to it ? Look, we have arrived, said 'Ali, as if ex-
pecting an immediate and munificent reward. Is this all ? I
asked. There is nought but this, he replied. There is the well
before you. Round it the sand and grit mixed with countless
generations of camel-dung to form a grassless turf absolutely
innocent of vegetation except a few bushes of unattractive
Shinan. The bare sands and the bare steppe closed round us
and we seemed to camp in an abomination of desolation,
littered far and wide with date stones from Jabrin, the residue
of Badawin meals.

My companions had certainly never spoken but soberly of
Maqainama and were in no way responsible for the disappointment of my illusions. Eight years ago the well was
unknown outside the domains of the Murra. Major Cheesman
had then brought back the rumour of its existence from his
sojourn in Jabrin. I had been sceptical of the very name,
which sounded strange for Arabia, but in that I was wrong for
not only was the word correctly reported by Major Cheesman but I have since discovered another well of the same
name in the Summan north-eastward of the Hasa. Major
Cheesman[1] had, however, constructed a legend round this
mysterious watering in the great desert which seemed at least
too good not to be true, and I had pitched high my hopes of
probing it to its foundations. At or near a dry well (possibly
that of Umm al Ramad itself) south of Jawamir he had found
a piece of granite, and from Salih he had heard of the existence of Maqainama ' six days' march from the south of
Jabrin ' with ' some very deep wells ' visited by the Murra
' in years of exceptional rain '. The wells were reported to
have been dug by the Bani Hilal, while for the granite Major
Cheesman found the nearest match as far afield as Assuan.
The two were accordingly linked up by reference to Sumerian
tradition, which produced the name of Magan to suggest a
plausible explanation of Maqainama (or Magainma as he
wrote the name). And Magan was the source of the diorite
used by the Sumerians in making their statues—a good
enough reason in all conscience for supposing that it also
produced granite, of which the piece found by Major Cheesman might have been a fragment chipped off a block in course
of transportation *via* Jabrin to Gudea's capital at Lagash.
The weakest point in the chain of the argument was the fact
that Magan (or Maganna as its proper name might have been
—a step nearer to the strange Magainma) was interpreted as
meaning ' the place where boats go to '. That shook Major
Cheesman's confidence in its identification with a spot so far
remote in the middle of the desert but, neither he nor Mr.
Thomas having apparently realised the estuary character of
Jabrin and the Jiban, it had fallen to me to discover that at

[1] *In Unknown Arabia*, pp. 266-7, 297, 308, 342, and 345.

one time in the past Maqainama itself must have been actually on or very near the sea.

Such in brief was the problem as posed by Major Cheesman for future investigation. It remained for me to discover the ruins and quarries of ancient Magan and I now stood on the very spot in which I had hoped to find them. On the way thither I had made, at secondhand, the, at least interesting, discovery that somewhere near the sea coast at the mouth of Wadi Sahba there was a district called Majann (in full Majannu, also pronounced Magann or Mayann and actually shown in Major Cheesman's map as Mijan), in which Salih and Humaid reported the existence of extensive ancient ruins. Major Cheesman had indeed suggested that the same name might well have been used by the ancients for both the seaport and the inland capital on which it depended. He had not, however, connected Mijan and Maqainama as he might have done, but his theory easily stood the test of the new light I could throw on the problem, while I could actually envisage an arm of the sea or estuary linking the two places.

Another discovery I had made in the course of our march through Jafura and Jabrin to this point was more disturbing. Fragments of granite were by no means as rare as might have been supposed. The frequent gravel patches of the desert were full of them, worn and polished by wind or water ; by no stretch of the imagination could it be postulated that all such fragments had dropped from quarried blocks in course of transportation. And, whether their presence was due to the action of rivers or floods flowing across Arabia or to release by denudation from an underlying conglomerate as had been suggested by Mr. W. Campbell Smith[1] of the British Museum—both alternatives amount after all to much the same thing—I was already aware that the greater part of Western Arabia represented a core of granite and igneous rocks which must obviously have been the ultimate source of the fragments in question.[2]

Major Cheesman's piece of granite had thus lost its special significance, but there was still no reason to suppose that there might not be granite and diorite quarries at Maqainama

---

[1] In Unknown Arabia, pp. 423-4.   [2] See Appendix.

if that spot was to be equated with ancient Maganna. It was, therefore, disappointing to find at first sight nothing suggesting the existence of any source of rocks suitable for the attention of sculptors though, undaunted by an initial reverse of this kind, I spent the period of our sojourn at the well in scouring the Summan uplands to a depth and breadth of several miles in search of enlightenment. The Summan in this neighbourhood, as also at many points within my ken further north, is of a whitish sandy limestone overlying sandstone, and the possibility of its containing anything in the nature of granite must, I think, be dismissed from our minds.

In a bushy depression of the Summan, a little way off the broad camel-tracks—doubtless partly an old caravan-route between Maqainama and the Aflaj province and partly the pathways of grazing camels going to and from the water—I found a single, delightful bronze arrow-head of ancient man. But otherwise there was no trace whatever anywhere of the human handiwork of antiquity—not even the sherds and bangles of Jabrin and 'Uj—to support the supposition that Maqainama might formerly have been the site of a town or city or even village. I came therefore to the conclusion that it never was, never could have been more than it is to-day—a desert well.

Its great depth—I found by measurement that the distance from the mouth to the water-level was no less than 171 feet (33 fathoms according to local reckoning)—precluded the idea that it might be the work of modern or even comparatively recent Badawin. It was obviously dug by the representatives of a more serious civilisation. The arrow-head, fired from an ancient bow perchance at a gazelle, proved conclusively that ancient man had frequented these parts. And the caravan-tracks to the Aflaj were evidently part of an old route which, linked up in due course with the deep well of Bir Fadhil to the east, suggested to my mind an ancient east-west trade route running from Gerrha or Majann on the Persian Gulf to the important mart of Mecca.

I had thus to my own satisfaction placed the problem of Maqainama in something like a proper perspective. Salih

had told Major Cheesman that the water-supply here was intermittent and dependent on the seasonal rains, but that is
incorrect. The water of the single well—and there is only
one not several—is inexhaustible and the camping of the
Badawin around it depends not on the water itself but on the
state of the neighbouring pastures; for the nomads only congregate where there are pastures, and it matters little to them
whether there is water or not for, with good fresh grazing,
they and their camels can go for months without it. Of recent years, however, the district round Maqainama has
suffered from a steady drought, and the well has only been
used by visitors of passage like ourselves or raiding-parties or
Badawin travelling with their families and camels between
the southern and northern pastures. On one point my companions were in entire agreement with Major Cheesman's
informant. The water of Maqainama, like that of Bir Fadhil,
is considered excellent and as good as any in the desert—it is
sweet to the taste and beneficial to the bowels of humanity in
strong contrast with the violent and foul purge-water of the
southern sands. I did not taste it myself except in tea,
coffee and cooked food, but the reputation of the water was
such that I did not omit to bring home a specimen for analysis.

No sooner had we settled down in camp than my companions repaired to the well-mouth and worked at it amain
until, in about 15 to 20 minutes, they had removed first the
overlying sand and then the covering[1] of skins and rafters
which, as at Bir ibn Juhaiyim and elsewhere, serves to protect the deep shaft from suffocation. The bucket attached to
a long rope, always carried by nomads and travellers where
deep wells may be encountered, was then harnessed to a
camel and lowered to the water. With a little expert dangling it filled, and the camel was ridden or led down the long
incline of the well-mound dragging the rope over a pulley set
up on a wooden bracket. As the water came to the surface it
was poured out into our great dish for the waiting camels.
Then our skins were filled, and so the drawing and drinking
went on during the 48 hours of our sojourn, when the covering was replaced as carefully as possible to keep the well intact

[1] Such covered wells are known as *Mutabbaq*.

for the next comer. A hostile raiding party might leave such
wells open to spite the home tribe or even fill it in with sand ;
and even the owners (Hamad ibn Nautan of the Miqlin subsection of Al Jabir) might do the same to deny its water to
an enemy. Otherwise the desert rule requires the cover to be
replaced in the common weal.

To avoid all possibility of drawing from stagnant surface
water I delayed taking my specimen until the morning of our
departure. The well had been tapped continuously for our
needs, including bathing though I had not indulged myself
with a bath. The bucket was lowered, filled and raised to the
surface. The water came up quite tepid though unfortunately I did not take its temperature, and I filled a bottle as it
were from the fountain-head. I sealed the cork carefully with
wax, labelled it and brought away what seemed to me as pure
a specimen as possible of the excellent sweet water of Maqainama.

It was duly analysed in the Research Laboratory of the
Anglo-Persian Oil Company, Limited, at Sunbury ; and the
official report on it was as follows :

' Sample labelled Maqainama.

This sample is highly polluted with sewage.

Hydrogen sulphide, 9 parts in 100,000

Free and saline ammonia, 14 parts in 100,000.

Albuminoid ammonia, 5 parts in 100,000.

Total solids (dried at 100° C.), 26 parts in 100,000.

Total inorganic solids (dried at red heat), 10 parts in
100,000.

Wanklyn condemns a drinking water containing more than
0·0082 parts in 100,000 of albuminoid ammonia.'

On this interesting report my friend Dr. G. M. Lees commented : ' The presence of albuminoid ammonia and free and
saline ammonia shows dilution with camels' urine without
any doubt. Are you sure that it was a clean sample from the
well and not *via* a drinking trough or any intermediate
stage between well and bottle ? ' I have already explained
the elaborate precautions I took to get a genuine specimen of
the water which is considered so excellent. It is astonishing
to know that the albuminoid ammonia content of Maqainama

water is more than 600 times in excess of the potable proportion. The conflict between European science and Arabian
practice is manifest, but *quot homines tot sententiae !* One
can scarcely perhaps expect the West to appreciate the virtues
of camel urine tempered by countless generations of seepage
through sandstone rock.

The halt at Maqainama occasioned further widespread
backsliding from the rigours of the fast coinciding with the
fortunate discovery that one of our camels had reached the
end of its working tether. What was wrong with it I never
knew but they sought my approval for its slaughter. That, I
replied, is a matter for the Amir to decide. And Zayid was
bored with the fasting. So the animal was couched and slain
on January 24th, the first casualty of our expedition and
that somewhat fortuitous. There was, therefore, meat in the
camp these days and for many days thereafter, for the residue
was salted by Zaid the cook, who daily dished out suitable
portions for our meals until the last of the animal was put
away into human receptacles about three weeks later. We
took advantage of a complete day's halt at Maqainama to
send the camels out to the Summan pastures under a small
guard, which was reinforced by my small party when I rode
out to inspect the country along the Aflaj route. Those who
were not fasting remained behind to look after the camp.
The country was a bare broken upland, which from the parallel of Maqainama extends south about 30 miles or more to
the fringe of the great gravel plain of Abu Bahr which, as will
be shown in detail later, carries the central steppe down to
the sands of the far south. Here and there the barrenness of
the Summan is relieved by shallow saucers or depressions
fairly well covered with vegetation and I counted as many as
ten different kinds of desert plants.[1] In an acacia bush we
found the old nest of a raven, and in one of the depressions a
Jerboa was dug out of its burrow, while a few small birds
were seen. Otherwise, apart from the arrow-head[2] and a few
lizards, there was little enough of interest.

[1] *Salam, Hadh, Nussi, Fani, Hithra, Sa'dan, Ramram, Kurraish, Duraima,
Qarnua*—see Appendix.

[2] I named the depression in which I found this relic Raudhat al Rumh
(the coomb of the spear).

The journey to Aflaj takes four days from Maqainama, the first two being spent in the Summan and the third in the sands of the Dahna, beyond which they traverse the gravel plain of Haraisan. In the latter is the only watering of the route, the well of Jabaliya, four fathoms to water when there is any, for it is a *Mishash* or waterhole dependent on the rains. For some years now it has been reckoned dead. From Maqainama to Sulaiyil by the direct desert route avoiding the Aflaj is 12 days, but fast camels have been known to do the journey in 8 days. This route is entirely waterless and lies for the most part in the sands until the neighbourhood of Sulaiyil is reached. Sometimes water is found in the rock-pools of Makiniya, while the oasis of Hamam near the end of the journey is not far from the direct line. Salih claimed to have done the journey from Abu Dhabi to the Hasa (some 400 miles) in 6 days, but such a record cannot be regarded as authentic. The man was not above exaggerating his achievements to add to their picturesqueness. The route from Jabrin to the Aflaj direct is known as Darb al Falaji, crossing the Summan and Dahna in two days to the watering of Abu Humaidh beyond the latter, whence one day brings the traveller to the Maqainama road at Jabaliya.

On the way back from our outing in the Summan Salim had a bad fit of nose-bleeding but seemed none the worse for it in the end. The camels came in from the pastures independently of us and, when I was summoned to dinner, I was surprised to find all my companions armed to the teeth. It was a wonderful scene under the full-moon that night, nearly a score of hardened desert veterans gathered round our piled-up tray of rice and meat, half-squatting, half-kneeling, rifles in hand and bandoliers at waist. With their free right hands they ladled the food into their mouths, while their senses were taut. What news ? I asked ; have you seen tracks ? No, they replied, but as we came homeward at sunset and halted for the prayer, 'Ali smelt the smoke of a camp-fire. It may be but grazing *Badu*, or it may be raiders seeking the water. Unless they are many they will not trouble us—but caution is better.

I had not till then realised that a highly developed sense of smell was among the virtues of the desert and it was only 'Ali who had sensed the smoke. Yet I had no doubt that he had done so, and in due course we had reason to know that we had not been alone in the desert that night. The visitors had doubtless noticed our occupation of the water and had not been strong enough to claim their turn. So they had given us a wide berth to march on till Fate placed the camels of our friend, Jabir ibn Fasl, at their mercy. They were a small party of brigands from Najran seeking prey to devour.

It was an anxious and watchful party that gathered round our camp-fire for supper before dawn, the traditional hour in Arabia for the inception of military operations. And there was joy when the sun rose to warm cold feet. We loaded up and marched away from Maqainama without regret, but with the first serious item of our programme duly accomplished. The next objective was Wabar.

CHAPTER II

FORGOTTEN RIVERS

' From Maqainama onwards there is nought more but the Rub'
al Khali until you come to the settlements. There is water to
the right of it and water to the left of it, but that is the Rub' al
Khali.'

WE had, as I reckoned, entered the Great South Desert when
we passed out of the Juba basin at Hafaïr. Now we were
properly embarked on the sands as we set our course roughly
eastward from Maqainama for Bir Fadhil. And Suwid swept
his arm comprehensively round to south and west as he
imparted to me the information with which I have opened
this chapter.

I have no doubt whatever in my own mind that, while the
Arabs in general know and use the term ' Rub' al Khali ' to
indicate the vast, vague, unknown wilderness of the Great
South Desert extending between Jabrin and the Hadhramaut
in one direction and between Oman and Najran in the other,
the actual denizens of the area—the Badawin tribes—are
perfectly familiar with the term and use it in two senses, the
one more comprehensive and vague than the other but both
definitely geographical in import and contrasting with such
descriptive terms as *Madhma*[1] (land of thirst) and *Mahmal*[1]
(bare region).

Apart from the fact that the Badawin have a limited
application of the term—this was perhaps not appreciated
before—as well as its common and wider connotation, my
view as here stated accords with the traditional acceptation
of the name ' Rub' al Khali ' both in Arabia and beyond its

[1] These terms, as applied to the Empty Quarter and similar wastes, are
more often used in the plural forms *Madhami* and *Mahamil*, but exceptions are frequent and the latter word is also used geographically, *e.g.*
Mahmal (a district in Central Najd), *Haml* (part of Jafura) and *Mahamil*
(desert between Wadi Dawasir and Bisha).

127

borders until less than a decade ago.   The late Dr. Hogarth,
one of the greatest European authorities on the exploration
and geography of Arabia, would probably have been surprised at the suggestion of any other interpretation.   And
Sir Percy Cox, who spent more than a generation of distinguished service at Masqat and other places in the Persian
Gulf and studied the project of penetrating into the Great
Desert himself, has informed me that in his opinion the term
was well understood by the Arabs of his experience as applying to the whole of the Great South Desert.

With such support behind a long tradition, sanctified by
literary and classical usage through many centuries, it would
perhaps be unnecessary to labour the matter further.   But
both Major Cheesman and Mr. Bertram Thomas have suc-
cessively within the past few years suggested that the
honourable term ' Rub' al Khali ', whose traditional English
translation of ' the Empty Quarter ' I have taken as the title
of my work, is no more than a chimaera of ' ancient writers '
and geographical ' text-books '.   Their views are entitled to
consideration, and I made it my business during these months
of wandering to ascertain the practice of the desert by studying and collating the conversational references of my companions and others to the scene of our activities.

Major Cheesman[1] deals with the matter somewhat briefly
and dogmatically.   In one passage he refers to ' the Great
South Desert of Arabia, often marked on maps as Ruba al
Khali, or more correctly the southern half as " Ahqaf " and
the northern as " Al Rimal ".'   Elsewhere he mentions ' the
Great South Desert, the Al Rimal (or Ruba al Khali of
ancient writers) ' and, in a footnote, says : ' In the Hasa the
northern part of the Great South Desert is spoken of as Al
Rimal, and the southern as Ahqaf, and Ruba al Khali is not
even understood.'

Mr. Thomas[2] in a chapter devoted to ' A Geographical
Note on the Rub' al Khali ', says : ' The entire area of South-
east Arabia . . . is . . . marked on our maps as Rub' al Khali.
. . . The meaning is sufficiently literal to have an application,

[1] *In Unknown Arabia*, pp. 228 and 310.
[2] *Arabia Felix*, pp. 180 *et seq* ; also pp. 262 *et seq*.

and the term is one that is familiar to literate Arabs elsewhere
who have learned geography from text-books, but the tribes
who live in the Rub' al Khali neither use the term nor understand it in its geographical sense.'   He does not so much as
mention the name ' Ahqaf ', and he does not discuss the
connotation of the term ' Al Rimal ', though he uses it as indicating the whole of the great sands through which he
passed up to Bunaiyan and the waterless desert to westward
of his route.   Like Major Cheesman, he boldly and uncompromisingly substitutes it for ' Rub' al Khali ', which is
expunged from the map of Arabia in the most cavalierly
fashion.   Mr. Thomas does however use the latter term quite
freely for convenience and as the title of his map.

Such then is the evidence for the prosecution.   Exactness
of geographical nomenclature is not, of course, to be expected
of the Badawin, but they do know what they are talking
about and they care little whether one term, when written
upon paper, overlaps another when similarly put to unnecessary uses, while they know that the features represented
by such terms do in fact overlap and mingle *in situ.*   The term
' Sawahib ', for instance, and the long parallel dune-ranges
which it is used to indicate, inevitably encroach not only on
Rub' al Khali (in the narrower sense which I shall shortly
discuss) but on the southern part of Al Rimal and swallows
up the whole of Al Khiran.   Similarly the Tuwal or deep well
area to the north bestrides part of Al Rimal and part of
Summan, while the Summan itself is partly Rub' al Khali and
partly not.

When I went down to Wadi Dawasir in 1918, skirting the
northern fringe of the Empty Quarter and often discussing its
contents and character, my companions, among whom was a
well-known representative of the Murra,[1] used the term
' Rub' al Khali ' quite freely and intelligently.   And now,
while plans were being made for my expedition, that was the
term used both by the King and his Ministers and others
concerned.   It was used by Ibn Jiluwi.   Sa'dan shivered at
the very sound of it ; and the Qusaibi brothers and other
friends of mine in the Hasa thought I was mad to venture

[1] Jabir ibn Faraj of the Buhaih, since dead.

I

into a tract whose name was so forbidding. So far at any rate Rub' al Khali was the commonest name in men's mouths, while in the Hasa the more intelligent people understood quite well the term ' Al Rimal ' as used by the Badawin roaming the great desert with their cattle. At starting, therefore, my impression was that the generality of folk in the Hasa used the terms ' Al Rimal ' and ' Rub' al Khali ' as synonymous, while elsewhere only the latter term was used of the whole area.

Nevertheless I maintained an open mind on the subject and was more interested to know how the Badawin themselves named the scene of our intended investigations. And I certainly had a sufficiently representative collection of men to throw light on the matter—six of the Murra from three different sections, two men representing different clans of the Manasir and three men from two different sections of the 'Ajman, to say nothing of Zayid and Ibn Ma'addi, both with considerable and the former with very considerable experience of the Great Desert.

So far as possible, and until I had formed a fair idea of their actual usage of the various terms of desert topography, I avoided anything in the nature of leading questions and simply jotted down in my notebook at the time any sentences in the conversations of my companions that struck me as interesting on any topic whatsoever. As I used my notebook incessantly all the time while riding and at our halts they did not know that I was recording their *obiter dicta* and were certainly not concerned to choose their language. The terms ' Al Raml ' (the sand), ' Al Ramla ' (the sand region), and ' Al Rimal ' (the sands) occurred frequently in their conversation and I could not but notice that people like ' Ali Jahman, Salim, Salih, and others used these terms as of a familiar region of which they had no feeling of horror. It was, however, common knowledge at an early stage of our proceedings that our programme included a march from Shanna or the Hadhramaut to Sulaiyil ; and the term ' Rub' al Khali ' was at least as frequently on their lips as ' Al Ramla ', which was certainly more often used than ' Al Rimal ', either generally of the whole area of ' the sands ' as understood by them or

with the addition of a local name to specify the particular
sand region intended, *e.g.* Ramla Maqainama, Ramla Shanna,
etc.

What then was the distinction they intended to make
between ' the sands ' and ' the Empty Quarter ' seeing that,
so far as I knew, the whole area in question was an ocean of
sand ? It was a distinction of two quite definite facets—on
the one hand pastures and on the other water. And it soon
became evident that in fact the various pasture regions
generally bore the names of the wells on which the Badawin
camped, Ramla this and Ramla that. Sanam was an exception but was none the less a grazing area with wells, and
there are other exceptions, but in general the rule held and
every well had its *Hadh* belt or *Khilla* belt or some other
kind of belt. But Qa'amiyat was just Qa'amiyat, Hawaya
Hawaya and Shuwaikila Shuwaikila (each divided up into
plant zones, of course), and those tracts and others were
always referred to as being districts of Rub' al Khali.

In seasons of good rain the Badawin might take their
cattle to pasture in the waterless tracts, but normally they
only frequent the water-bearing areas where they could
themselves settle on the wells while their camels sought herbs
to graze on in the neighbourhood. And such areas of normal
occupation are grouped together as a whole under the terms
' Al Ramla ' or ' Al Rimal '. The waterless tract is the
Empty Quarter *par excellence* and I have placed at the head
of this and other chapters typical *obiter dicta* of Suwid
and others, which emphasise the distinction that troubled
them.

'Ali Jahman had been visibly shocked when I asked him
about Shuwaikila. I have been into Qa'amiyat, he had said,
and into Hawaya to hunt the Oryx ; but all that and Shuwaikila and beyond are of Rub' al Khali. Ask Suwid of
them or Salim for they are of Dimnan. We others only go
into it for the Oryx-shooting. And later, when we were
three or four days out from Shanna in the waterless waste,
Farraj said : This is what they name Rub' al Khali—the land
of the Oryx. And Salim, as he rode with me on the last lap
of our journey, was to say : This is the Rub' al Khali ; no

man comes hither ever.   But perhaps the most epigrammatic
of all their utterances on the subject was that of Suwid, which
I have placed at the opening of the chapter on the ' Waterless
Waste '.

That the Badawin of the Great Desert—the Manasir and
Murra between them span the whole breadth of its thousand
miles from the Oman frontier to Najran—know and use the
term ' Rub' al Khali ' admits of no doubt whatever.   Some
of the border tribes mentioned by Mr. Thomas may not use
the term freely as they probably have active cognisance only
of the section to which the term ' Al Ramla ' applies, yet I
cannot but doubt their wholesale ignorance of the name and
its special significance.   But God knows best, as the Arabs
would say in such case, and I have no hesitation in restoring
to the Great South Desert of Arabia the name by which it has
been known to the Arabs before and since Shahrazad related to King Shahriyar the tale of the cobbler Ma'ruf, who
was transported by supernatural agency into the midst of
the Rub' al Kharab[1] and anticipated my own discovery of
Wabar.

I would state the final result of my researches into the
matter in the following formula.   The whole of the Great
South Desert is Rub' al Khali in contrast with the inhabited
world.   A great part of it, commonly frequented by pastoral
nomads and containing countless wells, is known to them and
their nearer neighbours as Al Ramla or Al Rimal, while a
part of the latter containing only briny wells is again sub-
divided from it under the name of Al Khiran and another
section with more palatable water is Sanam, another Tuwal
and so forth.   What remains after subtraction of the waterful
area is Rub' al Khali *par excellence*, the waterless desert, the
Empty Quarter—empty even by the reckoning of the Badawin.   The name ' Ahqaf ', common enough in literature, I
have never heard but on the lips of pedants and pedagogues.
It may perhaps be known and used by the Hadhramaut
Arabs, of whom I have no experience.

I have dealt at some length with an important aspect of a
great problem and must return to our marching through the

---

[1] Burton rightly equates this name with the commoner Rub' al Khali.

sandy downs of Ramla Maqainama. A fair wind blew upon us from the south and the gap gradually widened between us and the long, dark line of the Summan until it disappeared from our view and left us engulfed in an ocean of sand. It was a gentle, pleasant country somewhat similar to Jafura, now bare and now fairly thickly dotted with vegetation, mostly *Ghadha* but with patches of *Hadh* and other herbs. My companions seemed limp and lifeless after the richness of their feasting, and the baggage camels lagged behind. After little more than two hours' marching we found some fair pasture and halted for nearly an hour to let them come up. I found plenty to interest me—plants, insects and the like—but the slowness of our march annoyed me and, when we resumed, I insisted on walking. I found no difficulty in keeping pace with the baggage animals and amused myself with a little time-keeping, which showed that I was pro-gressing at the rate of about 50 inches per second—rather less than three miles an hour. It was pleasant enough walk-ing over the sand, but we came to a gravel plain about two miles wide like a broad ribbon running across the sands from south to north. My feet felt the difference at once and even the camels trod gingerly. My companions liked not my walking, which was a silent reproach to themselves, and about halfway across I yielded to their entreaties and the argument of my bare feet to mount. For a while I kept to the snail's pace of the baggage until there was a general speeding up, whereupon I went forward with some others.

Afar off they named to me a thick clump of perhaps a dozen *Ghadha* bushes as Ghadhawat ibn Huqai, called thus after a Marri who had perchance slept there or fought or lost a camel. At 3 p.m. we halted for prayers, and at 5 we camped for the night near the eastern extremity of Ramla Maqainama overlooking another broad gravel strip—Hidba Buraika.

The only incident of the march had been the sighting of a bustard which was shot at and missed. I had collected some Mantids and there were some moths[1] at my light in the even-

---

[1] Of 24 species of moths collected by me in the Rub' al Khali, no fewer than 16 are provisionally regarded as new to science. See Appendix.

ing. A very disagreeable dust-laden north wind arose during
the early hours and covered everything with sand. Abu
Ja'sha came and pegged down my tent-ropes in case of accidents, but I slept peacefully enough, vaguely dreaming of
Wadi Dawasir traversing a vast gravel flat strewn with the
relics of an ancient civilisation.

Next morning the sky was clouded and the air cold and
clammy. Everything was grimed with sand and the sun was
feeble in the extreme. We had done about 25 miles the first
day and this day we did as much, traversing Buraika (over
the gravel to sands), Hawiya (over sands with much *Ghadha*
to gravel) and finally into the pastures of Madara where we
camped before 4 p.m. as the atmosphere, now warm and still,
had induced somnolence all round. Salim had stalked a
hare unsuccessfully while we halted to watch him, and the
Ghadha-covered sands had yielded a host of black beetles
with golden bands upon their shoulders. Also the *Saluqi*
bitch had chased a fox without result over the gravel strip,
which struck me as an ideal landing ground for aeroplanes. A
little Oryx dung had been seen but there were no traces of
the animal's recent passage.

Camel-paths running south and north in the Buraika
gravel were pointed out as leading to the Qasab watering,
but 'Ali declared that there had been no rain in this area for
seven or eight years. Yet there seemed to be a good deal for
camels to eat, rather dry but not dead. Far off to the south-
east appeared the dune-range of 'Arq al Ghanam, beyond
which, they said, lay similar ranges[1] a day's journey away or
more. Just before reaching camp we passed an old, deserted
raven's nest in the fork of a *Ghadha* bush.

On the third day (January 28th) out from Maqainama we
reached Bir Fadhil after quite a short march. The whole
distance was about 55 miles and, about two miles short of the
wells, we entered real dune country—a stormy sea of lofty
billows tossed here and there in disorder but generally facing
north with a rolling crest or incipient horseshoe hollows.
Once we had to descend a very steep slope of soft sand,
while a strong blustering south wind blew about us till

[1] 'Uruq al Abal and 'Uruq al Khilla.

5 p.m. when it dropped, leaving us to enjoy a clear, soft, warm night.

Short though it was this march had been a dreary one and our mournful procession had been strung out to a long column. Zayid rode ahead with Humaid and Salih, talking with his usual vivacity to a respectful audience. Not far behind but alone rode Ibn Ma'addi, reciting passages from the Quran which he knew by heart—during *Ramdhan* the ' reading ' of the book through as many times as possible is accounted for virtue. Far behind, Sa'dan and I rode along together conversing, and still further in the rear the rest marched in a solid phalanx chanting a monotonous shanty.

At Bir Fadhil, whose eponymous digger was a former Shaikh of 'Adhba, the premier section of Murra, though the watering is regarded as the property of the Buqaih Ghafran, we found four wells spread over a mile length in a wide depression of the sands. The original[1] shaft was out of action and half filled with sand as the result of a visit in the preceding April by a raiding party of the Sa'ar tribe. They had watered their animals and filled their skins but had not troubled to replace the usual cover. I cast a stone into its depths but there was no answering sound of water, though one would have thought that it would have been simpler to clear out the sand from a well in recent use than to dig a new one. Not so, however, the Ghafran, who had set to in the summer to excavate the shaft by which we now pitched our tents in a small patch of gravel almost hidden by the encroaching sand. How 'Ali knew the spot, apparently described to him by its authors—for he had never seen it— was a mystery, but he marched straight to it and dismounted at what looked like a low mound of sand. He and others, however, soon cleared away the latter and revealed the covering of rafters and skins over the well-mouth. It was found, however, that part of the cover had collapsed inwards, admitting a good deal of sand into the shaft. Consequently no watering was possible until Zayid, stripped to the waist,

[1] Styled *Umm* or ' mother ', while the others are *Jahliyat*, apparently meaning ' children ', though the word may refer to the fact that they are old forgotten shafts rediscovered and re-excavated.

descended to clear out the accumulated rubbish, which was hauled up by the others as he filled the leather bucket with fragments of sandstone rock, bits of wood and, of course, much sand. When it was cleared a camel was harnessed to the long rope and the watering began. I measured the depth with my tape and found it to be no less than 126 feet, while the drawing incline of the parent well was as much as 58 paces, say 143 feet. The latter's mouth was, however, situated in a raised mound, about 10 feet high and representing the accumulated mixture of sand, moisture and camel-dung through generations or centuries, while the mouth of the one we used was flush with the ground level. The extra depth of the older shaft, therefore, represents a fortuitous addition, and I saw the grooves scored by well-ropes in the stone blocks lining the shaft at its original mouth level. The other two wells (one excavated in 1930 and since abandoned) were completely buried but it seemed strange to me that the Badawin should be capable of such works. By further enquiry, however, I elicited the fact that the actual shafts have existed from time immemorial, while the ' digging ' of our well, for instance, by the Ghafran meant no more than its rediscovery and clearing. The shafts seemed to be sunk through a ruddy sandstone.

In this well area I came upon a small cemetery, the first seen in Murra territory and containing 10 graves in a rough circle round one of greater dimensions, probably that of a Shaikh. Each was marked at the head by a block of white stone. It is indeed strange that one does not see in these desert tracts more frequent reminders of the vanity of life, but the explanation is simple enough. At Jabrin bodies committed to the saline mud are soon reduced to nothing, while in the desert the sand conveniently veils the passing of man. I picked up a small fragment of basaltic scoria which Hasan assured me was of the ' walking stone ' type he knew, but it was also suggested that it might have been brought here to be ground into a powder they use for the eyes. Or it might, according to others, have been used as a pounding stone[1]

[1] Called *Haid al Rawah*. No one could say where such fragments might have come from. See Appendix.

or pestle. The floor of the depression was, like that of
Maqainama, strewn with date-stones, bits of leather and
other unconsidered trifles eloquent of much human occupation of the site. 'Ali told me that about two days to the north
lay the well of Juwaifa with another, 'Uwaiya, to east of it
at about the same distance from Bir Fadhil, two days east of
which is Fadhila, another deepish well. All this northern part
of the sands is thus fairly liberally sprinkled with waterings,
and Mr. Thomas' map, of which fortunately I had received
a copy before starting on my journey, showed a continuous
series of wells all along the route followed by him. I gathered
from it, however, that the country westward of his line of
march was waterless, and this impression seems to be confirmed by his book.[1] I was naturally anxious to keep as far
from his route as possible, while 'Ali's desire was to go south-
east from Bir Fadhil to a well named Umm al Hadid, which
Mr. Thomas had not shown on his map and which from
'Ali's accounts I suspected of being the reputed site of Wabar
or very near it. The indications were that it was not very
far from Faraja on Mr. Thomas' route, but I was anxious
to miss no ancient or extant waterings further west and I had
ascertained in the course of conversation during these weeks
that 'Ali knew of certain old wells along the fringe of the
really waterless desert. It was important to put these on
the map and I, therefore, insisted on proceeding southward
rather than in the direction suggested by my guide.

That was accordingly the direction in which we struck out
next morning after watering the camels, filling up our 32
waterskins with the last sweet water we should see for some
time—that of Bir Fadhil ranks high in Badawin estimation
though doubtless similar to the water of Maqainama—and
replacing the cover over the mouth of the well. At 10 a.m. a
fresh south wind was blowing as we marched along a range[2] of
dunes, whose half-formed horseshoe hollows faced north-
west below their sharply chiselled wall-like crests. It is all
drought, this earth, said 'Ali encouragingly. But there was
a fair amount of rather dry *Ghadha* on the lower sands, while
before us lay the dark expanse of a great bushy, gravel plain

---

[1] *Arabia Felix*, p. 266 and Appendix III.   [2] 'Arq al Ghadha.

with the dune range of Numaila afar off beyond it. I dawdled on with Salim, now again our guide, observing the activities of a Bifasciated Lark, while Salih unsuccessfully stalked an eagle which had perched out of our way on a dune crest.

When he rejoined us we descended an easy slope on to the gravel plain of Shuqqat[1] al Khalfat while our companions as usual lagged in the rear. Suddenly I observed a white object on the ground and, before I could take in its significance, we were marching on masses of them. Look ! I said to Salim, shells of the sea ! I must dismount. He was off his camel in a trice, performing a sprightly war-dance as he gazed down at a cluster of bivalves. For nearly two hours we remained with others of our party riveted to that spot, while the baggage went ahead. Apart from Wabar itself this was perhaps the most interesting and dramatic discovery of the whole journey. The place was simply littered with shells, and among the shells we collected a good assortment of the most delightful flint implements of antiquity, the first of which was picked up and brought to me by Farraj, while Zayid, grubbing under the gravel, brought me a lump of what he imagined to be disintegrated mud of man-made walls ! It was evidently alluvial soil of an old river or lake and appeared to lie in bands which certainly created the illusion of wall-foundations.

Years ago on the way down to Wadi Dawasir I had crossed a number of wide torrent beds which were reported to run out into and lose themselves in the desert to eastward against the sand barrier of Dahna. I had assumed that the ancient city of Wabar must have been on the banks of one of these in the days when water flowed in them ; and I had always hoped that the exploration of the sands of the Great Desert might reveal the traces of a great civilisation in a once fertile land such as Sir Aurel Stein has unearthed in the dried-up river beds of the Central Asian desert. Mr. Thomas had apparently found no trace either of such channels or of such civilisation, but he had found an universality of sand which seemed to render such discoveries unlikely.

---

[1] *Shuqqa* (plural *Shiqaq*) means a ' cut ' or ' slice '—generally indicating a gravel valley or plain with or without vegetation but not very broad. *Raqqa* is used for hard plain, gravel or rock.

When we found the fossils at Qarn Abu Waïl and Anbak, 'Ali had told me of another shell deposit known to him in the desert, but that was to the west of Shanna, and it was a pleasant surprise indeed to come upon another at this point. The sands between Maqainama and Bir Fadhil had been streaked with broad glades of gravel and grit, but they had produced nothing of especial interest and seemed to me to be but the last kicks of the Summan as the steppe petered out under the sands. From Bir Fadhil onwards, I had supposed, all would be sand and nothing but sand. But that was far from being the case. Between it and Tuwairifa greater or smaller gravel patches and exposures of the underlying bed-rock were pleasingly frequent, while further west was reported a large gravel plain called Ra'la with Sahma and Abu Bahr beyond it south and west. Clearly, therefore, the western (waterless) part of the Rub' al Khali was less sandy than the eastern, while here in Shuqqat al Khalfat we had a gravel plain some 10 miles long, as far as I could judge, and three miles broad. A thick covering of bushes gave it an air of unexpected fertility, while the shells made it certain that at one time in the past there had been water here. The absence of any trace of fossilisation suggested a comparatively recent date, and the flint implements found in association with the shells set me off imagining ancient man in occupation of the banks of an old river or lake, or visiting them to hunt with spears and arrows the beasts that came down to drink.

The northern edge of the plain seemed to shelve or sink down towards the foot of the dune range which we had crossed to get to it, and I formed tentatively the opinion that I had in all probability encountered part of an old river-bed, whose upper reaches might be sought in the Wadi beds of the Aflaj province and south of it, which I have already mentioned.

Only one factor—and that a very important one—remained to be determined. Were the shells of marine or freshwater origin? I had no means of deciding that point and knew that I would have to wait till I got back to England before the question could be answered. Meanwhile I registered the opinion I have stated and the hope that it might be right. And on the strength of that hope I drew dotted lines on my mapping sheets connecting the shells of Shuqqat al Khalfat with a great river system traversing the desert from the Aflaj. Wadi Maqran, as the greatest of the western channels known to me, seemed to be the most appropriate name to adopt for the whole.

My companions applauded the fancy that had bridged 250 miles of hopeless desert with a river. We collected all we wanted of the bivalves, and in due course the experts of the British Museum diagnosed our finds as freshwater[1] shells. Unfortunately they have proved to be of species which have existed continuously for a long period and still exist. It has, therefore, not been possible to determine either their age or the approximate date of the beginnings of desiccation in Arabia. The flint implements found in association with the shells, however, have been classed[2] as being of Neolithic and Bronze Age types, but the date of the evolution of such types in any country can only be deduced with certainty from their geological associations. The rivers of the great desert would at any rate seem to have flowed until the very dawn of history if not within historic times. And if 5000 B.C. be considered as the approximate date of the passing of the Neolithic culture in Arabia on the analogy of the Libyan Desert, as suggested by Miss Caton-Thompson, the onset of desert conditions in the Empty Quarter must have developed contemporaneously with the early beginnings of serious civilisation in such countries as Egypt and Mesopotamia. Such a civilisation might indeed have made a beginning in these parts only to be stifled by Nature's hostility ; and there was nothing in the nature of the case to preclude the possibility of discovering ancient ruins in the Rub' al Khali. In any case our knowledge at the moment was too limited to be anything but encouraging. We had actually found evidences of human activity in ancient times amidst the apparent relics of a river, and we passed on hoping to add to

[1] See Appendix.

[2] By Mr. Reginald Smith of the British Museum and Miss G. Caton-Thompson.

the tale of our discoveries the city which legend has represented as the supreme achievement of the ancient Arabians. And it is perhaps only surprising that, while a comparatively recent date must provisionally be assumed for the inception of Arabian desiccation, no trace of Palaeolithic or even Mesolithic culture has been found among the flints collected during our expedition. It may be presumed, therefore, that the relics of such earlier cultures (which must surely have developed under conditions so favourable) may yet be found, if ever the spade is used to reveal the contents of the lower levels of the alluvium, on whose surface we made our discovery of shells and flints.

'Ali had left us to our shell-collecting and gone on with the baggage. A hare had, however, led him astray and he now met us, as we passed out of the gravel into the rolling sands of 'Arq Numaila, with the results of his collecting—the hare, a Palestine Short-toed Lark[1] and a whole family of ravens. Of the last he had shot the father, wounded the mother and secured her alive, and annexed the family of three exceedingly hideous, blind, naked, wide-mouthed babies. We did what we could to keep the living alive, but they died in our despite at intervals during the next few days. For the youngsters Zaid, the cook, made me a pickle of salt and water in which I consigned them in my ignorance to a hermetically-sealed tobacco tin. Some days later I took it into my head to see how they were progressing, but no sooner had I eased the lid than the whole caboodle exploded in my face with a report like a pistol shot and a stench than which I can imagine nothing more noisome. I fled precipitately from the mess, abandoning the trophies to the desert sand and the tender mercies of a pair of their relatives that sat by awaiting our departure before prospecting our leavings.

We marched on over the Numaila sands, interrupted at intervals by patches of gravel, in some of which we found shells and flints while others produced nothing. Thanks to a late start, a long delay at the shell-deposit and the nearness of the Numaila well, we camped by what had once been a watering at 2 p.m. after a total march of only 10 miles. And

[1] See Appendix.

where is the well ? I asked. There, yonder ! replied 'Ali pointing to a sandhill which could be differentiated from those that surrounded it far and wide only by a vague litter of very ancient camel-dung here and there. Of the well itself, buried under a smooth barrow of sand, there was no trace whatever and I wondered how on earth our guides had managed to find the spot. I would perhaps have questioned the existence of the well but for a remarkable incident. There had been water here, they told me, at 23 fathoms, but the well had not been visited by herding Arabs since the great drought had set in some eight or ten years back. 'Ali and Salim had both visited it before then, but Ibn Humaiyid, who had been there as a child, remembered having secreted his toys in a certain spot. To that spot he now went and from it unearthed a score or so of small, flat clay discs, pierced through in the centre, which the Badawin children use in playing a game called *Darraj*.[1] How the game is played I did not exactly ascertain, but their attempts to explain it left me with the impression of a combination of draughts, halma and tiddlywinks. I added the discs (of which we found other stray specimens at a few places on our route) to my collection and photographed a group of our guides on the tomb of the well.

The higher flights of desert-craft are as uncanny as the soarings of an Einsteinian brain. The ordinary man cannot fathom the intricacies of thought that lead to results either palpable or pleasingly intelligible. One gasps alike at the familiar handling and dissection of atoms and the unerring detection of a virgin by her footprints. In both cases the responsible factor would seem to be not instinct—as presumably is the case with animals seeking food, water or mates—but education. The habit, derived from generations of instruction on particular lines or under particular conditions, of observing the material facts and applying a certain train of reasoning to the facts observed can alone account for the miracles of the expert. The memorising of experience is a necessary corollary to the achievement of such a habit. And so in the Arabian desert the good guide is he who ob-

[1] Meaning ' wheels ' or ' rollers '.

serves carefully, deduces accurately and remembers faithfully. The desert man knows every dune and ridge and fold
as the shepherd knows his individual sheep. From each one
to the next he will guide you unerringly until you come to the
desired objective, but from afar he may deceive you and
himself if you ask him to point out its bearing. He follows
the path dictated by his own memory and experience, while
the best guides can do as much on the mere description of a
fellow-expert, for in their science they all use the same terms
and symbols as men of learning do all the world over. Yet
outside their own sphere—this strange sand-sense of the
great desert—the Murra did not appear to be gifted with
great brains or quick perceptions. 'Ali, it is true, had gleams
of intelligence and flashes of curiosity about things beyond
his ken ; but Ibn Humaiyid, Suwid and Salim, all experts in
their own limited sphere, were far from quick in the uptake.
Salim, indeed, seemed at times to make vigorous efforts not
to understand anything that impinged on his senses from an
unaccustomed angle, and often I amused myself trying to
make him do so—generally with ultimate success if I could
get him alone and far from all possibility of appeal to Zayid
and others, who were only too willing to play the interpreter.
And it was always a treat to hear him chuckle aloud as the
light dawned on him. You are intelligent, he would say,
more intelligent than I am ; do you get me ?

The gusty, dusty north wind, which had greeted us at Bir
Fadhil and had dropped during the day, now got up again to
plague us through the night, nearly upsetting my tent and
sprinkling everything with sand. The minimum temperature during the past few nights had been 50°—at Maqainama
it had dropped to 41° on the last night—and at dawn, the
wind having dropped, it was pleasantly cool under a clear
sky.

We got off at 8 a.m. to march over a typical ' desert ' landscape of low rolling billows broken here and there by scattered ranges of higher dunes like breakers on the swollen
bosom of an ocean. Patches of vegetation, dead these eight
years, varied the yellow monotony and occasionally we came
almost with a shock upon a thin line of fresh *Andab* grass,

which our camels mowed down in their stride with long
scythe-like sweeps of neck and head. These grasses and some
bushes of *Hadh* suggested that there had been some very
slight recent fall of rain, but generally the drought reigned
supreme and there was no sign of life in the waste.

Between the parallel dune-ranges[1] lay shallow sandy valleys with frequent patches of the bedrock exposed and sprinkled with gravel. My experience of the previous day encouraged me to visit as many of these as possible, and it struck
me as strange that such marked features should be nameless.
Doubtless they are liable to effacement by the movement of
the sands and in any case they were of little interest to a
pastoral community. My companions indeed seemed to
resent my frequent detours to visit them, though they
showed every sign of satisfaction when one such patch, larger
than most, yielded a harvest of flints in the gravel overlying a soil of markedly alluvial character. We celebrated the circumstance by naming the valley Raqqat al
Shalfa.[2]

After mid-day the dust-laden wind revisited the scene
though it was behind us and seemed to act as a spur to the
camels. Gaily we marched along over the rolling sandy
downs beyond Raqqat al Shalfa until suddenly in the midst
of that dead world there appeared a swallow struggling
gamely along northwards in the face of the blustering wind.
It seemed to experience as much delight in the encounter as
it gave me, fluttering familiarly round and between the slow-
marching camels for full five minutes when, apparently
realising that time was short and the way long before it, it
circled round us once more and disappeared for ever. It
looked to be in perfect condition to judge from the sheen of
its burnished blue-black plumage, and it showed no sign of
distress. Fortunately for it, my gun was with 'Ali who was
far out on our flank seeking hares, and I thought fondly that,
safely delivered from the dangers of such a meeting in the
perilous desert, it might be in England before me. Almost
immediately afterwards we found and captured a lizard,

[1] 'Arq al Sabat, 'Arq abu 'Afina and others.
[2] ' The beach of the spearpoint.'

while two locusts and a few beetles completed my bag for the afternoon.

The camels disliked the gravel patches almost as much as my companions and most days, on arriving in camp, some animal or more than one had to be attended to. The sharp stones, on which the men walked and ran with complete unconcern, tore the tender pads of the sand-bred animals to ribbons and they marched dabbing the desert with red spots of blood. The Arabs' treatment for such troubles consists of simple botching. A strip or round of leather is neatly cut out to the required size—in modern Arabia the rubber of discarded inner tubes of the motorist are often used instead of leather and we had a few sections of such material with us—and soaked with butter which is also liberally smeared over-the pad to be doctored. Strong men then hold down the struggling beast on its side while the cobbler—generally Abu Ja'sha in our party—threads a stout bodkin with a thin leather thong and draws it through patch and sole, repeating the process until the former becomes more or less part of the latter. Rough ends are then cut or smoothed off, and the camel rises, apparently none the worse for the operation, to face more bravely a new world of gravel or grit. My always tender feet could sympathise with a camel's ordeal on rough ground, but the Arab, regardless of years or sex, has inherited an enviable hide underfoot.

Ever and anon as we laboured on over the sand-ocean we had views of dune-ranges near or far ; and after some time we passed into a plain, some three miles wide and consisting of long alternating strips of low sand and gravel with scanty herbage, to which we gave the name of Shuqqat abu Nahar (' daytime ') for the reason that it formed the threshold, as it were, of an extensive tract of once much frequented pasture lands known as Marbakh abu Laila (' night '). It formed indeed a dark band against the horizon. In former times, said Salim, when there was life in these parts, it was so black over there with the bushes that they named it so. That was probably no more than an extempore piece of aetiology, for I doubt not that the name is derived from Abu Laila, the surname of the Shaikhs of the Zayid branch of Ghafran.

K

It was a gently undulating sand plain, more white or grey
now than black for little remained of the old pastures than
the half-buried stumps of dead bushes. It was mid-afternoon
and the baggage-train ahead of us seemed to be wilting. The
customary halt for the afternoon prayer was too much for
us and, though we remounted after it to continue the march,
we only rode for a quarter of an hour before giving it up as a
bad job. At our snail's pace it was impossible to reach
Tuwairifa before sunset and, as we intended to spend a night
there in any case, we might just as well leave ourselves
something to do (only seven miles as it proved) on the morrow. The afternoons of these desert marches were always
weary, dreary, drowsy affairs, especially when the wind was
in the south. That was not the case now, but the sand driving
before the gusts of the north wind had much the same effect,
and we were fasting. Three weeks we had now done of the
month, and it was more the sense of restraint than anything
else that was beginning to be irksome. With three pots of
tea and a bowl of camel's milk each day between sunset and
dawn I knew not the pangs of thirst, though there were
moments when a draught of cold water would, I thought,
have been the best drink in all the world. For the rest it was
coffee that mattered, and they seemed to find some sort of
respite from their yearning if only they could be at rest preparing the stuff for the critical moment and watching the sun
creep down to the horizon. It would have been more sen-
sible to get over as much ground as possible while all chance
of actual refreshment was taboo, but there is little sense
in men who march resenting every step that increases
the distance from home. And there was little or no
game to produce the necessary diversion in their gloomy
minds.

We camped by a row of low dunes in a desolate patch of
dead vegetation, and the night turned astonishingly cold
after the wind had dropped at sunset. The thermometer
recorded a minimum of 37°, and I shivered as I issued from
my warm, comfortable tent for dinner in the open as usual.
But there was still some meat left of the camel killed at
Maqainama. Try some of this, said Salih holding out a bit

of tripe, it is very good. It was hard and crisp as crackling with a strange flavour—quite good.

Next day there were again many patches of gravel among the shallow sands and we came upon two low groins of pebble-covered bedrock which strongly suggested the alignment of a Wadi. Zayid and Salim had dismounted with me to prospect the ground for flints when the former picked up a very nice arrow-head. And look, he said, the sand has dug up a well ! Do you know it, Salim ? No, replied the other, there are no wells known hereabouts but those of Tuwairifa. But it is a well, perchance, of the ancients.[1] I have never heard of any well here. 'Ali and Ibn Humaiyid were consulted and declared that no such well was known. For years no one had been in these parts and the wind had worked unseen to discover a former shaft. There was at any rate no mistaking the familiar raised ring dipping to a hollow choked with sand, and we agreed to name it Bir Maqran to commemorate my theory regarding the source of these ungainsayable indications of forgotten rivers. Keeping still within what seemed to be the banks of a valley we came after about two miles to a bulge of it containing the five wells of Tuwairifa.

We had now encountered fragments of old valley formations at intervals spread over a length of nearly 40 miles from north to south. The wells of Tuwairifa like those of Numaila and Bir Fadhil were reputed to be some 22 fathoms deep, and it seemed clear that the whole area overlay a deep-down table of sweet water. At the same time there are the great Wadis of the Aflaj tract (from Sha'ib al 'Ars to Wadi Maqran) some 200 miles to the west to be accounted for. In the fragmentary nature of the available evidence it would be impossible to say whether these valleys united in the desert to form a single river coming down to Tuwairifa and turning thence northward to Numaila and Bir Fadhil and so to the sea, or whether rather they came down independently into a great delta plain in this deep-well tract. In any case the sea cannot have been very far eastward of this region in those days, for the shallow brackish wells along Mr. Thomas' route seem to point to such a conclusion. My suggestion is, there-

[1]He used the word *Jahliyat*.

fore, that we have to do with an old forgotten river or rivers
or a delta running down to a sea or bay in this neighbourhood.
We have deep wells, freshwater shells and numerous relics
of human visitation to support the theory, while the existence
of a vast marine bay in the eastern tract of Rub' al Khali
would seem to be borne out by the shallow briny stratum of
water underlying the tract known as Al Khiran, to which we
shall come in due course.

The evidence of altitudes above sea-level does not, however, suggest a single valley trending northwards from Tuwairifa, as Numaila and Bir Fadhil[1] both lie at a higher level.
The land surface dips eastwards from Maqainama to the Bir
Fadhil and Numaila tract, which appears to be nearly level in
that longitude and contains the shell-deposit of Shuqqat al
Khalfat, while south of Numaila the land slopes southward
to the valley tract of Tuwairifa. This drop in altitude corresponds with a similar fall from the northern part of Aflaj to
the Maqran neighbourhood, and it may, therefore, be that we
have to do with two valley systems rather than one—the
Wadis of Aflaj proper trending eastward to Bir Fadhil and
Numaila, and the Maqran system flowing to Tuwairifa
parallel to but south of them. This at any rate seems the
most reasonable tentative conclusion for the time being.

As we approached Tuwairifa up the valley the gravel
patches were scored by the usual camel-paths radiating from
any desert well, but I noticed among them three rather
remarkable parallel lines of sinuous tracks, marked more
deeply and running fairly close together. After a while the
sand covered them but they reappeared in the gravel beyond.
My companions agreed that they were remarkable but could
not explain them, and I was left with my own conjecture
that they were possibly portions of an old caravan route
which touched at this watering on its way. The lines I saw
lay south-west and north-east, leading possibly to Maqainama
or more directly to the Aflaj.

[1] Bir Fadhil is 775 feet above sea-level; Numaila 800 feet; and
Tuwairifa only 600; while Maqainama is 850. These altitudes are, of
course, only approximate, being the result of the computation of my
Aneroid and Boiling Point Thermometer readings.

The five wells of Tuwairifa lie in a sandy hollow with a dune range some 40 or 50 feet high running along the north side of the valley. Abandoned by the grazing Badawin eight years ago when the drought began, they have been choked with sand. The main well is, however, clearly traceable, while the others were not difficult to locate by exposed portions of their raised lips and the usual litter of debris cleared from the shafts—at the bottom of one of which, they told me, lies the corpse of a man who was entombed years ago by the collapse of the shaft while he was engaged in clearing it out. The water is said to lie in a stratum of rock—presumably sandstone—but the pits are sunk through a considerable depth of alluvial soil which is liable to cave in, as it had done on that occasion. Grinding stones, fragments of marine shells obviously brought here by man, flint chips, *Darraj* discs and an Arab horseshoe were among the trophies collected from the rubbish heaps.

'Ali and Farraj had gone off wide of our route in the morning with my gun and a supply of ammunition in the hope of finding something to shoot. I had told them not to spurn any small birds they might come across, and they now came in with a very satisfactory bag of four hares, two Bifasciated Larks and two Wheatears.[1] Before sunset 'Ali accompanied me to the top of a dune overlooking the country all round. He seemed to be anxious as they are apt to be when encamped on a well, for a raiding party might well look in at so remote a watering in the hope of finding it opened up. However my glasses reassured him that we were alone and unwatched. What a scene of emptiness ! I remarked. The wells dead and all around us the country parched with drought—nothing but low rolling sands ! But what a country it was in those days ! he replied. Ten years ago, or it may be twelve, I saw Oryx here—yes, plenty of them—in these sands. Ah ! that is the very crown of sport, the shooting of the Oryx. And you, your fortune is good for you will be the first stranger to see the Oryx in his own country. Ay, if God wills we shall certainly shoot them before long when we get down to better

[1] For the identification of all my ornithological specimens I am indebted to Mr. N. B. Kinnear of the British Museum. See Appendix.

pastures—in abundance too. And the children of the Oryx
we will catch alive for you that you may take them to your
country even as the Christian did last year—I had told him
that Mr. Thomas had secured live specimens to bring home,
and of the present of a pair of animals which years ago
Ibn Sa'ud had sent to King George. And I will guide you
among the dunes that you may shoot them yourself. Yes,
have no fear, we shall see them in plenty—if God wills.
They follow the pastures—the food of the camel is their food
—whether on sand or steppe, though they prefer the steppe
if the grazing is good. Yet the sands are their refuge from
man and danger. This place was indeed full of them and the
wild-cat too and foxes in plenty, but this eight years'
drought——!

We descended the slope as the sun began to set and rejoined
our companions for the breaking of the fast. With three
waterless days behind us and at least three more to come
there was much talk of a long march on the morrow, but we
had spoken of such things so often only to break down either
when it came to making an early start or to marching
through a whole afternoon that I did not pay much attention to their words. This time, however, they had meant
what they said, and it was only 3.30 a.m. when I was woken
by shouts announcing the readiness of our morning supper.
Immediately afterwards I set to work as usual on my journal
and collections, but they demanded my tent, which, with my
approval, was removed from over my head as I sat at my
tasks. By 4.30 the baggage train had actually moved off
under the guidance of Salim, who shared with 'Ali the mono-
poly of the great secret of the sands. It was still dark, of
course, and the air cold and crisp without wind. Indeed the
conditions were almost wintry again and the thermometer
had registered a minimum of less than 34°. I continued my
work with a pot of tea to warm me up, while the party
left behind with me huddled over the fire drinking coffee till
prayer-time, when they wrapped themselves in their mantles
to sleep till sunrise. It was nearly 8 a.m. before we started
and the day remained deliciously cool throughout with a
maximum temperature of 68°. A north wind started lightly

with sunrise and gradually increased in strength and gustiness to die down altogether at sunset.

Before us lay the vast expanse of Bani Mukassar, a tract of several long parallel dune ranges. We seemed now to be in the very midst of the Great South Desert and the short lengths of dunes we had seen amidst the lower sands hitherto now gave way abruptly to dune barriers mountainous by comparison. Between the first two ranges lay a broad valley of rolling sand with considerable patches of the gritty or pebble-strewn rock floor exposed. On reaching the first range we skirted along its flank in the tracks of our baggage animals until, nearing the crest by a lofty dune, I called a halt to survey the scene from its summit. The wind swept the sand in a continuous sheet from its crest as we sat on the peak looking down into the gravel valley below and far out beyond it over range upon range of dunes like the one on which we were.

With Zayid and 'Ali I descended the steep soft slope of sand—perhaps 200 or 250 feet in elevation—on the further side to prospect the rock floor for flints or shells. Our camels, loudly protesting, were pushed or dragged down the slope, plunging almost knee-deep into the soft sand at every step. The range seemed to extend to a total length of about 5 miles along the flank of the valley, running NE. and SW. No sooner had we reached the bottom than we began to find flints, and a little further on we came upon the unmistakable traces of another unknown well—Salim afterwards agreed that no well had been known to exist in that position—which we christened Bir Mukassar. It lay about 5 miles ESE. of Tuwairifa and proved to be the last vestige of human activity in this area of ancient floods.

Beyond it lay the desert sands uninterrupted. The rest of the party had continued in the tracks of the baggage, and we saw them coming over and down the slope of the range far ahead while we slanted across the valley to cut them off. A steep downward slope of soft sand took us over the second range, while an easy passage was found through the third, beyond which we traversed a rolling sandy down tract to the further extremity of Bani Mukassar. Its width from side to

side was about 5 miles, and beyond it lay the district of
Sa'afij, in which we remained for the rest of the day and for
the greater part of the next.

It differed from the preceding tract in being an ocean of
sand billows frequently streaked with short ranges of higher
dunes like the breakers of a reef-strewn sea. The dune ranges,
instead of being long and continuous, were long but broken
up into short echeloned lengths; and our course, which entered
the area through a gap between two such runs of dunes, with
the deep bushy valley of Shuqqan al Birkan just beyond
them on our right hand—this valley is said to run south-west
for a considerable distance—ran from gap to gap through no
fewer than 10 of these intermittent ranges until we emerged
on an upland of sandy downs without any dune features to
break its ocean-like regularity. There was little of interest
in the whole tract except that the *Abal* bush now reappeared
on the bare sandy downs after a long absence from the scene
—somewhat grudgingly it is true, but none the less welcome
to the camels, which had been showing signs of thirst as the
result of many days' restriction to a diet of rather dry *Hadh*.
In one of the *Abal* bushes near our track we found an abandoned raven's nest, and on the second day we observed two
pairs of ravens apparently contemplating matrimony and
nest-building, while other individuals were seen from time to
time. Small birds were also comparatively numerous—two
kinds of larks and a Wheatear—while our hunters got
several hares.

Our men had certainly been as good as their word, and it
was 5 p.m. before we came up with the baggage party just
as it had selected a site for the evening's camp after twelve
hours of almost unbroken marching. We had covered nearly
30 miles and had thus accomplished our best marching performance since the beginning of the expedition. While the
tents were being erected I walked up to a low rounded sand
barrow to survey the scene with the lad Muhammad who had
taken up his position there to keep an eye on the camels,
which had been turned out to graze on arrival in camp. 'Ali
soon came up to join us and, as we sat there conversing, I
could not help wondering how on earth and why a great

city had grown up in the midst of such desolation. The
following day would answer that question, no doubt, and
'Ali spoke hopefully though perhaps he had begun to wonder
whether he had not raised my hopes too high. And there
was something else that troubled his avaricious soul. He
directed the conversation into an easy channel, talking of
raids and such things. He was explaining to me the system
of the division of any booty captured in such expeditions.
The Shaikh or leader of a raiding party would, of course, get
an extra share beyond that of himself as an individual and
that of his camel and any other mounts provided by him for
his poorer and camel-less attendants. Thus to every man
there would be one share and to every camel a share payable
to the owner and not the rider. A fifth of the whole would be
set aside for the Government or tribe, as the case might be,
and any principal man would get an extra share in that
capacity, while the chief of all would get yet another. Then,
of course, there would be the guide, an important personage
on such occasions, who would get a share in addition to anything earned in his various other capacities. Often, said he,
I have acted as guide to such expeditions and thus gotten an
extra share in the booty. But say—and he darted a sudden
glance at me full of entreaty and yearning—did Ibn Jiluwi
make it clear to you that I was to be the guide of this expedition ? I answered him truly that I had been assured of a
sufficiency of guides for each part of our wanderings. But
fear not, I added, it will be well with you if you serve me well
in what I want of you. And you see these glasses—I will
make them a present to you in addition to other rewards
when we arrive in the Hadhramaut. His eyes flamed with
cupidity. Far be it from me to suggest rewards ! he replied.
I have no desire but to serve you and him that sent me with
you, and I was angry that day when I heard you promising
rewards to Salim and Suwid for the piece of iron. Remember
that I am your guide, not they, in these parts.

Nearly three weeks had passed since the conversation he
referred to, but he had not forgotten, and his mind was agog
with jealousy and anxiety. Next morning the baggage was
started off at 5.30, again under the guidance of Salim. And

at 8 a.m. the rest of us started off in search of Wabar. 'Ali
was very attentive. I mounted and he walked by my side
leading Na'riya. At length in a quite normal and natural
manner we became separated and I noticed him on our
right flank still leading his camel. As usual, I thought, he is
seeking tracks of game and, as I became involved in conversation with Sa'dan and Ibn Ma'addi, I thought no more of
the matter. The scene was quite featureless—a low calm
ocean of gentle billows. It is like the country round Faraja,
said Ibn Ma'addi, whither I went down last year on the
business of Ibn Jiluwi. We watered at Bid' al Halfa and went
down to Bir Fadhil by way of Qasab. Between Bir Fadhil
and Faraja we watered at Fadhila. Faraja is buried now as
we left it uncovered—we were out to punish some of 'Ali's
folk, the Ghafran, so we left their well to perish. Now we
must send our camels to water at Ibrahima, where they say
is good water though further off. I knew that Mr. Thomas'
party had watered at Faraja and it was after his passing—
about a month later—that the punitive expedition had gone
down south to Bir Hadi and Shanna. The Sa'afij district,
some 40 miles across along the line of our easterly route, is a
part of the great Sanam tract. Beyond it eastward lay a
similar area called Tara'iz whose gentle swelling is disturbed
here and there by isolated hillocks of sand. 'Ali had been
careful to describe this peculiarity to me, and I recognised
the point that marked our passage from the one district into
the other. A solitary cone rose perhaps 50 feet from the
general level with a hollow of the horseshoe type facing south
but half filled-in with sand. Perhaps it was in course of formation, or it may have been in an advanced stage of burial,
for the sand in the dip was very soft and the marks of a hare's
passage across it suggested a more ponderous animal, so
large they were and deep. This must be the first of the
Tara'iz, I exclaimed looking round instinctively for 'Ali to
confirm my conjecture. I then realised I had not seen him
for nearly five hours and in a flash I knew that he had given us
all the slip—for only one conceivable purpose. He had made
up his mind to secure all the promised rewards for himself.
That annoyed me and I expressed resentment at being left

guideless in a wilderness where, in all conscience, no guide could have added very much to the geographical knowledge I sought. I felt however that such commercialisation of a dramatic situation was inappropriate. I had pictured our picturesque caravan appearing suddenly before the derelict remnants of old-time splendour. 'Ali was taking the gilt off the ginger-bread, and I was angry.

We marched on rather gloomily and I hoped that after all we would not come to our destination that day. The peerless monotony of the desert scarcely held promise of anything likely to disturb its unruffled calm. The afternoon was far advanced and at 3.30 we saw far ahead—miles ahead—the straggling line of our baggage caravan, still marching. By the time we caught it up it would surely be time to think of camping and, to make that more probable, I insisted on stopping for prayers soon after 4. My companions, however, had no desire for delay and I could not spin out the halt longer than 10 minutes. The prayers over, they were in their saddles at once and on we marched trying to overhaul the baggage.

Suddenly afar off to the right appeared a solitary rider ! He seemed to be gesticulating, but I held on. Look, said Zayid riding up to me, it is 'Ali summoning us to come in his direction. Look, I replied, there is the baggage with Salim far ahead. I will follow in Salim's tracks. He is our guide. 'Ali has deserted us long since. He can come after us if he will but we will camp with the baggage when we come up with it. We can look for the iron to-morrow. I am weary and have had enough for to-day. We held on and 'Ali came trotting frantically towards us. God give you life and strength ! shouted some of the men as he approached near enough. If God wills, good news ! I kept silent, marching straight on as if I heard not. Come this way, shouted 'Ali. Salim has erred from the path. It is there behind me ! He says, repeated Zayid, that we should turn to the right, to the south, whence he has come. It is there. I know, I replied, but I shall go on to Salim.

We marched on arguing, but it was in fact Salim that settled the issue. His party had noticed 'Ali's return to us and he had already deflected his course at right angles. I almost wanted to camp where we were and leave the ruins till the morrow, but I yielded to their pressure and we marched in the direction indicated by the disgruntled chief guide. For a while he rode silently by my side, having first ascertained the cause of my displeasure. I was not certain of the position, he tried furtively, and I did not want to lead you hither and thither over these sands. So you left us without a guide at all, I replied, to wander at our own sweet will! I told Zayid the direction to follow, he urged, and there were no hills or valleys in the way for me to name to you. It was all Sa'afij and Tara'iz. Yet you should not have gone without a word to me, I insisted, thinking now more of what lay before us than of his conduct.

Look you, Shaikh 'Abdullah, he went on hoping I had relented, I have found the castles. They are over yonder. We shall see them soon. And I give you good news—I have never seen so much of them exposed before. Often the sand buries them entirely, and I knew not till I saw them that we should see them at all. And look! he went on, I have brought a stone of one of the buildings to show you. From under his mantle, with an air of mystery, he produced a squarish block of vitreous blue-black slag as of a furnace!

CHAPTER III

WABAR

From Qariya strikes the sun upon the town ;
Blame not the guide that vainly seeks it now,
Since the Destroying Power laid it low,
Sparing nor cotton smock nor silken gown.

Hear then the words of 'Ad, Kin'ad his son :
Behold my castled-town, Aubar yclept !
Full ninety steeds within its stalls I kept,
To hunt the quarry, small and great, upon ;

And ninety eunuchs me within its walls
Served in resplendent robes from north and east ;
And ninety concubines, of comely breast
And rounded hips, amused me in its halls.

Now all is gone, all this with that, and never
Can ought repair the wreck—no hope for ever !

A visit to Wabar had at my request been specifically included by Ibn Jiluwi in the programme of our operations.
He had a vague idea that it was somewhere in the Empty
Quarter, but of all my companions only a few knew the
legend. And only two of them could connect it with anything within their ken. Those two were 'Ali Jahman and
Salim ibn Suwailim, while Suwid and Ibn Humaiyid had a
vague second-hand knowledge of the locality. Inevitably
our conversation during the past weeks had turned frequently to the topic, and at the head of this chapter I have
placed a free rendering of the somewhat corrupt text of a
ballad snatched as we rode from the lips of 'Ali. Its source
I do not know—nor did he—but he happened to quote the
second line as we sought the almost vanished well of Hafaïr
ibn al Adham near the edge of Jafura, and by coaxing and
wheedling I got the rest out of him, making him repeat the
poem frequently until I had the text as complete as it was
ever likely to be. He apparently knew no other poem relating

157

to the legendary city, and I was particularly intrigued by the
form in which its name appeared—Aubar, the plural of
Wabr.[1] He pronounced the first syllable as a deep rich O,
a letter which, of course, does not occur in the Arabic alphabet.

Ya'qut, the classical authority for the legend (which he
repeated from Hamdani and others), gives the name as
Wabar ; and it was certainly in that form that I first heard
tell of the city from the companions of my journey down to
Wadi Dawasir in 1918. On that occasion Jabir ibn Faraj
had told me of a wondrous block of iron ' like a camel '—he
probably meant in size though I thought he might be referring to a statue—in the midst of the southern sands. He
declared he had seen it himself and gave me an indication—
bearing and distance from the Aflaj where we were at the
time—of its position. In speaking of this block of iron he had
used the term ' Hadida ' which I took to be merely the Arabic
for ' a piece of iron,' while he had also mentioned that it was in
the midst of some ruins called Jafura. From another source—
either from another of my companions or somebody met in
the Aflaj—I heard of a group of ruins in the same sands, from
which Badawin had been reported as picking up relics of
human antiquity. For this locality also I got a bearing and
distance from the Aflaj together with the name of Wabar and
the details of its legend, which was supposed to link the
ancient city of 'Ad ibn Shaddad (? Kin'ad) with some (comparatively recent) ruins known as Qusairat 'Ad on the border
of the Aflaj province.

In such circumstances information is inevitably elicited
somewhat vaguely and in driblets, but I pieced the material
together as best I could and published the results of my
investigations with an account of my first wanderings in
Arabia.[2] I also attempted to indicate roughly on the map
the resulting positions of the two localities under the names
of Jafura and Wabar.

The former name caused Major Cheesman a good deal of

[1] Meaning ' camel-hair ' or ' coney.' *Cf. Ahl al Wăbăr* =people of hair-
tents (*vide* Burton, *Arabian Nights*, note on 977th Night).
[2] *The Heart of Arabia*, Vol. II, pp. 221-2.

difficulty and perhaps a little disappointment, for on his journey to Jabrin he skirted the whole of the western fringe of Jafura, which he thus found to be a long way north of the ruins indicated by me. That the use of the name was an error is ungainsayable, but the error was, I am convinced, Jabir's not mine, though I may have been responsible for it by pressing him to name a locality without realising that he had in fact already given me the local name in Al Hadida. His section of the Murra, the Buhaih, centres in effect on the Jafura sands and in the circumstances he may have thought in desperation that that name was good enough for such as me.

In any case I was on that occasion left with the impression of two quite distinct ancient sites in the Great South Desert at a considerable distance apart. And I registered the hope and intention of exploring them and other parts of the Empty Quarter some day if possible. So far as I was concerned the project rested there for many years and I heard no more of the mysterious ruins which I could not forget. Meanwhile Mr. Thomas had been hearing vaguely of the same things during his sojourn in Oman, and at an early stage of his journey of last year across the Rub' al Khali he was shown by his guides a broad band of caravan tracks leading north-west out of the fringing steppe into the sands of Ramla Shu'ait. That, he was told, was the road to Ubar.

His spelling of the word is interesting as showing what purports to be the local pronunciation of his guides—men of the Karb, 'Awamir and Kathir tribes, whose borderland character may have exposed them to foreign linguistic taints. The word itself is an impossible Arabic form, and Mr. Thomas does not seem to have realised its obvious affinity with the classical form of Wabar until the fact was pointed out by me.[1] Nevertheless there can be little or no doubt that the legendary city of the sands, referred to in the classics as Wābār or Aubār and in dialectical usage as Ūbār or Ōbār, is one and not many. This point indeed scarcely admits of argument, though it is obviously open to those who will to seek the ruins elsewhere than at the spot which I had now

[1] *Arabia Felix*, pp. 161-3.

reached with the specific object of finding them and with guides professing to be able to locate them.

On the strength of the information gleaned by him Mr. Thomas suggested on his map a ' probable site of the ancient city of Ubar ' approximately in Long. 50° 30′ E. and Lat. 19° N. That spot is more than 200 miles south-east of mine, and it may be that there are ruins there, though the catalogue of relics found between Mitan and Fasad by his Rashidi companion Mayuf, who ' had long ago forgotten the precise site,' is not particularly impressive. My own experiences did not tempt me to divert my wanderings in that direction when I might have done so from Shanna. Nevertheless the caravan tracks—if they are more than camel paths leading from the steppe pastures to waterings in the sands, which are numerous in the neighbourhood in question—are intriguing enough and merit consideration. To judge by their direction they might well lead to the once important and prosperous province of Aflaj, which would doubtless have been a customer of the exploiters of the Qara frankincense forests. In that case they would probably have passed through the watering of Tuwairifa, where, as already recorded, I saw similar tracks of the same orientation though on a narrower front. And incidentally they could scarcely have failed to pass by or close to my suggested site for Wabar.

At any rate Mr. Thomas, like myself in 1918, was left with the impression of a ruinous site somewhere in the sands, while later in his journey he was told by his Marri guide of the very ruins that now lay before me and of the great block of iron of which Jabir had spoken to me. At Faraja one of his men collected some potsherds and broken glass from a neighbouring patch of the exposed desert floor—we also found such things at many spots on our route—and he was told of a well called Umm al Hadid ' with a tradition of remains—two large blocks of so-called ironstone—whence its name.' As a matter of fact the group of three wells known as Umm al Hadid—one of which was actually dug by Salim our guide in the distant past—is only two miles from Faraja. I visited them in due course and, finding no trace of any iron, was told that the name of the well was merely

derived from the iron at Al Hadida, which again is the site
of Wabar. It was indeed to the ruins here that Hamad ibn
Sultan doubtless referred in speaking to Mr. Thomas of the
' foundations of a fort once to be seen but now covered over
with sand.' And Al Hadida lies only 10 miles south-west of
Faraja and Umm al Hadid.

So much for the previous history of the investigation of the
problem of Wabar. Early in my present journey I began to
have some sort of idea of what I might expect to find. But
the impression conveyed to me—as it had been in 1918 and
as Mr. Thomas gathered in 1931—was definitely one of two
sites at some distance apart. I had pricked up my ears when
'Ali, in speaking of the Faraja neighbourhood, had mentioned
the wells of Umm al Hadid. That had recalled Jabir's
mention of Al Hadida ; and Salim, as the author of one of
the three wells, had been called upon to enlighten my curiosity. Yes, he had said, it was many years ago I was in those
parts with grazing camels and we dug out the well as the
other two were choked, but it is not there that lies the iron.
That is half a day to the eastward, perhaps more perhaps
less, God knows. It is long since I saw it, but I did see it with
these eyes and I could find it again. We used to graze our
cattle there in the pastures, but God knows, it may be buried
in the sand. Yet I can take you to the place and perchance
we may find it. But what will you do with it ? You cannot
carry it away. It is very large. How large ? I asked. Well,
he replied, it is long since I saw it, but my memory is that it
is very large, a great block of iron, perhaps as big as a camel,
or smaller a little, or maybe larger. Perhaps, I suggested,
we could cut a bit out of it to take away and leave the rest.
You could do that, he replied delighted at my intelligence—a
favourite theme with him—for So-and-So did take a bit of
it and had it fashioned into a knife in the Hasa. Could you
find me that knife ? I asked. If So-and-So would sell, I
would buy it. God knows, he said, but that was long ago—
he may have it yet or he may not. It was from that iron the
wells took their name, for it was Sa'id, the father[1] of Jabir
whom we saw at Jabrin, who sank the original wells.

---

[1] More probably grandfather, I think.

L

I have given as nearly as possible the gist of conversations that spread over many days. I had asked him of the ruins of which Jabir had told me. No, he had replied, I saw no ruins—nothing, only the iron. But could you find the place, I asked, if the sands have covered it ? If God wills, I will show you the very spot ; and we can dig to it if the sand is not too deep. And I will reward you, I declared, if you show me the iron itself, but I must see the iron. Suwid and Abu Ja'sha were with us when this talk of rewards took place. How much will you give him ? they asked. I will reward him, I said, but how much do you think it is worth ? A lot of money ! said Abu Ja'sha. Yes, a lot of money ! echoed Suwid. Well, tell me, I replied, how much do you think ? Would you give him 30 dollars (£1 10s.) ? he suggested. That is a lot of money, I urged ; you are greedy of gain, you folk, but it is not worth all that. Say 15 dollars. No, let us say 20. They beamed approval at such a princely offer and we closed on that.

And there *are* ruins too, volunteered Suwid ; I have heard speak of them but I have not been in those parts. Well, I replied, I will give rewards for any ruins you will find me there or elsewhere. They speak of a city, he went on, the city of 'Ad ibn Kin'ad—Obar ! Do you know where it is ? I asked. No, he replied, but 'Ali does. It is a great city he says full of mansions (*Qusur*).[1] So 'Ali was roped into the conversation though I had now to walk warily. The offer of a substantial reward for the city as a whole might have resulted in the disclosure of an isolated hamlet and the concealment of the rest. The best policy was a small reward for every separate building and I offered five dollars apiece on that basis. Everybody seemed delighted except 'Ali. They would dig up the whole desert to make it give up its hidden secrets for such recompense. But 'Ali had held his peace, brooding gloomily. Why share such profits with any one ? He had laid his plans before he began to talk freely on the subject and, as far as possible, he kept his information for my private ear. I heard through Sa'dan that he and Zayid had expressed resentment at my wholesale offer of rewards.

[1] The word *Qasr* (plural *Qusur*) is used of any kind of mansion.

Do you know where the ruins are ? I asked 'Ali. Ay, I know, he replied ; it is years back that I saw them, walls as of castles—he used the plural form ' *Al Iqsar*,' which by European corruption has given us the Luxor of Egypt—and yet a strange sort of walls, all black as if burned with fire. God knows if they be castles indeed, yet they say it was the city of 'Ad. If it is not all covered with sand—sometimes the sand covers it all so that nothing can be seen of the ruins, and at others it digs them up. I have seen them, five or four maybe, but there must be many more. And do you know the iron too ? I asked. Only by the description of others, he replied. It is not in the ruins but away from them, perhaps an hour or more, but God knows. I only tell you what I have seen. Is it near Umm al Hadid ? I asked. Ay, it is near, not far, he answered cautiously. If you pray the noon prayer at the castles you may drive the camels to the water by the afternoon prayer. That is as I remember it, but I know the place exactly and will take you there. And, I asked on another occasion, have you heard of or seen any other ruins anywhere in the sands. There are none but these, he replied ; I know the desert as well as any other. Take it from me there are none but these.

Such was the contribution of my companions to the problem. At Jabrin a vague tradition of an attack by 'Ad and a ring of forts round the frontier suggested defence against a possible enemy in the south, although the ruins there visible are of too recent date to count towards the solution of the Wabar problem. At Maqainama a deep well obviously not the work of modern Badawin ; a bronze arrowhead ; and the deeply scored tracks of a caravan route : argued a nearer approach to the problem. Bir Fadhil contributed nothing but deep wells, but between there and Tuwairifa the discovery of ancient river-beds had been more than encouraging, if the theory of comparatively recent desiccation could be accepted. Moreover there were plentiful evidences of man in the flint implements found in association with presumably fresh-water shells, and on the buried sites of ancient wells ; while there was no reason to suppose that the men who had used them were not comparatively recent denizens of an once prosperous tract. At Tuwairifa there was again a river-bed with deep wells and the tell-tale caravan tracks.

But beyond that the sands had closed viciously over any further evidence there might be. And there were no other pegs on which to hang theories than the fables retailed by Yaqut in his fanciful ' Wonders of the World,' the Arabian Nights' phantasy of the Cobbler Ma'ruf's visit to the Rub' al Kharab (Khali ?)[1] and vague echoes of 'Uj and Kin'ad in such names as 'Aūj[2] and Jalī'ād.[3]

Yet we had found two rivers, and there was a third—the most important of all, Wadi Dawasir—still to be discovered. The fact that we had not yet crossed its traces was all to the good. And what more natural than that one of the greatest capitals of prehistoric Arabia should be found on the banks of its greatest prehistoric river ? I had not encouraged myself to think in terms of Petra or Tutankhamon, but my brain had caught the very mood of the shifting sands—always in motion, gentle or violent, as the sea itself—and my dreams these nights were nightmare vistas of long low barrack buildings whirling round on perpetually radiating gravel rays of a sandy desert, while I took rounds of angles on ever moving objects with a theodolite set on a revolving floor. It was the strangest experience of my life.

And now I was about to draw the veil from the mysteries on which I had pondered so long with all the devotion of a pilgrim setting out for Eleusis or the seat of Jupiter Ammon. And incidentally we must have been within a mile or two of one of the very spots marked by me on the map 14 years before on the strength of Jabir's bearings and distances. I had wrongly labelled it Jafura and given the name of Wabar on less precise information to the other spot at some distance to the south-west. Yet if I had confined myself to the latter name and to the spot indicated by Jabir as the site of ruins and a block of iron, I should have been entitled to share the credit which must be accorded to the memory of a charming companion. It is certainly rare to get such

[1] Burton's edition, 998th and 999th Nights.   [2] *ibidem*, 989th Night.
[3] *ibidem*, 899th Night.

accuracy from an Arab guide at a distance from the scene
described.

For half an hour we marched on over the desolate sands,
rather wearily for the wind had gone round again to the south
and it was a sultry afternoon. Look! exclaimed 'Ali suddenly, and I had my first glimpse of Wabar—a thin low line
of ruins riding upon a wave of the yellow sands. I halted to
photograph that memorable, uninspiring scene, which
vanished again as we dropped into a shallow depression.
Within five minutes we had dismounted in a similar hollow
on the fringe of the ruin-field which now lay hidden behind a
low rolling ridge of sand. Leaving my companions to pitch
the tents and get our meal ready against sunset, I walked up
to the crest of a low mound of the ridge to survey the general
scene before dark. We had decided to devote four days to
the examinations of the ruins, so I could leave their detailed
inspection to the morrow.

I reached the summit and in that moment fathomed the
legend of Wabar. I looked down not upon the ruins of an
ancient city but into the mouth of a volcano, whose twin
craters, half filled with drifted sand, lay side by side surrounded by slag and lava outpoured from the bowels of the
earth. That at any rate was the impression that flashed
through my mind in that moment. I knew not whether to
laugh or cry, but I was strangely fascinated by a scene that
had shattered the dreams of years. So that was Wabar! A
volcano in the desert! and on it built the story of a city
destroyed by fire from heaven for the sins of its King, who
had heeded not the warnings of the prophet Hud—generally
identified with the biblical Heber—and had waxed wanton
with his horses and eunuchs and concubines in an earthly
paradise until the wrath came upon him with the west
wind and reduced the scene of his riotous pleasure to ashes
and desolation!

One could scarcely have imagined a more sensational
solution of the riddle of the Great Sands. And it must be
admitted that the two great sand-filled craters, encircled by
lofty walls of slag, did bear an absurd resemblance to the
tumbled remnants of man-made castles. Many of my com-

panions were already on the scene, burrowing in the debris
for treasure. As I descended the slope towards the first
crater, they came running up to me with lumps of slag and
tiny fragments of rusted iron and small shining black pellets,
which they took to be the pearls of 'Ad's ladies blackened in
the conflagration that had consumed them with their lord.
'Ali watched me with nervous concern as I picked up and
examined fragments of the surrounding slag. The sun was
near his setting, and I just had time to make a rapid round
of the crater rims before returning to camp to break the
fast.

That was enough for the first day, but my companions
were disappointed with my verdict. This may indeed be
Wabar, I said, of which the Badawin speak, but it is the work
of God not man. These are no castles of the ancients but like
the volcanic peaks of the Harra which you have seen doubtless on the way to Mecca, on your right hand as you go up.
These mouths are even as the mouths of the Harra thrust up
by the inner fire from the belly of the earth. No, replied 'Ali
stoutly, but they are the castles of 'Ad, son of Kin'ad. They
are his mansions for sure, and see how the bricks have been
burned with fire as they relate ! And what are these but
pearls ? Each of them had indeed already amassed a collection of the round black pellets to carry away in their saddle-
bags to sell for profit. Fear not, I replied, this is certainly
the place of which you spoke and you have led me to it,
'Ali, as you promised. And these are the castles of Wabar
as you say. I am content, but take it from me, they were
not built of men. And what of Salim ? Has he found the
iron of which he told me—big as a camel ? I went to the very
spot, replied Salim himself rather gloomily, but the iron is
buried under the sand. If God wills, we will find it to-morrow
by digging. God is bounteous, I replied, and, if He wills,
you will find it ; but to-morrow I shall go down with the
camels to Ibrahima and we can leave half our number with
the tents and baggage to seek out the iron. Let the camels go
down early to the water, and I will go later after them when
I have seen the castles again and collected samples of the
stones and such like.

Next morning I was up betimes to cast round the scene on foot to a distance of about a mile from the two craters. Having got far enough to satisfy myself that there were no other craters or signs of them beyond the main area I walked back over the rolling sand downs, making a minute inspection of every nook and cranny until I came to a patch of the bedrock. It was of a dazzling whiteness and apparently unburned, though it was broken up and presumably affected by the heat in its vicinity.

I then ascended a sand ridge that separated this patch from the beginnings of the crater area. From there I saw a fair-sized patch of mixed slag-like fragments and broken up bedrock about 200 paces southward of the raised NW. extremity of the larger vent (Crater B—see plan). To southwest and west of the same point lay another similar patch, while the crater itself, with higher walls on its north-west and south sides than elsewhere, measured 120 paces in diameter and 412 in circumference. A section of the circular rim on the north side was missing, however—the length of the gap so formed being 52 paces,—while two small patches of debris lay respectively NW. and NE. of this gap at a distance of 65 paces with an interval of 110 paces between them. The mouth of this crater sloped down from all sides to a central depression, though the thickness of the sand which had drifted into it made it impossible to ascertain the character of the actual floor.

The centre of the second and smaller crater (A—see plan) lay on a bearing of 313° (in a straight line with our tents beyond it) from the NW. corner of Crater B. Walking towards it I measured 140 paces to the edge of its outer fringe of slag, whose width on a gentle slope to the lip of the crater was 50 paces. Bearing slightly to the right at 345° to take a section over the central line of this crater I found an inner fringe of slag 10 paces wide whence it was 55 paces (including a narrow inner fringe of slag on the other side) across the mouth to the further lip, beyond which lay a glacis of slag to a width of 43 paces. The rim of this crater formed a more or less perfect circle with walls of uniform height all round. Close by the last point, at distances vary-

ing from 20 to 50 paces, were small patches of slag and
bedrock fragments to south-west and west, while at 190
paces to the north-west was a similar but larger patch. This
looked as if it might have emanated from a third crater (D
—see plan), which was, however—if it is there at all—completely obliterated by a sandridge some 20 feet high. A
fourth possible crater (C) appeared to underlie the hillock
from which I had first surveyed the scene. At any rate small
patches of slag fragments were to be seen protruding from
under its skirts at various places. And finally there was a
suggestion of yet another crater (E) similarly buried under
an extensive mound of sand.

Thus in a couple of hours I had gained a fairly complete
impression of all there was to see at Wabar, although I left
the actual mapping of the area to a later occasion. I had also
collected a fairly wide range of specimens of the slag and
other debris ranging from pieces the size of a man's head
to little bombs of fused stuff and the still smaller ' pearls.'
For the time being, therefore, I was free to go off on the
projected expedition to Ibrahima, in the course of which I
looked forward to touching and crossing Mr. Thomas' route
of the previous year.

At first we marched north-east—my companions being
Zayid, 'Ali, Salih and Ibn Musainid, with whom was the dog,
which, by reason of his intimacy with the affairs of the
kitchen, had long since adopted him as her guide, philosopher
and food-provider—along the indeterminate boundary separating the bare gently rolling downs of Tara'iz on the west
from the bare gently rolling downs of Sanam proper on the
east. After about half an hour's marching we passed by a
conspicuous conical sandhill known as Qauz al Ishara, which
is the Badawin's guide to Wabar—or Al Hadida as they call
it, for they do not, of course, use the ancient name in common
parlance. From this landmark onwards Sanam extended—a
dreary sand waste with scanty scattered shrubs. In nearly
three hours from the ' ruins ' we came to Faraja, our course
bending round more to eastward as 'Ali found the necessary
clues to the direction of the watering in circumstances that
made it astonishing that anybody could find anything at all

which was not exactly like everything else in that desolation. The only sign of life on the whole of this march had been a single Bifasciated Lark, whose piping announced its presence long before I could detect it tripping along the ground out of our way. In all these bare districts the desert birds seldom seem to take to their wings, generally preferring to run along the ground which provides them with almost perfect protection from birds of prey. A flying bird is often betrayed by its dark shadow on the ground.

The single well of Faraja, which normally has water at a depth of 10 fathoms, was out of action. Its shaft was completely filled in with sand, which was thus convicted of having done its work of destruction within the short space of less than a year. Only the merest dip within the slightly raised well-rim showed where it was in the typical dung-littered depression of a howling wilderness. This well is attributed, as its name suggests, to a man named Faraj of the 'Uwair Ghafran, the section of Ibn Jallab, the premier chief of the Ghafran group, who resides for the most part in the Qatar promontory as the guest and *protégé* of its ruling Shaikh, 'Abdullah ibn Thani. Mr. Thomas had camped near here and his men had drawn water from the well, while Zayid and his company had used it subsequently, but since then no grazing Arabs had visited the scene owing to the drought in these parts, and we found nothing of interest but date-stones, fragments of leather and a few bits of rock extruded from the shaft in the course of its periodic clearances.

There was nothing to detain us here, and we passed on over the bare downs to Umm al Hadid only two miles distant to the north-north-west. In an extensive depression of sand with a litter of gravel in parts the three wells are situated at the points of a small equilateral triangle. As already stated one of them had been dug by Salim many years before this, while the other two were the work of Sa'id ibn Fasl more than a generation earlier. All were now equally dead though not entirely buried, for their mouths stood out prominently from the sand with a showing of rock and stratified masses of camel dung hardened by age. The depth to water was 10 fathoms as at Faraja, which incidentally the

Badawin pronounce more like Frija. Salih stalked a few small birds round the wells, while the others had tracked a fox to its earth in the earthy mound of one of them and delved in vain to extricate him. Meanwhile I busied myself collecting Mantids and samples of the rock and gravel. I found also the relics of Badawin meals of olden times—a gazelle horn (*Rim*) and bones of the Oryx (*Wudhaihi*).[1]

Continuing our march now in an ENE. direction, we came very soon to an exposed patch of the underlying rock of somewhat curious character. It looked like fragments of weathered limestone of various sizes hollowed out by the dissolution of some of its constituents into the semblance of shells. We now hastened on at a trot under the hot after-noon sun, scarcely tempered by light southerly airs, while Al Aqfa kept pace with us, lolloping along in the shadow of Ibn Musainid's camel. As we approached the watering the sand downs began to be less bare, and in parts had a satis-factory covering of bushes which promised well for the camels after they had had their drink. That was all to the good, for 'Ali now reckoned on a long waterless, pastureless stage before us when we should leave Wabar to march south. We should not apparently come to good pastures before 'Ain Sala or Naifa, in whose neighbourhood there had been a little rain about two years back.

In due course we arrived before a charming, fairly exten-sive, oval patch of gravel—like a lake surrounded by the rolling, bush-covered downs of sand—in which lay the wells of Ibrahima with our camels in a group by the side of the most southerly shaft, which had been opened up by Suwid and the two herdsmen for their refreshment. They had just completed the operation as we arrived and Suwid, riding his camel to and fro harnessed to the bucket-rope, drew for our animals. It was their sixth day since watering at Bir Fadhil

---

[1] The Arabian Oryx is *Leucoryx* (also called *Beatrix*). The Arabs also call it *Baqr al Wahsh* (the wild cow), but I do not know the name *Baqr Bansolah*, to which my attention has been drawn by Sir Percy Cox who heard it in Oman. The name *Rim* is applied throughout Arabia only to the White Gazelle—never to the Oryx. Other local specific names for gazelles (of darker colouring) are *Idmi* and *'Afri*. The generic name for gazelles as a whole is *Dhabi* (rarely *Ghazal*).

and the intervening pastures had been very dry ; so they drank gratefully and greedily before being marched off to the downs to feed to their heart's content on the comparatively excellent pastures of this locality.

We ourselves settled down for a pleasant picnic without tents or other paraphernalia ; and Salih, foraging among the pastures, brought in some green sprigs of the *Abal* which, cooked with rice to make a dish called *Makika*[1] by the Manasir, made a tolerable substitute for fresh vegetables— rather tasteless but in no way disagreeable. It is curious that the Murra do not ordinarily know this use of the *Abal*.

The well we used had water at 10 fathoms, the stuff being compared by 'Ali with that of Birkan, accounted good for drinking. I did not taste it for I was still on my waterless régime, but I used the water for a good wash and it seemed to be richly flavoured with the urine of camels.

I had brought my theodolite and disposed of the requisite star observations before dinner. But otherwise I had treated this excursion as a holiday jaunt and was able to get in a long night's sleep for the first time since leaving Hufuf. A hawk-moth (of the Striped Hawk type) flashed round the camp-fire and my lamp but I failed to annex it to my collection, though I secured a few other moths while reading the London newspapers I had received at Hufuf and left unread till now on account of the pressure of other work. The latest paper bore the date of November 29th and I wondered, as I extinguished my lamp and lay down to sleep, how I should find the world when I again returned to its news. At the moment it seemed very far away—very far—and I was really tired from the strain of nearly a month's wanderings without any respite from the necessity of constant attention to the business in hand—especially during the night hours, which alone during *Ramdhan* were available for the writing up of notes and the packing and labelling of collected stuff.

However, I now made up for such arrears of sleep, slumbering under the stars from 9.30 p.m. till 4.30 a.m., when I was woken for supper. The night had been dewless and the morning broke mild and still. I felt wonderfully refreshed

[1] Pronounced *Machicha.*

and ready for the day's task, which I began with a vigorous round-up of desert Mantids on the gravel—I never saw as many elsewhere as here. I also picked up a worn marine fossil embedded in a pebble fragment and examined the buried sites of the numerous well shafts. 'Ali did not know how many there might be, but I counted six, three of which seemed from the familiar raised circuits of dung mould to be comparatively recent. There were probably others I did not see, but the one we had used appeared to be the only one in active commission.

Meanwhile my companions again watered the camels which were driven in from the morning pasturing in excellent fettle. And at 8 a.m. we regretfully left the most charming site we had yet struck for camping. Suwid was loud in praise of its pasture as we rose out of the basin to ride on a compass course set by myself due south. After nearly three hours on that bearing I turned due west in the direction of Wabar, and my companions amused themselves testing my sense of locality. I came through the ordeal well enough, but there was a chorus of admiration when at length we saw the cone of Qauz al Ishara straight ahead of us. Salih went into raptures over the advantages of a compass, and the rest were impressed, for it had irked them to be marching at my dictation towards nothing. They would have preferred to make a bee-line back to the ' ruins.'

On the southward tack I had myself set 'Ali a problem. You know, I said, that on this bearing we should cross the last year's tracks of Hamad ibn Sultan and the Christian. Can you find them ? You know both Turaiqa and Faraja and should be able to tell me when we cross their route. In due course we saw a domed ridge of sand, which 'Ali named Al Qasima, the pasture-divide between the two wells. We marched on a little and 'Ali stopped. We are now, he said, on the line between the wells but the sand has covered the tracks. He cast about, however, and suddenly pointed to something on our right. Do you see, he asked, the dung of their camels ? We turned aside to investigate, and there were a few pellets half buried in the sand. But how can you identify that stuff ? I asked. It may be of some grazing camel. No, not that, he answered. We know dung as we know tracks and other things. Look at these pellets—he had dismounted to examine them and handed me a handful —they are small and hard, not the rich large stuff of animals at the pasture. The camel that dropped these had come a long journey and thirsting. And they are of a year back, but God knows.

The evidence seemed satisfactory enough, and I added some of the pellets to my collection of desert curios. We saw also the tracks of a wild cat[1] that had passed this way only the previous night, and we came upon a migrant hoopoe, which gave me a thrill like the swallow of the Numaila sands. Salih fired at it with my gun after some elaborate stalking— only to hasten its passage. A raven's nest and another small nest were other diversions of the day's march, which proved somewhat tiring as the morning advanced and we passed beyond the area of good pastures into very bare country, which reflected the sun's rays with a soft but blinding sheen. Near the end of the march we came upon fresh tracks of bustard and 'Ali, following them up with my gun, brought back the only specimen of the bird to be secured during all our wanderings. We saw them and their tracks quite frequently, but the bustard is a difficult bird to approach unless one has plenty of time to spare for the necessary circumambulation of its hiding place.

From the conical landmark I put my camel to a swinging trot and was glad enough to get to my tent in time for an afternoon nap, for the southern breeze had made me drowsy and the air was sultry though the temperature was only 80°. Have you found the iron ? I shouted to my welcoming companions as I rode in—the iron as big as a camel ? No, they answered gloomily ; we found it not though we have sought it everywhere since you left. But Zaid (the cook) found a small piece of iron over yonder under a bush of *Rimdh*. Salim says it is not the iron of which he spoke, so we left it there. It is heavy. Well, I replied, we must find the

---

[1] Identified by Captain J. G. Dollman of the British Museum as *Felis ocreata* from a skull found by me north of Shanna. The Badawin call it *Hirra* (Murra) and *Atfa'* (Manasir), while the Desert Fox (? Fennec) is called *Tha'l*, *Tha'lab* or *Husni* (*Abul Husain*).

big iron if we stay here four days for it. But bring me the small piece too.

In due course it was brought before me, a lump of iron about the size of a rabbit—*Parturiunt montes*!—and very heavy for its size,[1] somewhat rusted and brittle on the surface. I assumed that it was a meteorite, and I cannot but think that it may have been, after all, the famous piece which distance and defective memory had magnified to the dimensions of a camel. At the same time it is by no means impossible or even improbable that a much larger fragment lies buried somewhere in those sands. If so, we failed to find it in spite of a special effort on the following day when the whole of our party turned out to the spot indicated by Salim —a gentle slope of sand southward of the larger crater—and proceeded to sound the depths with sticks or by stamping on the ground. Nowhere could we detect any sign of a hidden foreign body, and it would probably require the use of magnetic instruments to do so under existing conditions. I decided that it was not worth while to waste more time over the thing and it was agreed that we should march on the morrow.

By a curious coincidence the issue of the Geographical Journal—the only one I had with me—containing the text of Mr. Thomas' lecture and his map happened also to contain an article on a supposedly meteoritic crater at Bosumtwi in Ashanti. That led me to note in my journal that the ' volcanic ' craters of Wabar were ' perhaps depressions created by the fall of meteorites.' I did not then, of course, know how few and rare are the known meteorite craters of the world—perhaps only four or five in all—and I little guessed the interest that such a discovery in the Arabian desert would occasion in the small circle of experts competent to deal with such matters. Still less did I guess that the very same issue of the Geographical Journal, to which I have referred, had, in connection with Mr. Thomas' lecture, a note by Mr. W. Campbell Smith, in which mention was actually made of what may well prove to be a sister fragment of the Wabar meteorite—perhaps, indeed, the original ' camel '—

[1] Its weight is 25 lb. and its dimensions 10 by 6 by 5 inches.

which has been in the British Museum for all but fifty years !

So far as I was concerned the search for Wabar and the giant iron was over. I could now honourably bequeath the task to my successors— to younger men or women who may not be deterred by my barren search for the fabled ruins from embarking upon similar enterprises in the great sands of Arabia. I had satisfied myself that there was no vestige of human antiquity among the ' castles ' to which 'Ali had guided me so faithfully and successfully ; and, if the only likely locality known to my guides had proved so disappointing, I concluded as the result of my researches up-to-date, as I was yet to do from my subsequent experience of the great desert, that there is little likelihood of ancient ruins being found anywhere in the Rub' al Khali. I think that the further conclusion is justified that the Empty Quarter in its widest sense has in all probability been unsuitable for human occupation—otherwise than by nomads—since a time long anterior to the beginnings of civilisation. The process of desiccation must have begun, and the great rivers must have ceased to flow, before the dawn of serious history—perhaps when the retreating ice-cap of the Pleistocene changed the climate of the earth's middle belt, stretching from the Sahara and the Libyan Desert across Arabia into the deserts of Central Asia. In the flints[1] and shells of those times we have the memory of men inhabiting a land made fair by flowing rivers—but they were the remote ancestors of those that built the first houses of which we have any cognisance.

What then of the legend ? So far as the Rub' al Khali is concerned it is a myth and no more. We must seek elsewhere the site that gave rise to it, and perhaps the clue to it is contained in the first line of the ballad that opens this chapter. That the great King 'Ad existed once upon a time can

[1] Miss G. Caton-Thompson, who has kindly examined the flint implements collected by me at various localities in the Rub' al Khali, is satisfied that they are all of Neolithic type and that none of them can be ascribed to Palaeolithic or Mesolithic times. As a rough guide to prehistoric chronology she equates the end of the Neolithic period with *circa* 5000 B.C. in the Libyan Desert. If we assume similar conditions in the Arabian Desert it would seem that the flowing rivers of the Rub' al Khali lasted almost to the beginnings of the earliest known civilisations (Egypt and Mesopotamia).

scarcely be doubted. His terrible fate is mentioned more than once in the *Quran*. Its memory may have been comparatively fresh, therefore, in the seventh century A.D. The corresponding disaster to the Thamudites of Madaïn Salih has a historical basis in the collapse of the Nabataean Power, and there is little reason to suppose that the 'Adites were a fiction of early imagination. It is apparently not known for certain who they were or where they lived, though it is generally supposed that they belonged to some part of Southern Arabia—the Yaman or Hadhramaut—whose ruins have not yet been exhaustively excavated or studied.[1] The spade may yet disclose the identity and history of 'Ad,[2] and it is natural enough that the required evidence should be sought in the first place somewhere between Shihr (i.e. Hadhramaut) and San'a, the capital of Yaman. Ya'qut places Wabar in that neighbourhood, and his sources doubtless derived their information (much of it absurd and purely fabulous) from earlier memories which doubtless go back to historical facts.

If, therefore, the poem which I have quoted is to be our guide and Yaman the scene of our researches, we must seek a locality named Qariya with a ruinfield to the west of it. I can only suggest that such a place is ready to our hand in a still unvisited locality on the road between Sulaiyil and Najran, whose rivers, Habauna and Najran, may well have watered the fringes of the desert eastward of the present limits of their oases within historical times. The name of the locality is suggestive enough—Qariyat al Jahiliyin, Qariya of the ancients or simply ' the village of the ancients.' The name suggests, like the poem, that Qariya and the ruins of Wabar are contiguous or near to each other—to-day the former is a desert well on the way to Najran and I could get no information regarding ruins. The neighbouring wells of

---

[1] Dr. Carl Rathjens of Hamburg has now for some time been engaged in archaeological work in the Yaman, and his results will be awaited with great interest.

[2] Reference should be made to a recent work by D. Van der Meulen and H. von Wissmann, entitled *Hadramaut* (Leyden, 1932). On pp. 56 *et seq.* will be found an account of ruins locally known as Dar 'Ad and ' dating probably from Sabaean times.'

'Uwaifara may, however, be suggested as a possible site for Wabar itself, which may be no more than a classical or literary corruption, as Mr. Thomas suggests,[1] of Ophir the land of gold, apes and peacocks ! In its proper Arabic form the name would be 'Afar, of which 'Uwaifara is but a correctly formed diminutive. The Greeks would have transcribed it ὄφαρ, which is Ofar or Ophir in our pronunciation. And finally in this locality we do certainly get nearer to country which still produces both gold and apes and jungle-fowl, if not peacocks—the granite massif of the Hijaz mountains within the seasonal rain-belt of the Indian monsoon.

If, however, the Yaman be not the scene of 'Ad's magnificence, there is yet another locality which might be probed with interesting results. Eastern Arabia, less well-known than the southern provinces, was nevertheless apparently the scene of an ancient civilisation. The *Tumuli* of Bahrain are well-known, and antiquities have been unearthed at the neighbouring island of Darin (? Darain, the twin palaces), while there are numerous ruins—ancient springs and irrigation channels and so forth—on the mainland between the Hasa and Kuwait, to-day a barren wilderness with scattered desert wells frequented only by grazing Badawin. Two of these wells indeed have names that startle—Qariya with Wabra to west of it ! Who shall say that they played no part in the history of the 'Adites ?

Such speculations, however, only dawned upon me slowly after my disappointment in the Rub' al Khali itself. I must now return to my lump of iron, which with the other material collected from Wabar was in due course handed over to the Wahhabi King and by him presented to the British Museum. Dr. L. J. Spencer, the Keeper of the Mineral Department, had no difficulty in determining the character of the finds.

The metal is, as I supposed, a fragment of meteoritic iron and the slag-like material is silica-glass or sand fused by the heat of the falling meteorite, the greater part of which must have evaporated at the stupendous temperature generated by its impact on the earth. Nothing was left of it but a few odd fragments which cooled rapidly enough to survive as

[1] *Arabia Felix*, p. 163.

M

evidence of the manner in which the craters were formed.
My material has proved to be a valuable contribution to the
study of such phenomena, but the technical side of it must
be left for Dr. Spencer[1] himself to deal with. By examination
of the fragment of meteoritic iron already referred to, which
has been in the British Museum since its purchase from a
dealer in 1885, he has come to the tentative conclusion that
the two fragments are of so closely similar composition that
they may well have formed part of the same meteoritic mass.
And the probability of the older specimen having come from
the so-called Wabar of the Rub' al Khali is reinforced by its
curious, somewhat vague and suspect history.

In 1885 the Nejed Meteorite, as it is labelled, was offered to
and purchased by the Museum authorities. The vendor was
a dealer resident at Bushire, who supplied the information
that in the spring of 1863 some Arabs encamped in ' Wadi
Bani Khalid ' had actually seen the meteorite fall during a
thunderstorm and had subsequently picked it up or dug it out
of the ground. The vendor had actually received it, presumably for a consideration, from a man called Shaikh
Khalaf ibn 'Isa,[2] who had apparently witnessed the fall. He
had given the above particulars and was still alive at
Hudaida in 1884.

Apart from the thunderstorm, which might have been an
accidental concomitant of the fall, there was nothing especially suspicious about this story. It did, however, arouse
suspicion in somewhat curious circumstances six or seven
years later. In 1892 another similar fragment of meteoritic
iron, and of approximately the same weight—the two were
respectively 131 and 137 lb. and so considerably larger than
mine,—was offered for sale to the British Museum with rather
more detail of information regarding its discovery. Unfortunately only the English translation of the accompanying
letter of explanation is extant, and certain possible emenda-
tions of the text have to be taken into account in considering
the matter. This fragment was also said to have been observed as it fell *during a thunderstorm* in the previous year
(1308 A.H. = 1890-91 A.D.) in ' *Wadi Bani Khalid*.' It was then

---

[1] See Appendix.   [2] Possibly a member of the ruling family of Bahrain.

dug out of the earth and forwarded by a certain Bin Nakhad bin Shaikh-el-Hurra to Shaikh Nasir bin Rashid, who in turn forwarded it *via* Qatif to Haji Ahmad Khan, who passed it on to the dealer. The Museum refused the specimen on account of its plainly suspect provenance, and it ultimately found its way to America.[1] There was now, however, good reason to doubt the details of the 1863 story, but there was no means of probing it to its foundations, and the matter rested there until the arrival of my meteorite this year.

I have carefully considered the correspondence and am entirely unable to suggest any identification for the ' Wadi Bani Khalid ' locality. It may well have meant no more than ' in the territory of the Bani Khalid tribe,' which evidently means Eastern Arabia and may have been used vaguely of the Hasa province in its widest sense,[2] which in 1863 was under Wahhabi rule and in 1891 in Turkish occupation. It struck me, however, at once that the name of the forwarder of the 1891 specimen offered interesting possibilities. It gave the man's surname with the additional information that he was the son (or nephew or grandson) of the Shaikh of a tribe or place called Hurra. I strongly suspect that the name should be Murra—it would not be difficult for a stranger unfamiliar with the tribes of Arabia to misread the Arabic M or ‌م for the unaspirated H or ‌ه. If that be so, can we identify anyone of the surname of Bin Nakhad among the Shaikhs of the Murra tribe ? I think so if we may again assume the possibility of a corrupt reading of an Arabic letter by an unfamiliar stranger ; and I find in my more or less exhaustive list of all the groups, sections and chiefs of the Murra that the leading Shaikh of the Jarraba group, to which belongs the excavator of the two original wells of Umm al Hadid (!), is Hamad ibn Nahhab. The two surnames[3] are too near and the circumstances too

---

[1] Field Museum of Natural History, Chicago.
[2] Including the Rub‘ al Khali.
[3] The two names in Arabic characters would be :—

ابن نخاد ابن شيخ الهره

and

ابن نخاب ابن شيخ المره

suspicious to leave me in any further doubt that the man who procured the 1891 meteorite from the same spot that had yielded its predecessor procured it from the craters of Al Hadida, from which the Umm al Hadid wells, dug by a member of the same family, derived their name.

The transaction had doubtless been profitable for the Marri, and it is perhaps not strange that his fellow tribesmen should have magnified the dimensions of such golden metal. But the camel had now been squeezed through the eye of a needle, and fragments of it had found their way to England and America long before I discovered their source and the secret of Wabar.

CHAPTER IV

BITTER WATERS

*This is Al Ramla, but the Rub' al Khali—the Rub' al Khali is
away yonder till you come to the mountains, the black mountains!*

WE were yet to spend many days among the wells and
parched pastures of Al Rimal, but the above was 'Ali's description of the situation as we rode away from Wabar on
the morning of February 6th. Two of the specific objectives
of the expedition had been disposed of and our thoughts
now centred on the third—the crossing of the waterless
desert. But first we must go down to Shanna, visiting the
frontier wells of the pasture lands.

The previous morning at Wabar I had found a heavy dew
on the ground—the first recorded by me for some days—but
there was none this morning, and the atmosphere was
pleasantly mild in spite of a raw, fairly strong north wind
as we made an early start on the longish waterless stage to
'Ain Sala.

It is strange that my companions had no idea of the
potential pecuniary value of the great iron which we had
not found. Doubtless the home tribe—the Jarraba—had
kept this knowledge to itself lest others might prospect the
locality and deprive it of possible future windfalls. And the
piece we had found had doubtless lain unseen since its discovery by the wind owing to the long drought which had
kept the nomads at a safe distance. The rewards I had promised were not claimed and, satisfied as I was, I deemed it
impolitic to pay them at the moment. A more suitable
occasion would present itself later on.

My party was thus somewhat depressed by the failure of
the guides to make good their early boasting and, to cheer
them up, I suggested to Humaid, who had hitherto been

without poetic inspiration, that he should compose a ballad
on the wonders of Wabar and the sacks of black pearls
which had rewarded their searching. Many weeks later
these were going the round of the dealers of Mecca with
disappointment in their train and my companions, distressed
by the collapse of their dreams of wealth, had to be content
with their earnings. For three months of really strenuous
work they got an average of L8 or L10 apiece—enough
under their conditions of existence to procure a wife withal
but not enough to buy a pedigree camel.

For the moment there was nothing for it but to set ourselves to the task in hahd and make as much progress as
possible amid surroundings as dull, monotonous and dreary
as may be imagined. A pair of ravens occupied our deserted
camp—it was here that we left behind the results of our
unsuccessful pickling,—and a light film of sand swept un-
ceasingly over the face of the earth around us. The gently
billowing desert was as a haze of steam rising from a vast,
simmering cauldron. And, when the wind dropped, the
soft, silky sheen of the sands struck painfully up at our eyes.

Apart from a sparse sprinkling of *Abal* the landscape was
very bare with only an occasional hummock of sand to break
the flatness of the picture. As I stood on one of these for a
general view I found it almost impossible to maintain my
position against the sheets of blowing sand which enveloped
me in their tiresome eddies. Till mid-afternoon we marched
still in Sanam with but an hour's break to rest.

Then the scene underwent an abrupt change as we passed
into the district of Majari Tasrat, so-called from the well of
Tasrat[1] a day's march to eastward, which is reported to have
sweet water at eight fathoms. Parallel to our course on the
right and beyond the limits of our vision lay the dune
ranges of Hibaka with the valleys of Shuqqan al Birkan
(already noticed in Sa'afij) beyond them and the sands of
Bani Zainan to their southward. The Tasrat tract is itself a
broad band of alternating ridges and valleys lying roughly
east and west. In one of the latter we camped that first
night, to resume our march at 7 a.m. under rather depressing

[1] Beyond Tasrat eastward is the well of Umm al Qaraïn.

conditions. A light, clammy northern breeze gently fanned a thick damp mist, out of which a very pale sun climbed feebly into the sky. Until well past mid-day visibility was seriously limited by the haze, but it mattered little. There was nothing to see that was different from what lay before our noses—a gradual *crescendo* of deeper and ever deeper valleys with correspondingly higher ridges as we advanced southward. The baggage train had been sent on two hours or more ahead of us but its tracks had already been obliterated by the driving sand. Here and there a patch of *Abal* bushes showed up like a fence on the higher levels, while at the foot of one ridge the thinnest imaginable line of green *Andab* grass created a veritable sensation. Two years ago they reported rain from these parts, said 'Ali, and look ! the first signs of its fruit ! Maybe there is life ahead. His hopes were not altogether fulfilled by our experience but some of the later valleys did look rather better.

We halted in one of them for a brief space at mid-day to let the camels feed on the *Abal*, which had now begun to be decorated with the characteristic pink tassels that give the shrub so jaunty an appearance in springtime. This valley was the first of a series similar to those of Tasrat but named Majari[1] Ma'shiya from the watering of that name at a day's journey or less to the eastward with briny but potable water at 11 fathoms. Beyond it to the east lies the watering of Manjurat[2] al Hadi near Mr. Thomas' route and named after the famous grandfather or more remote ancestor of his Marri guide. Another desert plant that now reappeared for the first time since our passage out of Jafura was the *Alqa*, green and already putting forth its tiny yellow blossoms. A few Desert Warblers were seen in these parts and some solitary locusts had been noted, but I was not prepared to see a butterfly. At first I thought the sudden flash of brown was an optical illusion, but I soon discovered that it was not. I may have seen a score or more of them thereafter during a month's wanderings in

[1] *Majari* (plural of *Majra*) means " channels."

[2] *Manjura* means " carved out " from the root *Najar* (carpentering). The name Miniyur, given by Mr. Thomas for another locality, is more properly Manjur pronounced with the typical softening of the J.

this tract of the sands, but I only captured the very last I encountered on the fringes of the waterless desert in Bani Zainan. I hoped that a butterfly—apparently the only[1] one of the Rub' al Khali, though I thought on several occasions that I saw another, a species of the Skipper family—in such a locality would be new to science, and many were the frantic efforts I made to secure a specimen ; but it proved to be a known species[2] after all.

This was the 29th day of *Ramdhan*, the last day of our fasting according to the calendar, and we fondly hoped as we camped in the next ridge-and-valley tract of Khillat Judair that we would awake next morning to normal life. The blustering north-east wind that had accompanied us all day dropped altogether at sunset, when all eyes were turned eagerly towards the western sky to seek the ' better moon.' The haze, however, defeated us, although Sa'd al Washmi claimed to have seen it and one or two others thought they had glimpsed the crescent. There is very little doubt that in all these cases the wish was father to the thought, and no one really took Sa'd's claim seriously. He disliked fasting too actively and too obviously to be a reliable witness. Nevertheless there arose a hubbub of argument and rasping wrangling as to whether the fast should be prolonged for a thirtieth day or the morrow be treated as the '*Id* of the feast. I announced my intention of completing the thirty days and Ibn Ma'addi, our spiritual guide, who with Suwid, Abu Ja'sha and myself had kept the fast without a break,[3] concurred. Most of the others followed suit, while a few decided to compromise by ' travelling ' next day and only the disgruntled three were left to celebrate the feast.

Far into the night, as I sat aloof at my work in my own tent, I heard snatches of their continued wrangling—raucous,

---

[1] I saw also one Painted Lady a few days later near Naifa.

[2] Identified by Mr. N. D. Riley of the British Museum as *Apharitis gilletti*, a species which occurs in Somaliland but was not previously known from Arabia, in various parts of which from Aden to Syria and 'Iraq the *genus* has hitherto been represented only by *A. acamas*.

[3] Salim and Ibn Humaiyid had only missed the ' day of the fog,' while Hasan also lost that day and compromised by ' travelling ' on the 30th day.

ranting, evil-minded talk, freely interlarded with mutual accusations of infidelity and irreligion.[1] The guiltier the conscience, the louder its protesting. On the whole the party had not distinguished itself during the month's ordeal. Apart from the four and a few others who had failed only on the 'day of the fog' the rest had ended up with greater or lesser debts to pay with Zayid, who had set a thoroughly bad example, and Sa'dan as easily the worst delinquents. In some aspects Islam is indeed an easygoing faith, leaving much to the individual conscience, with the result that those of bad faith get the better of the deal over their fellows—at least in this world.

Judair is a briny waterhole only two or three feet in depth about a day's march from our camp. It is considered unpotable for human beings but is poured out to the grazing camels. The Khilla or 'empty region' is so-called because it is innocent of *Hadh*, the characteristic pasture shrub of the south. The undulations of ridge and valley in this tract were steeper than those of the preceding districts. The slopes of the long dune ranges rose gradually from the north to a crest, from which there was almost always a steep drop into the valley beyond, generally of soft sand which necessitated careful attention on the part of the rider, as camels with all their experience have failed to develop grace in descending a sand cliff and prefer the headlong descent to the abyss in short, sharp, lurching leaps. On one such slope Zayid took a perfect toss from his precarious *Haulani* saddle, and on another Farraj strained his back with a similar accident. I managed to survive all risks by exercising a carefulness forced on me by constant anxiety for my instruments, which fortunately survived the three months of our wanderings without noticeable harm.

From Wabar (767 feet) we had ascended very gradually on a more or less southward course, but from the next tract —Hadh Faris, so-called from a watering to the eastward halfway between our route and Buwah—we began a slight descent to about the same level as Wabar near Bani

[1] To fast for safety on the feast day is, if anything, a worse offence than feasting on a fast day.

Jallab (730 feet), whence we dropped to 'Ain Sala (527 feet), beyond which to Naifa and Ziqirt the same lower level was maintained until we rose again towards Shanna.

Hadh Faris provided more variety of vegetation and more life than any tract since Wabar for, in addition to the tasselled *Abal*, there was a good deal of *Hadh* and *Alqa*, all fairly fresh. Two pairs of ravens were observed, the second in the neighbourhood of a newly built but eggless nest to which, after an initial flight, the hen bird returned rather boldly and unnecessarily only to be shot by Salih with my gun. The cock with hoarse cries of anger and distress intervened bravely to protect his wounded mate, and we rode on leaving Salih to deal with the pair. He eventually brought along the hen, now dead, leaving the disappointed widower to seek another mate, if he could find one unattached in that wilderness. Ravens, Bifasciated Larks and Desert Warblers had now come to be recognised by me as the commonest creatures in these regions, but a dragonfly was something of a surprise[1]—and not only one but three during this day's march and other specimens, of which I duly bagged a few, on the following days. They were all of the same species— a large dull bluish type already seen at Jabrin and in the Hasa—and I wondered whether they could be regarded as true denizens of the sands. If so, do they dispense with water in the larval stage or do they make do with the shallow, briny pools of Al Khiran ?

As we went south the dune waves became loftier, thicker and grander, while the deeper valleys between them seemed to be richer in vegetation. After some five hours of Hadh Faris we entered the tract of Bani Jallab, half-way across which—its width from north to south was about 15 miles— we camped for the night. The rugged nature of the country with its constant ups and downs over difficult ridges tended to retard progress, while a mild southern breeze, alternating with entirely windless intervals, created sultry marching conditions and frayed tempers already on edge with the night's altercations. Zayid, determined not to fast this last day and hoping to force the issue, had evidently ordered the

[1] *Hemianax ephippiger* Burm.

cook to oversleep himself, which he had done very successfully. So there was only tea and coffee for the morning
supper and we started the last day's fast fasting, so far as
solid food was concerned.

The day's proceedings were rather dreary in consequence
of all these factors, but there was some compensation in the
multiplying of indications that these better pastures had not
been neglected by the desert animals. A pair of horns of the
Rim gazelle was picked up from the sands, on which were
frequent traces also of the Oryx, whose dry dung, in places
fairly recent, has the sweet smell of musk. Our hunters
strayed from the course in high hopes of bringing back something to make high festival withal on the feast day. But
they all returned empty-handed except for a brace of hares,
and the party that assembled round the camp-fire for the
last formal breaking of the fast was in querulous mood.

It was Hasan Khurr al Dhib who first spotted the young
crescent high up in the sky several minutes before sunset.
It was fully ten minutes later that I saw it, while one or two
of the others under Hasan's guidance had picked it up before
me. The argument of the previous evening was of course
reopened, but my criticism of the afternoon's rate of progress—I had insisted on remaining with the baggage party
as a protest against the straggling of the rest and had announced my intention of walking for the whole of the next
day—took pride of place until the conversation was turned
into a channel of greater interest.

We had filled our waterskins at Ibrahima on February 4th
for a six days' march, but there had been no attempt to econo-
mise or control consumption. The water was now nearly
finished after only four days and Zayid urged that a party
should be sent to Naifa to bring back a supply to our next
camp. It was obvious that they had no intention of making a
vigorous effort to get to 'Ain Sala—which proved to be about
40 miles distant—on the morrow, and I strongly resisted the
proposal. But we have no water, said Zayid. I thought he
was exaggerating or lying and answered hotly : Well, you
can do without, surely, for one day, if I have done without
for more than a month. What's more, if there's but little

water, you can have it all. I want none of it, no, not even
for my usual tea, and you can have the milk of my camel too.
We can never arrive anywhere like this ; this is not marching.
We had indeed been marching less than 25 miles a day, as I
reckoned, since leaving Wabar.

Later in the evening Zayid came to my tent alone to plead
the common cause but I would not give way. Why can't you
do without water ? I asked. I can, you see. It will hurt us
to be without water, he replied unashamedly, and our skins
are empty. He departed evidently crestfallen at my
obstinacy and, taking counsel with the rest, slipped away
during the night with 'Ali and Humaid to get us water in
my despite and, as they hoped without doubt, to return
triumphantly with the carcase of an Oryx.

' Man proposes but God disposes.' I retired to bed unconscious of their scheming and leaving Sa'dan to skin two
birds and a hare by the light of my lamp. I was almost
asleep when there was a sudden roar and a tug at the tent
ropes. The tent came tumbling over my head, burying Sa'dan
in its folds and upsetting the lighted lamp. I rescued the
latter before any harm could come of the accident and fortunately I had packed everything away in the hope of an
early start. The gale blew upon us fast and furious with
stinging clouds of sand. I lay down in the open behind one
of my boxes for shelter, while Abu Ja'sha and others very
considerately built a barricade round me. The wind
howled and the sand blew most of the night, but I slept
fitfully.

It was nearly daylight before I was woken for the dawn
prayer. The storm had passed but our camp was a piteous
scene of wreckage. My protecting barrier had become part
of a decent-sized barrow. My tent had disappeared and we
had to dig it out of the sand. It was cold and raw and
miserable. And it was cheering to hear that there would be
no breakfast. There was but enough water for the day's
coffee drinkings. I declined the formal offer of my usual
tea, and our feast-day breakfast (after sunrise) was a lump of
dates and sand with some sips of coffee. I noticed that
Zayid and the others were absent but held my peace.

A little after 7 we began the march. I walked, and some of the others walked too as they often did at the beginning of a march. Salih joined me and we struck out on a bee-line course, leaving the camels to negotiate the dune ranges in their usual meandering way. We talked of Oryx and gazelles and the better country of the Manasir, but Salih was thinking of something else, while Sa'dan, riding but leading my camel, and Farraj with Salih's kept at a respectful distance within hail. I thoroughly enjoyed that walking up hill and down dale over the rolling sands, slithering down the steep slopes and toiling up to the crests. After nearly two hours of such progress we came to the top of a high ridge and I stopped to take in the scene. Suddenly a dark object on the summit of a dune caught my eye. What is that ? I exclaimed to Salih who was looking longingly in the other direction towards the camels. I thought it might be a raven or bush, but it looked somehow unfamiliar. Before Salih could look round it had slipped back furtively behind the peak. When I had explained exactly what I had seen he was all agog with excitement and nervousness. It may be the spy of a raiding party, he suggested, let us hasten to our companions. That was certainly the wisest thing to do in the circumstances, for our main body was half a mile away to the left. Salih urged me to hasten all I knew and gesticulated wildly to warn the rest that there was something afoot.

A hasty council of war was held when we rejoined them, while Farraj, Salih and others put their camels to the trot to spy out the land and the rest of us stood by the camels, preparing for battle. There was much brave talk and Sa'dan was among the bravest as he armed himself with my shot-gun—he, like me, had no rifle. Fear not, said 'Ali the herdsman, I will defend you. He and Muhammad and I remained with the camels. They had rifles, but I had only my ·22 pocket revolver.

In a minute or two, leaving a few men on our right flank, the remainder came back. Mount quickly, they said, and let us hasten, keeping to the left. As we did so, we saw our scouts returning to rejoin us, and with them were the enemy—Zayid and the other truants ! They had been caught by the storm before they had gone very far and had given up their self-imposed mission. The sand had obliterated their tracks and had washed out any hopes they may have had of tracking Oryx. So they had reconciled themselves to another waterless day and seemed to hope that their transparent stratagem had not been seen through by me.

Nevertheless they kept away from me while Salih and I resumed our walking, with a north-easterly breeze more or less behind us. Here and there we saw the droppings of Oryx and Salih obviously longed to be off seeking the quarry, but he remained loyally by my side as we kept easily ahead of the baggage. Zayid and Co. seemed to be making a satisfactory effort to register better progress, but an hour later we saw them halted some distance ahead. As we came up to them we found that they had propped up the carcase of a huge bull Oryx against an *Abal* bush. They had found it dead and half buried in the sand. Whether it had died of wounds or of drought—we had now entered a less favourable tract where there had been no recent rain and the vegetation was all dry—we could not say. But its carcase had not been touched. Only the paunch had collapsed—rotted by the intestines—otherwise the meat had dried intact upon the frame. I photographed the beast propped up against the bush that had shaded its dying moments and we cut off the head to carry along with us. Though dead, it was the first Oryx I had seen in its native land.

More than an hour after this interlude we passed into the district of Hadh 'Ain Sala—range after range of high whitish dunes. Salih liked the walking less and less with each passing hour but struggled gamely on, while I was thoroughly enjoying myself. I wondered whether he was really spent, for I felt not the slightest bit fatigued. I assured him that he might ride, if he would, without giving me offence. It was up to them to make the pace too hot for me if they disliked my walking. At length he confessed, with tears in his eyes, that he could walk no more and begged me to mount to save his face. We had been walking for eight hours and I yielded, but insisted on riding with the baggage. Less than an hour later I observed a state of agitation among the

advance party. Some of them, with rifles at the trail, were
speeding up the slope on foot. I thought that perhaps they
had observed an enemy or his tracks. But it was not that.
They had come upon the spot where a pair of full-grown
Oryx had enjoyed a siesta under a spreading *Abal* bush that
very afternoon. Everything was forgotten in that thrilling
moment—hunger, thirst, fatigue—and that was the end of
the day's march. We camped in a neighbouring hollow, my
tent being pitched in the pit of an incipient horseshoe
cavity of a lofty dune.

It was dark before the hunters returned—all unsuccessful,
but hoping for better sport next day. There had been no
dinner for them to miss, and I agreed now that a party
should go to Naifa to bring water next day to 'Ain Sala.
To my astonishment Salih, who but an hour before had been
crying out about his sore feet, had without a moment's
hesitation joined in the hunt, and he was one of the latest
to arrive back in camp. He came to my tent obviously
pleased with himself. Well, I asked, did you get an Oryx ?
No, he replied, but I saw one, a great bull too, and that near.
I drew a bead on him and pressed the trigger, but the cartridge misfired and at the sound the animal was gone. I
saw him no more, and here is the cursed cartridge. Do you
see the dent in its cap ? Yet he lied, and knew that I knew
that he lied. He smiled wanly at my scepticism but did not
press the matter.

Later on Zayid came to me mysteriously with the request
for my hurricane lamp—I had also a pressure lamp to attract
insects but was selfish about lending either as our paraffin
supply was none too abundant. What do you want it for ?
I asked. I want it, he replied. I insisted on his telling me the
reason. Well, he said, if you would know, we all heard as we
sat at the fire there the sound of a low whistling and we
think perhaps there may be raiders about and the whistle a
scout's signal. I gave him the lamp and thought no more of
the matter until next morning. It was nothing, said Zayid ;
we cast all around but found no tracks. It was a Jinn, said
Hasan with an air of conviction that surprised and interested
me. He was quite serious and they all seemed to agree with-

out demur. It did not seem to occur to them that such a sound could be anything but supernatural. I had often before heard of the Rub' al Khali as being infested with Jinns, but this was our first encounter with its spiritual denizens.

The morning broke cold, grey and very hazy with a gentle north breeze as we resumed the march. From time to time we came upon more signs of Oryx, and the dune ranges, lying uniformly north-east to south-west, seemed to be getting higher and steeper and softer, dropping southward like spent rollers of an ocean. It was a dull, dreary, dead country of sandy valleys, about a mile wide, between the waves with scanty, parched shrubs of *Andab* and *Alqa*, *Abal* and *Hadh*, and tufts of *Birkan* as we approached 'Ain Sala. It was a very short march of only 15 miles in all, but we broke it in the middle with an hour's halt. Almost the last of our water was used up for coffee, and the last remnants of the Maqainama camel were produced and grilled in the ashes to make up for a feast day that had been both breakfastless and dinnerless. The landscape now flattened out as seen from the north and the ranges looked lower but their downward dip was deeper. Slowly we approached the crest of a long winding range and Salim, pointing downwards almost at his feet, exclaimed : Look! 'Ain Sala! I looked down into a great pit 200 feet below us and saw a patch of rock.

For five days we had seen nothing but sand in a state of perpetual flux, and there was something strangely satisfying in the sight of rock. I dismounted to take in the scene while the camels fetched a wide circuit to reach the entrance to the hollow, which was completely surrounded by high steep slopes of sand in horseshoe formation except towards the south-west. A high point in the dune range immediately above the pit must have been at least 300 feet above its level but the ridge in general was from 50 to 100 feet lower. A pair of ravens circled round to witness our arrival and remained in attendance, though at a discreet distance, during our sojourn of five days from February 10th to 15th. Occasionally they even ventured into our camp during its

somnolent moments and might have been bolder with
impunity, for my shot-gun had now gone finally out of action
and all our efforts to put it right were unavailing. This was
something of a tragedy as we could scarcely hope to get any
more small birds though I continued to note their occurrence,
and even tried from time to time to shoot them with my
pocket pistol.

As I sat alone on a dune top commanding the hollow a
rifle shot rang out, echoing and re-echoing from slope to
slope. I saw a fox standing stock-still on the rock below.
For a moment it stood there before flight into the sands
beyond, where I followed it with my glasses as Farraj and
Al Aqfa pursued. The beast was obviously wounded—the
bullet had gone through its abdomen—and rapidly the bitch
overhauled it. Then among the bushes came the end, and
Farraj came back triumphant with his trophy, which proved
to be a Fennec or Desert Fox of the new subspecies[1]
collected last year by Mr. Thomas.

Having surveyed the scene sufficiently I went straight
down the steep soft slope towards the pit, whose geological
formation I examined while the tents were being pitched and
the camels driven forth to the pastures. About 50 feet
above the floor of the depression an intermittent stratum of
friable greyish sandstone appeared from under the heaped-
up sands. Downwards it shelved to a rock-floor of similar
formation, some acres in extent and curving round the actual
well area in an imposing semicircular cliff of 10 or 12 feet,
whose horns penetrated and lost themselves in the steep
surrounding sand slopes. In this area I found a few shell
fragments of freshwater[2] origin, but otherwise nothing but the
characteristic odds and ends of old Badawin camps—horns of
the *Rim* gazelle, cartridge cases, fragments of leather and the
like. But three fragments of stone picked up by me in
this locality have proved to be parts of a single small
stony meteorite.[3]

[1] *Arabia Felix*, p. 340. I brought back three specimens in all, which
have been provisionally labelled *Cynalopex sp.* by Captain J. G. Dollman of
the British Museum.

[2] *Melanoides tuberculata*—see Appendix.   [3] See Appendix.

N

Beyond the sandstone area, however, and isolated from it by the sand, I came upon an unique and fairly large patch of calcareous concretions, the nature of which I was completely at a loss to understand. It consisted of large and small single, double and even treble cylindrical tubes with rough, calcareous exteriors but smooth and polished insides. Mr. Campbell Smith[1] of the British Museum suggested that they could only be concretions formed round the 'branches and twigs of vegetation long since perished from the inside.' But the matter remained in suspense until, by a curious chance, a similar specimen of calcareous concretion was received at the Museum from a locality in Trans-Jordan. In this case the hardened reed, round which the calcareous matter had formed, was still intact. There could be little doubt, therefore, that the 'Ain Sala concretions were of similar origin, and we may suppose that a bed of reeds once upon a time grew in or near water on the spot where I found them. The 'Ain Sala tract thus becomes a possible candidate for the honour of being considered a relic of the old Wadi Dawasir, of which we had hitherto come upon no trace. In this case the Shanna valley further south, for which I have provision-ally reserved that honour, may prove to be the tail of the Najran valley system, for which also an ultimate destination must be found some day. 'Ain Sala and Tuwairifa, more than 100 miles apart, seem to lie approximately at the same altitude above sea-level and are separated by higher ground. They must therefore represent the remnants of different valleys, and it may be suggested tentatively that the district embracing Adraj, 'Ain Sala, Naifa and Ziqirt constitutes either a delta of Wadi Dawasir or an estuary of the sea. In the absence of any sign of fresh water underlying this neigh-bourhood I am inclined to prefer the latter alternative, though the former cannot by any means be ruled out of court.

The single well is sunk to a depth of seven or eight fathoms, as they say, through the sandstone rock, having a mouth only two feet in diameter and reinforced by a framework of wattle. In all probability its record of alternate life and death goes far back into the past, but its modern history—

[1] See Appendix.

and very short is the desert memory—begins with Al Nifl, a Shaikh of Murra, who came to these parts, sorely distraught with thirst in the course of a raiding expedition, and saw a vision in his fevered dreaming. Fear not, the voice had said, the water is at your feet. Next morning he had followed the ridge to where the rock lay exposed and had dug till he and his men came to water and thus saved themselves and their cattle alive. That was some 50 years ago and the drought had buried the shaft till the ' year of Hail ' by their reckoning (1921 by ours), when 'Ali Jahman had rediscovered and reopened the well. It remained in regular use for two seasons until the beginning of the eight years' drought, when it was again abandoned to the sands. We found it therefore dead and buried. Its water was, they said, always briny though drinkable.

It is indeed astonishing that a small patch of the bedrock surrounded by sands should remain more or less permanently exposed. It can perhaps be explained by the suggestion that in such deep hollows the wind sets up an eddy of the sands which serves to sweep the floor clean. It was indeed quite difficult to find a suitable spot for our tents, which were from time to time undercut by the sudden whirlwinds that descended upon us without warning and actually floored my tent on three occasions during our sojourn.

On arrival we used up the last of our water for a final brew of coffee and then had to wait in patience until the party which had gone to Naifa came in with full skins at 5 p.m. From that moment arose an activity of the bowels which, except for a brief period after Shanna, was to haunt us to the end of our desert wanderings and to make Naifa a byword among us. Curiously enough in my case the trouble started almost immediately after our arrival at 'Ain Sala and could not be attributed in its inception to that cause, though the Naifa water proved sufficiently powerful even in tea and coffee to aggravate my uneasiness. Its origin, however, I attribute to the discontinuance of the fast, for with the removal of all such restrictions I had, at the instigation of Salih and Humaid, browsed freely on the white blossoms and tender green sprigs of the *Abal* as we marched and at our halts, while *Makika* now appeared quite frequently on our menu. I can vouch therefore for the much-vaunted medicinal properties of the shrub.

It had been agreed that 'Ain Sala should be made our base of operations while Zayid and 'Ali went forth towards Shanna to recruit guides and guarantors for the proposed southward extension of our wanderings from any Arabs they might find in their path. We were to allow them six days and at the end of that period meet them at Ziqirt—a stage further south. Jabir ibn Fasl had warned us that we should find no one in the southern pastures as the grazing tribes had been packing up, as he left to come north, with the idea of getting to the protection of the southern mountains before the arrival of the punitive expedition which the guilty conscience of the Manhali Shaikh Saif ibn Tannaf imagined to be foreshadowed by the preparations for our expedition. Besides Saif himself our messengers were to seek out Hamad ibn Sultan, who had been Mr. Thomas' guide and was living with his wife among her kinsmen of the Rashid Kathiris— probably to be out of the way of the Wahhabi tax-collectors. Hasan ibn Kalut of the Rashid or one of his relatives would also be a desirable acquisition, while we should ultimately need representatives of the Sa'ar and Karb tribes. Zayid and 'Ali appeared to be going forward in all good faith to serve our ends loyally, but Jabir had spoken all too truly. They saw no signs of Arabs anywhere, and that very fact is as striking a tribute as can be imagined to the awe inspired by the name of Ibn Sa'ud. A party of nineteen men cannot be regarded as a serious menace to the war-like and turbulent tribes of the south, who can at short notice place 200 or 300 armed men in the field without difficulty. But it would evidently be a serious matter for them to challenge the representatives of the great King and, in any case, they preferred not to face the issue.

That night I had long consultations with the selected emissaries, and I gave them the choice of three ultimate objectives. An observation of *Polaris* gave our position as being a little south of the 20th Parallel while our Longitude appeared to be something in the neighbourhood of 51° E.

In these circumstances Qabr Hud[1]—the reputed tomb and
shrine of the prophet Heber—seemed to be the best objective on Longitude 50° E. and Latitude 16° N. as far as I
could ascertain from the available maps. That was therefore the task I set them, with Shibam (further west) and the
sea-coast (further south) as reasonable alternatives. Also
they were to hire a few fresh camels if possible and ascertain
the possibilities of replenishing our commissariat for the
ultimate waterless trek to Sulaiyil.

Look you, said 'Ali, you know what the *Badu* are like. These
people will want much money. You must tell us how much we
can go to. That is rather for you to consider, I replied ; I will
agree to what you consider reasonable. The money I have
brought is for the needs of our expedition. Waste it not lest
there be less for you all to share. But how much do you think?
insisted 'Ali. What do you advise ? I replied evasively. He
was for a long time unwilling to commit himself, and I told
them to consult among themselves and come to me with the
result. At length they came to me. We think, said 'Ali, that
they will not accept less than 100 dollars apiece. They are
Badu and greedy, and the Christian by all reports was generous
last year. What do you think ? I asked, turning to Zayid.
I agree with 'Ali, he replied, and it is cheap. They are
Shaikhs and, if you pay them well, they will serve you well.
Very well, I replied, let us agree to that. The prospect of the
expenditure of 400 or 500 dollars (about £20 or £25) did not
seem very outrageous in the circumstances.

Next morning we sat over the camp-fire sipping coffee and
eating dates while preparations went forward for sending down
the camels to water at Naifa. As we should visit the place later
I decided to stay where I was for a rest. Zayid and 'Ali would
go with the watering party and thence proceed to Shanna.
As we sat there a V-shaped column of geese or swans[2]

[1] This locality was visited by D. van der Meulen and Dr. H. von Wissmann in 1931. Their account is published in a recent volume entitled
Hadramaut. See also J.R.G.S., vol. lxxvii, No. 3, 1931, for an aeroplane
flight over the locality by Squadron-Leader the Hon. R. A. Cochrane. The
actual position, according to these authorities, is approximately Long. 49°
30′ E. and Lat. 16° N.

[2] My companions called them *Lau*.

passed far over our heads pointing northward. It was a lovely
sight in the midst of the desert. They will be going to Qatar,
said 'Ali, that is the direction and we often see them on the
coast there. Zaid, the cook, had reported seeing the tracks of
a Stone Curlew right down by the edge of the camp, and this
bird proved a regular visitor each night though we never had a
glimpse of it. Yet its persistence suggested some attraction
by the water or moisture of the well area, while the occurrence
of the earths of foxes in the near neighbourhood of the well
here and at Umm al Hadid—the same fact was observed at
other wells and suspected well-sites at later stages of our
march in this Khiran district—seemed to argue that the Desert
Fox does not eschew water and frequents its vicinity. I suggested to 'Ali that, if he would seek water to dig at in these
sands, he would do well to select suitable spots in firm ground
burrowed by foxes. The small desert birds were also here and
hereabout in comparative plenty, while on two occasions
during the daytime I saw a single Humming-bird Hawk moth.

Having sufficiently explored 'Ain Sala and its immediate
neighbourhood I decided on an excursion to the watering of
Adraj about 10 miles distant to the north-west. Thither,
accordingly, we proceeded on the 12th—a small party of seven
without tents or other *impedimenta*—to spend the night
there and return on the following day. The country traversed, with Salim as our guide, was similar to that we had
already seen when coming to 'Ain Sala. The pastures, however, seemed to be better while the only prominent feature
of the march was the long and fairly lofty dune range of
Hamran Adraj, lying north-east by south-west across our
path for several miles in each direction. Beyond it we
traversed a wide billowing plain bounded at the further side
by the higher range of Adraj itself.

Salim was not very certain of his bearings here, but turned
to the right along the foot of the ridge in the hope of finding
an easy passage across it. As we marched our camels became
excited at their—and my—first sight of the most beautiful
of all the desert bushes. The yellow cup-like flower and
frosted leaves of the *Zahr* made a charming picture indeed
in such surroundings and, though I saw the plant in plenty

afterwards, I never forgot this first impression of its almost exotic loveliness. I was surprised to hear that it does not rank very high as camel fodder in Badawin estimation, while the dung resulting from its consumption is regarded as having a lower calorific value than the product of *Hadh*. Our camels however made short work of the few plants we found, while I noticed that the tiny Desert Warbler (or perhaps some other bird, for I did not secure a specimen) was here in unwonted numbers, flying in companies instead of lurking about the bushes singly or in pairs.

Almost immediately afterwards we came rather unexpectedly upon the dip of the great horseshoe hollow of Adraj itself backed by the lofty dune which makes its range a conspicuous feature in the landscape. In a fairly extensive patch of the exposed sandstone bedrock lie the three ' dead ' wells which constitute this former watering. The water is said to have been at nine fathoms and the mouths of the shafts were easily enough distinguishable in spite of some encroachment of the sand on the lowest level of the hollow in which they lie between the steep sand-slope and a table of upstanding rock divided into four unequal sections and elevated about 10 or 12 feet above the well level. The surface of this table was of hard and rough calcareous appearance, but there was no sign of the 'Ain Sala reed tubes, though I picked up a small stony meteorite. Numerous thin specimens of fulgurites[1] or lightning tubes (formed by the fusing of the sand by lightning) were also found on the sands round this locality, and the Arabs have a theory that such tubes generally indicate the presence of water. We certainly found such specimens, however, on the desert sands where there was no suggestion of water, and there would seem to be no essential connection between the two. But it did seem to me that the exposures of the bedrock often had some relation to the presence of subterranean water, and it may be that such exposures tend to occur in low-lying old valley levels where of course there would presumably be water at a greater or lesser depth. Wilfrid and Lady Anne Blunt[2] also noted something of the same

---

[1] See Appendix.   [2] *A Pilgrimage to Nejd*, chap. viii.

kind in similar rock exposures in the great Northern Nafud.

Our visit to Adraj, delightful as it was in all other respects, was unfortunately marred by a minor domestic tragedy. I had gone up to the summit of the dune with Salim, who had then wandered into the desert in search of meat. He had returned to camp with a hare which seemed to me of an unusually light brown colouring. I passed it to Sa'dan for skinning, as we all sat chatting round the camp-fire, with a warning to exercise great care as I attached special importance to the specimen. The wretch, however, seemed to be in frivolous holiday mood and I had had to repeat my warning. After that I thought no more of the matter and we sat round our usual dish of rice after my companions had devoured the ash-grilled meat of the hare as a *hors d' œuvre*. Later on, as we still sat round the fire enjoying the pleasantness of the evening, Farraj, drawing something from the embers of the fire, asked casually where it had come from. It was the hare's skull ruined beyond repair and I could not refrain from giving expression to my wrath. Sa'dan, apparently undisturbed and quite unrepentant, allowed his silly tongue to wag impertinently and I suggested in momentary anger that the others did not do well to let such things happen with impunity. Seeing that I was genuinely aggrieved by the disaster Ibn Ma'addi suggested that the culprit should be bound and beaten, to which, perhaps stupidly but still in anger more at his continued impertinence than his error, I gave my consent. Thereupon they all fell upon him with the hearty roughness of their kind and belaboured him quite gently, as I thought, but at any rate enough to hurt his *amour propre* if not his body. He relapsed into rebellious sulks and had to be forced to assist me as usual at the theodolite. This work we accomplished successfully enough in spite of the tension between us, but the matter rankled in his cockney heart and he declared that he would work for me no more. Next day, having evidently thought things out to his satisfaction, he announced his formal resignation from my service, which I promptly accepted with the suggestion that I should pay him up to date. I then made enquiries for a volunteer to replace him and had several offers—but it was he himself that brought me my pot of tea and the hatchet was buried between us. He had taken his measure of me and we never quarrelled again—he was indeed indispensable and served me more than well, in return for which his final guerdon was considerably in excess of the earnings of any of the others.

The return journey to 'Ain Sala was made on a compass bearing set by myself—at first due south for nearly two hours and then due east as far as was permitted by intervening ridges. On this march, south of the next ridge beyond Hamran Adraj, we came upon a dark bluish hillock of rock in a sand-girt hollow of the desert, which seemed to suggest the presence of an old, forgotten well. We remained here an hour seeking in vain for shells or fossils, but we agreed that there must be a buried shaft somewhere in the hollow and bestowed the name of Bir al Makhfi or ' the hidden well ' on a locality which would certainly be worthy of further investigation when the Badawin return to this district under improved pasture conditions.

All this tract between 'Ain Sala and Adraj goes by the name of Hadh 'Ain Sala, while westward beyond the Adraj dune range begins the *Hadh*-less tract which they name Khillat Adraj, and which we were destined to traverse some weeks later. The pastures in this neighbourhood, though better than much we had seen hitherto, were nevertheless not of a character to attract the large herds of the grazing Badawin.

On reaching 'Ain Sala we found everything in order as we had left it, while Ibn Humaiyid, who had accompanied 'Ali and Zayid for the first part of their way only to prospect the approaches to Ziqirt and to locate it in his brain-map for the purpose of guiding us thither in due course, had safely returned. And the following day—warm, mild and windless except for occasional light northern breezes—we spent in rest and idleness. I scoured the surroundings in vain hopes of encountering the *Spindasis* butterfly already mentioned, and was glad to secure a couple of dragonflies. But, apart from the welcome rest amid tolerable pastures for the camels,

the chief advantage accruing from our prolonged sojourn at
'Ain Sala was the opportunity afforded for an useful series
of star and sun observations for the determination of its
Latitude and possibly also of its Longitude.

Next morning at 9 a.m. we broke camp and started off for
Naifa, the baggage pursuing the direct route while I, accompanied by Ibn Ma'addi and Farraj, made a slight diversion
more to the south to inspect two exposures of rock, which
they had noted the previous day while out in search of game.
Such patches of rock in the midst of the desert sands were as
interesting to me as uncharted islands in unknown seas are
to the wandering mariner, and I always found the Arab ready
to examine any spot where the presence of water might be
suspected.

After half an hour we came to the first exposure—a patch
of rock in a hollow of the sands which seemed to be an
incipient horseshoe. Here again we found a number of fox
earths and the sand was strewn with fulgurites. Only a well
mouth was wanted to complete the picture but we found it
not. So we christened the spot Al Sailan with reference to
its nearness to 'Ain Sala and passed on until, after about 20
minutes' marching, we came upon a regular hillock about
30 feet high situated in the pit of a typical horseshoe cavity
of the low, adjoining sandridge. There were other lesser
exposures of rock strata in the sand-slopes around, while
fox earths were numerous both in the flanks of the eminence
and on its summit. We again however drew blank for the
suspected well and contented ourselves with adding a new
name to the local map—calling the place Al Manifa, at
Farraj's suggestion, by reason of its comparatively great
elevation.

A few moments later we passed from Hadh 'Ain Sala into
Khilla Naifa, a tract of some half dozen rather bare dune
ranges of the now usual NE.-SW. orientation, which are
separately grouped under the name of Bani Riman on
account of the strikish whiteness of their colouring in contrast with the brown or ruddy hue of the sands we had left
behind. Tracks of bustard, hare and fox were seen abundantly, but we had little time to waste in search of game as

my companions were growing a little nervous of the growing distance between us and the main body now visible
afar off. Farraj, always inclined to be a little jumpy,
declared that that morning he had heard a distant rifle shot
as he had sat keeping a look-out on the 'Ain Sala ridge.
There might therefore be others in the desert besides ourselves, but it was at least as likely that the shot had emanated
from the rifle of Salim or Hasan who, with my permission,
had gone off on a short holiday in search of Oryx on the understanding that they should rejoin us on the third day at
Ziqirt. Or, suggested Salih who had come with us, it may
have been a Jinn doing a little game shooting.

The country became more broken, like a choppy sea, as
we went eastward, and the northern flanks of the Bani
Riman ranges were low and rounded though the southward
slopes were still deep and steep. A patch of good vegetation
on the way accommodated two larks and a warbler besides
producing a dragonfly and a Painted Lady—the first since
Jabrin and indeed the only one seen in the whole expanse of
the Rub' al Khali.

Under and on the south side of the third range lay the
watering of Naifa in an unusually elongated horseshoe
hollow, of which one side and the head formed part of the
main range while the other side was a projecting rib thereof
about half a mile long or more. The hollow was oriented
north-east and south-west roughly in accordance with the
axis of the dune-range itself, and was almost closed in by
sand at an inward curve of its projecting horns. The long
narrow approach corridor was well covered with *Abal*
bushes and spread out fanwise at its south-west extremity
into a broad rolling valley.

A single well, with its potent brine liquid at a depth of only
eight feet, lay in greyish sandstone at the inner (north-east)
edge of a small patch of the bedrock, from which the sand-
slopes rose steeply theatre fashion on three sides to a height
of 200 feet. We were merely marking time here to allow
Zayid and 'Ali to accomplish their mission, and I was in the
mood to enjoy as much rest as possible during these days of
enforced inactivity. It was 2 p.m. when we got into camp

and, as soon as my tent was pitched, I retired to it for a siesta, from which, about 3.30, I was woken by the usual noisy preparations for the afternoon prayer. After the prayer I remained outside enjoying the mild warmth of an almost windless afternoon, while some of my companions worked or washed noisily at the well, and Sa'dan sat monkey-like on the summit of the knife-edged rim of our crater, to which he had ascended.

Quite suddenly the great amphitheatre began to boom and drone with a sound not unlike that of a siren or perhaps an aeroplane engine—quite a musical, pleasing, rhythmic sound of astonishing depth. Only once before had I heard the phenomenon of the famous 'Singing Sands'—near the tumbled dunes of Badr between Yanbu' and Madina in July, 1928,—but on that occasion I had heard them only from afar. Here at Naifa the conditions were ideal for the study of the sand concert, and the first item was sufficiently prolonged—it lasted perhaps about four minutes—for me to recover from my surprise and take in every detail. The men working at the well started a rival and less musical concert of ribaldry directed at the Jinns who were supposed to be responsible for the occurrence. You wait, said Abu Ja'sha, noticing my annoyance at their unseemly intervention. Just wait till the evening and you will hear them letting off their big guns, much worse than this. That unfortunately did not happen, but for the moment I was content to realise that the key to the situation was Sa'dan, seated on the top of the slope. It was evident that the music was being engendered by the sand sliding down the steep slope from under him.

It seemed moreover—but this was probably an illusion—to stop when he rose and walked along the ridge for about 50 yards, and to start again when he sat down, though on this occasion the booming was fainter than before and only lasted about a minute. Again he moved on, following the summit of the cirque, and again there was no sound while he was actually on the move though, on his sitting down, the concert resumed quite as loudly as on the first occasion to last about three minutes. There seemed no doubt whatsoever, therefore, that the music was produced by Sa'dan's movements from one undisturbed zone to another and, when he came down, having had enough of that form of amusement, I went up in his place armed with a bottle (to collect a sample of the sand), note-book and watch.

I found a very light north wind (or north-north-east) blowing from behind the dune-range which enclosed the hollow. The summit was about 200 feet above the well, and the slope of the sand, converging on the depression in an almost perfect arc representing perhaps two-thirds of a circle, was exceedingly steep and soft, though by no means uniformly steep all round. And it seemed to me that the music only arose when the sand was sliding down the more steeply inclined parts. I could not therefore produce the phenomenon absolutely at will unless I happened to be on the brink of a section suitable for the performance. On three separate occasions, however, music followed on my disturbance of the loose sand at the summit—a loud, harmonious, organ-like booming.

I stood on the brink of the amphitheatre and pushed the thick soft sand of the summit downwards with my feet. Thereupon one or more broad shute-like bands of sand began to move steadily down the slope, setting up a distinctly audible frictional sound—just such a sound indeed as one would expect in the circumstances, a loud sound of rubbing or grating as of a rough body sliding over a sandy floor. This sound—in which was no suspicion of music and which would not be audible at any considerable distance—increased in a steady *crescendo* until the moving mass seemed to have progressed about 50 feet down the slope, whereupon the quality of the sound changed abruptly from the grating to a booming.

The loudness of the sound seemed to depend on the quantity of the sand in movement, but in all cases there was a *crescendo* of sound which only diminished slightly before stopping altogether quite abruptly—as abruptly as the engine of a motor car—and simultaneously, as it seemed to me, with a sudden cessation of all movement on the slope. Each item of actual booming lasted between two and three minutes on the average, while the distance traversed by the sand while singing seemed to be from 50 to 70 feet.

Having twice manipulated the show with complete success, I started off a sort of *Grand Finale* and soon had the sand cliff booming and droning in the most effective manner. Bottle in hand, I now plunged down the first 50 or 60 feet of the slope and threw myself in a kneeling position on to the singing mass, into which my knees penetrated to a depth of 12 inches or so. I then thrust the bottle deep into the soft, moving, singing sand and, as I drew it out, noticed a remarkable suctional sound as of a trombone. A similar sound resulted from the drawing out of my knees from the slope, and also as I plunged my hands into the mass and drew them out again. It also seemed to me that there was a hollowness deep down beneath the surface, but it would probably be difficult to be certain of that. Furthermore as I knelt on the moving sand I experienced a curious but quite unmistakable sensation of a subsurface throbbing and pulsing, as in a mild earthquake.

It seemed immaterial whether the sand was set in motion on the sunny or shady side of the cirque as I got good results from both—the time being soon after 4 p.m. and the northern side of the hollow being in the shade. But all my efforts to get music out of the lowest 60 or 70 feet of the slope resulted in nothing. At 7 p.m. that evening—without the assistance of any foreign agency though it happened that our camels were actually coming into camp at the moment down the corridor opposite the centre of the singing cliff—the booming started again, but was not as strong as it had been during the afternoon and only lasted about half a minute, after which the concert came finally to an end, leaving me free to notice one of the loveliest meteors I have ever seen.

At 8 p.m. the half moon stood half-way between Venus in the east and Jupiter in the west—the two great planets being seemingly at their most brilliant. The night was light as day and the sands lay silvery under the illuminations of heaven like mountain snow. Suddenly with a flash as of an explosion a huge ball of flame passed across the sky from the neighbourhood of Canopus in an easterly direction—travelling slowly but maintaining its brilliance until with another flash it disappeared. That night at Naifa was the best of all our nights, an unforgettable climax to the unique experiences of the day.

At 7 a.m. next morning—before we started on our march for Ziqirt and with the thermometer registering 45° Fahr. in the shade—I went up to the crest of the cliff only to find there was no more music in the sands. Try as I might I could not get the slightest sound out of them except the initial grating. Their sliding was sluggish and seemed to stop short of the musical zone. And the same afternoon at Ziqirt—a similar great cirque with knife-edged rim round a deep rock-floored hollow—there was again a booming of the sands as Farraj ascended the steep slope to keep a look-out for our returning envoys. But it was a feeble, short-lived —perhaps half a minute—moaning rather than a booming, and our efforts to produce better results ended in uniform failure.

Such then was all my experience of ' Singing Sands ' in the Rub' al Khali. The phenomenon is familiar enough to the Badawin, and Mr. Thomas had heard it in the dune country of Yadila (? Jadila) the previous year. It was only strange that the phenomenon should not have been met with more often.[1] I have recorded the facts of my observation in full as I wrote them down at the time in the hope that those better qualified to consider the how and why of the singing may have the fullest possible material to work on. It may however be permissible even in a layman to attempt an explanation of the matter on the basis of the thoughts that crowded upon him as he observed.

Since returning to England I have had an opportunity of making the intimate acquaintance of the so-called ' Whistling Sands ' of Porth Oer on the Caernarvonshire coast. I should describe them as ' squeaking ' rather than ' whistling,' and they certainly do not ' sing ' or ' boom ' or ' drone,' while they must be struck or kicked for each squeak they produce. I find it difficult to think that the

[1] Reference may be made to the chapter on ' Singing Sands ' in Lord Curzon's *Tales of Travel*.

problem presented by them is of the same order as that of
the desert booming. Yet Mr. C. Carus-Wilson, who is an
expert in such matters, failed to get any response whatever
from my specimen[1] of the ' Singing Sands ' of Naifa by
methods which set samples from Porth Oer and the Isle of
Eigg squeaking like a host of crickets. Whether the Porth
Oer sands would ever boom if piled up on steep Naifa-like
cliffs and set in motion I am not competent to say. The Naifa
sands certainly do not boom or squeak underfoot or when
kicked, and it may be that the Welsh sands would not squeak
or boom if pushed down a steep slope. Or it may be indeed
that, while only particular sands squeak at a touch, all
sands would boom under suitable conditions.[2]

Such questions are only for the experts. But there are
points about the Rub' al Khali sands which may be suggested
for consideration. The Porth Oer sands squeak even when
their subsurface is moist, provided that the actual surface
is dry, but the Naifa sands had no music in them at 7 a.m.
nor again, as I was to discover later on, after a comparatively
light sprinkling of rain. Yet they boomed mildly at 7 p.m.
after producing their full tone the same afternoon. Climatic
conditions generally—humidity, temperature, wind, etc.—
appear therefore to have some bearing on the subject.

In the next place the Naifa sands behaved differently in
the various zones of the musical sand cliff. The moving mass
began by grating at the top and continued by booming in the
middle, while they ceased to emit any sound at all on the
cessation of movement on the slope. Movement would
therefore seem to be an essential cause both of the grating
and the singing. It is difficult to say whether the volume
of the sliding mass is greater at the start or when the singing
begins. It is true that the sands, when they slide, set the
sands before them in motion, but the friction certainly stops
part of the original mass on the way while the final stoppage
of movement actually takes place on a steep incline. The
presumption is therefore that, while the mass gathers volume

[1] It should perhaps be admitted that the quantity of sand available for
his experiments was too small for the purpose.

[2] See note by Dr. Vaughan Cornish in Appendix.

as it goes, it also loses some in the same process until at a certain point the volume is not sufficient to maintain the forward motion. Yet the sand is booming—not at its loudest, it is true, but still definitely booming—at the very moment when sound and movement come simultaneously to an end.

If the shape or mineral composition of the grains is the dominant factor why should the sound start as a grating and develop into a booming ? The Porth Oer sands, for instance, have but a single note, with silence as the only alternative. Surely, therefore, there must be other factors in play among the desert sands. Is the booming a transmuted echoing of the grating as it reaches the requisite angle to the surrounding slopes or circuit ? Or is the transmutation effected by the formation of a vacuum or hollow space between the moving mass and the stable surface over which it moves ? Such a hollow would surely act as a sounding board, while its creation would presumably be gradual as the mass moves down the slope—perhaps due to the temperature of the atmosphere enhanced by the friction of the moving sand. Such questions, again, can only be answered by the expert, and I can do no more than record my impression that the change of sound from a grating to a booming seemed to be occasioned by the intervention of something in the nature of a sounding board.

My companions, being anxious either to get away from Naifa[1] or to reach without delay the rendezvous with 'Ali and Zayid, had represented the distance to Ziqirt as a full and energetic day's march. On that basis I had agreed to an early start and our caravan passed out of the Naifa hollow at 7.30. We had, however, not sent the baggage train ahead and it soon became evident that the march was to be slack and lifeless as most of our recent marches had been. Having negotiated the two remaining ranges of Bani Riman, we passed across two more ridges, apparently nameless, into the tract of Hamran Ziqirt consisting of four parallel ranges,

[1] Among the things collected here was a small piece of meteoric iron similar in composition to that of Wabar (see Appendix). It may have been brought and dropped here by some Arab visitor.

o

beyond the last of which a rolling plain ended in a deep, surf-like drop to the valley in which lies the watering of Ziqirt, nestling in a horseshoe hollow against the side of a high dune.

Early in the proceedings Al Aqfa had started a hare, and the march was practically brought to a standstill while almost every man in the party took a hand in an ultimately bloodless chase—the hare running the gauntlet of a long line of hunters in admirable fashion. After this disappointment the baggage party seemed to lose all heart and, in disgust at their lagging, I called a halt and went off with my butterfly net in search of insects in a wide valley with plentiful *Zahr* and other plants. If the animals are tired, I said, we can halt here as long as you like. It matters little to me.

This had the desired effect and the vanguard went on leading my mount, while I dawdled in the valley until the baggage came up, whereupon I continued the march walking. The conditions were pleasant enough for such mild exertion, and Sa'dan, whose camel had shown signs of lameness, joined me in my walk. Look you, he said, our companions were talking just now. They say there is no *Abal* about Ziqirt or other firewood. So they would camp short of the well to save themselves trouble. That is why they were marching slowly. There is Farraj, I said, with my camel. He would have me mount, but I would walk unless they are ready to march properly. So do you mount my beast in my stead when we come up with him. Farraj had indeed halted to await us and, as we came up, he called out : See, I have brought your camel, so mount now; the others are far ahead. Sa'dan will mount my beast, I replied, his is lame and he is tired, while I prefer to search for creeping things. See, the baggage is behind us, so it is no matter. He would not believe that I preferred walking if the conditions of our marching permitted, and he began to tackle me on the subject of my chronic dissatisfaction with our miserable rate of marching ; but his cavilling was turned upon himself when from the ridge we looked down into a depression in which the advance party had lighted a fire to make coffee. I left them

to it and went off again in search of insects, keeping generally
to the direction of our route so that they could catch me up
when they had had their refreshments.

They had obviously discussed my attitude and concluded
that it would be better to march properly themselves than have
me walk. That was more than the most callous of them could
stand. So I mounted when they caught me up and Farraj
rode with me, evidently determined to get to the bottom of
things. I like walking, I assured him, but I hate this slow
rate of marching. Surely it is better for us all to get to the
well quickly and pitch our tents. Then you can have your
coffee, while I can walk about as I like seeking these insects
and bits of rock. Tell me, he replied; we notice two things
in you. Firstly you are hot-tempered and easily get angry
if we do not as you please. And secondly you are ever ready
to disbelieve what the guides say. Tell me, he went on very
frankly and confidentially, were you like that from the day
God created you? or what is the reason for it? Surely you
know that the guides do not lie deliberately, and this is their
own country where they know every bush and every hummock. Why then should you suspect them of lying? As for
the guides, I replied with equal frankness, I know that they
know this country and you say they do not lie deliberately.
Do you remember that day marching down to 'Ain Sala,
when I wanted to go aside to visit Adraj on the way and 'Ali
told us it was distant a day's journey? Afterwards we went
to Adraj, as you know, and when I drew it on my map I
found it was but an hour's ride from our route. Tell me, did
'Ali really not know or was it otherwise? You speak sooth,
he replied, 'Ali lied but he was thinking of our need of water.
Well then, I went on, only this morning Ibn Humaiyid,
who is our guide now and went with 'Ali and Zayid to spy
out the way to Ziqirt, told us to hasten, as you know, saying
that we would not come to the place before sunset if we
marched hard. You have seen how we have marched this
morning. You all stopped to hunt that hare and you stopped
again for coffee and I have walked on my feet. We have
marched slowly and it is but noon. Now tell me—how far is
Ziqirt? Ziqirt! he exclaimed, why, that is yet afar off, very

far off. God knows if we will come to it by this evening.
Ibn Humaiyid says it is yet a long way off. Look you! I
answered, do you see that great dune before us a little way
off, perhaps an hour's riding ? That is Ziqirt ! Now, what
say you ? That Ziqirt ! he almost shouted with indignant
dismay, who told you so ? Do you know better than the
guides ? No, I replied very suavely, but Ibn Humaiyid told
us all that Bani Riman was five ranges, two before and two
beyond the middle one in which is Naifa ; he told us that
beyond them were two more ranges without name, and
beyond them Hamran Ziqirt, five ranges with the watering in
the last of them. We have crossed four of these and there
is the fifth before us. I have counted them and you have not.
That is the difference. Only there is no *Abal* there for firewood, though God is bountiful. But say, is Ibn Humaiyid,
who came here but yesterday, in error or is it otherwise ?
And as for the heat in my heart, may be that God put it
there when he created me, but it is you folk that enflame it
with your contrariness.

So we tried to understand our mutual differences as we
rode on towards our companions in advance, who had come
to a halt at the edge of the rolling plain at the further side of
the fourth range. Oh, Shaikh 'Abdullah, shouted Ibn
Humaiyid as we came up, look you, the well is yet distant
and this is the last of the good pastures on the way. We
would spend the night here, and when the camels have had
their fill, they will march better in the morning. Very well, I
replied, but it is too early yet, so let us march but an hour
more to yonder ridge and we will camp beyond it. The game
was up as they all knew only too well, and we crawled on
for less than an hour over an easy gradient of undulating
red-brown sands which shaded off imperceptibly into the
whiter masses of the dune summits. And from the top of
the range we looked down into the cup-like rock depression
of Ziqirt, only 15 miles from Naifa. A short day's march to
the eastward lies the watering of Bainha with that of
Dahbuba only a mile from the latter westward.

An eagle, a pair of ravens and some larks and warblers
had been observed during the march but, with my gun out of

action, our bag was empty. I dismounted on the ridge and visited the conspicuous conical peak already mentioned before descending the steep sand-slope to the hollow, where our animals, having fetched the necessary circuit to get to the narrow bottle-neck entrance to the well depression, arrived about the same time as myself. The chief feature of the locality is a very imposing display of the underlying bedrock which stands up in a regular cliff, about 40 feet high (as measured from the bottom of the depression) and 262 paces (about 650 feet) long from the point where it emerges from the steep sand-slope round the head of the great cirque to that at which it disappears again under the sandy floor of the entrance valley. The general direction of this face of rock, whose upper surface is exposed to a width of about 200 feet, is from ENE. to WSW. with a slight south-westerly kink at about mid-course. So far as I could judge, this rock (presumably a calcareous limestone formation overlying the characteristic sandstone of the floor and well-shafts) has a gentle dip of 5° from NW. to SE. and a similar inclination along its main axis from NE. to SW. On a higher level than the platform and southward of it, as also near its western extremity, I found some curious mounds of a gypseous character, while along the face of the cliff, where it falls to the level of the wells, is a glacis of sand thickly strown with the debris and large blocks of the blue-grey calcareous rock. I found a single rough flint and innumerable fragments of Oryx bones—doubtless the remains of many banquets,—but otherwise there was little enough to occupy my attention during the time of our enforced idleness while we awaited the return of our emissaries.

Whether or not there were wells here in former times, the known or remembered history of this locality goes back only to the days of the Wahhabi ruler, 'Abdullah ibn Faisal, the uncle of the present King, who ruled the country from 1867 to 1890 with an interval of several years, during which his hostile younger brother usurped his throne. In those days, probably about 1870, one of the Ghafran Shaikhs, Muhammad ibn Suwailih of the Banna section, had enrolled himself as a young man in 'Abdullah's army and was in regular attendance on his sovereign at Riyadh. He was of course accompanied by a following of his tribesmen with their tents and families, and with him was his own family consisting only or mainly of his mother. According to the honourable custom of Arabia the maintenance of the whole party devolved on the State Treasury, and it so happened that one day the steward in charge of the distribution of rations sent away the young Shaikh's mother empty-handed. She informed her son, who immediately sought the royal presence with vigorous complaints against the dispenser of the royal hospitality. Get you to work for your mother ! the prince had replied peevishly. On my head ! Muhammad had replied, the ordering is the King's ordering. With that he had withdrawn with his following into the pastures of the Rub' al Khali, whence he had fared forth with seven other kindred spirits to make war on the world. The little band soon came to be known as *Al Ziqirt*[1]—' the gens d'armes ' as we might say—by reason of their constitution as a military force under active service conditions, *i.e.* without women-folk or other encumbrances. The wilder spirits of the southern sands—from the Rashid, Manahil and other tribes—hastened to join the campaign of raiding and highway robbery that was initiated by the gang, whose first act had been to establish a base of operations in some unknown and unfrequented spot. Having selected a likely looking place they had proceeded to dig these wells, by which we were now encamped, and the watering has ever since commemorated in its name the memory of their once famous exploits. Another district, far off to the north, and north-eastward of Haradh, has earned from those same exploits the name of Hawaïr al Ziqirt—apparently a pasture tract with depressions liable to retain water for a few weeks or months after rain.

Of the three wells of Ziqirt one appeared to be quite ' dead ' although the marks of the haulage ropes are clearly visible—deeply scored in the rock mouth of the shaft. The

---

[1] The term is derived through the Turkish from the Italian ' sacurta ' or French ' securité,' just as the common Turkish (and Arabic) word for police, ' Sharta,' is derived from ' sûreté.'

second, similarly dead, was all but hidden from view by the
covering sand, while the third we found—somewhat to our
surprise for 'Ali had reported it dead—merely covered over
in the usual way. It was accordingly opened up for the
watering of the camels and was found to be about 20 feet
deep. It is a brine well and is regarded as potable though
more potent than that of Naifa, wherefore my companions
eschewed it as we had full skins of the latter to last us till
Shanna.

To ease the strain of our recent disagreements and to encourage a sharp look-out I had on our arrival offered a
reward of 10 dollars for the first man to spot our returning
envoys. But night came upon us with never a sign of them,
and the only incident of the late afternoon was the arrival
of Salim and Hasan, hungry, thirsty and disgruntled after
their long, vain search for Oryx. Next day—the last of
our tryst with Zayid—the dune tops were manned by eager
searchers while Farraj, stealing a march upon his fellows,
borrowed my glasses and went out far afield to win the dollars.
The afternoon wore on without result, and I was beginning
to resign myself to the prospect of another wasted day, when
Farraj came running into camp a little before sunset. Good
news ! he cried, I bring you good news of the coming of
Zayid and 'Ali. I saw them afar off yonder and I came
quickly to tell you. Come they alone ? I asked, or are there
others with them ? I saw but two riders, he replied. And
a few minutes later I saw Zayid and 'Ali riding down through
the narrow entrance of the depression.

They had been to Bir Hadi and Shanna and Turaiwa and
scoured all the countryside, but nowhere had they seen any
signs of Arabs. So they had returned empty-handed. You
should have gone further, I suggested, into the dunes of
Qa'amiyat. Perhaps you would have found the tribes there
hunting the Oryx ! It was a bow drawn at a venture, but
their sudden, startled, guilty look suggested that the shaft
had gone home. They had visited the wells, it is true, and
had drawn blank, but they had spent several days seeking
not Arabs but Oryx. I was only afraid that their report
would augment the general desire to get back home as soon

as possible out of this abandoned wilderness. But I was determined to resist any such tendency with all my vigour. For many days now I had endured the constant and inevitable friction engendered by the struggle between the insistent urge of my own fixed and unalterable purpose and the solid weight of the innate national inertia thrown into the balance against me by the united body of my companions. Their passive resistance had to be resisted at all costs. Surrender to it would mean failure, but the victory had to be won by a slow process of attrition, and I comforted myself with the reflection that in a month or so at most they would all forget their present woes in the satisfied contemplation of the earnings of their travail. Step by step we had progressed ever away from their home fires, but each step had been achieved only by the smallest margin as the momentum of a purposeful mind triumphed at each stage over the inert mass ever ready to recoil from any arduous objective.

After dinner that evening I summoned Farraj to receive his reward and encouraged his petty soul to think of the further guerdons to be won by further service. Then I was free to attend to Zayid and 'Ali, who came to my tent to discuss our plans for the future. I began well by making each of them an unexpected present of 30 pieces of silver for their recent exertions. Look you, I said, all these last days we have marched but little and the camels are rested. Time is short and I would get to the south without delay, that we may turn back through the Oryx country to Wadi Dawasir and thence home to Mecca for the pilgrimage, to which there are but two months from now. So let us march well to Shanna—the country is empty before us and we have nought to fear—and then we can decide whither to direct our march. Maybe we can leave our camp there and go down southward with only a small party. But let us start early on the morrow. They had probably agreed among themselves not to go beyond Shanna on any account but did not attempt to argue that point now. The immediate objective was enough to agree upon, and the matter was settled in the most amicable manner.

A load of anxiety was thus removed from my mind and I

was left to enjoy in peace the charm of another astonishingly beautiful night. The light of the moon and the two great planets, reinforced by the more modest brilliance of Sirius and Canopus, was seemingly filtered to the earth through a veil of haze, and the solid sand-cliffs round our camp took on the appearance of a gossamer curtain suspended before some fairy stage.

Next morning (February 18th) the baggage train was got off at 6.30, carrying with it our destined morning meal of rice all ready cooked in its cauldron. An hour later we started up out of the hollow and over the intervening plain to the Bani Khuwairan tract—a belt of short tumbled ridges and disordered dune groups which here interrupts the normal symmetry of the long parallel ridges of the Sawahib area. For about five miles we laboured through this maze, in which the *Abal* reappeared after its short absence in the Ziqirt district and the *Zahr* continued in unwonted profusion. All went merrily as a marriage bell until we came to the first of a series of parallel dune ranges lying NE. and SW., which constitute the district known as Bani Nasir from the conspicuous conical hillock of Huqna Nasir in its midst. Here to my dismay we overtook the baggage animals in spite of their good start and, somewhat foolishly, I suggested amid signs of universal satisfaction that we should dispose of our meal without further ado. The yellow flowers of the *Zahr* were here in abundance, making a charming scene for our picnic, and I was minded to seek insects while the rest had their coffee. Unfortunately I had not noticed that there was no *Abal* in this particular spot, and I was horrified at the suggestion that a second halt should be made for coffee when we came to suitable fuel. Good-bye, I thought, to all hope of any real progress. And, suiting my action to the thought, I continued the march on foot in company with the baggage train while my own party hastened on to find a desert hearth for their coffee. 'Ali, doubtless thinking of the pleasant shekels of yesternight and of others to follow, pursued me on foot to the conical sand-peak of Huqnat al Mish'ab where, slightly in advance of the baggage, I was enjoying the view. Torn between his own internal clamour for coffee and a genuine desire to accompany me, he exerted himself to the utmost to deflect me in the direction of the others but, failing in that object, sped away to share the stimulating liquor.

I continued walking and, as a matter of fact, walking was definitely pleasanter in that lovely, soft, sandy country with its steep ridges than the devious, lurching progress of the labouring camels. However, after three hours of it when Sa'dan came up with my steed, I mounted without protest and so we continued over the frequent ridges until the latter part of the afternoon, when we halted for prayers at a small patch of dazzling white gypsum exposed amid the sands, in which just before we had passed over the widespread and still unobliterated tracks, about a month old, of camels at pasture—presumably, they thought, those of Jabir ibn Fasl and others who had been with him before he went north.

An hour later we entered the district of Bani Jafnan with its prominent eponymous cone (Huqna Jafnan) a little way off to the south-west. In this tract the characteristic parallelism of the Sawahib formation is resumed, but its outstanding feature is the marked frequency of horseshoe hollows enclosed within sharply inclined, wedge-shaped shutes. In one such pit at the very beginning of the tract we found a small exposure of the rock-floor underlying the sands, where the discovery of a fox earth and other indications convinced us all of the concealed presence of a buried well. We labelled it Bir Jafnan and passed on to camp amid excellent and varied[1] vegetation on a wide gently rolling plain between low, bare dune ranges.

We had only marched about 25 miles during the day but, even so, the latter part of the journey had been accompanied by the music of loud protests from the trailing rear. Farraj, who was with 'Ali and me in the van, acted as amplifier to the unwelcome strains and lectured me on the proper care of camels. I pointed out that we had taken a fortnight over a march of about 100 miles and suggested that the camels could graze by moonlight. He declared that that was un-

[1] *Zahr, Abal, Andab, Alqa* and *Birkan.*

thinkable, but did not refer to the point later on when the camels were rounded up and driven into camp after two good hours in the moonlit pastures. The night was certainly as light as day, and the conditions were so pleasant that I dispensed with my tent, preferring to sleep under the sky.

There had however been an undercurrent of tension in our ranks all day for a curious reason. Quite early in the proceedings I had asked Abu Ja'sha how he was feeling and was a little astonished at his rough reply, which doubtless voiced the sentiments of the whole party. Rotten, he had answered, for have we not all laboured for you alike ? And yet you pick out two only of our number to gladden with gifts. We do not deny that Zayid and 'Ali deserved what they got, but we all deserve it and we object to their getting something while we go empty. Come, come ! I had replied, those gifts were for a special service, and you will all be remembered when the time comes—when we get to the Hadhramaut, and that is why I want to hasten over these stages, that I may reward you the sooner.

That did not appease their evil, envious souls and the next to take up the argument was Farraj himself, who had not informed the others of the gift he had had from me and whom I did not betray. But the comedy deepened when Zayid appeared before me and poured his 30 shekels upon my pallet, declaring that he had dishonoured himself in accepting them of me. I told him candidly that such behaviour was offensive to me and warned him to think again. He persisted, however, and I sent for Abu Ja'sha. Here, I said as he came up, here are 30 dollars for you ! He had declared that in such circumstances he would never have accepted a gift for himself alone, but now as he stuffed the silver into his bosom I did not spare him. It was you, I said, who made all the fuss and pother about my giving money to those two. And see how God has rewarded you ! Without a word he bundled the coins back out of his bosom on to my bedding. I immediately took up the pile and threw it aside on to the sand. Please yourself, I said, take it or leave it. It matters not to me, but leave me in peace, I have work to do. He then picked up the money and went back to his fellows, while next morning I summoned him to pick up one coin that he had overlooked. I learned afterwards that the money had been returned to Zayid, whose well-meant effort to force me to a general distribution of bounty at a most unsuitable moment had thus been frustrated.

In spite of this incident—and possibly because of it—a very special effort was made next day to record better progress than heretofore. In the midst of my slumbers I sensed an unwonted activity in the camp at an atrociously early hour and the baggage actually started off before I was aroused by an unusually early call to prayer. The baggage thus got a start of more than two hours on us, and I wandered about after dawn stalking an eagle which had taken up its position on a peak of the neighbouring dune range. I managed to get within reasonable range, but the shot from my little revolver only disturbed the sand close to the bird, which flew off to appear no more. The tracks of bustard were very plentiful here but the haste of our marching allowed of no pursuit although on one occasion three of them got up from under our feet. Wheatears and warblers were also seen in plenty and, as I was packing up, I had become aware of a little tragedy. The previous day we had secured a hare and Sa'dan, having skinned it, had laid the pelt and skull— thickly smeared with arsenical soap—by my bedside to dry. In the morning I found no trace of either, and the tell-tale sand soon revealed the identity of the thief, who was none other than the *Saluqi* bitch. She must have swallowed both skull and skin, and it was evident, as she marched with us that day, that she was feeling acutely the effects of her surreptitious, poisoned supper. At every other bush she lay down uneasily seeking shelter from the sun and scrabbling away the sand to get at the cool under-surface. But by the evening she had more or less recovered from her indisposition.

Meanwhile we made excellent progress over the ridges and valleys of Bani Jafnan—an immense sandy expanse of sea-like troughs each beginning with a lofty rounded wave break-ing southward. The general colouring of the tract was a light brownish red with a very copious covering of the desert vegetation, in whose midst here and there we observed a good deal of camel dung from the previous season's grazing. On two occasions we passed by small exposures of the underlying rock in horseshoe cavities of dunes and, at about noon when we came up with the baggage after more than four hours' marching, Farraj, who was an intelligent and observant desert craftsman, called our attention to the first shrub of *Hadh* marking our exit from Bani Jafnan into the fairly extensive tract of Hadhat abu Khashba, so-called from a cone peak of that name lying about a mile north-eastward of the ridge on whose summit we halted for lunch. By this time 'Ali and some others were positively fainting for a sip of coffee and we were all, indeed, so hungry after a really good morning's work that we proceeded to over-eat ourselves. Whether that was the cause or, as some averred, the excess of salt in the Naifa water after several days in the skins, we all showed signs of weariness during an unusually sultry afternoon with the result that all idea of making a forced march to Shanna during what remained of the day was abandoned.

Just before our lunch halt we had crossed the tracks left by Zayid and 'Ali on their outward journey to Shanna, while mild consternation was created in our ranks by the discovery almost immediately afterwards of the fairly recent tracks of a considerable raiding party. It was this discovery that necessitated our halt at that moment for it was essential that the matter should be investigated. They are of Sa'ar or, maybe, Dawasir, declared 'Ali, for their camels are of the steppe and not of the sands. You see how heavily they have trodden. It may be ten days ago or less that they passed, perhaps six or seven but probably before Zayid and I went down to Shanna. We saw not the tracks then for we passed here during the night.

As we marched a brief diversion was created by a snake which charged, upright and rapidly zig-zagging, through our ranks and took refuge amid the tangled roots of an *Abal* bush. After a vain search we set fire to the dry shrub but failed to coax the reptile out into the open again. Another halt was called at a small exposure of rock in a characteristic dune hollow, and a cursory search was rewarded by the discovery of a sprinkling of spiral shells. And so we came at about 3.30 p.m. to our evening camp at the edge of an extensive patch of gypsum, facing a horseshoe cliff, with a steep escarpment whose summit stood some 40 feet above the sandy pit-floor. This exposure seemed to be of sufficient importance to be christened, at 'Ali's suggestion, Umm al Qurun—a name which the following morning we extended to include a similar but smaller outcrop of rock in a neighbouring hollow about 500 yards away.

By now I was utterly weary and glad enough to camp after a march of only a little more than 20 miles. The salt or the sultriness had suddenly sapped my energy, and I lay down to sleep soundly for an hour or so in the lengthening shadow of one of my boxes. On this occasion as at our last camp I dispensed with the tent and the night was delightful. The great sheet of white gypsum glistened in the bright moonlight and the sands around us seemed to enclose the scene with a veil of mystery.

Next morning we still marched for more than an hour in the Hadhat abu Khashba tract, which was dotted with frequent rock exposures, to one group of which—a wide, flat, plate-like circle of grey-blue rock with two small patches of white gypsum near it—we gave the name of Umm al Sahnain.[1] The country had now degenerated into a broken, reddish down-tract with frequent short lines of dunes, until we came to a long double ridge beyond which we entered the *Hadh*-less tract of Ramla (or Khilla) Daugha, whose name-cone lay at some distance to our right out of sight, commemorating the fruitless labours of some of the Ghafran in an attempt to dig down to water through a rock exposure in its side. A little beyond this point we halted on the north side of a ridge overlooking the rolling downs and valleys of the Shanna country to give Zayid and another sufficient time to prospect the approaches to the well before our oncoming.

After a decent interval, during which 'Ali had pointed out to me all the familiar landmarks of what he regarded as the home pastures of his own folk, we slowly resumed our march. Three bustard flew away before us, and a little

[1] Mother of two plates.

colony of five warblers was disturbed by our passage.
Everywhere about us lay smaller or greater patches of rock
and gypsum, to one of which we turned aside at sight of a
fox going away across its bed of greyish clay or loam lightly
sprinkled with grit. Here we found a number of flint implements and some bits of stone which have proved to be
fragments of a stony meteorite[1]; and the occasion seemed
worthy of commemoration. So we named the spot Umm
al Tina from its earthy nature, and an hour later, passing
along but at a little distance from an almost continuous
valley of exposed gypsum patches, we came to the *Ultima
Thule* of our southward wanderings.

[1] See Appendix.

CHAPTER V

SHANNA

The land of foes, the land of fear!
—ZAYID.

THE well of Shanna, situated though it is at the meeting of all
the southern tracks, dates back only to the season of 1929-30
when for two reasons a large body of the Ghafran Murra
found themselves foregathered in the neighbourhood with
their tents and their cattle. The northern pastures of the
Hasa, whither this section of the tribe is wont to betake itself
in the winter months after its customary summer sojourn in
the heart of Al Rimal, had become uncomfortable by reason
of the alarums and excursions of Faisal al Duwish, who had
raised the more fanatical and unreasoning elements of the
Ikhwan in rebellion against their liege-lord the Wahhabi
King. Loyal and peaceful tribes had thus become liable to
attack by the fanatics, while on the other hand their assumed
loyalty was liable at any moment to bring down on them an
unwelcome invitation to take up arms in the Government's
cause against their erring brethren of the faith. A discreet
distance from the scene of action had thus become an obvious
desideratum during the early autumn of 1929 and the Murra
had the advantage of the vast expanse of the Rub' al Khali
wherein to choose a safe retreat till the storm should end or
abate. That advantage was however somewhat circumscribed
by pastoral conditions, and it was only in the Shanna neighbourhood that rains had been sufficiently recent and abundant to offer favourable pastures for the Ghafran camels. The
supreme drawback of the district lay in the disagreeable
salinity of its numerous scattered wells, from which a large
part of the tract has derived the name of Al Khiran[1] ; and it
was this disadvantage, of more moment to the men and

[1] Plural of *Khaur* (*Khor*), meaning ' marine estuary,'—*cf*. Khor 'Abdullah
near Basra—or simply ' salt water.'

224

women of the tribe than to their camels which drew a good
part of their liquid nourishment from the succulent herbs of
the desert, that sped various members of the Ghafran far and
wide over the country in search of pleasanter sources during
their prolonged sojourn in what they normally considered to
be only summer pastures.

It was our chief guide, 'Ali ibn Salih ibn Jahman, that
lighted on Shanna, a typical hollow amid the desert sands
with exposed patches of the underlying gypseous rock on this
side and that. It was in just such spots that experience had
taught the desert tribes to look for water, though they had
no means of divining the character of the liquid that might
be found. They would dig and trust to God, and it was a
merciful dispensation of Providence that, if the water was
salt, they would come to it at comparatively shallow levels
without too great an effort of labour. The deeper they went
without discovery of moisture the more certain it became that
they would either never come to water at all or would find it
less briny than that of the familiar shallow pits. So they
would dig on, having nothing very much better to do ; and
'Ali had dug down his narrow shaft in the soft gypsum to a
depth of 55 feet before he came to what he sought and called
it Shanna—sweet water, if you please, with just a taint of
bitterness therein, the best water of all the neighbourhood.
From that day to this Shanna has been the cynosure of
grazing or raiding tribesmen, a fount of life in the southern
sands and equally for that reason a source of death and
danger. None approaches Shanna but with circumspection ;
none remains there, on the well itself, longer than may be
necessary to water the beasts and fill the skins. We were
offending against the canons of the desert in occupying the
well for 48 hours, but were we not the King's men with the
King's camels ? Yet we remained nervously, our tempers
frayed as much by the uncertainty of our plans as by the fear
of unwelcome visitors.

Some days earlier Zayid and 'Ali Jahman, having scoured
the countryside in vain for signs of grazing Arabs, had visited
Shanna and scored the King's brand-mark in the moist sand
by the well's mouth by way of declaring our identity—a

P

precaution calculated to warn off all but those who might be
strong enough and willing to provoke the King's wrath.   As
Jabir ibn Fasl had told us at Jabrin there were none such in
the desert at this time.   The southern tribes, receiving news
of our expedition from Saif ibn Tannaf the Manhali Shaikh
who had hurriedly departed from the Hasa only a few days
before us on the rejection of his gifts and overtures by Ibn
Jiluwi, had retired to the southern mountains, while such
Murra elements as had remained in the south with the Rashid
relatives-in-law of Hamad ibn Sultan ibn Hadi—Bertram
Thomas' guide of the previous year and a near cousin of 'Ali
Jahman—similarly preferred to keep at a safe distance from
our path lest our purpose might be to collect the taxes which
for the moment they were not bothering to pay into the
King's treasury.   So the desert was empty and our scouts,
preceding us by about half an hour, were able to signal ' all
clear ' as we approached the well from behind the dune-
range skirting the northern edge of the valley-like depression
in which it lay.   Not only was there no one on the scene, but
no one had visited the place since the departure of Zayid and
'Ali some six days earlier.

At the foot of the sand-slope leading down to the hollow we
passed by the grave of some desert notable slain in a tribal
skirmish during the last year or two.   Its oval outline was
decked out with blocks of gypsum from the 40 feet cliffs of
the exposed bed-rock extending in two sections, separated by
a considerable gap, across the Shanna depression.   In the
lowest part of the hollow lay the well, and at some distance
further to the south-west a small rock-marked semi-circle,
oriented exactly towards the north-west, indicated the direction of Mecca and the position of the place set apart for the
prayers of the faithful.   Here and there a desert bush of
Abal or *Hadh* dotted the scene.   Our tents were pitched forthwith, the camels watered and driven forth to the pastures of
the valley under the care of 'Áli al Buhaihi and the lad
Muhammad.   A fire was soon alight for the making of coffee.
Zaid and his lieutenant got to work with their preparations
for dinner and others sped off, rifle in hand, to the surrounding sand-peaks to keep the customary vigil against possible

enemies or chance visitors. I sallied out to examine our surroundings and to collect such specimens as Shanna might provide for the British Museum—rocks or insects or other things.

Climbing the cliff to eastward of our camp I found myself
on an extensive patch of gypsum, roughly circular in form
and sinking gently from its outer perimeter to a smaller circular depression lightly covered with sand and grit. Its somewhat crater-like appearance, together with the roughened
surface of the gypsum, churned up as if by the wind, suggested that this might possibly be the desiccated site of an
ancient lake or pond; but I found nothing either to confirm
or invalidate such an impression. Near by, however, I came
upon a small circular shallow pit, only three feet in diameter
and four inches in depth, which I took to be an ancient and
buried well-mouth until some of my companions disillus-
ioned me with the information that such hollows are made
and used by the Badawin women for the extraction of dye
for their leather goods from the juicy shoots of the *Abal* bush,
pounded on sheets of leather laid over the pit, until they
yield their tannin.

A long line of scattered, discontinuous patches of exposed
gypseous rock extended south-westward from this point up
the valley between the dune-ranges on either hand lying
about a mile apart. The valley itself was fairly thickly
covered with the desert scrub of various kinds including the
charming yellow-flowered *Zahr*, apparently unknown or
but little known in the northern parts of the Rub' al Khali.
At Shanna itself the northern dune-range cuts straight across
the gypsum valley-bed which, however, continues beyond it
in a north-easterly direction for a mile or more. The whole
line of these exposed patches of the bed-rock suggested very
strongly to my mind the possibility of its being in fact the
dried-up bed of an ancient river. The very fact that the comparatively deep sweet-water well of Shanna lay in the line of
the supposed valley tended to confirm such an impression.
But it was not till the following day that my search for
further evidence was rewarded by the discovery of a considerable quantity of little spiral fresh-water shells[1] in the hollow

[1] *Melanoides tuberculata*, see Appendix.

itself at the foot of the cliffs. All the available evidence
points, therefore, to the conclusion that the Shanna hollow
and valley represent the site of an ancient river or fresh-water
lake ; and I was glad to think that I had discovered better
support than mere conjecture for the theory I had advanced
after a study of Mr. Thomas' land-levels some months earlier[1]
that the shallow depression shown by his figures in the Shanna
neighbourhood might well be the eastern continuation of the
great Wadi Dawasir channel whose upper reaches, trending
slightly south of east, I had seen at Sulaiyil in 1918. Such a
theory was indeed to find further substantial confirmation in
the desert westward of Shanna as I shall have occasion to
show in due course, but it must for the present suffice to leave
the facts, as ascertained up to the moment of our sojourn at
Shanna, to speak for themselves. It may however be suggested that the underlying gypseous surface of the Khiran
tract, whose existence is proved by the occurrence of frequent
exposures amid the tumbled sands, and the shallow salt-wells
of that area, contribute strong evidence of the existence in
these parts of a great marine bay or gulf formed by the uplift
of the mountains of the Oman and Qara provinces during
or after the Eocene epoch. Such a gulf might have been
gradually filled up by the silt of the rivers pouring down
into it from every direction, or might have been raised
above the sea-level partly by that process and partly by a
tectonic uplift of the land-surface until the whole area was
exposed to the devastating influence of blown sand from
the ' desert's dusty face ' and became what it is to-day—an
ocean of dunes.

It seems indeed probable that Shanna itself lies not far distant from the point at which Wadi Dawasir in ancient times
poured its waters into the sea, whose shore-line, still clearly
recognisable in the Miocene cliffs of the Jiban tract, may
well have run southwards along the Summan uplands west of
Jabrin to form a bay near Maqainama, whence it would
have run east round the deep-well salient of Bir Fadhil and
Tuwairifa (near the mouth of Wadi Maqran), to continue
thence again southward along the western side of the 'Ain

[1] J.R.G.S., December, 1931, pp. 574-5.

Sala-Ziqirt tract to Shanna. From here the line would have run east to Muqshin, whence it would have worked northward along the western foot of the Oman mountains to rejoin the present Persian Gulf in the neighbourhood of Masandam. Such a line is of course largely a matter of conjecture but may surely be regarded provisionally as being in general accord with the known facts until other sections of this vast unknown area are traversed and examined by future explorers.

A gentle north-east breeze, soft and warm, breathed over us that afternoon as I wandered up the valley towards our grazing camels to seek out Muhammad, always a willing ally in my designs on the elusive lizards and birds of the desert. My shot-gun being now hopelessly out of action, I was reduced to using a pocket revolver on the tiny targets presented by small birds, distant and restless. I had just missed a shrike—the only one seen during the journey—when from afar off towards the north-east a rifle-shot rang out clearly in the still air. I imagined that one of my companions had perhaps fired at a hare for the pot, but we were soon undeceived. We were about a mile from the camp, and the movements of our distant companions left little doubt that the shot had been fired as an alarm-signal. There seemed to be a general movement towards the ridge beyond our tents, and Muhammad was able to interpret the raucous sounds emitted in our direction as orders to drive in the camels. In a moment the quiet peaceful valley seemed to be alive with human activity, and I helped Muhammad to round up the nearest camels while 'Ali did the same for those further away. Slowly we moved towards the tents trying to interpret, as we went, the significance of the little knots of our companions occupying scattered points of vantage some distance beyond them or moving hither and thither under cover of the dune-ridges. Leaving Muhammad to drive in the animals to camp, I struck across the valley to ascertain the cause of the commotion from a group of men occupying the summit of a great dune. The warning had, it appeared, been fired by Farraj who, as he kept watch, had spotted three men riding towards Shanna from the eastward. If only he had remained hidden and silent those men would by now have been our prisoners, and we should have been in a strong position to bargain with their friends, few or many, following in the rear. But Farraj had lost his head. The three men ' saw him and beat it '[1] at their best speed away from us. Our people had seen and followed their tracks for some distance before abandoning the chase. We had gained no advantage from our superior position, and all that night we remained (while I slept) precariously on the alert. The night was cold enough in all conscience for those on guard on the exposed dune-tops, and it was a chilly crowd that gathered round our camp-fire to make coffee before the dawn prayer next morning.

Meanwhile Zayid and others had spent much of the night arguing and quarrelling with me about our future plans. And we had made no progress towards a decision. I had indeed become convinced that the whole incident was a put-up job, a false alarm deliberately conceived and played through at some inconvenience to the players for the purpose of putting an end to our wanderings. The more I think over the details of the matter, the more convinced I become that that was the case. What think you ? said Zayid, sidling into my tent with Salih and seating himself humbly on the sandy floor. I think nothing, I replied curtly ; Farraj is an ass to have shown himself like that and frightened away those three men, who would have been able, perhaps, to guide us to the wells of the south. Let us follow up their tracks in case we may come to their encampments. We cannot do that, he answered in the sanctimonious lisping accents so characteristic of him. Look ye, the land of the *Muslimin* is away behind us from here to Jabrin ; before us lies the land of the enemy, the land of fear. We cannot venture into it without peacemakers.[2] We are frightened. We are in danger. We must not linger here. We must go back. What think you, oh Shaikh ? I think, I replied, that we should go forward to the southward as you promised me we should. Surely, Zayid, you are not frightened at sight of three men ! It was true

---

[1] *Shafuh wa taqqu.*

[2] *Silm*, plural *Sulūm*, the word generally used for the usual northern term of *Rafiq* (or *Rabi'a* in the south) meaning ' introducer ' or ' guarantor.'

that we had no one in our party who knew the way to Thamut or Qabr Hud, the southern wells which I regarded as our obvious destination, and that we had no one qualified to introduce us to the Manahil or Sa'ar, whom we might expect to encounter in that direction. To walk into their camps without introduction would be tantamount, said Zayid, to delivering their ' bread and butter at their door-step.'[1] We were in fact more or less ' stymied ', but it was worth taking a risk. Zayid however was unhelpful and Salih, though blatantly obsequious, was useless. We deferred further argument till next day when 'Ali Jahman would have returned from his cold vigil far out in the desert. So I left them to ruminate the proposition that it would be worth their while not to be too frightened.

After the dawn prayer—the night having passed without alarm—we resumed the pow-wow. Zayid and the others had made up their minds not to venture further south on the line suggested by me, and I was compelled to admit to myself— though I did not do so publicly—that there were reasonable grounds for their attitude. They suggested as an alternative that we should travel south-east with Dhufar as our ultimate objective. There, at any rate, they would find provisions wherewith to replenish our depleted stores. That was a pleasant prospect, while the return journey might be made by sea if it had by then become too hot to prolong our desert wanderings. For me such a plan had but little attraction beyond the possibility that we might light upon the Rashid and Hamad ibn Sultan near the Shisar well and with their help arrange to cut back westward into the Hadhramaut border, whence we might strike up across the waterless desert—an essential objective of our expedition. Otherwise we should be merely covering ground already fully explored by Mr. Thomas. Another alternative was to turn north-east into the eastern Khiran area in the hope of finding grazing tribes settled on the wells. But that would take us further away from the waterless area and I feared it might be difficult to entice my companions back to Shanna—especially if we found no Arabs—for the great adventure, though I was

[1] *Rizquhum* and *ahlihim.*

strongly attracted by the prospect of examining the country around Ramlat al Shu'ait in which Mr. Thomas had suggested a possible alternative site of Wabar (Ubar). I felt however too strongly that the prospect of discovering ruins in this area was but a slender one. So I rejected that alternative and again pressed for a southward prolongation of our march, while my companions suggested that, as the season was already far advanced, we should lose no more time in making the attempt on the waterless desert itself. I kept that alternative mentally in reserve while maintaining my pressure for acceptance of my original plan, and I warned my friends that the consequences of their obstinacy might be unprofitable and unpleasant for themselves in the long run. We discontinued the argument for the nonce and I resumed my exploration of Shanna leaving them to think matters over with Sa'dan to watch their deliberations on my behalf.

Salih strolled out from the camp to seek me out as I sought shells in the ancient river-bed. Of all my companions he was the most charming : the glibbest of liars but ever ready to face public exposure with smiling equanimity : the frankest self-seeker though incurably optimistic in spite of regular disappointment : the champion and betrayer of all causes and persons : the friend of all and enemy of none by very reason of his naïve and simple dishonesty. None rode a camel more gracefully in the manner of Oman. Large dark-brown eyes and long curly tresses combined with a lissome figure and deep, rich, soft voice to give the manliest of men the charm and grace of a woman. Love was his chief obsession—love of women, love of money, of food, of ease and all things good. His belch was a portent, deep drawn from the uttermost recesses of a healthful, untroubled stomach, loud, lingering, lusty and eloquent.

He came to me now, a self-appointed envoy, to betray the deliberations of his companions and Sa'dan later confirmed the details of his treasonable report. My warnings of the King's possible wrath, coupled with my pressure for a southward extension of our wanderings, had given them all seriously to think. To the south they would not go—on that they were fully determined, every man of them. My dis-

pleasure was therefore inevitable though of little moment
except for its possible reverberations in more powerful quarters. The King would be angry on my account ; he might
be furious ; he might be terrible in his dealings with those
who had betrayed their trust and mission. Ibn Jiluwi had
charged Zayid to avoid avoidable danger. That was pre-
cisely what they were now seeking to do, though I would
doubtless put a different interpretation on their conduct ; and
Ibn Jiluwi might be angry with them if he thought that the
King might be displeased with the manner in which he had
discharged the task allotted to him. Which way lay the best
hope of salvation ? They had offered to conduct me to
Dhufar, they had offered to wander at my will in Al Khiran ;
and they had suggested the march across the waterless desert
from where we were. But nothing seemed to satisfy me short
of seeking death or danger amid the black mountains of
Hadhramaut. That they would not face without guides and
peacemakers, so their choice lay between the King's wrath
and their own master's. Zayid and others of the party had
already experienced punishment at the hands of Ibn Jiluwi—
imprisonment for a period with food enough though without
the solace of female society. That could be endured again.
Suwid bore in three places the terrible scars of Sa'ar daggers
which had left him for dead on a never-to-be-forgotten
occasion. He could not speak of that day without horror and
agonised remembrance. He would not face that again. But
what of the King ? What would he do in his anger ? That
was the question, and my companions had agreed that the
safest course was to return forthwith to the Hasa, to risk the
wrath of Ibn Jiluwi and to trust to their own ability to persuade him that I had been dangerously unreasonable in my
demands on their patience and endurance.

Thus dramatically confronted with the spectre of complete
failure in circumstances which I had certainly not foreseen
at any stage of our wrangling arguments, I had to change my
tactics. Returning to my tent I summoned Zayid and 'Ali
for a consultation, and in a few minutes more than half the
party was foregathered round my pallet. We argued and
wrangled. I protested that I would on no account go back

to the Hasa. They could abandon me if they liked but that
would be very serious for them. They would get no reward
from me and would certainly have to face the direst wrath of
those who had sent me hither. On the other hand I would no
longer insist on the southern journey if they were really afraid
of its consequences, and I would guarantee them against the
King's wrath by satisfying His Majesty that I had willingly
embarked on the crossing of the waterless desert from Shanna
rather than from a more southerly point. But the crossing of
the waterless desert was an essential part of my expedition.
Ibn Jiluwi had warned them of that before we started and any
failure in that direction would certainly bring down punishment on their heads.

Surely but steadily the feeling of the assembly veered
round to agreement with my proposals. The prospect of some
Oryx-hunting in the waterless desert appealed to those who
would do the hunting. The emptiness of the desert reassured
the more timid of our companions. And there was always the
comforting thought that the enterprise could be abandoned in
favour of retreat northwards to the nearest water in the event
of its proving unfeasible or excessively uncomfortable. So we
agreed in principle to the compromise of a westerly march to
be begun on the morrow, and for the time being an atmosphere of friendliness resumed its sway over our counsels. We
broke up to meet again half an hour later for the mid-day
meal, after which—my companions being present in full
force—our new pact was duly sealed by a distribution of
largesse. I had intended, I explained, to distribute presents
among you on our arrival at the Hadhramaut border, but we
have abandoned the idea of going so far to the southward. So
Shanna has become the farthest limit of our outward march,
and now by agreement our faces are turned homeward to
Mecca across the Empty Quarter. I want now to give you
some sign of gratitude for your exertions which have brought
us so far. My further and final thanks you shall have at
Mecca in due course, but take now this bag of dollars and
divide it among you as you see fit. Sa'dan, as my servant,
shall have no part in it, so you are seventeen to share the
money.

May God reward you, Shaikh 'Abdullah, they replied in unison. How much is there in the bag ? asked Ibn Ma'addi. Five hundred dollars, I replied ; whereupon there was much counting up on hands and some searching of souls. There would be 30 dollars apiece with 10 dollars short. Well, said Ibn Ma'addi, Zayid and 'Ali had money the other day from Shaikh 'Abdullah. Surely it is they that should get less now. As you please, said Zayid, but cut it all from me. Have no fear, I interposed, I will make good the deficiency—come, Abu Ja'sha, do you divide the swag among them. So little Ja'sha's father counted out the silver, thirty pieces to each man sitting round the fire, starting from the right and working round against the clock till he came to Zayid sitting at his left hand. It was a tense moment. Give me twenty, said Zayid, and keep thirty for yourself. Give him his full tale of thirty, I interposed, unwilling that our leader should remain dependent on my generosity. So they all had thirty dollars but Abu Ja'sha, who looked a little crestfallen and sheepish under so public a test of his unselfishness or optimism. I moved away back to my tent and privily secreted 20 dollars under my pillow. A little later I sent for Abu Ja'sha to move out some of my baggage in readiness for the morrow's march—he was the handy man of the party. Have you had the ten dollars? they asked him afterwards. He did not disappoint me, was his evasive reply, from which they knew just enough to salve their guilty consciences but not enough to excite their cupidity.

Our future course being thus decided by general agreement, I left the details to Zayid and his fellows with a suggestion that, if they wished, I should have no objection to their making the proposed attempt on the Empty Quarter without tents or other heavy *impedimenta*, which might be sent back with such of our men and camels as would find the waterless desert too much for their powers of endurance. That is certainly what we ought to have done in the circumstances. Both 'Ali Jahman and the Dimnani guides declared that they had never heard of any previous crossing of the desert from Shanna or anywhere in the Khiran district to Sulaiyil or its neighbourhood. 'Ali's experience extended to the Qa'amiyat and Hawaya tracts, whither the Ghafran Murra are wont in favourable seasons to wander to a distance of four or five days' journey from Shanna, Ziqirt and Naifa in search of pastures for their animals and Oryx or *Rim* gazelles for the pot. But in such cases they would always return in due course (when their camels needed water) to their base-wells and would thus never have occasion to penetrate further afield into the inhospitable desert. Similarly, as they well knew, hunting parties frequently enough visited the heart of the waterless desert from the Aflaj and Dawasir districts to shoot Oryx for ultimate sale in their home markets, where the flesh of the unicorn is considered a great and invigorating delicacy. Indeed a complete carcase, properly cured by drying in sun and wind, might well fetch prices as high as L10, or even L20 in a season of scarcity. Such parties would, however, inevitably return from the hunting-grounds to their familiar waterings and would never want to visit Shanna or other such desert wells even if they could locate them. Suwid had penetrated from Sulaiyil with such parties to the districts of Al Jalada (Jilida) and Raida on more than one occasion, while Salim knew the Oryx grounds southwards of Wadi Dawasir towards Najran and had crossed the northern fringes of the waterless desert between Maqainama and the Aflaj district and from Bir Fadhil direct to Sulaiyil. Indeed, as they declared, only the more adventurous of the Murra Arabs—men like 'Ali Jahman, Hamad ibn Sultan, Ibn Nifl, Ibn Fasl and some others—would go forth hunting in these generally rainless and pastureless districts, while any raiding party that might have occasion to traverse them in any direction would of necessity skirt the desert fringe and keep within reasonable reach of the borderland waterings in order to call at them in case of need.

There was thus obviously no useful object to be served under the normal conditions of Arab life by a direct crossing of this vast waterless wilderness from side to side and, though it was and is perhaps difficult to believe that such a crossing had never been attempted or accomplished before just for fun or from sheer love of adventure, I can only place on record the fact that neither from my own companions nor from anyone that we met at Sulaiyil or elsewhere could I learn of any such attempt or achievement. It is therefore possible, and perhaps even probable, that while no substantial part of the waterless desert has actually remained untrodden by human feet, we were the first party to venture into it with the intention of emerging on the other side. We were certainly the first to embark on such an enterprise with tents and heavy baggage, and it seemed to me before we set out that my companions were guilty of bad desert-craft in deciding to make the attempt under so great a handicap. We were to suffer dearly for such folly. We were in due course to find ourselves on the brink of a disastrous failure. But we were to learn from our experiences a lesson that perhaps pointed the way to ultimate success. For the moment the apparent light-heartedness and cheerfulness of my companions led me to suspect that our enterprise might not prove as alarming as I had imagined, but I was at a loss to guess their motives which in the light of our subsequent experiences seem clear enough. In the first place there was a reasonable prospect of good Oryx-hunting and the Arab is a born hunter as well as a lover of meat and an optimist. The lure of the chase and its savoury results appealed strongly to my companions, while on the other hand they doubtless held in reserve the thought that, if hunting failed and the march proved unpleasant, they could always break away from the venture before it was too late and retreat to the more northerly wells which would be within reasonable reach during the first few days of the journey. And it was this factor doubtless that decided them against parting with the more bulky of our stores (the great bags of rice that we carried) in order that they might at least have plenty of food on the easy return journey by the water-route on which perhaps many, if not all of them, were still counting.

All day long their preparations went on apace. The 32 waterskins, some of which had got torn and cracked during the journey up to date, were overhauled and botched and greased before being filled from the well and laid out in rows for loading on the morrow. Our stores were similarly divided up into suitable packs, and everything made ship-shape for an early start. The camels were, of course, out at the pastures and a desultory watch for enemies or visitors was kept up all day from the scattered dune-tops, though our decision to

return homewards across the empty desert seemed somewhat
to have abated the nervous strain of the previous afternoon.
In fact everyone seemed remarkably cheerful. In a fortnight,
with luck, we might be back in the civilised world where the
horror and danger of our present situation would be forgotten. And above all there was good silver in every saddle-bag
with hopes of more in due course in every breast. A good
meal of rice and butter and dates after sunset made every one
happy and cheerful. Salim, our guide to be, even spoke of
10 days as the prospective limit of our labours, and I found
it necessary to strike a note of warning lest we should go
forth in too extravagant a mood. By my calculations the
distance before us was some 360 miles as the crow flies, and I
wagered that we could not do it in less than 15 days at the
most favourable rate of marching achieved by us during the
past weeks. It behoved us, therefore, to be careful of our
water and to put away thoughts of any food that would require water for its cooking. They agreed cordially enough
for they had just disposed of a good dinner and were glad
enough to see me cheerful in spite of their victory in the day's
arguments. In fact there was no ground for despondency on
my part, for we were on the very threshold of a great adventure which for fourteen years I had regarded as the goal of
my ambition.

That night our sentries were posted only on the nearer hills,
and the unknown terrors of the south were forgotten with our
decision to avoid them. To-morrow, why ? to-morrow we
should be homeward bound over an utterly empty and waterless waste. We should there at least be safe from enemies, so
we slept comfortably in anticipation of that security and,
when we assembled for the morning prayer in the chill darkness of the pre-dawn with the thermometer registering only
40° *Fahr.*, our scouts came in from their watching—most of
them, poor wretches, just tittering with cold. We warmed
them up with coffee, and the camels were brought to the well
for a final watering before the great ordeal awaiting them,
while our cooks prepared our own last meal of rice. Unfortunately we made a better show of it than the animals, which,
having imbibed gallons of water only two days earlier on our

arrival at Shanna, seemed almost unwilling to drink. For that we were to suffer some days later but we could not think of such things at the moment, and our preparations for a start went forward without fuss or haste. I gave up my tent to be packed and loaded, and spent the few remaining moments of our sojourn by the well in an eleventh-hour appeal for a change of course to the southward. Such an appeal was doomed to failure, as I knew. Far off beyond the rolling sandy downs dotted with desert scrub lay that southern horizon of the land of death which none of us had seen and none should see, whose very name inspired in my companions a vague brooding sense of fear and gloom.

By 8.30 a.m. on February 22nd all was ready for our march, and off we started up out of the hollow into the valley south-westward—nineteen men and a dog with 30 of the 32 camels that had left Dulaiqiya 47 days earlier. They now carried well-filled boxes of desert specimens, to say nothing of 32 skins and two barrels of Shanna water. And I chaffed my companions as we went, rhyming after their crude desert fashion :

> We came to Shanna and saw foemen three ;
> We fled away for fear of treachery,
> Seeking the Wadi where good onions be ! [1]

They smiled wanly, eyeing me askance and wondering whether perhaps I might betray them after all. Little could they understand the joy that bubbled over in my heart as we breasted up into the great desert at last ! As little did I fathom the dark scheming of their treacherous minds as they marched with me into the unknown.

[1] *Yaum jina ila Shanna shifna ahl thalatha*
Wa sharadna minhum khaïfin min al khabatha
Raïdin al Wadi fiha khair wa karratha.

PART III

RUB' AL KHALI

Q

CHAPTER I

' THE VERITABLE DESERT '

'Tis this—that which they named to you as the Empty Quarter!
—'ALI JAHMAN.

DESPITE the long and strenuous journey before us we had agreed to make the first day's march a short one to enable me to visit and inspect all the wells to westward of Shanna. The main body with the baggage was to march direct to an agreed rendezvous under the guidance of Salim, while my smaller party, including Zayid and 'Ali Jahman, was to make the necessary detour by the wells and in due course rejoin the rest during the afternoon. The baggage-train got away some ten minutes ahead of us and passed out into the desert over the left bank of the Shanna valley in a north-westerly direction, while we marched up the valley itself south-westward to the wells of Arfaja about a mile away and situated in the deep hollow of a horseshoe sand-cliff. Part of the hollow was occupied by a considerable hillock of ex-posed gypseous rock with steep 40-feet cliffs, between which and the sand-slopes round it lay two wells. One of them was in fact no more than a trial shaft which had been abandoned in despair by its excavators before any moisture had been reached ; but the other had reached the water table at a depth of seven fathoms though it had never yielded a satis-factory supply and had soon been abandoned. Its shaft had subsequently been filled in almost to the top by blown sand from the desert, which will doubtless one day obliterate this memorial of the human labour which led ultimately, and during the same season, to the discovery and exploitation of Shanna. In ten minutes from Arfaja we came upon a great dyke of sand lying in the form of a double horseshoe, right across the valley at a great southward bend of its course.

243

Upstream of the dyke the wind had scooped out a deep pit, in whose sandy bottom we found two wells known as Bir ibn Suwailim after our Dimnani guide, Salim ibn Suwailim, who had originally dug them out about 25 years ago, when these southern sands would seem to have enjoyed their last considerable cycle of good rains and good pastures. Subsequently drought had driven the Arabs and their camels elsewhere, and Salim's wells, left to their fate, had been swallowed up by the sands until their site was rediscovered and cleared in the 1929-30 season by 'Ali Jahman, truly a great desert pioneer. As at Arfaja the water was found to be similar in quality to that of Shanna, but its depth was nine fathoms— a fact that suggests that the diggers at Arfaja might have met with better success if they had sunk their shaft to, say, 10 fathoms. After a single season's use the tribesmen moved away from the watering of Ibn Suwailim, and again the sands did their work upon the site.

The valley now ran up in a southerly direction through a maze of dunes rising from the desert floor to heights of 200 or 300 feet and scattered about and across the trough in little groups of two and three. Here and there a small patch of the exposed bedrock attracted our attention, while after labouring along, up hill and down dale, in a most tiring manner for about three miles we found ourselves on the 300 feet summit of a steep sand-slope with the pit of Mamura immediately below us. 'Ali had done his best to persuade me to march direct from Bir ibn Suwailim to Zuwaira in order to avoid this difficult patch of country, but I had explained to him that it was absolutely necessary for me to see a locality with my own eyes if I wished to place it on the map. So hither we had come.

A hare—one of a dozen we encountered during this day's march through comparatively good pastures—went away as we descended into the bottom, where we found several lizards for my collection. A party of Murra had occupied this locality during the season of 1929-30—the 'day of Sibila' as it is called in Arabian chronology after the great battle near Zilfi which gave Ibn Sa'ud the final victory over the rebel Ikhwan—and 'Ali, prospecting as always for water, had found it at a depth of only three fathoms—good Shanna-like water but far from copious. So the well had been abandoned and it needed 'Ali himself to locate its position amid the sands which had completely obliterated all trace of it. Near by lay a considerable patch of exposed gypseous rock, whose surface, whipped into little rigid wavelets, suggested the bed of an ancient lake or lagoon.

Beyond it westward the valley-bed, curving round between lofty ridges of sand, appeared in numerous patches of exposed bed-rock until, crossing a low transverse sand-ridge, we descended into the depression—still obviously part of the same valley—of Zuwaira. Close under the sand-slope on our right we came upon the single well of the locality, a shaft of five fathoms, which 'Ali had sunk in the year (1928-29) before Sibila and which, though covered over, had evidently been used by visitors only a few weeks before our visit. The sandy soil round the well still showed signs of moisture, and my companions counted the tracks of fifteen camels belonging doubtless to some raiding party. Here were the dead embers of their coffee-fire and there they had prayed, while two men were shown by their tracks to have gone off on foot to keep watch from the hill-top while their fellows got on with the nervous but necessary task of watering their camels and filling their skins. The very sight of such tracks, old as they were, brought on an attack of nerves in my small party, which chafed impatiently as I carried out my usual routine search for objects of scientific interest. The men who had passed that way might, for all we knew, be due to return by now. They might have encountered our baggage-party, they might yet encounter ourselves. The more pity that we had divided up our strength and the more reason to make haste to rejoin our companions. Yet our short halt was not in vain for Zayid picked up a flint implement to add to my collection. So we resumed the march with no great delay over a great, undulating rose-pink tract of downs lying between lofty ridges more than a mile apart, thickly covered with the lovely *Zahr* plant. Our course lay nearly due north now for about three miles with the exposed bed of the valley appearing in patches on our right, until from an intervening sand-ridge we looked out upon a veritable lake of gypsum gleaming white in the hazy sunshine.

Here lay Turaiwa, the last of the desert wells westward of Shanna, dug by 'Ali during the 1929-30 season, a single shaft descending 13 fathoms to a stratum of briny water like that of Ziqirt and other wells of Al Khiran. The gypsum lake was, perhaps, therefore the relic of an arm of the sea rather than part of the old river-bed, which doubtless splayed out into a delta as it approached the bay. Like Zuwaira, this well had recently been visited by Arabs, though my companions could not agree as to the approximate date of their passing. Its mouth had been carefully covered over in accordance with local custom, while the rock-marked niche of the praying-place and the presence of an *Abal*-dye pit on a patch of gypsum lying a few feet higher than the level of the well-mouth proclaimed that Turaiwa was a rendezvous of grazing Arabs accompanied by their tents and womenfolk as well as a place of call for casual travellers.

We had now completed our programme so far as it concerned the wells of the Shanna district, and our immediate objective was to rejoin our baggage-train as soon as possible. The country through which we marched all formed part of the tract vaguely known as Ramla Shanna or the Shanna sands—a country of typical *Sawahib* character with long parallel sand-ridges at intervals of a mile, more or less, and undulating scrub-dotted valleys or depressions between them. Here and there the underlying rock of the desert lay exposed amid the sands—white or blue-grey in colouring.

About 10 miles west of Shanna the general character of the desert changes. The sand-ridges no longer run in parallel strips but lie scattered about the landscape in wide theatre-like arcs, generally facing southwards and containing within their great embrace extensive tracts of sandy downs and valley bottoms of rock or light sand. This tract is known as Al Qatarat. About five miles on from Tuwaira we came to a halt in one of these bottoms for a short midday rest and the usual refreshments while our camels grazed. The blue rock of the desert was here seen exposed and descending from north to south in two 20-feet ledges—a shelving beach as it were or more probably a river bank, but with no sign of gravel. Throughout the afternoon, during which we marched about nine miles in all, the scene remained unchanged, and our course lay over hill and dale along an interrupted series of similar patches of rock, while from the summits we crossed to pass from bottom to bottom we looked out over vast panoramas of rolling sand-hills and ridges and isolated horseshoe dunes. A hare lay doggo under an *Abal* bush while 'Ali, attended by an audience of four men and their mounts disposed in a semicircle round the quarry, blew it to bits with a rifle-bullet at a range of a few yards. We only got two of the many hares we saw and Al Aqfa, the *Saluqi* bitch, had fed too comfortably at Shanna to be in training for the chase. A mild diversion was caused by a monitor [1] lizard which took refuge in a bush and scattered my companions as it darted out to seek other cover. With a gentle tap of my riding cane I seemed to break its back and it lay on the ground snapping helplessly at us, but at this period my slender supply of methylated spirits had been exhausted and all our efforts to preserve the specimen ended in failure. A single dragonfly was perhaps the strangest of the day's encounters, while three butterflies were also seen though not captured. They were the most elusive of all the desert creatures and I only caught one in all these days of desert wandering.

Late in the afternoon we espied two men on a sand-ridge afar off and rightly assumed that they were members of our baggage-party on the lookout for our arrival. A few minutes later we were in camp, having covered a distance of rather more than 20 miles during the day by our roundabout route. Shanna was about 15 miles away, as the crow flies, and some 150 feet below us. A day's journey to southward lay the tract of Ramlat abu Dhulu'—a lofty sand-range with lower ridges extending westward to the high dune massifs of Al Qa'amiyat. So ended the first day with little progress achieved, but conditions had been favourable enough, promising better things for the days to come.

At 2 a.m. the baggage was started off to get the full

[1] *Waral* or *Ruwaili.*

benefit of the cool night-hours, while with a few companions I slept on till dawn. I dawdled over my morning packing. Suddenly Salih, from an eminence commanding the plain behind us, shouted for my glasses and announced the presence of suspicious moving things far off. He failed to substantiate his report but in the desert all alarms must be taken seriously—true or false,—and we lost no time in loading up and moving off.

Many weeks earlier 'Ali had confided to me that he knew of a locality full of shells in these southern parts, and I felt it was now time to remind him of his promise to lead me thither. He had indeed not forgotten. He was not altogether sure of the locality but imagined that it was not far off. He had turned aside once or twice during the previous day to examine the exposed rock patches we had passed in case they might prove to be the spot he sought, and here and there we had found small scattered lots of the little spiral shells seen at Shanna. We had clearly therefore been following a river-bed or traversing a delta but now, within a mile of our camp, we came upon what looked from afar like another of the numerous patches of exposed rock we had seen so often. There it is, said 'Ali. What? I asked. The shells I spoke of, he answered; 'tis many years since I passed this way and saw them. I was returning from hunting the Oryx in Qa'amiyat and I paid but little attention to such things. But when you were so excited at sight of the shells in the Jiban I remembered. We rode on to the edge of the exposed patch and I noticed a scatter of little white spirals. Further on we came upon a few bivalves[1] and I dismounted. We remained there nearly an hour, collecting the freshwater shells in hundreds and thousands, while our scouts kept watch on the neighbouring ridges for fear of foes. Nowhere did I see any trace of flint implements as at the northern locality, but here was clearly a considerable stretch of an old river-bed. A mile further on we found another similar patch with a more modest deposit of shells. Thus for something over 20 miles we had found sporadic evidences of fresh water in ancient times. Nothing but a

[1] *Unio terminalis*—see Appendix.

river could fully account for such a phenomenon and I had little hesitation in assuming as a working theory that we had in fact been exploring the lower reaches of Wadi Dawasir, the great river of ancient times that issued from the 'Asir and Yaman highlands to pass by Dam and Sulaiyil into the great desert. At least we can say that the theory is not inconsistent with the known facts. What do you call this place ? I asked 'Ali. It has no name, he replied. Then let us name it Abu Muhairat, I suggested, ' the father of shells.' Forget it not that you may, perchance, tell those who come after me, for the shells are the shells of a river—not sea-shells as we saw in the Jiban—and the river is Wadi Dawasir. He speaks sooth, said one of the party, yet we knew it not till this day for we *Badu* have no knowledge. Now 'Ali had long coveted the cloak of Sa'dan, who had brought two with him in the hope of selling one to his own profit, and I knew they had been haggling over the price of it, for 'Ali had declared that 20 dollars was more than he could pay. I will give you the 20 dollars, I said to Sa'dan, only say nothing of it to any soul. So I rode with Sa'dan as we left the scene of the great discovery and 'Ali drew up to us to know whether I was pleased with his guiding. I drew the cloak from Sa'dan's saddle and threw it over to him. It is yours, I said, but find me more flints or shells if you know of any. This is the limit of my knowledge, he replied, but say nothing of the cloak to our brethren lest they envy me. I will put it privily away this night when we reach camp.

So we passed on. A desert lark piped about us and sidled away to safety. A *Spindasis* butterfly appeared again, and we passed from the massed sand-theatres of Al Qatarat into the gently undulating tract of Hadh Qa'amiyat with the roseate dune-massifs of Qa'amiyat proper forming a great mountain wall across our southern horizon. The great peaks seemed to rise about 500 feet above the general desert level, and among them, according to 'Ali, lay the true haunts of the Oryx, a shy animal that travels far and fast over steppe and desert in search of food but retires ever to the almost inaccessible sand-mountains for safety against surprise or pursuit. We crossed the recent tracks of a party of eight or ten men of the Sa'ar tribe going towards Shanna—perhaps the party whose scouts had frightened and been equally frightened by us only four days before. And then we came upon young sprouts of the *Andab* grass, which told of recent though slight rain in these parts. Inevitably we paused until our camels had obliterated that thin splash of green from the desert landscape. The *Andab* is ever the first of the herbs to come to life after rain, and the *Abal* runs it close. But *Alqa*, *Birkan* and *Zahr* need more coaxing. Of them all the *Abal*, with *Hadh* a good second, lives longest in the lengthening drought : and the Badawin from long experience can date back falls of rain with approximate accuracy by the state of these bushes in various parts of the desert.

We marched over a long succession of vast saucer-like depressions with high rims and easy slopes down to greater or smaller exposed patches of the calcareous or gypseous rock-bottom varying in colour from a deep greyish-blue—the colour of Dorset cheese—to white and grey. Some of these patches had from the distance all the appearance of vast lakes. In some the rock shelved back in a serious of distinct steps into and under the enveloping sand ; while in others the surface lay flat with a covering of grit and gravel dotted here and there with larger fragments of rock.

From this basin-tract we passed into Hibaka Qa'amiyat, a district of parallel sand-ridges running SW. and NE., close together with narrow valleys between them, and easy enough to negotiate. Half a day's journey to the north lay Sanam al Hawar, an area of low dunes picturesquely named ' the humps of the camel-colts,' while the high ranges of Qa'amiyat still ran parallel to us on the left hand not far off. A charming landscape it was indeed, but how lifeless ! Afar off ahead of us an eagle was soaring about in stately solitude, seeking food. Nearer to us a raven watched our passage through the desert from the safe vantage of a dune-peak, while desert larks appeared from time to time. A long whitish snake with upreared head and flicking tongue charged through our advancing column ; and 'Ali was off his mount in a trice chasing it as it fled to a neighbouring

bush. His efforts to catch it by the tail were amusing but
futile—perhaps happily !

The parallel ranges gradually merged into a stormy sea of
dunes and ridges without symmetry except that the horseshoe hollows seemed regularly to face south-west. On one
steepish slope 'Ali, who led the way up, dismounted to
scrape away the uppermost crest of sand for our easier
passing. The dune summits stood about 200 feet above the
depressions, while the general level of the sandy downs and
ridges lay about half-way between the two. We halted for
the afternoon prayers and coffee on the open downs, where
we found the horns of a doe Oryx on the ground, where she
had apparently died of hunger. The horns were 29 inches
in length. Another raven appeared to investigate the cause
of our halting, and shortly afterwards as we marched over
the downs we sighted our baggage-animals ahead. Our
camp for the night was by a ridge of the Hibaka, near which
Farraj had located the earth of a Fennec fox and captured
its inhabitants, a male and a female, alive. A small snake had
also been taken during the march by the transport folk, and
that night the bright glare of my pressure-lamp attracted a
large company of moths [1] and other insects, including the
first grasshopper seen by me in the Rub' al Khali. It had
struck me as altogether extraordinary that, while butterflies
and even dragonflies had been comparatively plentiful from
time to time, not a single grasshopper had been seen in
country apparently so suitable for its activities. On coming
into camp we had seen the tracks of a Stone Curlew
(*Karwan*), but had not seen the bird itself. We had marched
about 25 miles during the day but, with two days counted
out, had only done about 46 of the 360 miles that had confronted us at starting from Shanna. The climatic conditions had, however, been satisfactory enough with temperatures ranging from a minimum of 46° *Fahr.* at night to
about 85° in the shade by day. The sun was hot in the
afternoons, of course, but it would be difficult to imagine
more perfect nights with a full moon shining down upon us

[1] An astonishingly large proportion of the moths collected in the Rub' al
Khali appear to be new species—see Appendix.

in the wilderness, while the morning marches were a sheer
delight. Our spirits sank as the sun neared the meridian,
and my companions whiled away the afternoon boredom
with their barren, cheerless singing.

On the third day we marched 26 miles—a fair average
day's march for laden camels—over what remained of the
Hibaka tract, a barish rolling weald of sand, into the still
barer downs of Hamra, practically without scrub of any kind,
and ultimately into the scantily-covered tract of Abal
Khadim with its gently swelling bosom of ridges and wide
valleys. Soon after starting we came upon an exposed patch
of gypsum and grey-blue rock, where we found a rich profusion of spiral shells, wherefore we named the spot Abu
Sabban. 'Ali shot a hare, which in due course we stewed for
breakfast at our next halt and ate with dates. The wind was
now coming from the south-west, a hot quarter, and steadily
gaining strength ; and we ploughed on rather drearily over
a landscape that reminded me strongly of Jafura. The
baggage-animals also had evidently been labouring, as we
had only made about eight miles when we came upon the
spot where the advance-party had performed their dawn
prayers and refreshed themselves with coffee. Not long
afterwards we actually sighted them in the distance but our
rather long halt for breakfast gave them time to get ahead
again, and we saw them no more though the sun went down
on us and we quickened our speed in the rapidly deepening
gloom. We were beginning to wonder indeed whether we
might perhaps have missed their route as the blowing sand
had rapidly obliterated their tracks ; but at length we saw a
large bonfire far ahead of us and soon rejoined our companions in camp at about 7.30. It had been a tiring day for
us all and there was a good deal of wild and angry talk in
camp, as of men tired and hungry and dissatisfied. But it
was nothing more than that. They would have been satisfied enough if I could have agreed to night-marching all the
time but that was clearly impossible. We had come to see
the country and not merely to traverse it, while I had the
support of those who still hoped to see and shoot the Oryx.
On several occasions during the day we had come upon old

dung and tracks of the animal, while during the afternoon
we passed a great spreading *Abal* bush in which a pair had
evidently rested during the heat of the day—perhaps yesterday or a day or two before. Smell the dung, said 'Ali,
passing a few pellets up to me as I halted to view the spot;
it is like musk, very pleasant to the nose. In another spot
we saw tracks, about four days old, of a full-grown pair and
a young one. Our spirits began to rise and we hoped for
something better on the morrow. So our plans held good,
and the transport again started off at 3 a.m.

During the day we had collected some lizards. A pair of
ravens had been seen, and a few larks and tiny warblers,
charming little creatures that played hide-and-seek with me
amid the branches of an *Abal* bush and only left that shelter
for another when I became too bold in my innocent quest
(for my gun was out of action for good). It was interesting
to see how these little birds fly from bush to bush almost
invisibly in long graceful swoops close along the ground—to
avoid the keen eye of hawk and raven. A *Spindasis* butterfly
and two dragonflies were also seen, and in one spot we found
the horns of a dead *Rim* gazelle. The wind veered round to
the south and the heat increased. Then in the afternoon the
wind dropped altogether, and the sun blazed on us without
mercy. Said 'Ali : The Rubʻ al Khali they talked of to you,
this is it ! it is three years since any rain fell here, and you
will see the *Zahr* no more until you come to Harmaliya [1]—
five or six days hence. It was indeed a desolate scene with
the scantiest of scrub and during the last two hours before
sunset the sun struck us in the face from straight in front.
It was like marching into a furnace.

We began the fourth day's march under a sense of combined strain and expectation. During the night the abandon-
ment of our enterprise had been seriously canvassed and my
lack of sympathy with our strained camels provided Farraj
with an opportunity to read me a lecture. If your beast is
well, said he, then you are well ; but if she wilts, then you
wilt. Very true, I said, but it is you folk that think not

[1] In fact we never came to this locality and I never ascertained its exact
position.

twice of increasing the strain. We have to cross this Empty Quarter, and I but ride straight on, neither thinking of retreat nor thinking of diversion. But look for instance at Zayid and Salih, who rode off just now on the trail of an Oryx. All day they may ride their beasts after their quarry and return at nightfall unsuccessful, disheartened and tired. Then they will chide me for my obstinacy and want to return to water. That is always your way.

Soon after starting on the day's march and just before passing from the Abal Khadhim tract into the very similar bare rolling country of Hadhat al Qata—indeed the only difference was the scanty appearance of *Hadh* amidst the *Abal* and *Alqa*—we had come upon the tracks of four Oryx, and our men lusted to be off after them. Zayid drew up to me with a cringing request for permission to follow up the tracks, and I was glad enough to think that I might have some hours free of his company. To Salih I replied that he could please himself, and off the pair went at a steady walk which soon took them out of sight on our flank. 'Ali had unsuccessfully pleaded for similar liberty. Look you, he had said untruthfully, we have come to the end of the country I know. Beyond this there is no guidance in me, but Ibn Humaiyid knows it all and I can go and seek out an Oryx for you. I can do without the Oryx, I had replied, and I want your company. So he rode on sulkily far ahead, while Farraj danced attendance on me.

An hour later we passed the spot where the advance-party had prayed and made coffee. It was 9 a.m. and they must have left the spot barely an hour and a half before, yet over their fresh tracks lay the still more recent trail of a full-grown bull Oryx ! That was too much for us all. Lovingly they read the message of the tracks aloud—how the great beast had sauntered along from the north cropping a bush here and there as he passed : how he had stood transfixed for a moment as he came upon the ploughed-up channel of our baggage camels : and how finally he had galloped away for dear life from the scent and signs of danger. 'Ali pleaded with tears in his eyes, and I yielded. Farraj strained at the leash, and I acquiesced with the reproach that I would soon be left entirely alone. Off they went, and we went on.

Very soon Farraj came back, protesting that he could not bear to leave me so ill-attended. Look you, he said, we would never have left our dear families and come out on this business but for two reasons : hope of profit and fear of punishment. I have no desire but to serve you, but it is Zayid and 'Ali that are to blame for all our troubles. You will surely not let their behaviour involve the rest of us in loss. Tell me what you want and I will do it. He was the lack-wit of our party—ever resisting but repenting, repenting but resisting—but the frankest of them all in naïve self-seeking. I had appealed to his cupidity the previous evening with some small pecuniary compensation for the trouble involved in capturing the two foxes—and for a bitten finger of which he had made the most, quite shamelessly.

Up hill and down dale we marched on. Here and there a small patch of exposed bluish rock in the bottom of a valley claimed our attention. The vegetation became scantier as we went, and all that there was was dead. Soon the rolling downs became absolutely bare, and the hot sun blazed down on them until the sand glared again into our faces mercilessly. Now and again the higher sands produced a mirage like sheets of glass. Not a bird did we see all that day, though once we heard the piping of an invisible lark. A dragonfly astonished me in such surroundings and thrice we saw a butterfly—flitting shadows that caught my eye for an instant and disappeared into the enveloping sheen of sand-reflected light. Two gargoylish lizards crouched in the sandy fire as we passed and were duly consigned to my ever-ready bottle.

We passed from Hadhat al Qata into Khillat al Hawaya about mid-day—a vast down-tract of rounded ribs of soft sand lying SW. and NE. as usual, with occasional lofty dunes to vary the monotony. It was easy going, but the heat was intense without relief. At 2 p.m. we halted by an exposed patch of the underlying bedrock for a short rest. I spread my mantle over the branches of a moribund *Abal* bush and scraped away the heated upper layer of sand to make myself a couch in the shade. I slept until I was summoned to coffee, and we disposed of the afternoon prayer before resuming the march.

Far away now to our southward lay the long line of the Hibaka, whose northerly extremity we had traversed the previous day, with the Qa'amiyat uplands beyond it; while to our north the Hawaya ridges extended a day and a half to the Bani Jallab tract, westward of which lies Al Jalada[1] (apparently a gravel plain), with the northern Hibaka (or Hibaka Faraja) on its northern side. The downs gradually changed in character to form a series of more or less parallel ridges (always lying SW. and NE.), which we crossed in wearisome succession at intervals of a quarter mile or more. Very hot it became as the afternoon wore on and our spirits drooped. Yet every now and then a cool zephyr breathed upon us from the east, fragrant reminder of the oncoming night. At the hottest of the day the shade temperature had touched 93°, but at 10 p.m. it was only 65°, and the minimum of the night in camp was 50°. We camped at 5 p.m. near the western edge of Khillat Hawaya and our hunters dribbled in about sunset from their futile hunting. The camels had felt the day's strain, marching through a pastureless wilderness, but there was less talk of giving up. We were now a hundred miles away from Shanna and at least as far from any water, while Zayid and 'Ali had evidently devised a plan for the morrow to their own liking. The baggage-train was started off before 2 a.m., and after the chatter and clatter of their starting we slept in peace in the cool desert while the waning moon went its way over us through an almost starless sky.

I awoke before dawn as usual, and over our morning coffee and dates after the prayer it was announced that the camels of Zayid and 'Ali were missing! Having come in rather late the previous evening, they had been left to graze in the moonlight and had strayed away. An hour was wasted in looking for them—a precious hour of the day's coolth—and then it was proposed that the rest of us should start leaving Muhaimid with one camel, carrying water and provisions, in attendance on Zayid and 'Ali, who would track

[1] More probably, perhaps, Sahma or Ra'la. See p. 316.

down their lost beasts and follow in our trail. They might as well have made a clean breast of their plans, which were too obvious to call for comment. They would have to-day for another long pursuit of the elusive Oryx and—most significant of all—our future plans could be reconsidered if they failed again. By nightfall we would still be near enough to water to go back and, viewed in the light of such a pact, the developments of the day fall into a clearer, if ominous, perspective. Meanwhile there was nothing to be done but to make the best of a bad situation and hope for the best. But I did privately register the hope that Zayid and 'Ali might not meet with success in their selfish quest. So we started off on our fifth day's march with Farraj riding the animal that carried my boxes, Ibn Humaiyid as guide and Salih in attendance. All went merrily enough and we joked and laughed, nominating Farraj to the Amirate, left vacant by the desertion of Zayid, and Salih as his deputy. And I offered to wager a large sum that the hunters would return disappointed. Meanwhile we could be happy without their company. And we were happy enough as we struck out over the bare, easy, rolling downs, streaked at wide intervals with ridges of sand so low as to be scarcely perceptible. Farraj characteristically made the most of his uncomfortable perch on my boxes as evidence of his will to service ; and I chaffed him, pointing out how he dominated us all as from a throne raised aloft. How well it would be, I said, if we could always march thus without Zayid and 'Ali ! You and Salih could take it in turns each day to be our leader and ride upon the throne, as rode the Arab virgins in the good old days in a litter leading their tribal warriors into battle. I am content, Salih interposed hastily, to leave that honour to Farraj, and I can serve you better catching lizards for you or turning aside with you to collect rocks and shells—and perhaps flints—from the bare valley-bottoms on the way. And at intervals, when the conversation flagged, they would strike up their barren singing to break the silence of the desert.

After an hour we passed into Qasba Hawaya, and they pointed out to me the dried-up stubble of the *Qasab* grass

R

which differentiates it from what had gone before. After
good rains, said Ibn Humaiyid, this is good grazing country
and the Arabs come hither with their milch-camels to seek
the Oryx. And they remain out until the camels need water,
themselves living only on milk and the meat of the chase.
But it is the great ones only who do that—people like Ibn
Nifl and Ibn Jahman and Ibn Suwailim. It is a hard life.
But there has been no rain in these parts for seven or eight
years now, and none come hither these days. Gradually the
country had become more undulating with rounded dunes
and low ridges. But it was amazingly bare.

The light, cool breeze of the early morning dropped, but
for an hour or two the conditions remained pleasant enough
though the air was deathly still. The silence—once broken
by the sweet piping of an invisible lark—was astonishing.
And the dunes and ridges merged into a sea of billows without order, tossed and tumbled by the conflict of desert winds.
A little way off to the southward a group of lofty pink dunes
towered above it all, and we went by the tracks and dung
of a solitary Oryx, which had passed across this wilderness
two days earlier questing for pastures further north.

Suddenly there appeared before us the trough of a great
valley-bottom cleaving the rolling downs from south-west to
north-east. In its bed we saw a long series of exposed
patches of the underlying rock, which we turned out of our
way to visit in search of shells. We found none and climbed
up the long and weary slope beyond to enter, on its crest,
the district of Hadhat al Hawaya, a tract of deeper valleys
and higher ridges which extend in uniformly parallel lines
for some 40 or 50 miles westward to the Shuwaikila country.
Here the *Hadh* bush reappeared after a long absence, dead
like everything else though occasional tufts of green raised
hopes that were doomed to disappointment. As the day
drew on to noontide and the sun blazed down on us without
mercy it was easy to believe that never in 20 years or
more had rain fallen in this district. The dry *Hadh* shrubs
had gathered mounds of sand about their half-buried heads
and even the hardy *Abal*, the longest-lived of all the desert
plants, had not survived the strain.

Its long, blackened roots lay spread about the sandy floor round the perished relics of once great thickets, whose gnarled and writhing branches proclaimed the agonies to which at last after a gallant struggle they had succumbed exhausted. Drought and famine stalked the land with drawn swords of flaming fire, breathing hotly upon us who ventured thus into their domain. It was impressive but it was depressing, and I was oppressed, maybe, by a premonition of failure. Grimly and in silence we marched on over an endless succession of valleys and ridges, hoping that each crest would gladden our eyes with a vision of pastures ahead, but hoping in vain. Nevertheless it was a pleasant landscape —these rolling downs and deep valleys of Hawaya, where Death reigned supreme, and a single raven waged perpetual war against the little creatures that dared to live against such odds, larks and lizards and tiny warblers.

It occurred to me, as we passed through the various belts of this great sand-desert, that the sharply defined limits of *Hadh* and *Qasba*, *Hamra* [1] and *Khilla* and the like must in some way reflect the chemical character of the sands themselves or of the soils and waters underlying them. Each plant has a more or less definite life-period dependent on the frequency of rains, the hardiest coming to life out of death or dormancy upon the slightest encouragement and lasting through the years under the greatest provocation, while the tenderer herbs shrink from rebirth until tempted by copious rainfall and wilt as soon as the drought resumes its sway. But a systematic study of the plants themselves and of the sand and bedrock of their habitat would certainly yield interesting and important results, especially if correlated with the study of similar or comparable plant-zones in the Sahara and other great desert tracts of the world. The untutored eye could detect no outward and visible explanation of the zone phenomenon. It merely noted the beginnings and the ends of the *Hadh* belts, outside which all was *Khilla* dotted with *Abal* or naked *Hamra*, with minor zones of *Qasba* and *Birkan*.

[1] *Hamra, Hamrur* (pl. *Hamarir*), apparently used only of sand-tracts absolutely destitute of any kind of vegetation.

In a space of about four hours we had crossed as many valleys, well-marked channels between broad gently sloping ridges. In each case the wind had scoured out the bed to expose patches of the calcareous rock below, of which we collected samples while searching in vain for shells and fossils. Here and there in the sandy hollows we found queer, thin tubes[1] of coagulated sand, which my companions regarded as evidence of subsoil water in the neighbourhood and which they often find near the known wells. These proved to be fulgurites or lightning-sticks, formed by the fusing of damp sand by lightning and the adhesion of sand to the fused mass in such a manner as to form a thin tube. Our specimens are puny little things compared with many in the British Museum, but the frequency of their occurrence in the rainless, or almost rainless, desert is remarkable enough.

Some of these ridges flattened out at the top into broad plateaus of a gentle switchback character with shallow undulations and occasional moraines of low rounded dunes in large groups. Far and wide it was an unimaginably bare wilderness, and our nerves seemed to be at high tension as we faced the prospect of hour after hour of the same desolation, labouring on in the growing sultriness of noon along the furrow ploughed ahead of us by the passage of our baggage-train. Not once had we drawn rein since starting and the time drew nigh for a short halt for a breather, with coffee to cheer the heart of man. We had crossed the third valley and slowly climbed the long slope beyond it to the ridge crest, whence we looked forth on yet another valley with rolling downs beyond. Our general course had been WNW., but now almost due north of us, as we scanned the horizon, we saw a tent silhouetted against the slope of the further ridge. It was evidently one of our own tents, pitched for the first time since leaving Shanna, for we had discarded all unnecessary trouble and comfort to save time. The tent foreboded ill ; the sudden change of direction was ominous. It was scarcely past midday and I railed in natural wrath against the transport folk for their wretched marching. The light-headed Farraj took up the challenge with a hysterical

[1] See Appendix.

outburst. We toil for you in vain ; we strain the camels till
they break—all in vain. You are ever displeased and
critical. Would you have them march on in the fire of this
noontide sun ? They are perchance resting for an hour or
two. Yet he knew, as I felt instinctively, that the tent foreboded more than ill—perhaps disaster. Could one be anything but critical and on one's guard with companions who
would readily have sacrificed the whole object of our endeavour to their own miserable comfort ? In such circumstances the Arab does not show up to advantage. He clings
frantically, desperately, to life, however miserable, and,
when that is at risk, loses heart and head. Greed of filthy
lucre alone makes him pause from flight, and gradually he
may be brought round to a more reasonable attitude if he
can be made to feel that all the troubles of the past may have
been in vain if he shrinks from those of the future. At
Shanna it had been fear of human foes that had produced
rebellion, and I had submitted with a good enough grace
though not without a struggle. On the way I had frankly,
though vainly, tried to bribe 'Ali Jahman to turn south
while it was still not too late, but he had shrunk from the
prospect of incurring the hostility of his companions. And
now it was the waterless desert, the fear of thirst and death,
that made women of these men. I could not, would not
yield. We had come 140 miles. A third of the journey was
behind us and a steady effort would carry us through if only
they would play the man. They were, of course, weak and
disheartened with hunger for we had had nothing but dates
since Shanna. I was famished myself and could sympathise
with their condition. I felt like Moses in the wilderness when
the multitude clamoured against him, but I could produce
neither water nor manna.

So we marched on wrangling towards the distant tent. In
half an hour we reached camp to hear that five or six baggage-
animals had collapsed from thirst, hunger and exhaustion.
One of them was actually sheltering against the sun under
cover of the tent at the time, while two or three others were
similarly indulged when in due course they were brought in
from the desert with the loads of which they had been

relieved for a time to let them recover from the strain. The
position was just about as serious as it could be and some
reconsideration of our plans would obviously be necessary.
We were at a crisis of our fortunes, but the battle had yet to
be joined that would end at midnight in my own discom
fiture.

My tent had been pitched near the other when we arrived
but, after depositing my goods and chattels in it, I hastened
to join my companions, whom I found in surly mood and
openly mutinous, attributing the debacle of the day to my
insane insistence both on embarking upon such an enterprise
and on marching through the heat of the day. I tried to be
conciliatory in the circumstances and pointed out gently that
night-marching would have defeated the whole object of our
journey. I went on to declare that at Shanna I had strongly
urged the division of our forces and the despatch of all our
heavy baggage by the comparatively easy route by the wells
to Riyadh or Hufuf, so that we might attempt the waterless
crossing with a light and well-equipped party. It was therefore they who had brought about the present disastrous state
of affairs by neglecting my advice. I had moreover warned
them at Shanna that the journey would take at least 15
days while they had clung foolishly to Ibn Suwailim's
optimistic estimate of 11 or 12, and thus had only themselves to thank for the disappointment of their hopes. We
had in fact done exactly one-third of the distance in one-
third of the time allowed for by me, and there was no reason
to talk of abandoning the enterprise. I certainly would not
do that. I would go on alone if necessary and they could go
back and tell their master that they had abandoned their
guest in the desert. And now, I continued, our course is
clear enough. We can send back the baggage-animals to
Naifa, whence they may either return to the Hasa or rejoin
us at Wadi Dawasir by way of Bir Fadhil and the Aflaj.
The rest of us could continue the march direct to Sulaiyil,
where we should await the arrival of the baggage. The only
course was to be firm and unyielding with as much concilia-
toriness as possible, but my frankness merely fanned the
flames of mutiny as they sat silent and brooding round the

embers of the coffee fire. The coffee cups were passing round.

'Abdul Rahman, the coffee-man, scion of the dour clans of Dhruma and usually too absorbed in his coffee-making to take much part in the general conversation, looked up with a snarl and jerked out some offensive remark about my lack of consideration for others. I rounded on the assembled company and chid them. I came over to your tent, I said, to discuss the situation with you that we may make plans for the future. I did not come to hear expressions of your ill-temper, and it astonishes me that you should all sit by and let such a remark as that be made in your presence with impunity. I, at any rate, will not stand that from any of you. With that I tossed my untasted cup on the sand and rose to leave the tent. Ibn Ma'addi, doubtless remembering the Sa'dan incident at Adraj, interposed with an olive branch. If you wish it, he said, we will give 'Abdul Rahman a beating for his insolence. No, I replied as I walked away, I do not wish it; I have forgiven him. But if any of you wish to discuss matters with me, he must come to my tent. I come no more to yours. At such a crisis it was obviously undesirable to make enemies gratuitously, while I also reflected that 'Abdul Rahman had probably had a gruelling day of it with the breakdown of the camels. He was perhaps also contemplating death from thirst as a very real possibility. High words and ill-temper were inevitable in such circumstances, and I was full of sympathy for the unfortunate wretches though by no means disposed to yield to their clamour for an ignominious retreat. So I left them to their talking, and fragments of their wild conversation floated over to my ears as I settled down to plot out our whole march from Shanna to this point. I had had no time to do such work during the past five days and it was imperative that I should know roughly without delay our actual position in the great waterless desert. Sa'dan brought me my customary pot of tea and the gossip of the enemy camp, whence emissaries came from time to time to resume negotiations with me about our future movements. By sunset I had finished my task and, as soon as it was dark enough, I made

and worked out the necessary astronomical observations to
check the accuracy of my compass traverse. Our progress
had been certainly a little disappointing though I had dis-
counted such a contingency in advance. Two-thirds of the
desert journey lay before us—a matter of ten days, though
these might be reduced to eight with a reasonable amount of
night marching. Could the best of our camels do it ? That
was the great question, while there could be no doubt, whatever, that the baggage-animals must make with all possible
speed for the nearest water. There was little to choose in
the matter of distance between Naifa and Shanna, but wild
horses would not have dragged my companions back to the
latter. They feared it as the plague, and there was no
reason why their preference should not be conceded. For
the camels (and to a lesser extent for the personnel) it was
literally a question of life and death. And four of the camels
lay there before us in a state of complete collapse. Nothing
but water would revive them for further marching, and there
was no water to spare if all claims had to be considered.

Meanwhile the stream of visitors to my tent had enabled
me to devise a scheme which was at least feasible and accept-
able though not acclaimed with the enthusiasm demanded
by our parlous situation. The absentees, Zayid and 'Ali,
were to be encouraged to accompany the baggage back to
Naifa, while I insisted that Ibn Suwailim should go with my
party as guide for he alone knew the general direction and
conditions of the march before us well enough to act in such
a capacity, though even he had never traversed the desert
on any line southward of Faraja and Maqainama. Sa'dan
would, of course, go with me, for he both desired to do so
and was indispensable for my work, and that made a nucleus
of three, to which Salih adhered unconditionally, thus making
four. Farraj hedged, torn between fear and greed—and
never have I met an Arab so vacillating and uncertain in
temper—but eventually decided to throw in his lot with me.
Humaid would not be parted from Salih and that made six,
while Suwid, who had publicly denounced the scheme as
sheer madness, came to my tent alone and very mysteriously
to indicate by wordless signs that he too would be included

in my party, which was duly completed by the inclusion of Abu Ja'sha, the indispensable handy man. On my part I agreed readily enough to a reasonable amount of night-marching—a concession that I could scarcely refuse in the circumstances seeing that we should in any case have scarcely enough water to see us through to the end, for we should have to spare some for the weariest of the camels and leave the baggage-party with sufficient to bring them to Naifa.

As the hours passed by with no sign of Zayid and 'Ali we agreed that the desert party should make a start with the first appearance of the moon, due sometime after midnight, as there was clearly no time to be lost. The interval was spent in making the necessary dispositions to give effect to our plans. The available food supplies were divided up and the camels destined for our party selected. In due course everything was ready and I had just completed my star observations when we heard afar off the grunts and chatter that portended the unwelcome return of Zayid and his companions.

As I had anticipated with dread, all our carefully worked out plans collapsed with Zayid's arrival in camp. He was quite naturally furious that any plans should have been concerted in his absence, and neither he nor 'Ali was inclined to be communicative on the subject of the day's hunting, which had at any rate provided no venison. They left it to be understood that they had toiled all day in search of their lost camels and they had a colourable grievance in our decision to relegate them unconsulted to the returning baggage-party. From the first moment Zayid declared himself against our scheme. After the inevitable cup of coffee which enabled him rapidly to take stock of the situation, as I could gather from the privacy of my own tent by the voluble protests made in the other, he came over to discuss matters with me. He was charming as could be and honey-tongued in his protestations of devoted service. Look you, he said, I cannot desert you thus ; I will come with you myself, for my face would be blackened for ever if I left you now to your fate. The way is far and there is not sufficient water and the camels are dead. We will, however, do what you wish. We will perish with you. We will take the best camels and all the water that can be spared and what matter ? We will put our trust in God. If God so wills, we will reach Sulaiyil alive, but blame not us if we all die of thirst in the desert. You saw to-day how many of the animals broke down. They cannot march without pastures to fill their bellies. There are but two or three of them that are fit for the journey. Why, even my mount and 'Ali's are more dead than alive. But whatever you wish we will do. I have done my duty in warning you of the danger we shall be running, but the ordering is yours.

The advent of Zayid had clearly changed the situation. He could make or mar our enterprise, and I could not trust him to make arrangements that would give us a sporting chance of success. I felt that I had lost my throw with Fate, and I turned to the only alternative—a faint hope of ultimate success to weigh in the balance against the certain failure of the plans we had made so hopefully. Look you, Zayid, I said, your coming has spoiled my plans and you have turned my companions against me. Either let me go with my men and the camels we have chosen or give me your word of honour here and now. If I agree to go back to Naifa now with all our party intact will you give me your word of honour that, when we have rested and refreshed our camels, you will ride with me again across the Empty Quarter, even to Sulaiyil, as you gave me your word to do at Shanna ? That was part of your charge from Ibn Jiluwi, and I warn you that Ibn Sa'ud himself will be wroth with you and the rest of them if you fail in this matter. I cannot go back except across the Empty Quarter. I give you my word of honour to that, oh Shaikh Abdullah, he replied blandly, and the matter is of God's will. For a moment I wrestled with myself and saw that there was no reasonable alternative to putting my trust in any sense of decency that remained in him. The men were all so obsessed with fear of Zayid that they could do nothing on their own initiative. Salih and Farraj, who had solemnly given me their hands in token of loyalty to the afternoon's bargain, cut but sorry figures in their sudden and complete collapse. And in the few moments that remained before a final decision was reached I listened to a loud altercation proceeding in the rival camp. He cannot go, I heard, without a guide ; so let Ibn Suwailim tell him straight out that he will not accompany him. Rise Salim and tell him that we may get back to the watering without delay. And a moment later Ibn Suwailim was led into my tent by Suwid, repeated his lesson like a child and went his way.

Thus it was finally agreed that we should all return together to Naifa and that the baggage-train should start off as soon as the moon had risen. Of the whole nineteen of us, I alone was unhappy that evening, while the rest set about their remaining tasks with a good will worthier of a better cause than ignominious retreat. The Empty Quarter had routed us. We had come about 140 miles—a five days' journey—into its inhospitable, drought-stricken wastes, and now we were to flee from its terrors. We were at least 140 miles from the nearest water and by the time we reached Naifa our camels would have done some 280 miles of the waterless desert unavailingly. They would have gone nine or ten days without water, and most of that time through pastureless lands. But our decision to turn back enabled us to devote four or five skins of our precious water to the relief of the seven or eight animals most seriously affected by the day's agony. In fact the decision to turn back was celebrated in our camp by what sounded to me in the darkness as a veritable orgy of water-wasting. The camels sucked the precious liquid from the leather tubs into their aching bellies, while some few, which had not reached the end of their tether, were subjected to the process of ' snuffing.' [1] This is an economical method of refreshing camels by administering a kettleful of water through the nostrils to cool the head and brain. The silly beasts struggle violently under such treatment, which is presumably painful enough at the time, but there would seem to be no doubt about its efficacy for the purpose in view, and I was to observe the process frequently enough during the fortnight that now remained of our wanderings in the Empty Quarter.

[1] *Nashuk, yatanashshakun.*

The men, too, were duly catered for. A large cauldron of rice was set to boil on the camp-fire and at midnight I was summoned to partake of the feast. I was however too weary of spirit and body to worry about food and remained in bed, while my fellows apparently enjoyed their first square meal since our departure from Shanna. I was still on my régime of tea at suitable intervals—generally thrice but sometimes only twice a day—and I had tasted no water since leaving Hufuf 51 days before, though a small supply of camel's milk, growing less day by day as the pastureless deserts shrank the udders of our milch-animals, served to vary my diet and lend me strength. All through I had certainly suffered less from thirst than my companions, who drank copiously whenever they had water in plenty to drink and thus, like foolish virgins, tended more and more to need liquid refreshment as the available supply grew daily less. These experiences convinced me that moderation in drinking is the best antidote to thirst in desert conditions, and it may be that tea has virtue quite out of proportion to the amount consumed. My companions seldom indulged in it and then spoiled it with sugar and milk.

It was in utter weariness that I lay down to sleep that night, and sleep came not as I revolved the disastrous experiences of the day and wondered what of good or evil the days to come had in store for me. Soon after the midnight rice-feast the baggage-train moved off into the darkness with a half-moon to light the way. The great retreat had begun, and peace descended upon the desert which had vanquished us. The struggle had been great and grim, but the suspense was over. And at last sleep blotted out the nightmare of the day, the worst day of the whole journey from beginning to end and perhaps the most terrible of all my experience. Yet good cometh out of evil, and so indeed it was to prove in the end. It is but rarely that one can look back on failure with such satisfaction.

CHAPTER II

RETREAT

Nor Muslims' land nor land of infidels—the Empty Quarter!
—'ABDUL RAHMAN.

THE call to prayer roused us before dawn to the day's work. The night had been chilly as we lay in the open, having sent the tents ahead, and we warmed ourselves round the fire sipping coffee. Our supply of dates was all but exhausted and little remained of them but the two skins which had been provided for my personal use by Ibn Jiluwi and which I had rigorously refused to broach, placing them under the special charge of Sa'dan to be used only in some extremity. The public store had been scandalously squandered without thought for the morrow, and even the camels had been surreptitiously fed on dates to make up for poor pastures. We had indeed been using up our stores at the rate of double rations each day and now we had to depend on rice alone, which involved a daily expenditure of water on which we had not reckoned. Ibn Suwailim optimistically estimated that we might reach Naifa in three days, while I protested that we should ration ourselves on the assumption of a five days' march. But the optimists triumphed, and the dawn of the fourth day saw the last of our water consumed. A vigorous forced march brought us to Naifa at midnight that day, but many of them had leisure to repent their lack of foresight during the blazing march of that afternoon.

Soon after 6 a.m. we started off eastward (or slightly north of east) along the trough of the fourth Hawaya valley, a great channel about 500 or 600 yards in width and running between parallel ridges which became dune-massifs as we advanced and finally culminated in a great moraine of rounded hillocks at the eastern extremity of the depression. Hitherto we had merely crossed these valleys from side to side and saw them extending into the distance on either hand. It was interesting therefore to follow one of them down its course, and our generally eastward march gave us many opportunities of repeating the experience during the next few days, as the line of least resistance coincided roughly with our desired direction. Such valleys vary a good deal in length, perhaps from three to eight miles, and our plan was generally to march up their centre and cross the moraine tracts in which they ended to the next, and so forth. Here and there we passed by patches of the underlying desert surface swept bare by the wind and covered with light grit.

Every now and then the sands told the tale of some animal of the baggage-train fallen by the way or couched to have its load readjusted. And in one spot we gleaned a harvest of onions which had fallen unobserved. We divided them among us and ate them with relish for we were famished. I had spurned the proffered feast of the previous evening and had had nothing but dates for six days, with a strictly limited ration of sweet biscuits, which had been my only luxury during the whole journey (to be eaten with my tea). I was weak with hunger and weary in spirit. To some extent perhaps my long abstention from water had something to do with the state of feebleness, which only now, in these early moments of desponding, I recognised with some feeling of alarm. Doubtless also the long days of strenuous exertion on a meatless diet accounted for part of my weakness, and it seemed unlikely enough that any meat would be forthcoming, for even the hares seemed to have abandoned the droughty waste and we had seen none for several days. There was nothing to do but struggle on, and I rode aloof from my companions, silently, rejecting the solace of their society and chatter to mark the disappointment that lay as a gulf between us. Everything, I felt, depended on leaving them to ponder the probable consequences of a final failure with the knowledge that my ultimate approbation and bounty could only be secured by acquiescence in my objective. That had now become an obsession—the crossing of the waterless waste— as the exploration of the Great South Desert in general had been for the past fourteen years. I had developed a curiously impersonal attitude towards myself and my surroundings. My brain and soul were in conflict with each other in a setting altogether unique. Why quarrel with companions in adversity who in the endeavour to save themselves alive were but holding me back from senseless disaster ? Why not agree with them to shirk the struggle with hostile Fate and return home in peace and goodwill ? But why live ? replied my soul ; we had done much already of what I had yearned to do all these years, but it was not enough. This yet remained to do—the virgin wilderness never crossed by man, perhaps uncrossable. To shrink from that now on the very threshold was unthinkable. Everything must be risked on that great throw. 'Tis only thus that the great victories are won, and what of nineteen lives in comparison with the thousands sacrificed by every general that history has honoured ? My brain saw clearly enough the logic of my companions in their perversity, while my soul recked of nothing but the goal. Twice had my companions triumphed over me, at Shanna and amid the sands of Hawaya. The third round would settle things once and for all, and my will must bend them to submission. I had to reckon with Zayid alone, the evil genius of our party, the devil incarnate as he seemed to me those days, who dominated the rest in a manner altogether astonishing. He was not loved but feared.

Thus along the valleys and up over the tumbled moraines we marched hour after hour. Our camels, now turned towards water and salvation, dragged along wearily but gamely. In the valleys we seemed to be ascending steadily, and at the end of our first day's march the aneroid showed that we had risen nearly 200 feet. Our milch-camels had gone on overnight with the baggage and I had not had my usual ration of morning milk, while the thin stuff of the night before showed how the animals were suffering from the drought.

A small pair of Oryx horns was found on the sands as we passed and a couple of butterflies (*Spindasis*) flitted by in the sunlight, while at one spot we saw three ravens together. Otherwise there was no life in the desert and nothing to

attract attention but the occasional patches of rock exposed by
the wind. A light southerly breeze blew most of the morning,
obliterating the tracks of the advance-party, whose halting
place for the dawn prayer we had observed earlier in our
progress. They had apparently taken four hours or more to
cover a distance we had negotiated in less than two. It was
clear that they were labouring under the loads. We went
by a tract in which the ridges were ranged one behind
another in sweeping semi-circular ribs, like the seats of a
theatre, grouped about the end of the valley.

On resuming after our morning refreshments in a gently
undulating upland with a fair amount of *Abal,* on which
the camels browsed the while, we passed from the *Hadh*
tract into the *Qasba* with its characteristic stubble of dry
grass and lofty dunes dotted with *Abal.* It was a long
weary pull up to its tumbled plateau of bare but shapely
knolls, to the right of which lay the trough of a valley
whose numerous bare patches, spread over a length of two
miles, gave one the impression of a continuous river-bed. The
south wind gathered strength and the marching conditions
were pleasant enough. A short halt was called as we descended into the valley, skirting one of its bare patches, for
my companions to have a drink of water, for the scarcity had
made the whole available supply communal property to be
shared out, like and like, with solemn formality. The
thirsting camels craned round their long necks to nose the
bowls of the precious liquid, but there was none for them.

We passed by an ancient raven's nest in an *Abal* thicket.
Sheets of sand swept over the desert's face under the strength-
ening wind, which had become a little tiresome, and smoke-
like streamers blew from every dune-top. We had by now
lost all trace of the route followed by the baggage-party
though we knew that they could not be far ahead. Yet we
saw no sign of them. The explanation was soon forthcoming.
Afar off in the rear we saw a man running apparently in pursuit of us and, as he drew near, we recognised 'Ali Jahman.
He had seen us passing and the baggage-train was away to
our left and behind. So we halted to let it come up and I was
weary enough, both physically and spiritually, to be glad of

so early a break in the day's march. The wind dropped a little during the afternoon and had veered slightly round to the south-east. It remained cool, and the day had produced a welcome miracle. It was not till 5 p.m. (we had halted at 2) that the baggage-animals trailed into camp slowly, drearily, and wearily. Four or five of them had collapsed during the day, and the men in attendance had been kept busy adjusting and readjusting loads to relieve the worst cases. Some of them had been ' snuffed ' to keep them going, and one of them had given birth to a premature calf which had been slaughtered at once. The meat was triumphantly brought in dangling from the flanks of various beasts of the party, but the mother had been allowed a respite from carrying a load. I bring you good news of fat, 'Ali had said as he came up. And perhaps now, I suggested, we shall have more milk for we have had little of late. No, he replied, the old cow will yield no milk till she has drunk her fill of water. As a matter of fact she never gave a drop—the strain had been too great for her. I was just about dead-beat at this time and sat listlessly among my companions round the fire while they cooked the tender meat in the ashes. I was as ready as any of them for the welcome nourishment and took my share in every round of the good things that came, hot and fresh, from the fire. That seemed to put fresh life into me and I went back to my tent with a strange sense of well-being. A pot of tea completed the good work, and Zaid cooked a small dish of rice for Sa'dan and me.

Zayid came to me during the evening to press for some night-marching. The camels were in a bad way and our water supply was dangerously low, while we had only covered some 20 miles on the first day. We had far to go and we must cover the ground more rapidly to avoid disaster. I was in a comfortable mood for negotiations after long privations and in a fairly strong position to turn things to my advantage. They could not force me to march by night and I claimed but little of the available water. I could at least demand that they should be as abstemious as myself and I knew that that would trouble them. Look you, Zayid, I said frankly, it is you that

s

have baulked me at every turn. The rest of our companions fear you and would gladly follow me but for such fear. It is you alone that can help me in my plans ; the rest are utterly useless. Will you do as I wish if I do as you wish in this matter of night-marching ? You have given me your word that we shall go up again from Naifa into the desert when we are rested. Will you assure me again now that that is indeed your intention ? If so I will march as may be necessary by night that we may get to Naifa the quicker. The strong one is God, he replied with all his native glibness, and if it be of God's will we shall go up again as I have promised you. We will send the baggage back by the easy way, and a few of us with as much water as possible will accompany you across the desert. So we patched up a truce in our long fight, and it was agreed that the transport should set out at midnight while the rest of us would start three hours later. On that basis preparations were now made and the baggage went off with the usual fuss and clatter while we slept on till 3.30 a.m., when for the first time since starting out on our expedition we marched by moonlight. I could console myself with the reflection that I already had a sufficiently good idea of the country in these parts. An hour or two of marching in the dark would be immaterial and a pleasant experience in itself. Our general direction was slightly north of east with Altair and Deneb as our guides, while the moon gave enough light to show the general lie of the ridges and valleys and the Southern Cross accompanied us on the right hand. But all the advantage of our propititious start was dissipated when we halted for the dawn prayer at 5 a.m. and my companions —eight of them rode with me—insisted on brewing coffee, for which they were ever faint after three or four hours of marching. That seemed to me wretched backsliding in the circumstances but I refrained from comment or criticism, having adopted the attitude that the ordering of all our movements should rest with Zayid alone. On the first day of our march Farraj had reined back to ride with me. You know, he said, that I at least would have gone forward with you if you had decided to continue the march to Sulaiyil. I am indeed ever at your service, and sustenance is from God.

It is too late to talk like that now, I replied, you and Salih had a chance last night to show that you were men. But you failed me and now everything is in the hands of Zayid. If I want any help or service I shall henceforth seek it of him. Salih had wisely kept aloof from me, while 'Ali, thoroughly disgruntled by the events of the night at the Hawaya camp, elected to march for the first two days with the baggage. Ibn Humaiyid was an adequate, if uncommunicative and uninspiring, guide for the nonce, and I was glad enough to be quit of 'Ali, who had played me false and was scarcely likely to be of further practical use to me. I had indeed registered a determination that he and Farraj should not be of the desert party when we should set out from Naifa. It was pleasent enough sitting round the fire in the morning chill with coffee and sweetened milk (from Humaid's mount) to cheer ourselves withal. A gentle breeze blew from the south-east as we resumed the march over the undulating upland with occasional transverse ridges, behind which the stars which had directed our course vanished one by one into the growing pool of daylight. The sun itself appeared above the horizon about 6 a.m. and the real day's work had begun with ourselves only about five miles to the good.

As we passed soon afterwards into Khillat Hawaya the country resembled a storm-tossed sea, with the axis of the sand breakers lying NE. and SW. Here we saw the fairly fresh tracks and night lodging of a pair of Oryx, and I observed that there was greater abundance of vegetation, with the inevitable *Abal* most in evidence and some *Alqa* here and there—a favourite herb of camels and Oryx. Patches of blue-grey rock varied the monotony of the sands, on which I found embedded the fragments of an egg of some small bird, possibly the Desert Lark, which we saw two or three times during the day. We saw by their traces that the baggage people had halted for the dawn prayer only ten miles from their starting point—a poor result for some five hours marching. But the camels were played out. To-day was the seventh day out from the last serious watering, and practically nowhere in all that time had we found sufficient green food to correct the natural consequences of such abstinence.

In such circumstances flatulence is a common and dangerous malady among camels, to cure which the Arabs resort to a curious device. They sew up the anal orifice or plaster it over with a dough of camel-dung, and then tie down the tail, fastening it to the saddle with a cord passed under its belly and between the legs, so as to prevent the emission of wind. Sha'la, the camel which had been confined the previous day, had been treated thus during the night and looked comically uncomfortable enough in all conscience, but my companions had no doubt that she would not have been able to march at all without such attention.

The cool south wind of the morning gradually freshened to a steady, strong blow and the sand drifted over the landscape in sheets, entirely obliterating the route of the advance-party. They had however taken warning from the experience from the previous day and had set up beacons of *Abal* branches on the dune-tops at intervals along their path. The glare from the sand was rather trying during this march and it seemed to me that the whole country around us was in movement attuned to the wind. It is long indeed, said the homesick townsman 'Abdul Rahman, since we saw a real mist. For weeks and months we have seen nought but this blowing sand. No country is this of the *Muslimin*, nor yet the country of the infidel—just the Empty Quarter !

Shortly before halting for our pre-noon break we had passed by a group of three exposed rock-patches on our left hand, one of which was depressed in the centre to a small crater-like hollow, half filled with sand. It was possibly an ancient well, long buried and forgotten, but we did not stop to investigate it closely and merely contented ourselves with giving it a name—Bir Hawaya—to commemorate our conjecture regarding it. The *Abal* bushes about our camping place seemed to be full of caterpillars, and later on I caught a dragonfly, but still the general aspect of the country was bare and dreary. We continued our march over a wide gently rolling plain with scattered dunes of some height and occasional low ridges. Afar off we caught sight of our baggage-camels ahead though it was barely noon. They were obviously labouring and a little later we saw them halted while preparations were being made to pitch the tents. On coming up with them we found no fewer than seven of the animals sheltering under canvas against the sun. Many a collapse there had been by the way, and matters looked none too cheerful with only a third of the whole journey behind us and our water seriously reduced. But we could not expect miracles of the heavily laden animals in such conditions, and it would be merely courting disaster to send them out again to march in the heat of the afternoon. At the same time they had to get on by hook or by crook, or perish in the wilderness. We accordingly agreed that the only thing to do now was to divide up into two sections and let the baggage-party march all night and as far into the day as possible in an effort to get to Naifa as soon as it could. The other section, reduced to six persons including myself for there were only six camels considered perfectly capable of bearing the strain involved, would continue the former routine of a short march before dawn followed by continuous marching till near sunset. 'Ali, now recovered from his sulks, volunteered to accompany us as guide—perhaps in order to retain his mount, which was the best of the whole company; Zayid remained faithful to me, and Salih and Humaid completed the little party with Sa'dan. Everything was thus satisfactorily arranged and I went off late in the afternoon to explore the valley in which we were encamped. At no great distance I came upon a series of exposed calcareous cliffs, about 15 feet high, lying up against and half buried by the lofty sand ridge forming one side of the valley. A number of the familiar little spiral shells was all that rewarded a diligent search of the bare ground at the base of the cliffs, from which I collected an assortment of rock samples. The short walk had almost exhausted me and I wondered vaguely whether I could get back to camp. I was once more desperately hungry—my whole body seemed to be clamouring for food but I knew that a good meal of rice was preparing against my return to give the new arrangements a good start. I made no attempt to respond to the call to prayer at sunset and sprawled weakly on the sand devouring a couple of raw onions, which I now generally carried in my pocket with a few peppermint tablets against such a

contingency. I then crawled slowly back to camp, where the
whole party assembled round a substantial mess of rice, from
which I was literally the last to rise. Unfortunately Sa'dan
had without any previous warning announced during the day
that my supply of tea was exhausted. I had told him to keep
the leaves of my last pot for a second brew and it was weak
stuff that I had to put up with that evening after dinner. The
same leaves were used for a third brew before I retired to
sleep, leaving something in the pot to drink cold—and it was
deliciously cold— before starting on our march in the early
hours of the morrow. And yet again those leaves served for
our common refreshment after the dawn prayer, boiled up
with water and milk (again from Humaid's camel for my cow,
now almost dry, had been sent on with the baggage) and
sweetened with sugar and cardamum to suit the taste of the
majority. I had, it is true, a small private supply of tea for
emergencies, but this I was saving for the hoped-for final
attempt on the waterless desert. So for the next few days I
was without the comfort of tea, while our daily supply of
milk was almost negligible. I came to the conclusion that at
Naifa it would be well to make a virtue of necessity and
abandon my waterless régime, which could be resumed on our
departure thence for Sulaiyil.

Meanwhile we had sped the baggage-train on its weary
way through the darkness at 7.45 p.m. hoping that we
would not see it again until we ourselves reached Naifa.
The night proved unusually prolific of moths, mostly of
one species of Noctuid,[1] whose larval food plant is presumably the *Abal*, now in full bloom with its dull red tassels
and little white edible flowers. Of the latter, mixed with
rice, the Manasir made me a dish of *Makika*, which they recom-
mend one not to eat with meat, which it is liable to harden
to the consistency of leather. From time to time in the
extremity of my hunger I browsed on the raw flowers as we
marched along and I was to discover in due course that the
dry twigs of this plant, slightly crushed in a mortar and mixed
with hot water, made a fairly satisfactory substitute for tea.
Its colour was all that could be desired but the liquid was

[1] Apparently a new species.

somewhat bitter to the taste and constipating in its effect—
an antidote, as I was to learn, to the powerful salts of the
Naifa water. The green sprouts of the *Abal* are pounded up
by the Badawin women to make a dye, and its dry wood is by
far the best fuel of the desert—altogether a beneficent plant,
and as widespread as beneficent. In Najd they call it *Arta*
and seem to ignore most of its possible uses.

At 3 a.m., after an all too short but refreshing sleep, we
were on the move again, steering half-way between Altair and
Vega ; but we had not been going two hours when they began
clamouring for a halt. The dawn will soon be upon us,
they said ; it is time to pray, by which they meant it was time
to think of coffee ! The fire was soon ready and the water
aboil, while I lay stretched on the sand and slept blissfully till
they roused me for the prayer. Then we sat round for the
sorry but welcome thimblefuls of milk and coffee that fell to
our lot. And soon we were again in the saddle to ride into the
dawn—a pinkish flush slowly widening in the sky to our right
front until the sun's golden orb flooded the vast ocean of
rolling dunes with the light of day. A pair of larks piped
to each other in the cool, still air of the morning—the
notes of the sexes being, as I thought, very different—and a
raven sailed past us presumably to prospect for food at our
last halting-place.

We passed by a lofty dune of peculiarly beautiful lines and
curves, but were taken aback to find that the advance-party
had halted for the dawn prayer only a little way beyond it.
We had come but twelve miles or so from our night camp and
it was difficult to believe that the baggage-train had made no
better progress than that in the nine hours that had elapsed
between their starting and the time for prayers. Yet there
was no mistaking their traces—the spot where they had
lighted a fire for their coffee and the line formed in the sand
by their prostrations. They had probably had trouble in the
darkness and gone astray, but the simple fact remained that
they had made little progress and there could be little doubt
that we would after all catch them up again.

To our right and converging towards our front lay the
tract known as Hadhat al Qata. At intervals a group of

Hadh bushes showed that we were marching on the frontier
line between it and the Khillat, in which for the most part we
remained till the very end of the day's long march. A line of
green *Andab* grass announced our re-entry into regions which
had had rain during the last year or two. The undulating
plain gave way shortly to the typical long parallel dune-
ranges of the *Sawahib* formation, which extends unbroken
from here, as they declared, to distant Muqshin in the southeastern sands. We ploughed steadily on over the eternal
switchback of ridges and valleys, slanting across the latter
and following the former until we found suitable spots at
which to cross them. The wind had sprung up from the
south-west, pleasant enough at first though growing warmer
rapidly, and I noticed that the sand trails in the lea of the
desert bushes now pointed to the north or north-west—auto-
matic recorders of the prevailing winds of a district over a
period of days.

At 10.30, having marched five hours since our last refreshment, we halted for coffee—and they had made also a substitute tea of cardamum and sugar. So far this day we had had
nothing whatever to eat except a few raw onions, but we had
not far to go as it proved for our next meal. Starting off over
an upland of high rolling downs and ridges, we continued over
a regular switchback of gentle undulations until, towards 1
p.m., we crossed a steepish ridge to find the hollow below us
occupied by our advance-party in camp. The last part of the
march had been blazing hot and we rejoiced at a sight which
was also somewhat disconcerting. Again a number of the
camels were sheltering against the sun under canvas and our
own animals, as we came up, made a wild dash for the same
cover, trying to enter the tents—rider and all. We had much
ado to couch them in the open to off-saddle, and I had to
share my tent with three camels and some of my men.
However Zaid was already well on with his preparations for a
meal, and in due course we composed ourselves for an afternoon siesta after a substantial and satisfying dinner of plain
rice. The camels looked unutterably miserable and were
indeed utterly exhausted, though happily unconscious of the
supreme effort which they would shortly be called upon to

make. A butterfly tempted me out into the open but I soon
returned to shelter, and slumbered until the call to prayer
roused the camp to action. Shortly before 5 p.m. we loaded
up and marched off—once more an united company. The
country was much as before though the hollow dunes faced
north instead of south-east. An hour later the sun sank below
the horizon behind us and we halted to pray. In the gloaming we marched again, over the same scenery of long ridges
separated by wide valleys, with Jupiter to mark our general
direction. Zayid rode stripped to the waist to enjoy the
coolth and we marched for an hour and a half to the edge of
Khillat Adraj, whence the baggage-train went straight on
while my small party of six halted for a night's rest. We had
made good use of February's extra day, having covered more
than 30 miles, but something like 50 more, so far as we could
judge, still remained while our water was all but exhausted.
I lay down to rest without thought of anything else and was
soon fast asleep. My companions made coffee and milk but
did not wake me, so I remained supperless and it was 2.30
a.m. when I was roused for the long march before us. It was a
delicious night, cool and windless, and the waning moon was
just above the horizon.

Two hours later we halted for prayers within the borders of
Hadh 'Ain Sala, and there we used up the very last of our
water in a final effort to brew courage and endurance. The
carefully hoarded tea-leaves of yesterday were produced by
Sa'dan and worked up with water and milk for the fifth time.
Coffee was of course indispensable and with the little that
remained of the water, after these primary calls on it had
been satisfied, Salih sat apart at a second fire and cooked us a
modest breakfast of rice liberally buttered from the leather
jug he carried at his saddle-bow. That certainly filled me with
cheerful strength and once more we started, Salih taking advantage of his successful and much appreciated cooking to in-
gratiate himself with me once more. Did you like that rice ?
he asked ; I cooked it for your sake and for the sake of the
Amir (i.e. Zayid). I seek ever to serve you both. I admitted
that I had enjoyed my meal, perhaps rather grudgingly, for I
have never been able to appreciate and never encourage this

curious Arab weakness for vaunting an obsequious desire to
please. Another national characteristic, somewhat akin to
this, is the constant anxiety to be the announcer of good or
pleasing news—in the hope of reward. It is less objection-
able, of course, and has an intelligible basis of origin, but it
has a tendency in Arabia to discourage the purveying of true
news which is more important and to encourage exaggeration
or even suppression of material facts. But the East in general
has no squeamishness about working for rewards. What else
indeed should one work for ? The philosophy of Arabia is
definitely materialistic both in its metaphysics and its ethics.

Two and a half hours later, after passing across a valley
with considerable profusion of *Hadh* and *Alqa*, we re-entered
Khillat Adraj, and I realised that practically ever since leaving camp in the morning we had roughly been following (now
on this side and now on that) the line of demarcation between
the tracts of Hadh 'Ain Sala and Khillat Adraj. Good news
for you, of fat, shouted Salih riding up to us from the rear
where he had been lagging behind with 'Ali Jahman. I
thought they might have caught a hare lying asleep in a bush,
for we had heard no shot, but it was nothing as commonplace
as that. 'Ali's camel had shown signs of premature confinement under the strain of such marching, and the interesting
event was expected at any moment. It was, to say the least,
inconsiderate of the beast to choose a time when every
minute counted towards salvation. A halt was called in the
interests of the expectant mother and Salih gathered sticks
for a fire in exultant expectation of the meat which would
soon be cooking in its ashes. I went off in search of insects
while Zayid composed himself to sleep under a bush and 'Ali
and Humaid girt up their loins for the midwifery. The camel
gazed about her miserably as if not quite knowing what was
wrong. The midwives made several fruitless attempts to
hasten the delivery, but each time the half-protruding head
withdrew into the womb. The mother alternately stood or
lay on her side in apparent pain until at last 'Ali secured a
good purchase on the head as it looked out pathetically on the
strange world of sun and sand. He then began to pull amain
and the recumbent mother lashed out viciously at each tug

on her vitals, 'Ali and Humaid performing acrobatic feats the while to avoid her kicks without letting go their hold of the infant. Finally it came away in their hands with a great gush of liquid as the mother again lashed out with a final agonised kick, snarling the while and at once laying her long neck on the ground with a sigh of weariness and relief. The midwives had nearly fallen over in their effort to get clear of her, while after a few moments she rose to her feet and went off to browse on the *Abal* bushes as if nothing had happened. The calf meanwhile looked more dead than alive after such treatment and we crowded round to hear the verdict, for that which is born dead is not lawful meat. For a moment we stood in suspense over the inert mass, but soon the limbs made a feeble movement and the body was convulsed with a breath that was half sigh. It lived and the knife was put to the base of the throat. The warm, red blood gushed forth and it lived no more. By their reckoning it was a calf of nine or ten months but in every respect it seemed to be perfectly formed, though with the birth moisture still upon the skin it looked very naked with little hair except on its head and forelegs. The rest of the body was covered very lightly with a soft down, almost invisible until the skin dried.

My companions immediately set to work skinning and carving up the carcase into convenient joints. The share of our absent companions was meticulously set apart to be conveyed to Naifa, and a portion similarly preserved for the evening meal. The rest was cut up into suitable fragments and thrown upon the embers of the fire, whence after a perfunctory roasting they were withdrawn to be eaten. In ordinary circumstances I do not think I could have brought myself to partake of such a meal, but our immediate circumstances were far from ordinary and I could have eaten anything, cooked or raw. At any rate I did my share of the eating and very delicious it was.

The whole affair had only delayed us an hour and a quarter, and we went on our way rejoicing. The unfortunate mother was granted a respite from carrying a rider, while 'Ali rode pillion behind Humaid. To prevent flatulence and its consequences her tail was tied down in the manner already described, the after-birth protruding from it sideways until in due course it came or was pulled away. The vegetation was distinctly more copious than any we had seen for many days and was more abundant on the Hadh 'Ain Sala side of the dividing line, into which we passed again soon after resuming our march. Here we found fresh *Andab* and *Alqa* in some profusion besides *Hadh* and *Abal*, and our camels nibbled at them as they went though very gingerly it seemed, for they were now so distraught with thirst that they could scarcely eat anything except during the cool hours of the night. They just dragged along as our men urged them forward over a vast gently rolling light-brown plain extending into the far distance on our left, while our view to the southward was cut short by a range of lofty dunes, along whose north side our course lay.

A lark piped to us out of the blazing sky, following the sound to earth with a stone-like dive. And I thought as we went that the *Hadh* in its fresh green garb of springtime was by far the prettiest of all the desert plants of its kind. Its colour is a charming greyish green and its sprouts are studded with rings of inoffensive spines. What a difference a little food makes to man! 24 hours earlier I had felt very faint and feeble with hunger, but now the world was all smiling and cheerful, and for an hour or two of the march I was chewing a tender grisly bone of the infant camel to keep fresh the memory of that blessed meal.

Far away to the right at the northern extremity of Hadhat al Qata lay a group of four or five dune-ranges to which they gave the name of Bani Fazran, and the country over which we marched was generally of the typical *Sawahib* type. At 2 p.m. I thought we had done a long enough bout of marching to justify a short halt to tide over the worst of the afternoon. 'Ali objected strongly. Look you, he said, I don't know this country at all well. By day I can find my way but, if we get benighted, I am lost. I cannot get you to the water in the dark. Nevertheless I insisted on a halt for I knew that he was lying. There was no water left for coffee and his one desire was to get to Naifa without delay for a dose of the gentle stimulant. During the two hours of our halt I dozed peacefully in the shade of an *Abal* bush overspread with my mantle.

At 4 p.m. or a little later, after prayers as usual, we resumed. There were some clouds in the west as there had also been for a short time during the night ; and there seemed to be an unwonted cooling of the air. I rode bareheaded to get the best of the light breeze that fanned us, while the feeble sun sank rapidly towards the edge of the world behind us. Every day in the great deserts one breathes a sigh of relief as he gets low enough in the sky to lose his strength and one can think contentedly of the twelve hours or more that lie ahead, of coolth and darkness, until he comes again. The nights are seldom anything but delightful, but this afternoon somehow seemed abnormal though we knew not then what it portended.

We halted for prayers at the crest of a great ridge as the sun sank in a blaze of gold and purple. Up to this point we had covered about 30 miles, and I should have been content to leave the remaining distance till the morning, but my now thirsting companions clamoured insistently to press on. I yielded to their pressure and we marched through the growing dusk along the broad valleys and over the steep ridges until we crossed the familiar range of 'Ain Sala about 7 p.m., the buried well by which we had camped before being at some distance to the north-east of this point. 'Ali, who was now riding Zayid's mount while the latter bestrode the so recently confined Na'riya, made no mistake in his guiding despite his earlier disclaimer and we pressed on. The strain was telling on my own camel and she began to lag till I wearied of urging her on. A change was suggested, and I rode a less elegant but faster animal which had hitherto carried the little baggage (instruments and the like) which I could not dispense with. That greatly improved our rate of progress, but it was a long cry from 'Ain Sala to Naifa and there was much arguing in the dark as to whether we had not strayed from the direct line. 'Ali led us straight into what looked like an impassable mountain barrier. Straight up its steep face he led us to its crest and I gasped at the thought of the perilous descent on the other side. But immediately below me gleamed our camp-fires in the snug hollow of

Naifa itself, and we had struck the summit of the ridge at the very point where a gently sloping corridor led down between two great buttresses towards the well. 'Ali had surpassed himself. He had a sense of the desert shared only by the very best of his own kind. It was something incredible, altogether inexplicable. I thought, said I to him, in the midst of my companions' paean of thanksgiving and congratulations, that you did not know your way in the dark. God guide you ! he replied, the camels could not have lived another night without water. He said nothing about coffee !

We trailed down into Naifa. It was well past 11 p.m. and we had done 45 miles during the day, a magnificent performance for camels on the ninth day without water and for men exhausted by hunger. The sky had suddenly clouded over heavily to north and north-east, and frequent flashes of lightning told of a distant storm.

Have you any water there ? I called to Zaid as I passed his kitchen camp. Yes, indeed, he replied, and here it is, cold as snow. May it refresh you ! In a trice I was off my camel and holding the grateful bowl to my lips—the first water I had tasted in 55 days. I drank slowly and with relish till I had drained it to the last drop. And then I filled again and drank. And yet once more—a third bowl. Only then was I satisfied, and never in all my life have I tasted such nectar. Yet it was the water of Naifa, foul, briny stuff with all the properties of the salts called Epsom or something stronger. I had broken my long self-imposed rule of abstinence from water, and I felt amazingly refreshed by the experience. Zaid had lost no time since the arrival of the baggage-train about an hour after sunset, and we soon sat down to a stupendous dish of rice. The camels were watered at once, and I spread my bedding in the open for a well-earned rest. The great retreat had been successfully accomplished without any casualties. We only needed time to recuperate and reorganise our forces before facing the final bout of our great tussle with the desert.

CHAPTER III

RECUPERATION

'Tis well with thee if thy steed be well, but faints the rider of
fainting beast—FARRAJ AL 'ARQANI.

THE night was rough and stormy. The wind swept from
time to time in howling, violent gusts across my bed, covering
it with sand. But I slept soundly enough till nearly 5 a.m.,
when I was woken by a gentle patter of rain-drops, which
lasted for about fifteen minutes. I lay on my back open-
mouthed to catch the drops, and relapsed into slumber to be
woken again by the call to prayer. At 8 a.m. we had a sharp
but short shower, and for the next hour there was an intermittent spitting of rain. The sky remained overcast but
there was no more rain that day, though about 10 a.m.
violent squalls swept down into the hollow from the north-
east, making things exceedingly uncomfortable for us and
uprooting our tents, which we made no attempt to pitch
again until the wind had abated somewhat. Later in the
afternoon, the sky remaining overclouded, the wind dropped
to a gentle north-east breeze with promise of more rain. It
was indeed a blessed day, that second of March. The Arabs
were as happy as sandboys and all day long paid visits to
the surrounding dune-tops, from which they shouted out to
us in the hollow the news of the weather around us. At first
the rain seemed to be for the most part in the north-east,
while later on it had transferred its attention to the south-
west, whence came occasional flashes of lightning and the
low growl of distant thunder. Only in the west and north-
west, which were of primary concern to me, there were no
signs of rain that day. I waited anxiously for some indication
of the general temper of my companions and asked no leading questions about conditions in the west. But I had one

uncomfortable moment when there was talk of Bir Fadhil.
I kept silence.

Our first concern after the dawn prayers had been inevitably for the camels, which had drunk but gingerly overnight in the extremity of their thirst. They were now again
led down to the well, where they had their fill. They
crowded greedily round the great metal tray, which served
them as drinking-trough as well as ourselves for dinner-table
and dish. The men had much ado to keep it full of water as
a dozen long necks jostled for the liquid and as many pairs
of lips sucked it up with manifest signs of satisfaction. The
sated beasts withdrew for a while but stood about the well,
returning every now and then to the trough for another
swig, and at last the last barrel had had its fill. The animals
scattered to browse on the *Abal* bushes in and about the
hollow while the herdsmen, 'Ali al Buhaihi and Muhaimid,
breakfasted and collected the rations necessary for their
sojourn of three days in the pastures beyond 'Ain Sala,
whither it had been decided to send the animals to recuperate from the fatigues and privations of their recent march
and to gather strength for the coming ordeal.

Meanwhile there was an important question for us all to
discuss and decide. We still had plenty of rice, but there
was nothing left of the dates except the two skins of my
private store, which I had uncompromisingly earmarked for
the party that was to cross the waterless desert. We could
take no rice on that journey as we should have no water for
its cooking, but dates alone would scarcely suffice us and the
baggage party could not be expected to do with nothing
but rice. Meat was an obviously desirable addition to our
diet and there were only two possible sources of supply.
Game we could no longer hope for after our recent experience
in the desert, but the slaughter of a camel would provide us
with flesh for many days, and we had agreed in principle
during the march that we might reasonably celebrate our
arrival at Naifa by the sacrifice of one of our animals to our
urgent need. The individual had already been selected, one
of the victims of our original breakdown—a beast with more
beef than stamina. And now had come the moment for

giving effect to our plan. After the watering of the camels I
suggested that the intended victim should be detached from
the rest of the herd now ready to go to the pastures. I
noticed however that there was a good deal of hesitancy
among my companions, who, one and all, desired the meat.
They awaited Zayid's approval, without which not one of them
would have stretched forth a hand against an animal of Ibn
Jiluwi. Had we not earlier at Wabar abandoned one of the
camels to almost certain death rather than slay it for the pot,
when lameness rendered it unfit to march with us ? Ibn
Jiluwi could have no reason to cavil at that, but he had been
known to visit with his heavy-handed wrath myrmidons
who had lessened the numbers of his stock to appease their
hunger on an expedition. Zayid would not pronounce the
fateful word and the matter hung in the balance. I exerted
all my influence to secure meat for the company and went
as far as to command Abu Ja'sha to do the deed. He hung
back regretfully and I had to argue the point out with
Zayid, whom I assured of my acceptance of full responsibility. His unwilling opposition slowly relaxed. Abu Ja'sha
sought out the intended victim and led her to the kitchen
camp, where her blood soon flowed out upon the sands.
There was much rejoicing in the camp. The skinning of the
beast was the work of a few moments, and a portion of the
meat was handed to the herdsmen to take away to the
pastures. The camels trailed off out of the Naifa hollow into
the desert, while the men left behind in camp concentrated
whole-heartedly on the various functions of butcher and cook.
I accepted a tit-bit rapidly roasted in the ashes of the fire,
but reserved my main energies for the meal which Zaid was
soon getting ready. My companions, however, spent most
of the morning cooking and eating choice portions. And Al
Aqfa, the *Saluqi* bitch which had starved with the rest of us
for nine days, during which she had had practically nothing
but date-stones, was not forgotten in the general good
fortune. She must have absolutely gorged herself with raw
meat for, when I saw her, she was making a pathetic effort
to drag herself towards a bowl of water only a few yards
distant. On reaching it she flopped down on the sand and

T

lazily, though contentedly, lapped at the liquid with an outstretched paw on either side of the receptacle to steady it. So twice a day, while we remained at Naifa, we feasted nobly on a great dish of camel-meat and rice, which did much to restore our wasted strength, while the harm that might have come of such indulgence was duly rectified by the Naifa water.

After my initial orgy of the previous night I had made up my mind to drink freely of this water during the days of our sojourn here—especially as there was no tea available—and to resume my waterless regimen as soon as we started off on the march across the desert. To this programme I adhered, and to it I probably owed the fact that, at my next weighing about three weeks after my return to Mecca, I turned the scale at a weight well above my normal. I had certainly lost no substance as the result of my ninety days in the desert, and by an accidental indulgence in an unsuspected ' cure ' I had triumphantly restored the health of earlier years which long residence in the Hijaz had shown signs of sapping. But these discoveries were for the future. At the moment I was conscious only of the unpleasant and exhausting aspect of the Naifa stuff, which was so salt to the taste that I successfully tried the experiment of adding a liberal quantity of Eno's fruit-salts to it at each potation (while my one and only bottle of Eno's lasted). That certainly had a sweetening effect, which was much appreciated by some of my companions, who also delighted in the fizzing of my strange sherbet. The Naifa water is a very powerful aperient of the Epsom salts type and its potency may be gauged from the fact that the leather skins in which we carried it across the desert were found to be badly corroded by the salts. Their effect on the tough camel-meat consumed by us must have been somewat similar, for the frequency of our exits into the privacy of the desert became a jest and unfailing source of merriment in the camp. How they all loathed and cursed the stuff and its inexorable effects ! I alone insisted on the hygienic advantages of our amazing situation. There are rich men, I said, in my country, who would willingly spend much of their wealth to be in our place, if they only knew of this water. And when the King asked me at Mecca whether we had found anything of practical significance in the desert I told him that at Naifa (and presumably in the whole tract of Al Khiran) he had all the makings of an attractive health-resort if he was minded to develop its possibilities. By a curious coincidence the very name Naifa is an exact palindrome of Afian, the usual Arabic form of the name of another famous source—Evian. A sample of the water was in due course analysed in the Research Laboratory of the Anglo-Persian Oil Company at Sunbury-on-Thames and was found to contain a high percentage of salts [1] in solution, to wit Chlorides and Sulphates of Sodium, Calcium and Magnesium. ' It is not surprising,' wrote Dr. G. M. Lees to me in this connection, ' that the water had the effect which you described. . . . I have looked up analyses of various European mineral waters, but there are none that correspond. It has too much chloride to be considered potable in this part of the world. It is like, say, Baden water with additional ordinary salt and less sulphate in proportion. Its origin is probably from rocks rich in gypsum and magnesium sulphate and salt.'

Having set apart the meat required for our more immediate needs, my companions did not neglect the requirements of the future. Previous experience had shown us that the salting of meat to preserve it was liable to create difficulties where abundance of water could not be counted on to slake the resultant thirst. It was accordingly agreed that the surplus meat of the slaughtered camel—and the quantity it provided was indeed astonishing—should be dry-cured in sun and wind without salt. The raw meat was accordingly carved in wide thin slices, which were spread out on every convenient *Abal* thicket for the drying. For a while the

---

[1] The details of the actual analysis, dated 6th August, 1932, are as follows :

Total solids dried at 110° C.		861 pts./100,000	
Calcium (Ca)	-	- 61·5	,,
Magnesium (Mg)	-	- 20·4	,,
Sodium (Na)	-	- 170	,,
Sulphate (SO4)	-	- 274	,,
Chloride (Cl2)	-	- 209	,,
Carbonate (CO3)	-	- 19	,,
Bicarbonate	-	- absent.	

stench in and around our camp was appalling, but our men were ever on the lookout to weed out the putrefying morsels from the stuff that was curing according to plan, and by the end of our sojourn there was a goodly mass of healthy-looking, well-dried strips of raw meat to be distributed among the two companies, into which we formed ourselves for our two different destinations. This raw dried meat presumably resembles biltong, which I have never seen or tasted, and the process is familiar enough to the hunters of Oryx and gazelles in the desert.

A pair of ravens took up their residence on the dunes of Naifa during our stay and hovered about the camp fondly eyeing the rich stores at our disposal, but without daring to approach near enough to do any thieving. They had good enough reason for their wariness for one of the birds had lost a leg to a bullet from Zayid's rifle on our previous visit to this locality. It seemed to be unaffected by its loss of a limb except that it was apparently unable to hop about like its companion. The only other tenant of the place besides ourselves was a Wheatear which during these days was a regular and persistent visitor to the well, whose water it presumably did not disdain. Its cheerful cheeping was a pleasant sound in my ears, especially in the peaceful silence of the early mornings. Our hunters prospected the desert in vain for hares though the two herdsmen reported having captured a brace while grazing the camels beyond 'Ain Sala.

Having disposed of the main preoccupations of the morning, including our first good meal, I decided to follow the example of my companions by having a bathe. Our dinner tray now served for a bath and Zaid, drawing up the water from the ten-feet depth of the well in the leather bucket, poured it over me time and again till I was satisfied. The water was pleasantly warm from the well—we generally left the luke-warm stuff to cool in the skins before drinking—and I thoroughly enjoyed the first proper bathe I had had since leaving the Hasa. I had moreover not indulged in a change of clothing all these weeks, wearing the same things night and day, till it now began to dawn on me from certain unmistakable and irritating indications that my body had become amenable to occupation by the companions of my companions and their camels. It was an interesting though somewhat disturbing thought and I decided precipitately on a complete change of raiment after my cleansing. A morbid curiosity led me to examine those parts of my discarded clothing which had been nearest my skin—and my conjecture as to the state of my body was confirmed by the discoveries I made. Thereafter I was more careful to avoid the risk of further visitations of those minute but not invisible beings whose very name is generally left unuttered.

Thus did our first day of rest draw to an end with all the omens favourable. The long tension of our recent trying march had made way for an atmosphere of contentment and goodwill. Our healthful bodies, subdued by long hunger, had reacted pleasantly enough to the influence of plentiful food and water. And I retired to bed early that night with a strange sense of well-being and optimism. For the first time in all the long course of our expedition the stars in their courses seemed to be fighting on my side, and I prayed that the stormy conditions might continue for some days more.

My prayer was promptly answered, for I was woken at 2 a.m. by the pleasant patter of rain on my canvas roof and for half an hour the showers continued. They ended with a short but heavy downpour, and I slumbered again while sheets of lightning lit up the great storm-clouds which seemed to be spread over the sky in every direction. At noon the temperature had been 84°, rising to 88° during the afternoon and falling to a minimum of as much as 70° during the night. The minimum night temperatures in the desert had been a good deal lower than this figure, ranging from 60° to 63° during the last few days.

Salih, seeking ever to please, made me some *Abal* tea after prayers next morning, and I found that it somewhat toned down the virulence of the water. At noon I enjoyed another bathe at the well, but the heat rapidly became very oppressive. I found it exceedingly painful to walk barefoot on the heated sand and by 3 p.m. the thermometer in my tent registered 97°. The storm conditions of the morning had given way to bright sunshine which blazed down mercilessly into our hollow, depressing everyone's spirits to such an extent that there again arose talk of beating a hasty retreat to the north. Sa'dan reported a suggestion that had been made by Zayid in conversation round the coffee-fire that I should be asked to give them a written guarantee of indemnity against the contingency of my perishing in the desert ! With such companions such a condition was clearly impossible of acceptance. But the matter was never actually raised in my presence and, when I sat at coffee with my companions after the afternoon prayer, I seized the opportunity of opening a discussion of our future plans.

You know, I said, that at the beginning of our journey we all contemplated finishing the expedition together so that we might reach Mecca in time for the pilgrimage. For those who are going with me across the desert to Sulaiyil there is still plenty of time to fulfil that arrangement, but we are agreed that the baggage-animals cannot march with us. I had hoped that they might go round by Bir Fadhil and Maqai-nama to rejoin us at Wadi Dawasir, but now the time is too short for that. I suggest therefore that the baggage-party should march straight to Riyadh, and I will despatch with them a letter to the Amir Sa'ud asking him to send those who want to do the pilgrimage by motor car to Mecca, while those who prefer to return straight to their families can go down to the Hasa with the camels.

I had already broached this idea with one or two of the men who happened to be at the well while I was bathing. They had approved it strongly and it was obvious that they had lost no time in communicating it to their fellows. At any rate I was astonished at the chorus of assent that greeted the scheme when I propounded it. Not a word was said about any written guarantee or other conditions for the desert journey, and I was able on the spot to take the names of those desiring to enroll themselves in the three parties envisaged by my proposal. Zayid and I had agreed that the desert party should consist of nine persons including myself, and the composition of this section presented no difficulty as I had firmly expressed my desire to exclude from it both 'Ali and Farraj. The two herdsmen being temporarily absent, there were only eight to be disposed of ; and of these only three wanted to go to Mecca *via* Riyadh, while the rest had no desire but to get back as soon as possible to their families. At that we left things for the time being, and I was all too pleased to see practically complete harmony re-established among us. The previous evening in a dream I had seen the great King at my side, distressed at my despondency. What ails you, he had asked, that you are so downcast ? Think no more of your trouble for I will put it right. The new harmony among us, coupled with a definite decision in favour of an attempt on the waterless desert, seemed to arise directly from the vision.

The changed weather conditions, the rain and squally winds, had had a remarkable effect on the ' Singing Sands ' of Naifa, which remained mute during our present sojourn, except for a fleeting moment at 4 p.m. on March 3rd, when I heard the familiar booming. So far as I could ascertain the inception of the concert had been entirely due to natural causes, for none of our people had been on or near the slope ; but the music lasted barely five seconds, and the despatch of Sa'dan up to the ridge to see what he could do brought no result. The conditions were doubtless unsuitable and, hot as it was at that hour, it would seem to me that the amount of moisture absorbed by the sands during the recent showers might have been a sufficient cause of their silence. Abu Ja'sha was however of opinion, quite seriously, that the *genii loci* were sulking on account of our indecorous hilarity during their musical demonstrations in honour of our first visit to their abode. They were thus lashing us with violent squalls instead of charming us with sweet music.

That night the storm continued with frequent lightning among the clouds to north and north-west, but there was no rain on us and the morning dawned fine enough with very light clouds high up and slowly moving northwards. Later on the north wind came down upon us in violent gusts, sweeping the hollow with sheets of flying sand, which threatened the stability of the tents and almost buried the great store of meat stacked by the kitchen. It was horribly uncomfortable in camp under the lash of the whirlwind, but the sky was for the most part overcast and the sun only struggled through feebly at wide intervals. It was, therefore, much cooler than it had been the previous afternoon, while I derived much satisfaction from the fact that such actual rainfall as could be observed was concentrated afar off to the west on the very line which we should soon be following.

During the afternoon I went forth again to the well for a bathe to escape the stuffiness of my tent, intensified by a regular gathering of the clans to bask in the sunshine of my new-born good humour, which was perhaps expected to result in a further distribution of bounty, though I had firmly made up my mind that no further rewards should be given until actually earned. The baggage-people would get their proper dues at Riyadh on handing over safely all the cases and packages scheduled in my letter to the heir-apparent—and I may anticipate the subsequent course of events to the extent of stating that all the baggage arrived safe and intact at Mecca. The men concerned also received the payments indicated in my letter, while those who went with me were duly rewarded after our safe arrival.

A few drops of rain fell while I was bathing, and at 5 p.m. a violent squall burst upon us from the north-east. It lasted intermittently for four hours. The whirlwind filled the deep hollow of Naifa with eddying clouds of sand. The ropes and pegs strained and strained again in the effort to hold the tents to their unstable foundation. Crash went the taber-nacle of my companions, levelled over their heads. Crash went mine as I clutched desperately at everything likely to be carried away. One of my precious killing-bottles, already a little cracked by some earlier accident, was hurled against a stone and smashed to atoms. And, crawling out from under the debris of the tent, we all sat disconsolately in the open while the stinging sand played upon us like a hose. We could scarcely stand steady as we lined up for the sunset prayer, and our dinner was eaten in circumstances of un-imaginable discomfort. How Zaid and Ibn Musainid had ever managed to cook it under such conditions was a mystery, and it was a miracle indeed that they had done so without a more lavish admixture of sand.

Before sunset I had gone out into the desert to have a look round, and the scene that met my eyes was truly amazing. Great black clouds of sand raced before the gale along the summits around us like squadrons of Valkyries, while from the higher dune-tops streamed as it were dark pennants in the wind and the desert floor was swept as by driving snow, sheet after sheet of white sand, like successive waves of a cavalry charge. It was a spectacle never to be forgotten, that desert in stormy mood with the roll of distant thunder and the blinding flashes that rent the lowering clouds. The tempest ceased as suddenly as it had begun, but the sky remained clouded and it was not till just before dawn that I was able to secure the very necessary astronomical observations for which I had waited so patiently all these days. Even then I was only able to deal with one star—Spica,— for the growing daylight cut short my observations of Altair.

So dawned the Day, the fifth day of March, the day appointed for our launching out once more into the waterless desert, for better or for worse. The camels came in during the morning according to plan, and all day long Zayid and his fellows toiled at the necessary preparations. The water-skins had to be botched and greased and finally filled at the well, 22 skins and 3 five-gallon spirit-barrels (in which we had originally carried oil for our lamps) being allotted to the desert party, while the remaining ten were to go with the baggage-folk, who would be able to draw water at intervals along their route. Division had to be made of the available stock of provisions and of the camels, fifteen of which would go with us and fourteen back with the baggage. The *Saluqi* bitch was to go with us, and up to the last minute almost there was no absolute finality about the composition of the two parties. Muhaimid, the younger herdsman, begged for permission to go to Mecca with us across the desert, and I was gratified to find that, while no one already enrolled in my party showed any desire to secede, several of the others now volunteered to join us and even begged to be allowed to do so. Farraj, doubtless thinking mainly of the better chance of divine ' sustenance,' was one but I firmly rejected his advances. Another was Hasan Khurr al Dhib, whom

together with Muhaimid I eventually accepted as additions
to our party, whose numbers thus rose to eleven. Among
the remainder there was much searching of hearts as to the
respective advantages of going to Mecca or to the families
waiting patiently in the Hasa. Farraj, having his plea for
inclusion in my party definitely rejected, changed his mind
no less than seven times that day and finally decided in con-
junction with 'Ali Jahman and Ibn Humaiyid to abandon all
thought of the pilgrimage and return to the Hasa. So all
these matters were in due course decided and disposed of,
and I embodied the arrangements made in a letter to the
Amir Sa'ud, of which 'Abdul Rahman was nominated to be
the bearer.

Meanwhile I had devoted all the available time to packing
up everything that was to go to Riyadh. For the desert
journey it was obviously desirable to carry an absolute
minimum of *impedimenta*, but it was no easy matter deciding
what to take and what to send back. In case of possible
accidents, which one had to envisage quite solemnly, I decided to send back all maps, observation-books, and my main
diary so that these at least should not be lost to the world in
the event of our failure to get across the desert. I accordingly wrote up my journal as far as possible to date before
finally consigning it to one of the returning boxes. And I
was writing almost up to the last moment, as far as was
possible with the frequent invasion of my tent by those of
the returning party who wished to reassure themselves that
they were not sacrificing the reward of their past and future
labours by deserting my person at this stage. Farraj was
the most persistent with 'Ali Jahman a good second. Oh
Shaikh 'Abdullah, said the latter, you know that I would
have liked to accompany you to the end, but the baggage-
train must have a conductor and I know the country it will
have to pass over better than any of them, while I have no
knowledge of the desert between here and Sulaiyil. But I
am at your service to go with you if you wish it. And you
know that the provisions we have for the baggage-party are
not enough for us. Will you not therefore give us just a
little money for replenishing our stores on the way ? And

where, I asked demurely, will you find provisions to buy in this desert ? We can buy what we want at Kharj, he answered, when we get there. To which I replied : Go to ! when you reach Kharj you will be but an easy day's journey from Riyadh. He retired unsuccessful but unabashed, and came again to express a hope that I had not forgotten to allot him a larger reward than the rest for his services as guide. You and the rest, I replied, will know the rewards allotted to each of you when you arrive at Riyadh. In fact every man of them was to get, and got, exactly the same as his fellows.

As the afternoon wore on our preparations approached completion. The camels were watered with every encouragement to drink their fill, which they did readily enough after their restful sojourn amid good pastures. We ourselves were summoned to a final dinner of camel-meat and rice soon after 5 p.m. The camels were loaded up, and half an hour later the baggage-party filed up out of the hollow into the desert and turned north-east. Farraj and 'Ali Jahman dallied a moment over the coffee-fire, where the rest of us were gathered for a final round of refreshment before starting on our long trek. As they rose to follow in the tracks of the baggage each of them saluted me with a kiss on the forehead. Forgiveness for our failings ! said 'Ali. There is nothing to forgive, I replied, but I thank you for your services. In the keeping of God ! And so I parted from eight of the companions of two months of wandering in the wilderness. The farewell of the Arab is manly indeed. With fair words on his lips he strides off into the desert and is gone. He never looks back.

CHAPTER IV

THE WATERLESS WASTE

Where there is no water, 'tis the Empty Quarter; none thither goes.
—SUWID AL AZMA.

THE sands of Naifa receded behind us into the gloaming as we marched north-west towards Adraj—eleven men with fifteen camels and a dog. The camels were festooned with water-skins and garlands of raw dry meat, which gave forth a fragrant odour in the cool night air.

Sunset being almost upon us when all was ready for a start, we had delayed for a few moments to accomplish the customary prayer-rites by the ashes of our camp-fire. The clouds had once more begun to gather over us as we then mounted to begin the great adventure. The omens were favourable. We were all in good condition, man and beast. The dunes of Arabia wore a mantle of Scotch mist, out of which a gentle drizzle fanned us at intervals as we went into the darkness. All we could see was the ghostly silhouettes of our companions marching along in ghostly silence. And thus for five hours over the familiar ridges and valleys of the Naifa-'Ain Sala district until we came to a great range on the confines of Adraj, where we halted for a night's rest just as Orion's Belt stood upon the western horizon. A single incident had caused a slight commotion during the march. Al Aqfa was suddenly discovered to be missing. She had missed her good friend the cook in our company, and had apparently gone off back to Naifa in search of him. We resigned ourselves philosophically to the sad loss, but our joy was great indeed when the familiar shape was seen once more sidling into camp soon after our own arrival. She had drawn blank at our abandoned dwelling-place and returned following our tracks. The intelligence of the desert *Saluqi* is almost human.

In the darkness we had laboured somewhat in negotiating the lofty *Sawahib* ridges, but a moderate northerly breeze with some slight drizzling rain had kept us cool enough and we marched bareheaded. Nevertheless we arrived in camp tired and hungry. Abu Ja'sha earned our gratitude by producing a substantial dish of rice, cleverly saved from the residue of our last dinner, out of the depths of his saddle-bags; and we set to with some of the raw dried meat, hastily cooked in the ashes and resembling leather, added to the rice. The milch-camels, after their days at pasture, also contributed abundantly to our comfort, and of course there was coffee to round off the proceedings before we composed ourselves for sleep. We had made a propitious start and all seemed well enough.

When we woke about dawn—having of course slept in the open as the tents had gone back with the other party—there was an appreciable dew upon the ground, as there had been also at Naifa the previous morning. A cool north breeze blew gently but steadily over the desert, while light clouds covered most of the sky with tufts of orange wool. We were glad of the movement necessitated by our preparations for a start to work off the chill of night, and we dawdled a moment over the fire to drink our drops of coffee. At 6.30 we were in the saddle clinging to the southern skirt of the sand-ridge until we came to a low col that enabled us to cross it and resume our general WNW. direction.

There was plentiful vegetation[1] in these parts for the camels to crop as they marched, and our progress in consequence was miserably slow, but I said no word. My mount was Na'riya, the heroine of the confinement in the desert, the best of all our beasts, strong and fast though a little rough withal. 'Ali Jahman had been loth to part with her, but our need had been great enough to override all sentiment and personal preferences. Two months ago she had been considered too obstreperous for my inexperienced hands to hold, but the long march had toned her down and she was a delight to ride, though I had to have my wits about me when mount-

---

[1] *Hadh, Abal, Alqa, Andab* and *Birkan*—i.e., all the staple plants of the southern sands except *Zahr*.

ing. I always insisted on doing that unaided and became quite adept, though the slightest touch of the knee on saddle was enough to launch her in full stride. My original mount, Al Bahraniya, had fallen to Zayid, also a good beast though inclined to be slow and a little heavy. But Zayid was the outstanding camel-master of us all, and could get the best out of her without visible effort.

Over the great rolling downs, becoming perceptibly barer of vegetation as we advanced, we struck, leaving the prominent peak of Adraj itself two or three miles to our left. The atmosphere, cool and clammy under the overcast sky, left nothing to be desired. And from time to time Al Aqfa started off on the track of a hare, apparently trusting to her eyes rather than her nose. The Arab certainly thinks that the *Saluqi* works by sight rather than scent, but it would be difficult to decide the matter definitely. Our dog certainly appeared to take short cuts where the little round dots of the hare's trail fetched a circuit, but she was also very quick to pick up any trifle of food one might fling to her from camel-back even in the dark, and I suspected that a sense of smell played some part in her activities.

The sand-trails now lay uniformly to the south of the tufts and thickets of vegetation in deference to the north wind which had ruled the roost since the break of the weather, but in some places we found them to the west. Salim, thoroughly enjoying his responsible status of sole guide to the expedition, generally rode with me in the lead. His camel, a huge and ponderous beast, carried two water-skins covered with pendent stalactites of raw meat, to which the rider helped himself freely from time to time. It is good, he said; eat a little and you will see. Well, give me a small bit from the piece you have in your hand, I replied. It did not look particularly appetising, but I found it savoury enough to the taste—good, strong meat too to ward off the weakness that comes of hungering. Salim and Suwid, both of the same clan, had laid in a communal stock of the stuff and also shared the contents of the four water-skins they carried between them. The one never drank without informing the other and inviting him to do likewise. I was soon recognised as a partner in their joint stock of meat, but I had again abandoned the practice of drinking water. Salim was like a great school-boy and prattled freely of all the good things he hoped to take back with him for his family from Mecca. You will speak to the King, he said, that he may give me an order on the royal commissariat in the Hasa for two sacks of rice and a sack of sugar—and coffee. We will surely buy coffee at Sulaiyil, I replied, or at Bisha if we go there. Thither come the coffee-caravans from the Yaman by way of Najran, and it should be cheap. By God ! he said, you are right ; you are a hawk and more hawk-like[1] than I. If God wills our way will be blessed —and, pray God, the King will be pleased with us. You will surely speak with him for us. He also wanted a mantle, for his own was of poor stuff and too thin to keep out the cold. I registered the intention of passing on the one I wore to him at the end of the journey, if successful, and in due course it became his property. It was a good, thick garment of Hasa weaving, and worth about L3.

During the early part of the morning's march we had some lofty and difficult dune-ranges to negotiate with occasional complexes of moraine-like character but, as we passed across the fringe of *Hadh* that marked the division between the 'Ain Sala tract and Khillat Adraj, we entered upon a great gently-rolling plain with low ridges at considerable intervals. Here there was neither *Hadh* nor *Birkan* and the *Andab* grass was dead or completely dry, but the *Abal* remained green and there was fresh *Alqa* in satisfactory profusion. We passed by some old Oryx-dung, but the only living thing we saw before our morning halt about 11 a.m. was a single Desert Warbler. Our lunch was of dates dipped in butter with coffee, after which we rested awhile to let the camels graze while there was still good vegetation. I improved the occasion by securing, at long last and after so many fruitless efforts, my first and only specimen of the *Spindasis* butterfly. The sky was lightly overcast all round us and a gentle easterly breeze was blowing when we resumed the march at mid-day.

The country rapidly became more and more bare with only

[1] *Saqr* =hawk ; the epithet *asqar* (very or more hawk-like) comes very near in pronunciation to *Azka*, the comparative of *Zaki* (clever).

scattered *Abal* bushes and very little (though still something)
of other plants. A raven appeared on the scene some way
ahead to emphasize the lifelessness of our surroundings. I
recorded the ridges and valleys as we went, a monotonous
task in an altogether monotonous world. The men sang
grimly to wear down their boredom. Salim discoursed to me
of his experiences in the desert. He had never done or
attempted its crossing from Shanna or Naifa, and had never
heard of anyone else having done it. We are surely the first
to make this journey, he said. Beyond Hawaya and Shuwaikila I have no knowledge of these parts except from the
talk of others. But once long ago I rode with Al Nifl from
the Aflaj district to Naifa, seeking out the Sa'ar folk to raid.
And another time I went from Bir Fadhil to Sulaiyil with our
grazing camels, when there had been rain in those parts. The
herds remained in the desert, and I went to the village to get
dates and other provisions. But this is the Empty Quarter ;
no one comes here, never.

So we trailed on rather wearily throughout that afternoon
over immense gently-undulating plains varied at intervals by
rougher patches formed by the confluence of dunes and
ridges. At first there was little wind except occasional
refreshing gusts from the north-west, while the clouds for the
most part were massed in the south and west. Gradually the
wind gathered strength, always coming from the same quarter, and the flying sheets of sand made the latter part of the
afternoon somewhat disagreeable. By 3.30 p.m. a mild gale
was blowing and stirring up a feeble sandstorm over a
considerable area, blotting out the view. We struggled on
but Salim was showing signs of weariness. I am thirsty, he
said, let us stop awhile for our companions to drink. Quite
firmly I goaded him on. We will lose time if we halt, I said ;
we are in the van and, as long as we march, the others will
follow. Look how far they are behind and lagging. Perchance they would like to camp now though the afternoon is
scarce half spent. If we stop it will mean camping here for
the night. By God ! he replied with a sigh of resignation,
this country has good pasture. It would do the camels good.
We shall come to pastures as good, I replied, before sunset.

There was in fact plentiful fresh vegetation of the usual
varieties, but we soon passed beyond it, and my prophecy
was not fulfilled. An hour later, after vain search for good
pasture, we came to a halt at Zayid's insistence—he had
trotted up from far in the rear to remonstrate against our
continued advance—in a narrow depression on the south side
of a long ridge of high dunes. We were still in the tract of
Khillat Adraj, and had marched some 27 miles during the
day—a fairly reasonable but not particularly good performance. However we had no reason to be displeased with our
record of 45 miles from Naifa since sunset the previous evening, and the weather conditions continued favourable.
Indeed the sky was fairly heavily overcast all over during the
evening, though we could detect no sign of actual rain in any
direction, and the wind, gradually moderating to a mild
zephyr, came from the north. The lifelessness of the country
was rather depressing, for we had only seen four birds in the
whole area covered—a Wagtail and another Desert Warbler in
addition to those already mentioned being encountered a little
before our arrival in camp. We had meat, however, to cheer
us at dinner, though they again made the mistake of cooking
the dried strips—this time in butter. Dates too we had—a
strictly limited ration doled out by Sa'dan, who was in
special charge of the two precious skins and had my strict
instructions to husband the supply on the assumption of a
journey of twelve days. There was coffee and milk as usual
and, last but not least, there was a pot of tea for myself from
my small emergency stock, which I had reckoned would last
out the rest of the march at my normal rate of consumption
of three (small) pots a day. With a march in prospect for the
early hours we were early to bed and the night passed without
incident except for a change of the wind from north to east.

I was roused from my slumbers an hour after midnight to
find a few drops of rain falling from a lowering sky. There
was still a light breeze from the east and a clammy moistness
in the air. With no food or coffee to delay our start we were
soon in the saddle, marching about due west over gentle
undulating sand-downs with only three ridges—and those of
no great difficulty—to negotiate up to 5 a.m. when we halted

U

for the dawn prayer and a light breakfast. The rain had been
with us intermittently throughout this march, and towards
dawn there was a good deal of thunder and lightning in the
south.

On resuming the march after an hour's halt we passed
almost immediately into the district of Hadh Bani Zainan, an
immense gently-undulating drought-stricken plain in which
practically all the vegetation except a few *Abal* bushes was
dead. The stumps and long-exposed roots of the larger
thickets were black as if they had been burned with fire. It
was indeed a desolate scene through which we rode, mostly in
silence. It was pleasant to ride bareheaded in the tempered
sunlight. The wind had dropped to nothing, and the sky
was trying to clear. Again there was no sign of life anywhere
though in two spots we observed Oryx dung. We were in the
very midst of the Oryx country, but our hunters had lost all
inclination for the chase. It was indeed amazing that during
all these weeks not one of us had ever had a glimpse of the
animal, which we had hoped so confidently to meet in large
numbers. 'Ali Jahman had even spoken of the possibility
of eking out our water-supply in emergency by squeezing out
the liquid contained in the tripe of the animals we should shoot.

Supposing one was very thirsty, I asked Salim as we rode
along ahead of our companions as usual, and had no water,
could one make shift with the urine of camels ? You use it
to wash your hair and as medicine for your stomach. Could
you also use it for ordinary drinking purposes if hard
pressed ? No, he replied, it would but make you more
thirsty, but we do sometimes get a deal of drinkable liquid
in another way. We take the undigested food from a camel's
cud and squeeze the water out of it. Have you ever gone
thirsting for a long period, Salim ? I asked. Perhaps two
days, but not more, he replied, and praise be to God ! I have
heard of men who have been longer without water ; perhaps
four days, but scarcely more, God knows.

As the morning wore on, patches of beautiful blue sky
began to chequer the wide-spread pattern of clouds and the
sun grew quite hot behind a thin film of haze. The atmosphere was rather stifling, and the surface of the sand seemed

to be quite firm and hard as the result of its recent watering. Here and there a jumble of short formless ridges broke the general monotony of the bare plain, while in one spot we saw a fine massif of high dunes about a mile or so to the south-west, white and grey, in the alternating streaks of sunshine and shadow. Everywhere the plants of the desert were parched and dead, and no living thing did we see till nearly noon when I was thrilled by the sight of a swallow. A swallow lost in that wilderness ! Round and round an *Abal* bush it was flying when we first saw it. Twice it circled round our little caravan in the friendliest manner, as it might do about a ship at sea, and then it disappeared over a ridge to return no more—apparently travelling northwards. Some days later we were to see its fellows in plenty at Sulaiyil—presumably on the main route of their seasonal migration. This one may have strayed from the flock or been blown out of its way. It would scarcely find water to refresh it short of Jabrin.

We passed on, marching parallel with a very long and unusually fine range of dunes extending as far as we could see to north-east and south-west. In due course we struck at right angles up its long, steep slope and down over its summit into an absolutely bare plain, where the sand lay in well-marked ribs across our path and its surface was sodden with moisture to a depth of half an inch. There had clearly been more rain here than we had enjoyed at any point, and we spoke longingly of the rich herbage which would soon be sprouting up in this area—too late for us, for we had not given the rain time to do its work. Perhaps in a month's time or more the Arabs of the great desert would be bringing their cattle here to enjoy the fresh pastures, and they would certainly find Oryx and hares in plenty for the pot.

The name of Bani Zainan[1] would seem to indicate the generally easy character of this tract of broad, featureless valleys and plains lying between distant low ridges in contrast with the tract of Hawaya[2] which signifies frequent, narrow depressions or valleys between high dune-ranges

[1] *Zain* = good, pleasant, while the common local term *Bani* (*i.e.* children of) seems to be familiarly applied to dunes and ridges.

[2] *i.e.* plenty, quantity, much.

resembling the long rolling breakers of a shallow sea. As distinct from either, the *Hibaka* or moraine formation is not unlike a storm-tossed ocean covered with ' white horses.'

We had marched no less than seven hours without a break when, at 1 p.m., it was voted desirable to make a short halt for refreshments in a wide rolling plain. There was not much for the camels to browse on, and with the sun peeping out more boldly through the gaps in the clouds, which remained thick only in the south, the atmosphere was inclined to be sultry in spite of a light northerly breeze. Just before halting we had seen the fresh track of a hare, as well as dung both of Oryx and the *Rim* gazelle, but it scarcely seemed likely that we should actually see any game under such conditions. There was nothing for game to live on, though again during the afternoon we met with gazelle and Oryx droppings so often that we began to hope there might be fresh pastures at no great distance ahead. And certainly there was some improvement in this respect, for we came upon strips of vegetation where there was a little *Abal* and even some green *Hadh*, to say nothing of occasional thin lines of *Andab*, which may have been the outcome of the recent rain or of an isolated earlier shower. At intervals Suwid or one of the others would dismount to scrape away the surface sand by way of testing the depth to which the moisture had penetrated. On one occasion they found the sand quite wet at a depth of six inches, and we actually passed by a fair-sized hollow in which a regular pool had evidently been formed by the rain, though there was nothing now left of the water. In another spot there had clearly been a shower of hail or very large rain-drops, which had pitted the sandy surface over a considerable area. But still there was no sign of any living thing, the record of the day's march being only a single Desert Warbler and a butterfly in addition to the swallow.

By 4 p.m. we had all had enough of the marching and settled down to camp on the north side of one of the low Bani Zainan ridges. The sky was then fairly clear overhead, while the clouds had been concentrated to the northward, whence came a steady though moderate breeze. The camels were

fortunate enough to find some green pasture in the neighbourhood of the camp, and I was able, for the first time since
leaving Naifa, to get some star readings. We had covered
40 miles during the day and had fully earned the all too short
rest that Zayid was prepared to allow us. For we were in the
saddle again before 2 a.m., marching now under a clear starlit
sky with a fresh, north-easterly breeze blowing across our
path. They call it *Na'shi* from the constellation of the
Great Bear, generally known to the Arabs as *Banat al Na'sh*.[1]

We had struck a patch of frequent ridges, crossing no
fewer than nine in the course of the three hours ending with
our halt for the dawn prayer. Salim, now no longer enjoying
the keen sight of youth, was nonplussed by the darkness.
Most of the time he walked by my side, leading his mount, for
he could tell by the feel of the sand under his feet the direction in which firm surfaces and easy summits were likely to be
found. Once or twice he got rather badly involved in soft
going and steep slopes, which spelled danger for our bulging
water-skins. The camel, when left to himself, will plunge
down such descents as if the devil were at his heels, and not
seldom there were collisions between two or more animals
playing that game at the same time. Fortunately our water-
skins in the end suffered no damage, for Salim generally
stayed behind at any particularly difficult slope either to lead
down the more refractory animals with his own hand or to
launch them on their descent one by one.

He soon tired and we halted somewhat earlier than usual
to get the coffee and tea ready before the time for prayers. It
was a still, cloudless dawn with slight dampness in the air,
and I seized the opportunity to get a little sleep while the
others were busy at the fire. In such circumstance sleep
comes easily and quickly, and it seemed but a moment later
that I was woken by Suwid's call to prayer. Our breakfast
consisted of dates with milk, tea and coffee, but I had consumed a good deal of the raw meat during our march in the
dark. So there was none of that hungry feeling which had
made the days of our retreat so irksome. Besides that difference everything seemed to be going very well. By this

[1] Meaning " the Bier."

time we had done about 95 miles or just about a quarter of our journey, and the fourth day was all practically to go.

Resuming our march just as the sun was coming up behind us, we were confronted by a gently-rolling down-tract, very bare and dead so far as vegetation was concerned but easy going. The vast ocean was streaked here and there with short runs of dunes in range formation, but in the daylight we were able to steer clear of them without losing ground. A Desert Warbler flew furtively from a thicket near our route to a safer distance, and I was surprised to see a kind of hawk which my companions identified as *Abu Haqab*, perhaps a Harrier. It is different, they explained, from the *Saqr* or falcon used in hawking, as also from the *Shabbut* or Sparrow-hawk. In all these tracts there were abundant signs of good recent rainfall, and I noticed curious little bubbles in the sand. We call them *Abyar al Sultan*,[1] volunteered Salih, in our country. Salim winked at me knowingly. He lies, he said ; we have no name for them. They are just holes in the sand formed by large drops of rain. The matter was perhaps of little moment and I kept an open mind, for the Manasir have little curiosities of lore and language of which their neighbours might well be ignorant. On the other hand Salih was a liar—undoubtedly. I had had experience of that on several occasions but could not resent his manifest keenness to keep me supplied with information about the great desert and its fringes. A curious trait of the Manasir is the important part played by women in their general scheme. I have alluded to some such matters in earlier[2] pages. Men are frequently addressed by the names of their spouses, e.g. *Ya shaugh*[3] *fulana*—oh husband of So-and-So ! In Najd one might know but would scarcely utter in public the name of a friend's wife unless she happened to be famous—or infamous !

It was curious that the exposed patches of gypseous or calcareous bed-rock, which had been so conspicuous a feature of the southern part of the desert, had nowhere been encountered during the days of our march from Naifa up to this

---

[1] Wells of the Sultan.　　　　　　　　　　　　　[2] *vide* pp. 77 and 81.

[3] *Shaugh*, meaning husband, is apparently dialectical—perhaps a corruption of *Zauj*, often transposed as *Jauz*.

point. We now however, at a distance of about 100 miles
from Naifa, came across and made a brief halt át a small
exposure about 100 yards long. It yielded nothing of particular interest, though it seemed to lie in a marked valley-
depression beyond which we plunged into a regular upland
of disordered dunes. Suddenly and for no apparent reason the
vegetation improved. The *Abal* bushes became more plentiful
with a good show of fresh shoots ; and there was some *Alqa*,
to say nothing of fresh *Hadh*. Lower your voices, growled
Salim ; these folk never think as they march—always chatter-
ing and singing. There might be an Oryx about in such pasture as this, and he would be gone at the slightest sound. To
judge by the frequent little heaps of dung-pellets this locality
had been discovered and made use of by the *Rim* gazelles,
but we saw nothing of them in passing.

At 10-30 a.m. we halted for less than an hour in a bare
upland tract with some *Abal* and *Hadh* for our camels to
browse on. On the way we had encountered some patches of
difficult dune country, and had observed at a little distance
to the right another small patch of exposed rock at the base
of a sand-ridge. Such exposures are generally termed *Shuqqa*,
and I asked Salim whether he had ever heard of the *Kharaïm*[1]
or glades in the sand of which I remembered having heard
years before from Jabir, my Marri companion of an earlier
journey. Salim seemed puzzled by the question. He had
never heard the term, but Salih, who happened to be riding
with us, volunteered some information on the subject which
fitted in very well with the impression left in my mind by
Jabir. They are like the *Shiqaq*, he replied, and yet different,
for they are more extensive. Generally they are the salt-pans
or basins at the tail of the *Wadis* that run into the sands from
the Qara country in the south. We call them *Kharima*, and I
have seen such about Muqshin. Salim looked sceptical for he
had never heard of such things, but on this occasion Salih
was right. Mr. Thomas[2] mentions these *Kharaïm*, which he
describes as a ' skirting corridor,' as a characteristic feature
of the desert on the southern fringe of the great sands.

The sky was cloudless now, but conditions remained cool

[1] Plural of *Kharima*.   [2] See *Arabia Felix*, p. 156.

with a northerly breeze blowing over the sodden sands. Our course lay almost dead straight over a great undulating plain of parched and withered scrub, in the midst of which we came upon yet another patch of exposed rock in a shallow depression, which we searched in vain for shells and flints. The capture of a couple of lizards produced a mild diversion by the way, and Al Aqfa, perched on the back on one of the baggage-camels for a rest during the heat of the day, was a source of innocent merriment. She showed an extraordinary lack of intelligence in making the best of what was, after all, a rather unusual privilege. Instead of lying at full length on the baggage and adjusting herself to its contours she insisted on standing upright at the imminent risk of being precipitated to the ground by each lurch of the camel. Clinging to the uneven surface of saddle and baggage as it were by the toes, she was engaged throughout her ride in trying to keep a precarious balance and looked exceedingly uncomfortable, though she was doubtless grateful for a brief respite from carrying her own weight over the rapidly heating sands. Her riding was, however, of brief duration for, as we entered a shallow valley with a good spread of fresh vegetation, a hare started up from under our feet—the first we had seen in the desert for nearly a fortnight—and the dog, leaping recklessly from her lofty perch, was immediately in hot pursuit, while various members of our party, wildly excited by the prospect of a chase with fresh meat to crown it, joined in the fun, heading the breathless quarry from point to point as it dodged and jinked before the jaws of death. At first it seemed almost certain that Al Aqfa would secure the prize, and we climbed the ridge beyond the valley leaving only Zayid in attendance to bring the meat along in due course. When he rejoined us, however, it was without the hare, which had taken refuge in a fox's earth and so escaped alive. There had been no time to dig her out.

Just before this pleasurable diversion Suwid had provoked peals of laughter with a misadventure which resulted in his taking a toss, camel and all, down a steep soft sand-slope on which he had ventured without due circumspection. The sand-covered folds between lofty dunes are often nothing but concealed crevasses and it is just as well not to step upon them. Generally there is nothing whatever to indicate the hidden danger, but the desert Arab has an uncanny instinct for such pitfalls and I often admired the sure judgment that at times led them up or across an apparently impossible dune-crest in preference to an easy-looking col which closer inspection showed to be nothing but a deep mass of soft sand. It was rarely that any of them came to grief—and that through their own carelessness entirely,—but in the course of our wanderings I had seen both Zayid and Salih laid low by such accidents as that of which Suwid was now the smiling hero.

We now rose into an upland of dunes and ridges with a good deal of *Abal* and *Hadh* in the narrow gullies between them. From the condition of the vegetation my companions deduced—and who shall say that they were wrong ?—that there must have been a fall of rain here not more than four or five years before. Since then there had been nothing to encourage the tenderer plants until now, and now once more the desert had drunk deep to blossom in due course like the rose. It is indeed amazing to think, as I write of this dreary wilderness of narrow depressions some few months after our passing, that it is now probably covered with a pall of green, to the delight of the Oryx and gazelles and other beasts that roam about it unseen and unmolested.

We passed by yet another exposure of the bed-rock under a ridge of this upland, and near by we saw a gentle spray of sand issuing from the burrow of a skink engaged in urgent repairs to its dwelling, whose roof had probably collapsed in the recent rain. The little beast worked with frenzied energy, loosening the debris within with head and front feet to push it out of doors behind him with his vigorous hind legs. We noticed also the recent claw-tracks of a raven, though the bird was nowhere to be seen.

We soon passed out of the belt of fresh vegetation. A vast, bare plain formed the transition from the Bani Zainan tract into Hadhat al Hawaya, whose outermost line of dune-waves —we could see four of them, each about a mile long, spread out before us as we approached—followed the typical

SW.-NE. orientation. The whole landscape looked very desolate and dead, as indeed it was. There was a good deal of *Abal*
and *Hadh*, but all dead ; and those who had clamoured for a
halt in the better pastures some way behind seemed to have
been justified by the unfavourable turn of events against us.
Let us press on, I said to Salim ; we may come to pastures
ahead. But I saw Zayid speeding up from the rear. We had
reached the third of the Hawaya ridges when he caught us up.
The afternoon is far spent, he suggested ; it is time we prayed.
As you wish, I said meekly in accordance with my declared
intention of leaving the ordering of our movements entirely
to Zayid. So we off-saddled to settle down for the night and
the camels went off in search of food. Around us the low
ranges of dunes rode upon an ocean of gently swelling downs.
Again we had done about 40 miles during the day. A third
of our journey was accomplished in three full days and a
bittock, while, with 120 miles behind us, we were now back
again at about the meridian from which we had retreated only
ten days or so earlier. Then we were beaten and felt it ; now
we were full of vigour and optimism, knowing that the real
trouble lay ahead of us but conscious that we had stolen a
long march on it without much effect on ourselves. The
camels had not had the best of luck in the matter of pastures,
but things might have been a good deal worse. We still had
some meat and our water-supply was well on the right side of
sufficiency—thanks to the cool weather we had so far enjoyed.

A cool north-east breeze continued to fan us, and a clear
sky gave me the opportunity of making more astronomical
observations. But the event of the evening was the appearance of the new moon of Dhil Qa'da, the third and presumably
last new moon of our wanderings, for the next, by the grace of
God, should find us at Mecca. Hasan, surnamed ' Wolf-face,'
established his claim to be the keenest-eyed of all our party.
His range of vision was astonishing and he actually picked up
the slender crescent before the sun had set. For some minutes
we sought it in vain and then Zayid saw it a second or two
before myself. Sa'dan was altogether left at the post and
never saw the moon till the following night. His early up-
bringing in an airless, windowless home at Majma'a had

dimmed his vision without damping his spirits. Another moon and he would be back again with his little wife at Mecca, but his thoughts often strayed in another direction. With his earnings in my service he might add to his responsibilities, and Bisha was renowned for its women. So they said and thither we would be going, and Sa'dan was pensive these days, pondering the pros and cons of bigamy.

It was a perfect night for sleeping under the stars—cool, cloudless and windless. All too soon they roused me and we marched through the darkness over a wide flat plain with Jupiter going before us. The atmosphere was extraordinarily luminous and the dark shapes of man and beast stood out sharply against a curious light, for which it seemed difficult to account. The planet was bright enough to cast shadows but could scarcely have been responsible for all the light that enveloped us, which was perhaps due to the reflection of myriads of stars in the crystal mirrors of the rain-washed sands.

We marched about ten miles in starlight and halted for refreshments and prayers somewhat earlier than usual soon after Jupiter had sunk below the horizon. By now the store of raw meat was nearly exhausted, but Salim and Suwid seemed to have an inexhaustible supply which they produced mysteriously in cautious quantities from the depths of their saddle-bags. I asked no questions and took the tendered rations, chewing them unobserved in the dark. Presumably the others also had secret stocks. At the halt I lay down to sleep until prayer-time, after which we had our slender ration of dates, dipping them in butter or milk according to taste before consigning them to our mouths. I had taken some time to develop this habit, so deep-seated in the Arabian character; but now all forms of food were grist to my mill. My companions squeezed their dates into cup-like receptacles, with which to ladle the liquid butter into their mouths, but that was more than I could stomach.

At dawn I found a slight dew upon the ground and on the bushes. The sun rose upon us from behind, disclosing a far-flung scene of long parallel NE.-SW. ridges with shallow valleys between them, averaging about a mile in width. The desert herbage was withered everywhere by the long drought,

which was of 20 years' standing in these parts. Hawaya
extends northward to the gravel plain of Ra'la which begins
half a day's journey westward of Tuwairifa and merges into
the great steppe of Abu Bahr, to which we would come in due
course. The width of Ra'la from east to west is a journey of
two days or about 50 miles. Occasionally we came upon thin
lines of green *Andab* with scanty *Alqa* and *Abal*, but the *Hadh*
was all dead.

An ancient raven's nest in the branches of an *Abal* thicket
told of better times long since, and we saw the fresh tracks of
some desert mice, but the only living thing actually seen in
that desolate waste was a lark. Far and wide the plain extended around us, for all the world like a great sea with the
occasional ruffle of a low, lazy wave. The breeze had veered
round from north to south, a menacing gesture, and we
braced ourselves to face the coming heat. The sun steadily
asserted its undisputed sway in a cloudless sky. The storm
was spent at last and the rest of our march would be grim
enough. Yet everywhere the signs of recent rain—in one
spot there had again been hail—spoke of blessings to come
when we should be gone.

Wearily, as the morning advanced, we approached the
western extremity of Hawaya ; and the long line of the Shuwaikila dunes appeared before us, afar off. A broad strip of
very dry *Sabat* grass seemed to form a natural frontier between the two tracts and we called a halt for lunch on the back
of a low rounded ridge which proved to be the last rampart of
Hawaya. On the whole we had found this northern part of
Hawaya gentler in its undulations—and more like Bani
Zainan—than it had been further south with its well-marked
ridges and valleys and tumbled moraines. Here the valleys
had generally been shallower and broader, while the dune-
ranges had been lower and easier. Apart from occasional
puffs of breeze from the south the air was very still, becoming
hotter every moment. We spread a rug and mantles over a
large thicket of *Abal* and huddled together in their shade,
while the camels stood or sat about listlessly, too weary of the
whole business to prospect for forage, of which there was
obviously none to be found.

We dallied an hour over our dates, coffee and tea. A lizard was captured and another eluded us, while a butterfly tempted me to vain exertion for a moment. Once more we mounted and marched. A derelict raven's nest marked our entry into Shuwaikila through a gap in its long, discontinuous outer ridge, whose north-eastern extremity was said to lie about half a day's journey to our right. A second ridge lay close behind the first and separated from it by a narrow depression, in which we found another old raven's nest in an *Abal* bush. A cruel glare struck up into our eyes from the very fine light brown sand, and we seemed suddenly to have passed into another world.

Perhaps it was merely imagination, for the very name[1] of this district in the deepest recesses of Rub' al Khali had conjured up visions of disaster in the minds of my companions two months before, when I had casually enquired of 'Ali whether he knew the tract. Mr. Thomas had shown it on his map on the strength of hearsay information, and 'Ali had looked at me quizzically as if wondering how on earth I could have any knowledge of things so remote. My companions now recalled the incident and laughed at their old terror. We were now hardened veterans of travel in the Empty Quarter and the dreaded district was but another stage on the path that pointed homeward.

As a matter of fact the great bulk of the Shuwaikila tract lay to south and south-west of us. We had struck but a slender tongue of it extending north-eastward along the western fringe of Hawaya, separating it from another district of the desert which we could already see before us in the distance. Beyond a gently undulating plain of firm sand with some dry vegetation of *Hadh* and *Sabat* lay a low barrier of dunes, and beyond that again as it were a glimpse of the sea, a firm dark blue line that thrilled us to the marrow. *Wallah*! ejaculated Salim, it is Sahma! the gravel plain that streaks the desert between the dunes. And there, beyond it, are the ranges of Al 'Awariq. It is

---

[1] Said to be derived from the root *Shakl*, signifying likeness—*Shakila* (dim. *Shuwaikila*) Hawaya, *i.e.* resembling Hawaya ; but such Badawin derivations are at best doubtful.

all even as I remember it for I came hither once in the
year of the *Jihad*—in modern Badawin parlance the ' holy
war ' means Ibn Sa'ud's victorious campaign against King
Husain and his dynasty in 1924-5—when I was with a raiding party and we came from the north. By God, I did not
think we should come to it in this journey unless perchance
we might strike a southern tongue of it after crossing the
Shuwaikilat,[1] which I reckoned to be three days' march
across. And lo ! we have traversed it in less than two hours.
We have come up more to the northward than I reckoned.
The Sahma thrusts out long thin tongues of gravel north and
east into the sands of Shuwaikila, which thus peter out
against the plain in a ragged and untidy fringe and actually
spill over into it in occasional isolated dunes or longer patches
of the type known as *Zubara*. The main plain, varying in
width from two to five miles, and even more in some parts,
appears from the distance as a great lagoon extending from
south-west to north-east and bordered by a range of dunes on
either side—Shuwaikila to the east and south and 'Awariq on
the other side, continued further west by the ranges of Bani
Ma'aridh. Topographically the plain is merely an eastward
bulge of the vast Abu Bahr gravel steppe, and geologically it
forms a transition from the unbroken steppe to the continuous and uninterrupted sands, which begin with Shuwaikila
and extend to the line of steppe which separates the Great
South Desert from the mountainous regions of Oman, Qara,
and Hadramaut. As I was afterwards to see for myself the two
sand-tracts of 'Awariq and Bani Ma'aridh are so frequently
interrupted by strips of Sahma-like character that the whole
area may be regarded as a single geographical unit of gravel
overlain in parts by dunes and sand-ridges, which will presumably in course of the ages cover the whole area with a
continuous mantle. It is of course just possible that the
reverse process of uncovering is in operation to expose what
is to-day visible of Sahma, but on the whole it seems more
likely that the sands are increasing their depredations on
the steppe rather than losing ground. Sahma appears to
mean ' streaked,' and the name fits extraordinarily well.

[1] Plural of *Shuwaikila*.

Apart from occasional puffs, which seemed to come in-
discriminately from all the cardinal points in turn, the
wind was in abeyance as we descended the last gentle slope of
Shuwaikila and stepped upon gravel for the first time for
about six weeks. The camels knew the difference at once and
minced along gingerly, for the gravel was sharp and hot.
Their soft feet suffered agonies, and the great animals from
time to time almost collapsed with a sudden buckling movement as they trod on something extra unpleasant. To add to
our troubles the afternoon had turned piping hot under the
naked sun. A Wagtail greeted us with its unfamiliar chirrup
and fled from us with graceful dives, but it was the only sign
of life in that waste scene. The only vegetation, if one may
call it so, was *Sabat* grass, as dry as tinder and so close cropped
by the desert winds that it was scarcely visible though it
tickled one's bare feet like needle points set on end.

As soon as we reached the main Sahma strip and struck
down the midst of it with the bordering sands on either side,
I dismounted to examine and collect specimens of the gravel,
which seemed in general to be very similar to that of the bare
spaces in Jafura and about Maqainama. The pebbles indeed
constitute a fairly complete sample of the igneous and other
rocks of Western Arabia, and I have little doubt that all the
pebble-strands of the central and eastern parts of the peninsula can be traced back ultimately to the great core of
primary rocks, of which the Hijaz mountains and the
plateau east of them are composed.[1] The gravel must have
been brought down to these eastern beaches by the action of
water, and we now know beyond all possibility of doubt that
great rivers flowed across this part of Arabia in ancient
times at least as far as the longitude of Shanna and Bir
Fadhil.

My interest in anything so ridiculously useless as gravel
disturbed my companions, who felt no inclination to stand by
in the stifling heat. Abu Ja'sha, the proud possessor of the
only umbrella in our party, rode past me apparently absorbed
in the weary task of goading on the few animals that carried
baggage but no rider. Others, as they passed, looked at me

[1] See Appendix.

askance, wondering perhaps whether I expected them to stop.
For the sake of peace I waved them all on and even told Salim
to lead my camel on behind the rest for I would soon catch
them up. So I was left alone to discover to my woe that it
was far from being such a simple matter as I had imagined. I
had not troubled to extract my sandals from my saddle-bag,
and my bare feet felt absurdly tender on the hot gravel and
sharp stubble. Far ahead the mirage glinted like a sea, and
the sun's heat made walking a serious business. I was glad
enough when I saw Salim rein back to await me and felt that
I had studied the gravel sufficiently when I remounted to
trail along after the now distant main body. Salim and I
held on over the middle of the plain, while the rest gradually
slanted across to the line of the 'Awariq dunes, which, I
noticed, were fairly thickly dotted with large and apparently
fresh thickets of *Abal*.

At length at about 4 p.m.—a slight south wind was blowing and the temperature must have been about 90° in the
shade—I noticed among our distant companions the familiar
movement which always presaged a decision to halt. The
staidly-moving phalanx broke up at a trot, as each rider
sought a suitable site for his night's rest, and in a moment
there was a couching of camels on the edge of the sands.
Salim eyed them longingly with the thought of coffee doubtless uppermost in his simple mind. I myself was tired and
weary enough in all conscience, but my watchful eye had
detected the presence of the little wingless desert Mantids
(*Eremiaphila*) in the gravel and I was loth to quit the plain
without a specimen or two, for I had seen the creature but
seldom since our visit to Ibrahima, where they had been
abundant. I dismounted again and sent Salim off with my
camel to camp, while I wandered about in search of my
quarry.

Having met with moderate success in my quest, I turned
towards my companions and arrived in camp quite worn out
with my exertions and extremely thirsty. Sa'dan brought
me my usual pot of tea, but that alone was not enough to
quench my thirst. Look, Sa'dan, I said, you know that during these days I have not insisted on having the milk of my

cow as I used to have before, day and night. With all provisions so short I have pooled it with the common stock, and
we have all shared alike in everything except the water,
which I have eschewed. But now I am dying of thirst and I
yearn for a bowl of milk. Go and arrange with Abu Ja'sha to
bring it me here when the camels come in and he milks them.
I must have my milk at least this one night, but arrange the
matter with him quietly lest our brethren be aggrieved.
Very good, he replied, it shall be done—it is nothing.

An hour later I summoned him from the camp-fire. What
of the milk ? I asked. Abu Ja'sha, he replied, has not yet
milked. See ! the camels are even now coming in from
grazing. You shall have the milk very soon. But another
half hour passed and still there was no sign of the milk. And
dinner was shortly announced. I strolled over to join my
companions for the meal and, there in the circle round the
fire, I saw two bowls of milk. I thought they all looked a
little sheepish but Abu Ja'sha greeted me jauntily. Look !
oh Shaikh 'Abdullah ! he cried, here is milk for you. I have
just milked your cow. Drink, and may it refresh you ! There
was clearly a challenge in his words, as if he said : Drink the
one bowl yourself alone, while the rest of us share the other.
And the challenge was deliberately made in public with the
connivance of the assembled company. I thank you, I
replied calmly, but let our brethren drink of it. Their need
is greater than mine. They have toiled greatly to-day in the
heat, and perchance they have been sparing of water, for we
have yet far to go. Ibn Jiluwi did indeed say that that
camel's milk was for me alone, but what matter ? All these
days we have shared it, and from now onwards it is yours
alone. I will drink no milk until we reach Sulaiyil. I have
sworn it, and from now onwards it is not lawful that I drink.
I might have dropped a bomb among them, such was the
consternation that ensued upon my words. The tables were
completely turned upon their knavish tricks, and they knew
that they had been beaten. They pressed me to change my
mind. Would you have me transgress an oath ? I asked ; is
not that unlawful ? Abu Ja'sha swore vainly that he had
but just drawn the milk and was on the point of bringing it

x

over to me when dinner was announced. All to no purpose. In the circumstances the others could scarcely drink the unwanted stuff, and it stood over while we dined—our dinner being dates only with butter to dip them in. I made no further allusion to the incident, and Salih gallantly created a diversion by announcing that the previous night he had been stung by a scorpion. He had probably done no more than tread on a spike or thorn, and there seemed to be no swelling of the foot or poisonous irritation. I went off, however, to fetch my bottle of iodine, and there by my bedside I found the bowl of milk! Abu Ja'sha, I called out loudly that all might hear, come hither! What is this? It is your bowl of milk, he replied ingratiatingly; I put it there lest you might be thirsty in the night. Did you not hear what I said? I asked; would you have me break my oath? Take it away and give it to our brethren that they may drink and, look you! bring me no milk hereafter until we reach Sulaiyil. After that I shall keep my cow to myself, and I swear now that I shall not share a drop of her milk with any of you. Till then it is all yours. Drink it and welcome! But our brethren will not drink, they say, he replied, so what shall I do with it? Drink it yourself, I said, or give it to the dog, if you like, but take it away. Ostentatiously he called to the dog, and Al Aqfa profited deservedly from our bickering. Sa'dan also, reproached for his privity in the night's unfortunate incident and manfully admitting his responsibility, took the oath upon himself to drink no milk these days, and I learned incidentally that Suwid had also forsworn milk some days before in consequence of a suggestion from one of the rest that he had swallowed more than his due share of the common bowl. It was certainly interesting to discover that, in the Badawin code, an oath taken in such circumstances is regarded as inviolable. The townsman is only honour-bound by the oath of divorce for, if he do the thing forsworn, his wife is automatically divorced and, by the sacred law, he cannot remarry her until she has been wedded (and divorced) by another man.

Our camp lay in the midst of well-grown *Abal* bushes on the border-line between the 'Awariq dunes and the Sahma plain, which at this point was about three miles wide. North-

westward, one behind another and apparently separated
from each other by tongues of gravel, lay the five dune-ranges
composing the 'Awariq tract, to a depth of about five miles ;
and behind them again were the low ridges, some seven or
eight in number, of Bani Ma'aridh. Our further course,
varying from WSW. to SSW., was designed to avoid the ups
and downs of the sand-tracts by skirting along the edge of
Sahma past the echeloned southern extremities of the various
ridges or lines of dunes. To some extent the sands spilled
over from the north on to the gravel in slender tongues and
isolated dunes, which in some places crossed the plain to lie
along the fringe of Shuwaikila. Generally speaking however
the gravel is bordered on the south by the latter while, apart
from the protruding tongues of hard plain forming bays and
estuaries in the sands, Sahma lies wholly south of 'Awariq
and Bani Ma'aridh. So far as I could gather from Salim's
rather vague information it joins up with the great plain of
Abu Bahr by a narrow corridor between Shuwaikila and the
southern extremities of Bani Ma'aridh.

The fifth night of our journey found us about 170 miles
out from Naifa—satisfactory progress on the whole—but the
best part of 200 miles lay ahead of us and we could scarcely
hope to do it in less than five or six days. Another night-
march was therefore necessary and, in spite of a rather
fatiguing day of warmth and unrelieved sunshine, we were in
the saddle again by 1.30 a.m. to march three hours in the
dark. We rode on the gravel with the sands immediately to
our right. And again I was struck by the curious incandescent effect produced by the conditions of night-marching in
this sand-country. The dark silhouettes of our camels seemed
to be surrounded by vague halos of light, and one could see
bushes and the outlines of the dunes with astonishing clear-
ness.

After the incident of the previous night our breakfast
party was somewhat glum and the camels were not called
upon to supply milk for anybody. Our fare was dates alone,
and only a meagre ration of them, for we could not afford to
be too optimistic in the rate of consumption of our sole means
of sustenance. I had had raw meat to chew during the night-

march, but there was nothing to indicate how much was left
and I preferred to ask no questions. The *Saluqi* bitch literally had nothing but our discarded date stones, which she
picked up from the sand and swallowed whole. No doubt
she was well inured to such a diet, and the bowl of milk had
been an unexpected godsend for her. Our camels were more
or less starving. But our only thought was to get on with
our marching as quick as possible.

The sun rose from a flat ocean-like horizon behind us soon
after we had resumed, and it looked as if we were in for a
gruelling day. Our animals suffered from the hard pebbles
underfoot, but it was considered more expeditious to march
on the gravel than to follow the undulations of the 'Awariq
sands, which lay close on our right hand. There had evidently been no rain in this neighbourhood during the recent
storm and the landscape was amazingly bare, though Salim
hoped for better things ahead and chid some members of the
party for singing as they marched. There might be gazelles
or Oryx about which we would frighten away before reaching
them ; or there might even be raiders or some hunting-party
within hearing. At the best, it seemed to me, these desert
shanties are poor and barren things, the ebullitions of empty
souls engaged on a thankless task. Singing was their only
antidote against boredom—singing and the jaunty anecdotes
of which the retailer was generally the hero. In the dark the
desert rule is against any uplifting of the voice for fear of
foes, but in the Empty Quarter our men honoured it more in
the breach than in the observance, while some of them contented themselves with an astonishing and unattractive
falsetto. Ibn Ma'addi was the worst offender in this respect,
but he was not an attractive character in any aspect and, to
my infinite relief, he generally preferred to lag along in the
rear. A scion of the Subai' tribe and native of Ranya, he
had been attached to our expedition in view of our probable
return to civilisation by way of Wadi Dawasir. Salih also
had a falsetto alternative to his customary bass, but in his
case it was more or less innocuous and he did not resent being
mocked at for such lapses into effeminacy.

The Sahma plain had broadened out to about four miles

now with numerous fingers extending octopus-like into the northern sands, which in response threw out occasional tongues of sand across our path. We crossed a mile-wide estuary of gravel, to which Salim gave the name of Janah Sahma, after striking across a considerable bulge of sand with a good sprinkling of *Abal* bushes. Here we actually saw a lark and recent tracks of a raven, which had however decamped from the scene, while a little further on the horns and skeleton of an Oryx lay upon the sand. The Sahma wing, on which we were, was said by Salim to run up north-east for a considerable distance, forming the dividing line between the first two dune-ranges of 'Awariq. The steady but slight rise of the land with our westward marching was imperceptible to the senses. A better speed-track than these vast plains of light gravel could scarcely be conceived and I thought with a shudder, as I rode on, that perhaps some day, after just such rains as we had had, this strange wilderness may be visited by motoring parties in search of gazelles and Oryx ! So far as I can form an opinion on the subject there is nothing but lack of water to prevent the penetration of motor cars into the very heart of the Empty Quarter down to about the nineteenth parallel or perhaps further. But the sand-desert eastward of Sahma will probably for ever remain inviolate. It would be sheer insanity to involve oneself with a motor car in such a maze.

My companions alternately slept in their saddles and burst into their dreary shanty-singing to relieve the monotony of the desert's dullness. During the early part of the morning a south-easterly breeze fanned us from behind, cool and gentle, and the plain was dotted with pools of mirage. We began to grow weary and about 10-30 a.m. decided on a brief halt to rest ourselves and our camels. We came to a stop on a low protruding ridge of the 'Awariq sands with a few miserable bushes of *Abal* upon its slopes. My camel had been showing distressing signs of thirst, and some of the others were in like case. They sat round us disconsolate, their ugly pessimistic faces seeming to regard the desolate scene with utter disdain. A few of them only straggled away in search of food, and I noticed that Zayid was the most active of the party in round-

ing up any animals that showed signs of going too far. In
such circumstances a thirsting camel might easily give one the
slip in an attempt to return to water. Its chance of success
would be slender indeed, but that would be little consolation
for an irretrievable loss, for we had no more animals than we
needed. The sun blazed down on us, and some of the men
clamoured to prolong the halt until the noontide heat should
abate, but Zayid resisted them firmly. It was madness to
waste time now. We were more than half-way across the
desert, having covered about 200 miles. We were about
as far from water as we could be—in any direction,—and
there was at any rate nothing to be hoped for either from
retreat or from the diversion of our course to north or south.
Nowhere in all the length and breadth of Arabia could our
situation in relation to water be paralleled. Even elsewhere,
for instance in the Libyan desert and the Sahara, such a
situation would be rarely encountered ; and the only
similar case of an outstandingly long journey between water-
points which has since come to my notice is that of Rohlfs,
who in 1874 travelled from the Dakhila oasis to Siwa, a distance of about 400 miles over waterless country, in 30 days.
But he experienced the blessing of a cloud-burst about a
third of the way across, which flooded the desert and enabled
the traveller both to water his camels and to replenish his
water-skins.

It is always difficult, and perhaps a little invidious, to com-
pare achievements *prima facie* of similar character though
necessarily conditioned by minor variations of time, season,
place and circumstances in general. Nevertheless Rohlfs'
journey affords so close a parallel to our own crossing of this
waterless desert, and his story (published in German[1] more
than half a century ago) is so difficult of access to the ordinary
English reader, that a brief account of the outstanding features
of his march, as compared with my own experiences, may not
be altogether without interest at this point.

In the first place his journey was undertaken under the
authority and patronage of the Khedive Isma'il Pasha just as

---

[1] *Drei Monate in der libyschen Wüste* by Gerhard Rohlfs, published by
Theodor Fischer at Cassel in 1875.

mine was under the auspices of the King of Arabia. In both
cases success inevitably depended on such august and powerful
backing—in mine most certainly. Secondly Rohlfs' objective
appears to have been to strike right across the waterless Libyan
desert westward from Dakhila to Kufra (a distance of about
400 miles), just as mine was to cross the waterless desert (375
miles wide) from Shanna or Naifa to Sulaiyil. My objective
was successfully achieved in ten days of strenuous marching, while Rohlfs, starting from Dakhila on January 26th,
1874, found on February 1st (seven days later) that further progress westward was hopelessly barred by the heavy
dune-country ahead. This check is therefore comparable to
our own breakdown from a different cause during the first
attempt on the waterless desert from Shanna. He had then
covered 105 miles while we had done 140 in two days' less time.
We had to retreat from that point a further 140 miles back to
water at Naifa, so that our camels did 280 miles in all without
water on that occasion. Rohlfs' problem was solved in a
different way, for, as he and his party were considering their
plans, the desert experienced the unusual phenomenon of a
heavy and long-drawn-out fall of rain. The camels thus had
an unexpected and presumably satisfying drink,[1] while the
iron water-tanks carried by the expedition could be replen-
ished. Rohlfs therefore determined to make north-north-west
for Siwa through the dune-country on a line parallel with the
oases of Dakhila, Farafra, etc., and at a distance from them of
about 100 miles on the average. Thus at no point during his
march of 285 miles from the point he calls Regenfeld (where he
had the rain) to Siwa was he more than 100 miles from the
nearest water, while about (or rather less than) half-way
through he was as near as 50 miles to the watering of Nasla. In
utter hopelessness of outlook, therefore, our situation, with 375
miles between the water-points at start and finish and the
nearest water not nearer than about 180 or 190 miles at our
central point, surpassed that of Rohlfs' party. Quite apart
from that however he carried so ample a provision of water

[1] Rohlfs does not in fact mention that they did, and on February 12th
stated that the camels had last been ' watered ' 17 days before at Dakhila,
but it is surely incredible that they should not have made the most of such
rain.

that at a point he calls Sandheim, where he halted for a whole day on February 12th, he was able to give all his camels a 'ration of water' if not a 'complete watering.' They had then done 17 days since their last regular watering at Dakhila but only eight days since the copious rain, while eight days later they arrived at Siwa. His camels thus did three waterless periods of eight days each, while ours did the first abortive journey from Shanna to Hadh Hawaya and back to Naifa (280 miles) in nine days and the final march of 375 miles in ten days, on both occasions without water except emergency rations for such animals as were in danger of collapse and occasional 'snuffing' all round.

His party seems to have lost as many as 20 camels during the venture although most of his animals were newly recruited and quite fresh at Dakhila, while we lost none though all our camels had done just two months of very strenuous marching under generally unfavourable pasture conditions before we set out on the long, final, waterless lap. Our camels moreover had to pick up what food they could get among the dead or moribund bushes of the Empty Quarter while Rohlfs' animals carried fodder for themselves, which possibly accounted for the optimism of his experienced old Badawin leader, Hajj Madjub, who 'guaranteed the camels to last from 40 to 50 days without requiring to drink' and in any case thought 'they would reach Siwa without being watered.' My men, in the known state of the desert pastures, certainly had no such optimism at the start and feared, on the contrary, that the camels would make serious inroads into our scanty water-supply. At the end only three skins remained of the 24 with which we started, and even so we had been very sparing in the use of water.

Yet it was perhaps in the matter of provisions for the human members of his party that Rohlfs' experience and mine con-trasted most startlingly. We had nought but raw meat and dates, coffee and a little tea, arriving at Sulaiyil literally with-out enough of anything for another meal. Rohlfs however records that on the last day of his march an inspection of his commissariat had revealed that 'there was still enough of everything for several days.' At starting from Dakhila he had

noted that ' besides water, camel fodder and ordinary[1] provisions I had been lucky enough to procure out of the stores
recently arrived from Siut, bacon, sausages, cheeses, wine,
chocolates and other luxuries, while one of the beasts carried
on top of its load a whole hen-coop containing 30 chickens! ' No
wonder that his average day's march was only 15 miles (18½ if
the five days' of halting be excluded from the reckoning) as
compared with our 35 ! If his expedition was a better model
of organisation, we can perhaps justly claim to have faced a
more searching test of the desert's inhospitality.

From all accounts the Libyan desert is worse off for vegetation than the Empty Quarter under the influence of a long
drought, but there the difficulty is met by carrying fodder for
the animals, while in Arabia the camels must do the best they
can on what is provided by niggardly Nature or go starving.
Therefore they must travel fast, and that is always the main
consideration in Arabian camel-breeding. On another point
Africa and Arabia present a curious and interesting contrast,
the Arab strongly preferring the female camel for his journey-
ing, while in the deserts of Egypt and Libya only the male
seems to be used for riding. In all our train we had but one
male camel—and he was a gelding much to the disappointment of an optimistic breeder in Sulaiyil, who turned up at
our camp with a female from his herd in the hope of getting
her covered by a bull of the renowned '*Umaniya* strain.

To spur his fellows to action Zayid, who had done most of
the coffee-making while the others slept wrapped in their
mantles, displayed great energy in loading up the baggage-
animals for the resumption of the march about noon. The
country was now a veritable chequer-board of alternating
patches of sand and gravel, over which we picked our way,
gradually diverging from the main Sahma plain as we cut
across the lower extremities of the 'Awariq ranges. The
heat was now intense in spite of an occasional puff of southerly breeze, and Salim as usual led the way with me, very
drowsily. Suddenly we were awakened from our trance by

---

[1] His supplies were on such a generous scale, indeed, that 'several *cwt.*
of dates and biscuits ' were jettisoned at Regenfeld before the march was
resumed.

as strange a sight as one could imagine in such surroundings.
There on our path, and crossing it from south to north, ran a
double line of tracks of a female camel with her calf! The
traces were fresh enough, perhaps a day old but scarcely
more, and Salim, electrified, swung round to study them with
rapt attention, following them a little way with never a word.
Then, as suddenly, he resumed his march as if satisfied.
Perhaps a hunting party, he muttered more to himself than
me, with a milch-camel which has strayed from them or,
maybe, raiders. Yet there were but the two tracks—of
yesterday too or perchance the day before—and it is strange
that they have not been followed up. We marched on a little
seeking other tracks but saw none. Pity 'tis, said Salim, we
cannot follow up those animals. The youngster would be
good meat, and the mother would give us milk. But they
are gone far by now. They must have strayed from their
party far hence, or we would have seen tracks of the searchers.
The men have doubtless hastened back to Sulaiyil thirsting,
or to Najran if they be raiders. Probably raiders ! he grunted
finally as if satisfied with his solution, and the cow was
probably part of their booty. She strayed from them in the
dark, seeking to return to her own folk. Look, she went
north, probably to the Aflaj. Maybe the raiders whose
smoke 'Ali smelt at Maqainama. Do you remember ? Thus
he mused as he went, and his conclusions met with the approval of Zayid and the others, when they came up with us.
And in fact his conclusions hit the mark almost exactly. At
Sulaiyil and Wadi Dawasir we were to hear in due course the
whole story. Our friend, Jabir ibn Fasl, had bethought himself of a plan after we had left him with my box of fossils to
convey to Hufuf. The money he had had for his trouble and
hospitality would serve to provide him and his family with
such necessaries and luxuries as might be purchased in the
marts of the Hasa. So he had decided to go down alone with
a couple of camels bearing himself and my box, while the
woman should drive his herd of some 40 head to the Dahna
pastures, perhaps 100 miles distant, and there await his
return at a specified locality in the neighbourhood of Rijm al
Shuwai'ar on the Riyadh-Hasa road. On the way thither

the unfortunate woman had encountered a small party of
brigands from Najran, whose camp-fire smoke had undoubtedly been smelt from afar by 'Ali Jahman that night at
Maqainama, and had been robbed of all the livestock of Ibn
Fasl. The raiders, with the charming old-world courtesy of
the road, had then left five camels, including one or two
weary animals of their own, for the woman to carry on with
and had driven off the rest on their hasty return journey to
Najran. The cow and calf, whose tracks we had encountered, must have strayed from them and been abandoned
as unworthy of a long search, which might have jeopardised
their safe return against the double chance of pursuit and
thirst. And, strangest of all, we heard later the almost
incredible news that the strayed animal and her calf had
actually returned to their lawful owner, who had in due
course arrived at the appointed rendezvous in the Dahna to
find himself the victim at last of the stern fate that pursues
the Arabian nomad all the days of his life even under the
peaceful conditions of Wahhabi rule. It is true that Ibn
Sa'ud has almost entirely eliminated the ancient pastime of
raiding from the life-programme of his own subjects, but his
vast dominions march with lengthy frontiers behind which
weakness, misrule and anarchy continue to breed the prim-
eval type of disturbers of the peace. Now and again, but not
so commonly as in former times, these brigands violate the
Wahhabi border-line ; and Najran has ever been a notorious
offender, though by a curious coincidence a Wahhabi expeditionary force was actually dealing faithfully with that
hot-bed of seditious unrest while this very gang of its turbulent citizens was pillaging the livestock of Jabir ibn Fasl
nearly a thousand miles away. Najran, after a bloody battle
costing several hundreds of casualties, made its formal submission to Ibn Sa'ud's lieutenant, Khalid ibn Luwai of
Khurma, during this same month of March. That was perhaps little consolation to Jabir in his tragic loss, and I was
sorry to think that, incidentally and quite unwittingly, I had
perhaps contributed to the disaster.

The exciting discovery of such tracks in a region so remote
had served to divert our attention for an hour or so from the

oppressive afternoon heat. All day long we had seen no
living thing except a pair of Wheatears in the neighbourhood of our mid-day camp. Death reigned supreme. The
scanty bushes were scorched and withered, with, here and
there, a tuft of green stuff surviving miraculously to be cropped
by our camels as they passed, though they were almost too
thirsty to eat anything. A pile of whitened bones and a pair
of horns, black and gracefully curved, betrayed the scene of a
gazelle's last agony. We passed by the hole of a desert
mouse, whose in-going tracks told us it was still at home, but
we were too tired to dig it out. The gravel-strips amid the
dunes and ranges of 'Awariq shone again with the mirage.
The heat was appalling, unbearable. Yet there was nothing
to do but set our teeth and march on till, about mid-afternoon, we had the satisfaction of passing out of the 'Awariq
tract into the parallel shallow valleys of Bani Ma'aridh bordered on either hand by low ridges of waving sand. Little
was changed, indeed, but the name. The dull monotony of
the stricken land was almost more irksome than the blazing
sun. See the camels, how they thirst ! said Salim ; we must
surely ' snuff ' many of them to-night, for they can bear no
more without water. We were again at a crisis of our fortunes and the possibility of a breakdown had to be envisaged;
but we had something in hand. Retreat being wholly out of
the question, we were ourselves in harmony—no slight matter
in such circumstances—and we had plenty of water provided
we continued to use it sparingly. We could afford to dose the
camels with enough to cool their brains, and that would make
all the difference.

The main Sahma plain was now far away to the left and
invisible, but offshoots of it were still much in evidence as we
marched south-west along the first broad valley of Bani
Ma'aridh. The rain of the previous week had not visited this
district and, to judge by the conditions of the *Abal* and *Hadh*
bushes, it must have been years since it had had any moisture
to absorb. Perhaps 20 years or more, suggested Salim.
A single Wheatear seemed to have the whole area to itself,
and there was some very old gazelle and Oryx dung. But
there was also something still more interesting—the frag-

ments of a complete ostrich-egg[1] lying upon and half immersed in the sand. I gathered them up for my collection. There could be little doubt that the egg had hatched out in this very spot, and it was difficult enough to believe that that event had occurred at least 40 or 50 years ago. Yet Salim and Suwid insisted that it must be so. Only the oldest men of the desert had seen the great bird alive in these parts when they went hunting with their fathers. To their successors the ostrich was but a myth from the dead past.

So we passed from the first valley across its bordering ridge into the second, at whose further edge along the third ridge of Bani Ma'aridh we came at length to rest in the midst of withered thickets of *Abal*. The long march in the heat with only a pot of tea at mid-day had exhausted me, and I lay down without ceremony to sleep in the lengthening shade of a dead bush. The sun was below the horizon when Sa'dan woke me with a pot of tea, and I felt refreshed enough to deal with astronomical observations and the other records which a traveller must keep. But I was beginning to wonder whether I could do another such day on my waterless régime with only a small allowance of dates and a steadily lessening quantity of raw meat to sustain me each day. With milk now cut out of my diet I reckoned that my total daily consumption of liquid amounted to five small pots of tea—perhaps four pints in the aggregate. When I joined my companions for our frugal dinner Zayid held out a bowl of milk to me. Drink, said he, and think no more of what passed yesternight. I cannot do that, I replied, with the oath upon me. But it is no matter. Drink ye, and I assure you that I bear no malice. So they drank and were refreshed ; and the hatchet was buried between us. After dinner they dealt with the camels. Four of them were found to need a proper drink, including my gallant Na'riya. A skin and a half of water was poured out to them in an upturned sheepskin over-saddle, for we had brought no bucket. A kettle apiece sufficed for the rest, poured into the nose. I slept while they were at the doctoring and half an hour after midnight we were again in the saddle. My thermometer showed a tem-

[1] See Appendix.

perature of 72° at the time but it seemed quite chilly with a
south-easterly wind. In the west a broad black band of clouds
gathered as we marched in the dark, until at our halting
before dawn half the sky was overcast. I slumbered as usual
while they prepared coffee and tea, and woke with a start at
the sound of the prayer-call. Have a care of Al Aqfa, I said
to my companions as we sat round the fire sipping our coffee,
for I saw her just now in a dream. I saw her standing at the
top of a long, steep flight of steps, unable to descend. And
there was a man behind her that pushed her, so that she fell
headlong to the ground, lying in a crumpled heap with a
broken leg. Perhaps to-day she will fall from the camel as
she rides—surely she likes not such riding. But have a care
lest we lose her. Fear not, they replied reassuringly, she will
not fall—God forbid ! But they apparently discussed the
dream among themselves during the march. It is nothing,
said Humaid to the others—he had the reputation of being a
seer as well as a poet—perchance Shaikh 'Abdullah will break
his watch to-day, but God knows. The remark was not
made in my hearing, but they were all aware of the tender
care I ever bestowed on the two precious chronometer-watches,
which I carried in a specially designed belt, always on my
person. A calamity was indicated by my vision and there
could scarcely be worse than an accident to either of them.
We moved off again in the twilight over a bare sandy plain
on the south side of the fifth ridge of Bani Ma'aridh. The
atmosphere was delightfully cool at this hour and heavy
clouds were gathered over the north-western sky, while the
two great stars of the Centaur—familiarly known to the
desert Arabs as the Cavalier and Muleteer [1]—shone brilliantly
in the clear south. The coffee and dates had put fresh life
into the men, who chatted and even sang until Salim, apparently grown nervous or perhaps still optimistically considering the chance of encountering an Oryx, protested snappily.
By God's face, he exclaimed, shame upon you that you sing
in the dark ! Red [2] men, he added for my private ear, do
not chatter in the dark—at night they keep quiet. But the
others paid little heed to him, and only Abu Ja'sha rode

[1] *Khaiyal* and *Zammal.*   [2] The Arab's equivalent for our ' white man.'

silent. Ever since the milk incident he had comported himself
like a whipped dog, and his usual he-man effervescence was
in abeyance. The sun, blood-red and woolly, climbed up
into the sky behind us over the vast flat plain, in which the
ridges seemed but gentle ripples on the surface. And almost
with the first streaks of daylight we saw the marks of a full-
grown bull Oryx on the sands. He had passed that way
three or four days ago, going north.

The character of the surface was gradually undergoing a
transformation, a mixture of sand and light gravel succeeding
to the sandy valleys and ridges behind us. All this, said
Salim, is part of the great gravel plain, on which the sands
are ever encroaching. After rain these plains soon become
covered with herbs, but now, as you see, there is no sign of
vegetation. Even the sand-slopes are bare and naked.
There were a few dead *Abal* bushes in the far distance to our
left, along a ridge. But here at least there were signs of
recent rain, and Suwid scrabbled up the sand to gauge the
depth of moisture.

At length we came to the last low ridge of Bani Ma'aridh,
dotted very sparsely with dead *Abal*. From its crest we
looked out on a dark immensity as of an ocean. It was the
' father of the sea,' the great gravel plain of Abu Bahr, protruding southward from the Summan steppe like a vast
promontory of *terra firma* in the midst of the great sand-
ocean. Vast and naked and flat it spread out before us to a
sea-like horizon, with only an islet of dunes far out in its
midst to the north-west to break its impressive monotony.
Along its hither fringe to the furthest limits of our vision to
south-west and north-east ran the low barrier of the Bani
Ma'aridh sands. A raven swooped down from the empyrean
to salute our passing, and a Wheatear took shelter in a
distant thicket, as with an instinctive tremor of hesitation
or excitement we launched out into the abomination of
desolation, blissfully ignorant of its extent and little recking
of the toilsome hours that lay before us until we should come
to the thrice-welcome sands beyond.

Bani Ma'aridh, belying the suggestion of troublesome
obstacles in its name, had proved to be an easy tract of firm

sand lightly covering a gravel foundation, while the half-dozen ridges that ran transversely across it at wide intervals were lower and easier than anything in the area of the true *Sawahib*. Abu Bahr on the other hand was wholly and simply true to its name—an ocean, unruffled, serene and silent, without a mark of any kind to guide the traveller. Salim seemed almost reluctant to strike out on what appeared to me the obvious course and for a while steered almost due south-west, hugging as it were the shore of Bani Ma'aridh with its scattered *Abal* bushes rather than risk the unrelieved wilderness that stretched out to the westward. It was then just 7 a.m., and he was possibly thinking a few hours ahead to our usual halt for coffee, when we should need fuel. It would be time enough to strike across after that important function. Yet he was uncomfortable about the matter, as I could see from his constant shading of his eyes to scan the hopeless horizon. Our water-supply was the supreme factor to be considered, and by going far out of our course we were merely increasing the total distance to be traversed. I argued therefore in favour of the direct course, and he yielded. You are right, he said, but, look you, I have never been here before and I do not know how wide is Abu Bahr. In it we shall find no fuel and we shall not reach the Rumaila sands before the noon heat. Shall we wait so long for our coffee ? But perchance, if God wills, it is not so far as that. My eyes see not so far as yours, so look out for the dune-range which should lie somewhere before us. I have heard men say that one may see the sands from afar off as one enters Abu Bahr from the east, and it is even so further north, where I have crossed it going from Maqainama to Sulaiyil. Tell me, do you see any ridges of sand ahead—you would see it for it is a line of high dunes ? I strained my eyes and assured him I could see nothing, but he changed direction to the west, and from that moment there was no alternative to going ahead as fast as possible. If he had only known that we should not sight Rumaila that day, he would surely have warned us to carry faggots from the last dead bushes of Bani Ma'aridh for a fire. We had had tea and coffee at 5 a.m. and we should have no more till the morrow

at 8 a.m. Twenty-seven hours without coffee ! That was a
supreme test of Arab virtue, and our great march across Abu
Bahr revealed both the Arab and his camel at their very best.
It was indeed a stupendous performance, just such a feat as
they sing of in their ballads and vaunt in the epics of their
ancient chivalry. It was the crowning glory of our whole adventure, though a crown of thorns very painful in the making.

From the southern limits of the Summan, according to
Salim, Abu Bahr extends for some 150 miles southward to
the line where the curved horns of Bani Ma'aridh and
Rumaila join to cut it off. Beyond these again to the south
lies Raida, apparently a tract of light sand or gravel, with the
undulating sand-downs of Al Qaunis to the east and a prolongation of the 'Awariq dune-ranges to the south. And
beyond that again lies Karsh al Ba'ir, regarding whose position Salim was studiously vague, for his knowledge was based
entirely on hearsay evidence. Suwid, however, had once
accompanied an Oryx-hunting expedition which penetrated
to a distance of six days' journey (perhaps 150 miles) south-
eastward from Sulaiyil. According to him the transition
from Al Qaunis to Bani Ma'aridh is effected by a sand-strip,
called Al Dhuhur, of four parallel dune-ranges. Beyond
Bani Ma'aridh he came to a tract of sandy downs named Al
Fuqar, and after that he crossed the 'Awariq dunes to
Karsh al Ba'ir (or Hawaya Ba'ir), which he described as an
intricate maze of irregular dunes, apparently of the moraine
type. Southward of those sands lies the bare gravel plain of
Jilida, which presumably extends to the lofty dunes of
Qa'amiyat.

Thus, as we marched on, I tried to puzzle out something
approaching a reasonable topographical scheme of the great
desert. The line of Bani Ma'aridh receded steadily in a haze
of fantastic hummocks floating on a vast mirage, and for an
hour or two a light breeze fanned us fitfully from the east
and south-east. But the sun worked up steadily to the
inevitable climax and we decided to brace our nerves for the
trials of the afternoon with a brief halt of less than an hour
about 11 a.m. My companions slaked their thirst and we sat
round to a meal of dates with butter to flavour them, while

Y

some of the camels were ' snuffed ' to cool their heads before
the day's heat had reached its worst. Suwid took the water
into his mouth and blew it into the nostrils of his steed,
while the only kettle was being used elsewhere for the same
purpose. It was indeed a strange scene—that bevy of camels
and men at rest in the midst of the featureless wilderness
with never a dry blade of grass or stick of fuel to vary its
barren gravel, stretching out to the horizon on every side.
I collected an assortment of its pebbles before we remounted
and cast about in vain for desert Mantids or other creeping
things. The world around us was dead.

An hour later we saw the distant shimmer of sands and
thought we might be approaching Rumaila, but were disappointed. It was but an isolated dune-group piled up on
the gravel. Afar off a dust-devil rose some 20 feet into
the air and, curling its tail upward, disappeared as suddenly
as it had formed. The sun blazed down on us and my companions drowsily dozed as they went—a relief denied to me
by lack of experience. Salim dozed with the rest, waking up
every now and then with a grunt indicating the desired
direction. I wondered how in such circumstances, half
asleep and with nothing to guide him, he could keep any
direction at all, but I checked his course frequently with the
compass only to be amazed at his accurate piloting. I asked
him how he managed it and he simply did not know. There
is perhaps an instinctive sense of direction in the men and
animals of the desert controlled by a sub-conscious percep-
tion of the motion of the sun and stars. Salim never had any
but the vaguest idea of the time as such—an hour simply
meant nothing to him—but he never seemed to be at a loss
for direction, at any rate if the sky was clear.

We had reached the worst patch of the afternoon, the
dismal hours between 1 and 3 p.m. Having had no sip of
liquid since 5 a.m. I was beginning to feel thirsty. The prospect of tea seemed very remote as we marched into the
mirage now gradually shifting to our front, and I began to
wonder how much longer I could hold out against the inward
craving for water. For a while I kept it at bay by eating the
few onions I had reserved for such a crisis, and when they

were done I resorted to sucking peppermints, of which during
these days I always carried a small supply in my pocket.
But for some reason the remedy would not work and I
seemed to be thirstier than before. They had offered me
water when we had halted and I had refused it with disdain,
but now I felt myself on the verge of asking for it. Yet I
resisted and marched on wrestling with myself—but only
for a while. At 2.30 p.m. Salim drew rein and dismounted
to drink. I am thirsty, he said, and do you too drink now.
The sun is hot and the water in my skin is cool. I had dismounted, if only for a few moments' relief from riding in the
sultry afternoon heat. He held the bowl towards me and the
temptation was too great. I sat on the ground and drank
the stuff—tepid and of a dark brown colour—till I had
drained the bowl and arose refreshed to resume my riding.
It was my first cool drink since Naifa, now about 250 miles
behind us, and I wasted no regrets on the collapse of my
waterless penance. The desert had defeated me and henceforth I could drink freely without compunction.

We pushed on again after so welcome a respite and it
was not long before I began to feel irrepressibly drowsy.
Whether it was merely the natural result of a series of short
nights or the afternoon heat or the water I cannot say, but I
was scarcely able to hold myself upright in the saddle when
a further welcome respite from the gruelling struggle came
with a halt for the afternoon prayer at 4 p.m. I improved
the occasion with another drink, which brought with it the
realisation that travel had done nothing to deaden the
potency of Naifa water. Tea had hitherto served to counter-
act its normal effect, but now the sense of fatigue returned
which I had experienced during the four days of our sojourn
at the source. Nevertheless we had now been marching with
but little rest since midnight and that may have accounted
for my weariness, at least in part. Marching now into the
sinking sun was as trying an ordeal as one could well imagine.
Yet there was no sign among my companions of the customary search for a spot to camp in. Zayid seemed indeed to
be inspired suddenly with the energy of a devil incarnate.
He sprang into the lead when the march began to flag and

chattered incessantly to those who rode with him, telling
them tales of his own experiences and achievements in many
a raid, tales of long marches and lean days on the desert
borders of Oman and tales of hospitality in desert booths of
the great Shaikhs with the coffee and the meat that make
glad the heart of man. The weary camels seemed somehow
to respond automatically to the new mood that had settled
on the men. The dreary drag changed suddenly to a race
with time during those last two hours before sunset. Never
in all my experience have I seen men drive and camels march
as they drove and marched that day while there remained
light to bring them to camp and fodder and fuel before nightfall. But the sun went down with never a sign of the
welcoming sands beyond the eternal gravel. And still we
went on.

We halted for the sunset prayer, and, absolutely deadbeat,
I heaved a sigh of relief that at last our labours were over for
the day. But I was mistaken, for no sooner had we got
through the service and partaken of another drink of water
all round, than Zayid gave the order to mount and continue
the march. I was too weary to protest or argue, and followed
suit meekly enough. To camp where we were would have
been to renounce all hope of coffee for the night, and that
was more than my companions could stomach. On the other
hand we had during the half hour before sunset seen frequent
traces of ancient camel-paths, scored in the gravel plain and
dating back many years to the epoch of rain and pastures
that had preceded the twenty years' drought. In those days
the Arabs had brought out their grazing camels as far as this
into the desert, the animals needing no water for long periods
and the men existing on their milk. It was, therefore, a
reasonable inference that there could not be much more left
of the gravel plain and that, perhaps, a short march would
bring us to the sands, where we could certainly hope to find
dead bushes to make a fire withal.' So we not only marched
but actually quickened our pace from a steady walk to a
slow trot of something like five miles an hour.

Everywhere now we saw abundant evidences of the recent
rain, of which we had indeed met with some slender indica-

tions far out in the midst of Abu Bahr. There was too an almost imperceptible rippling of the plain, whose shallow furrows seemed to have flowed abundantly with water quite recently. It was certainly a welcome sign of some more definite change ahead and, as the darkness finally descended upon us, I had the impression that the whole surface of the desert was progressively becoming more undulating and, to some slight extent, even streaked with thin lines of sand. I looked to see the time and discovered to my dismay that my wrist-watch was missing ! Rapidly we held a council of war to consider so serious a casualty, and I suggested that two members of the party should go back on our tracks to seek the watch. They could not have far to go in any case, as I had noted the time of our starting after the halt at sunset, but I could not go on without the watch. Their going back would save time as we could go on, leaving them to follow. Otherwise I must insist on camping for the night. But wait ! I added, let me search my saddle-bag—it held a good deal of my equipment and bulged rather widely at the mouth—lest the watch may have dropped into it from my wrist. And lo and behold ! there I actually found it intact except for the strap, which had given way under the strain of long wearing. Then there was general rejoicing, and they told me of Humaid's interpretation of my dream.

We continued the march, still trotting and walking in turns. And on and on we went, scarcely seeing anything but the ground immediately under our feet, seemingly a rolling plain with appreciable depressions though with never a sign of anything that looked like bushes or herbage. We might indeed have passed quite close to such things without observing them in the darkness for, to make the gloom more impressive, heavy storm-clouds rolled up across the sky from the north-east. After the heat of the day such coolth was indeed welcome, and a few drops of rain raised hopes of different conditions on the morrow. Meanwhile the one idea in the minds of Zayid and his fellows was coffee, while I could think of nothing but the urgent need of sleep. After all most of them had slept or dozed in the saddle all through that strenuous day, while their need of refreshment was no

greater than mine. If I could do without that, they surely
could ; and the moment was rapidly approaching when I
could no longer keep awake in the saddle, while the camels,
driven on by Zayid as if the fiend himself was behind them
and responding nobly to the heel, were almost at the end of
their powers of endurance. Furthermore there was not
the slightest hope of fodder even if we came to fuel.

About 9 p.m. I sounded Salim and Humaid and was not
less surprised than pleased to find them in agreement with
my view, that it was useless seeking fuel in that darkness
without any idea whatever of its whereabouts or distance.
Like that we might go on all night without success, and our
last state would be worse than our first. Let us rest the night
and sleep, I said, for even the hungry camels will be better
to-morrow for a rest now. Yes, added Abu Ja'sha, and the
camels are dead, but Zayid drives on as you see. Look you,
I said, I can go on no more without sleep. If any of you
know of fuel within five minutes or ten, let him lead on.
Otherwise I will halt here and you may do as you will. So,
with considerable relief I thought, the cry went up that
Shaikh 'Abdullah was weary and would halt. Back from the
front came sounds of voluble cursing and Zayid reined up to
protest at the folly of halting. It is but folly, I rejoined very
curtly as I tapped Na'riya to her knees, it is but folly to
march on blindly you know not whither. I march no more,
and here I sleep. You are the Amir and can please yourself.
There may be fuel near or far, within five minutes or five
hours. Seek it out as you please and I will come to you when
you have found it. I can follow your tracks in the daylight
to-morrow, but I can sit on a camel no more.

So with a muttered curse Zayid yielded, and the unfortunate camels came to rest at 9.15 p.m. after a forced and
furious march that had begun soon after midnight. Out
of the 21 hours they had actually marched 18 allowing
for the occasional short halts we had enjoyed, and the
distance we had covered in the time was about 70 miles.
The wretched animals just stretched out their necks on the
cool sand and remained motionless, while we unloaded the
gear and spread our beds on the desert for a well-earned rest.

Sa'dan brought me a bowl of water and a lump of dates for supper—it was all we had, and the camels could not be milked after such a day. But stay, I said to Sa'dan, there are two tins of fruit in my saddle-bag. Bring me one of them and lend me your knife. I had carried these two tins with me from Mecca to Hufuf, from Hufuf to the Empty Quarter, resolved not to broach them except in a crisis. And now was certainly the right moment for one of them. Yet a tin of peaches would be a mere drop in the ocean amongst eleven of us, so I shared it with Sa'dan alone to flatter my conscience. The fruit and juice were lukewarm with the day's heating, but delicious ; and I lay down to sleep as I had never slept before, while the clouds gathered about us with the music of distant thunder.

At last we had broken the back of the desert, which had so nearly broken ours in the dismal days of our retreat from Hawaya and again during the last two days. We had had to fight hard, and we had won through with a final effort that had strained us almost to the breaking-point. But we had won through, and there remained but a hundred miles or so to the watering. In six full days of marching since we rode out of Naifa we had covered 270 miles under conditions almost ideally unfavourable in the matter of pasture— maintaining an average of over 40 miles a day, which would be reckoned good going in easier circumstances. We had certainly had three cool days to start with, but the three that had followed had more than balanced that advantage, and we had every reason to be content with our performance. And the camels that had crossed Abu Bahr at its hottest and done 48 hours without a scrap of food had not come fresh to that ordeal. They had already travelled for two whole months in the leanest of deserts almost without respite. None but the best camels could have come through such a trial, and ours were certainly as good animals as any in all Arabia.

My companions were astir betimes next morning (March 12th), clamouring for coffee. A leaden sky with storm-clouds to north and north-east greeted my awakening, and we were soon on the move in the twilight gloaming. The air was

damp and clammy about us and the north-east wind, which
had blown throughout the night, chilled us as we marched.
We were still in the gravel plain of Abu Bahr, no longer
however a dead flat wilderness, but rather a low gently undulating steppe, bare and desolate with streaks of sand and here
and there an outcrop of rocky ground, which was a welcome
relief from the monotony of gravel. We had scarcely been
marching ten minutes when we came upon a strip of withered
Hadh bushes, which would have given us coffee the previous
night had we marched but a little further. Now, however,
it did not tempt us to stop. It is better, said Zayid, to go
on yet a bit that, perchance, we may find fodder for the
camels as well as fuel for our coffee. So we marched on
past two or three mounds of the outcropping rock, some 20
feet above the plain level, and noticed signs of a recent
flood.

Beyond them we came to a light spread of sand that
marked the transition from Abu Bahr into Rumaila, whose
first range of dunes lay upon our right hand, while the gravel
plain spread out on our left, gently undulating, dotted with
patches of rock and streaked here and there with tongues of
sand. Almost immediately we came upon a few green
bushes of *'Arrad*, the first edible vegetation encountered in
48 hours, and no power on earth could have got our camels
past them. Their hunger was terrible to watch, and we gave
them their heads to do as they willed until they had made
an end of the scanty herbs. Then we passed on into the real
sands of Rumaila, whose gently-billowing bosom was
scarred here and there by exposed patches of the underlying
bed-rock. Here was much *Hadh*, though withered and dead,
and Al Aqfa went off on her own, searching hungrily for
tracks of hares. Rumaila, a tract of broad sandy valleys
separated each from the other by long waves of dunes, is
generally regarded as a southerly continuation of the Dahna,
from which it is said to be separated at a day's journey northward of our line of march by a *Marbakh* or flat, sandy plain
besprinkled with *Hadh*, *Abal* and other herbage. In Rumaila itself there appears to be no *Abal* but we came upon
dry tufts of *Birkan* and *Sabat* stubble.

The valley beyond the first dune-range contained a considerable area of exposed rock, a greyish calcareous material. We passed by a small patch naturally hollowed out to form a pond, now dry though it appeared to have held water quite recently. Near by we found a thin line of green *Andab*, which the camels cropped to the ground as they passed. And we saw a pair of Chats and a desert lark as we crossed the second dune-wave into a wide plain, where a halt was called in the midst of a profusion of dead *Hadh*. The camels sat disconsolately around us or wandered about in vain search of fodder, while we settled down to the main business of the morning—the making of coffee and tea, which in due course we consumed with a meagre ration of dates. How comforting was that meal—the tea and coffee after 27 hours of forced abstinence ! And there was milk too for those who had not forsworn it. The north-east wind grew stronger as we dallied over our breakfasting—for Salih, having upset a pot of coffee on the fire in a laudable effort to make a second brew to eke out the first, had insisted on beginning all over again—and by the time we were ready to resume our march the sand was sweeping along the plain before it in long wisps which covered the countryside with a veil of haze.

It was pleasant riding like that over rolling downs of sand after the flat gravel of yesterday. A sense of well-being pervaded us after the refreshments of which we had just partaken, and the sun filtered but faintly through the light clouds which raced upon the earth before us in alternate bands of light and shade. Here too the recent rains had had time to coax life out of the dead wilderness. Tiny heads of green heralded the birth of desert plants, the succulent *Halam* and the *Sa'dan*, whose discarded burrs of past seasons strewed the sandy floor and stuck to the soft pads of the camels. They stamped petulantly as they went, to rid themselves of the irritating limpets, and every now and then we stopped to clear their feet of the spikes, counting on one occasion no fewer than 18 burrs on a single pad of my camel, Na'riya. The short thorns of the small circular discs cannot penetrate far enough into the gristle to do harm, but the irritation is intense, as I had reason to know when I walked barefoot upon the sands.

Little piles of camel droppings, judged to be a month old or so and half-buried in the sand, which had entirely obliterated the tracks of the animals responsible for them, started my companions on a lively argument as to their significance. At intervals they continued until we came to the spot where the party had evidently camped on its way and we could form a rough estimate of its numbers—some eight or nine animals perhaps. Doubtless a raiding party, and perhaps the one whose camp-fire smoke we had smelt at Maqainama, though at the time we could not tell whether we were on their outward or homeward route. Or perhaps the party which had lost the camel and calf whose tracks we had crossed in the very heart of the desert. On one point, however, all were agreed. The dung was even as the dung of our animals, camels of the desert marching through poor pastures. None but raiders would march thus.

Our westerly course carried us diagonally across the valleys and waves of Rumaila until at noon we halted again on its western fringe to collect fuel from the dead bushes along the base of its fifth and last range of dunes. Beyond lay the bare, low, undulating tract of Qaunis, where no bushes were likely to be encountered, while we had at least learned from Abu Bahr the folly of entering upon such an area without some provision against adversity. We had no desire for a long march this day, after the exertions of the previous one, and we contemplated no more than an attempt to clear the sands of Qaunis and a reasonably early halt in the steppe of Al Jidda beyond for a good night's rest.

Our water-supply was now found to be sufficient to justify further relief for the camels, which were duly subjected to the indignity of ' snuffing.' One of them was declared to be suffering from the ' evil eye,' [1] and the ' snuffing ' was preceded by an exhibition of wizardry, doubtless a survival from some ancient animistic rite of the early paganism of Arabia. Each one of us was required to spit into the bowl of water intended for the sufferer, and the strange medicine was

---

[1] *Mandhula (? Mandhura)*—*i.e.*, looked upon by an (evil) eye.

poured into her resisting nostrils, while half a dozen men held her firmly down for the operation, which was, apparently successfully, performed by Suwid. What the preceding symptoms had been I omitted to ascertain, but my companions appeared to be satisfied that the evil spirit had duly departed out of the beast. Perhaps it had entered into the doctors themselves, who now fell to quarrelling about the always elaborate ceremonial of their coffee-serving. Like and like the presiding genius of the occasion pours around to the assembled company, to each man a cup—once round and a second time, but each time missing out himself. And then with monotonous regularity begins the comedy. A third cup would be offered to the man on the pourer's right. 'Tis yours, he would say, and the pourer would drink. He would then pour again to him who had waived the cup, and the same thing would happen with the next in order and the next, until it becomes a matter of gauging how each man had fared in the distribution. And then begin the quarrels and argument of desert courtesy, generally culminating in a deadlock of all-round self-denial. 'Tis yours, no, yours, but never 'tis mine ! And immemorial custom leaves the last dregs in the pot to the pourer himself, who generally fares worst in the contest. It is little enough in all conscience to pick a quarrel out of, but the little is enough when nerves are stretched on the rack by desert travel. A careless word, and the flame leaps up out of smouldering embers.

On entering the Qaunis downs, whose northern extremity lay about ten miles to northward of our course according to Salim, we changed direction to the north-west. It was all very bare with a little *Sabat* stubble, but we had sport with a few lizards and for the first time in the waterless desert I saw a locust, a single insect only and that dead upon the sand. But here there was ample evidence of better days in the past, the droppings of grazing camels and scattered embers of deserted camp-fires. Hither, said Salim, the Oryx comes sometimes but rarely, though the *Rim* is plentiful when the desert blossoms after rain. Now they are all gone far off in search of pastures. We would find them perhaps to the north, but here, as you see, there has been no rain for years

until this month.   Yet see how the *Sa'dan* is sprouting everywhere.   There was indeed a sheen of delicate green upon the
gentle slopes and Suwid, with constant soundings in the
sand, found an average depth of two or three feet for the
moisture left by the recent rainfall.

Far off, perhaps six or seven miles, to the south-west
appeared the long sand-ridge of Mushaimikh, a familiar landmark of the Sulaiyil hunters.   It betokened our approach to
the end of Al Qaunis, from whose last ridge we soon looked
out indeed on a scene that filled us with rejoicing—a vast
blue sea as it were, the great steppe plain of Al Jidda [1]
backed by the distant coast of the Tuwaiq barrier.   ' The
veritable desert ' was at last behind us, and our eyes rested
once more on the borders of the sown.   Somewhere in the
folds of the great upland before us lay our destination,
Sulaiyil ;   and Suwid and Salim were able to identify the
isolated hillock of Abraq ibn Jaffal, where they had once
halted during a journey to Maqainama from the west.   It lay
far off to the north-west, and somewhere in the desert, about
15 or 20 miles from it, they remembered to have drawn water
on that occasion from a pool that the rain had formed in a
great rock depression known as Makiniya.   At first the
steppe was lightly dusted with sand, overflowing from the
fringes of Qaunis ;   but gradually we passed into an unrelieved wilderness of rock and gravel, dark of colour and all
but bare of vegetation.   A line of flat-topped hillocks stood
out from the higher ground behind them, the relic of an old
line of low cliffs, which converged on our course ahead from
the north-east.   From them the desert ran back to the hazy
horizon of the distant uplands, and again we rejoiced as we
marched on before the cool breeze from the east.   How
different it all was from yesterday, when we had suffered
torments of heat and thirst and uncertainty !   The very sky
had changed its mood, and the distant scene ahead, for all
its dreariness of aspect, was yet the home of men.   Verily
Tuwaiq is our father, exclaimed Sa'dan, whose own home
lay in a fold of this same upland barrier, some hundreds of
miles to the north ; yes, Tuwaiq is our father, as the Dahna

[1] In full Jiddat al Farsha ; also sometimes called Hidbat al Farsha.

is our mother. Laud to the Lord, that we see it again, coming from the empty world behind us. And to-morrow, maybe, if God wills, we may look again on the faces of men. Ay, and women too, for there may be damsels at Sulaiyil for us to wed. His thoughts were ever of his little wife at Mecca and of other women whom he might in due course introduce to the bliss of his minute menage in the Ma'abida quarter.

We had taken things easily enough during the day and settled down in camp for the night soon after 5 p.m. after a total march of about 25 miles. To the southward at a distance of some eight or ten miles the long ridge of Mushaimikh stood out prominently in the scene. Behind us the Qaunis sands lined the horizon with its long coast. Elsewhere there was nothing but the dark steppe stretching back to the rolling uplands, its broad bosom swelling up here and there to little paps. The sun set, the storm-clouds rolled up again from west and north, and we rested from our labours. There was a surprise in store for me when they summoned me to dinner, for Salih had cooked a dish of rice to celebrate the occasion. Very good it was too after the long and meagre monotony of dates and raw meat, for Salim's stock of the latter seemed inexhaustible and he had given me some during the day's march with the information that there was still a little left for the morrow. Whether the meat rations of the rest had held out in similar fashion I never inquired, but it was surprising indeed that there should be anything left to eat of the animal we had slain eleven days before. After dinner I attended to my theodolite observations with Sa'dan's assistance as usual, and then in privacy we shared the contents of the second and last tin of peaches before composing ourselves for the night's sleep.

A fresh east wind, with a little northing in it, blew throughout the night, which was deliciously cool though the temperature never fell below 72°. And the sky was heavily clouded over at 11-30 p.m., when Zayid disturbed the peace and slumbers of the camp with an ill-judged attempt to get us on the move again ahead of our usual time. Fortunately I looked at my watch when he roused me, and he retired disgruntled and grumbling at my obstinacy. He would have liked to make Sulaiyil by the following afternoon, but I saw no point at this stage in making a forced night-march which would deprive me of the pleasure of seeing the country by daylight. So it was not till two hours later that we were again on the move, and then it was so dark under the heavy clouds that obscured the sky and stars that we could not see more than a few yards in any direction, and Salim seemed unable to steer a course. At least my compass showed that we were heading north-west, while our bearing during the later part of the previous afternoon's march had been practically due west. Salim, in answer to my question, admitted that we should be on the same point as then and abruptly changed direction, asking me to do the piloting on that course by my compass as he was unable to steer in the darkness with neither stars nor landmarks to guide him. The others, recalled from their course, broke forth into oaths and execrations on the error of our ways, and I treated them to a discourse on the virtues of the compass, while we pursued our line in complete disregard of their protests. They remained sceptical but followed in our wake, discoursing loudly among themselves on the folly of trusting to instruments and other new-fangled things when a sense of direction was all that was needed to guide one aright. You may be right, I said, but Salim says we should march on the same line as we were following in the afternoon till we camped at sunset, and that is the line we are now on. But tell me, I asked, where is the great star—I referred to the planet Jupiter—which has gone before us each day of this night-marching ? They pointed without hesitation to the north-west, the direction which they had been following when recalled. Not so, said I, it is straight ahead of us behind the clouds, but God knows best. There was no convincing them and Salim put his childish trust in me. So we marched on at the best pace possible in the dark, while the unfortunate camels floundered about painfully on the sharp rocks of the plain. Then of a sudden there was a break in the clouds ahead of us, and the great planet shone straight down in our faces ! Salim went into raptures of delight : Oh, Shaikh 'Abdullah, 'tis you have guided us this night, not I, you and your compass. God is great indeed ! Look, you people, is it not so ? That star it is we should be steering on, and you would have had us go all awry. We should have struck Hamam and not Sulaiyil, if we had followed you. There was at least general rejoicing—for there had been genuine misgiving—that we were indeed on the right track, but they marvelled how I should have guided them in the darkness even with a compass. I showed them the luminous points, and they marvelled yet more at the notorious intelligence of the Franks. By the face of God ! ejaculated Salim, did he not know all about Shuwaikila before he had even set eyes on the great sands ? And did he not tell us at Naifa the direction and distance of Sulaiyil. By God ! it was very sooth he spoke then though we knew it not. I had indeed made a rough computation of the position of Naifa in relation to Sulaiyil and told them before starting that we should need 112 hours of actual marching to cover the 560 kilometres (350 miles), which I reckoned to be the approximate distance. In the end our total marching-time proved to be 111 hours, though we probably marched on the whole at a better average rate than five kilometres an hour and therefore covered a distance nearer 600 kilometres than the 555 suggested by my adopted rate—the distance between Naifa and Sulaiyil by our route being 375 miles.

The clouds closed again over Jupiter and I marched on in the darkness, musing how the great planet had seemed to follow the fortunes of my adventure from its earliest beginnings—when at Riyadh in November I used to wake at the Muadhdhin's raucous cry before the dawn to see him gazing down upon me from his mansion in the Sickle, seemingly mocking at me with its great query-mark. I had shuddered then in agonies of nervous irritation as the days went by with no sign of the King's will. And each day Jupiter, in all his radiance, had but renewed the question. Was it to be or not to be ? Then had come the great day of rejoicing when the King had spoken, and thence onward the planet had coursed nightly through the sky guarding us as we wandered through the desert, and each night he gained almost imperceptibly on the query-mark which ever followed him. And

then at last he had gone before us in these last night-marches
in the waterless desert with the Sickle above and behind him
until this last night when he appeared alone for an instant,
smiling through the clouds to vindicate my guiding. As the
dim light of the false dawn showed behind us he shone out
again in a band of clear sky between the horizon and the
rolling clouds, and as he sank to rest, Regulus, alone of the
Lion's stars, sailed out from behind the clouds—the stop
without the question—as if to mark the end of our tale. The
band of clouds sank behind the horizon obscuring the Sickle
to its setting, and the upper sky put forth all its brilliance to
applaud the happy issue of our last struggle with the dark,
while the Raven and the Bear, with Spica and Arcturus at
the apex, raised aloft their triumphal arch over our advance.
The thing was done, the great journey was all but over, and
we halted to pray and refresh ourselves with tea and coffee,
while the slow dawn extinguished the heavenly illuminations.

It was a great moment when we mounted again to resume
the march which would carry us all but home. The world
had transformed itself under cover of the darkness, and we
looked out now on a gravel plain, it is true, but a plain
streaked with stripes not of sand but of green bushes. The
earth seemed to pulse with moisture, and long lines of dark
green *Harmal*—a strange plant to our desert senses—
marked the shallow channels of the floods from Tuwaiq,
while at some distance to our left a broader band of green
betrayed the course of the great Wadi Dawasir, whose tail
of modern times peters out in the stony desert with nothing
but local rain to fill a channel that once upon a time—long
before man had learned to record his knowledge and experiences—had carried a mighty river into the delta of Shanna.
Something of its long story we had traced in our wanderings ;
the rest is buried in the sands. Here and there groups of
spreading acacia bushes dotted the channels in the gravel
and Salih extracted a little owl from the deserted burrow of
a spiny-tailed lizard.[1]

Salim and I led on over the great plain and the numerous
drainage-lines that crossed it from the north-west to south-

[1] *Dhabb.*

east, apparently trending from the slopes of Tuwaiq towards
the main line of the Dawasir channel. The plain appeared
as a vast chess-board of alternating dark and light patches,
in which, but mostly in vain, we sought fodder for the camels.
The *Harmal* is poisonous while the acacias, much to my
surprise, attracted only the disdain of the thirsting beasts,
but it was different when we came to a patch of scattered
Dha'a grass, half dead though revived to greenness by the
rains, round which they crowded, pushing and jostling, to
eat ravenously. It was but a mouthful or two all round—
little enough for starving animals now well on with their
third day of foodless marching. Never, said Salim, in answer
to my enquiry, have I myself gone so long without food for
my camels. Without fresh fodder they become thirsty and,
when they are very thirsty, they cannot eat until they drink.
But they can go on longer like this if necessary. They could
last five days, perhaps six, without food, but that would be
their limit. After that they would just sit down and die.
Yet, if God wills, we will yet see good (fare) for the beasts
to-day. So thought they all, and again they drove on the
camels over the foodless scene as if the devil pursued.
Zayid was in a foul temper and had discouraged the preparation of coffee at the dawn halt to mark his unappeased displeasure at my refusal to march at midnight. And Jupiter
had confounded his captious carping at the route dictated
by my compass. But the main ground of his objection was
the loss of precious hours which might have carried us into
Sulaiyil before nightfall, and he sought his revenge by
vicious, purposeful driving, as if to achieve that object after
all in my despite. I had too just an idea of the distance
involved to be disturbed by such a prospect, but I maintained a discreet silence when my compass informed me that
Salim, by some strange aberration of judgment, was heading
south-west instead of west on our original course. The
boundless desert lay before us and we could deflect our
course in the right direction when we would. A few extra
miles would do us no harm, though they would cheat Zayid
of his triumph.

So we marched for nearly five hours over an immense

z

whitish wilderness of gravel in which were frequent burrows of the great *Dhabb* (spiny-tailed lizard) but little or no vegetation except the now familiar lines of *Harmal* and acacias. Everywhere there was the sprouting of tiny plants too minute for the camels to notice, and we sought in vain something that would justify a halt for refreshments. Salim produced the last of his dry meat and we agreed that it would be pleasant to have some coffee if we could find something for the camels to browse on meanwhile. But the distant lines of *Harmal* led us on in the hope they might be *Dha'a* only to disappoint us when we reached them until, towards 10 a.m., I announced my intention of halting at the next patch of *Samr* (acacia) we might come to. Zayid redoubled his energies and went into the lead, but the others lagged in the hope that I would be as good as my word. I drew rein accordingly at the next bushes and went off after a hawk-moth that I saw darting from flower to flower of the *Harmal*, while the rest set to work with the pots and the fire. Zayid, left in the air, came back livid with fury and I said not a word, leaving the others to appease his wrath. But not to be appeased he sulked apart while we enjoyed coffee and dates. Thus a good hour went by and, when we resumed the march, I informed Salim about the error of his direction. With the mounting sun the desert had become somewhat hazy and the poor visibility made it impossible to see the distant uplands. Nevertheless Salim agreed that it would be safer to march west for a bit until he could pick up a landmark. We changed course accordingly, and Zayid came racing up from the rear in a perfect paroxysm of fury. What is this ? he cried ; where are your senses that you change direction ? The afternoon is upon us and you go wandering here and there in this desert. The water is there, there, he added challengingly, pointing south-west in the very direction from which we had turned away. I felt no inclination to leave Salim to bear the brunt of the storm and took up the challenge before he could answer, for in truth he was not very sure of himself. Oh Zayid, I answered, Salim is our guide and he has directed us over the desert all these days. What fault have you found in him that you question his guiding now ?

Are you, then, also of the guides that you can tell us where the water is, which you have never seen since God created you ? But you are right, Zayid ; you speak sooth indeed, for the water is indeed there where you say—ay, the waters of Hassi and Qariya on the road to Najran. But if it is Sulaiyil you seek and the wells of Latwa, that is a different matter, for they lie in that direction—and I pointed somewhat northward of west—it is there that I am going, and not your way ; but as for yourself, the ordering is yours. Yet look you, Zayid, we have crossed the Empty Quarter, and it is thanks to you, as I know, for it was yours to mar my prospects—as you did twice—or to make them as you have done now. Why do you, therefore, seek to quarrel now when there is nought to gain from it ? From Sulaiyil you can go home if you like not my company, or you can go with me to Mecca if you please. But from now onwards I need you no more, so let there be peace between us. We have wrangled enough, and I want no more of it. At any rate I go with Salim thither, and if you would see Sulaiyil, you had better come with us— but hold your peace !

He fell back to the rear, disgruntled and beaten, while Salim rejoiced like a child that I had spoken up for him. So we marched on over the wilderness, utterly bare and desolate, with nothing to bring us the assurance we sought of the landmarks that appeared not. He was underestimating the distance and that was all, but he was visibly becoming more and more uncomfortable. At length he stopped, shading his eyes to peer feebly into the uncompromising void. Look you, he said, I am lost. It is long, very long, since I was in these parts and I know them no longer. Fear not, I replied, but, if you will, let us turn more to the north-west. It is safer to go north into Tuwaiq than south into the limitless, waterless desert. So we turned north-west for half an hour, when at last there appeared afar off on our left a low ridge ending with a knoll surmounted by a cairn, while a broad band of *Harmal* and acacias to our right traced the course of a channel descending from the lower slopes of Tuwaiq. I cannot see well, said Salim, but if that yonder is a cairn it is surely Rijm al Ma—the cairn of the watering. Suwid, he

called out, do you go with another of the brethren to see if
that is the cairn. So off went Suwid with Salih while we led
on somewhat north of west. Almost immediately we came
to two or three camel-paths meandering across the desert.
Salim sighed with relief. Surely these will bring us to the
water if we follow them. And as we went other paths
struck into the general line, the paths of generations of
camels trailing from the desert pastures to the watering,
scored deep in the gravel plain. We went by a stone-lined
prayer-place of the herdsmen, and afar off there appeared
before us the line of dunes which they call 'Arq al Rammak,
the dividing line between the vast plain of Al Jidda and the
lesser plain of Al Farsha where the Wadi splays out into a
delta in the angle formed by the northern and southern
sections of Tuwaiq. A pleasant east wind blew freshly upon
us from behind to temper the sultriness of the afternoon and
the sky was leaden with dull clouds above. A few spots of
rain dropped from them as we turned aside into a thin
coppice of acacias for the afternoon prayer. Long since, a
month or more ago, a raiding party had halted here, and
there were plentiful droppings of the *Rim*, which evidently
frequented the spot in considerable numbers to eke out the
hot afternoons in the grateful shade of the bushes.

The wind increased in strength, veering to the south-east,
as we continued the march across the flattened right shoulder
of the Rammak dune-ridge, beyond which at last we looked
upon the broad line of thick bushes which constitute the
Farsha or flood-channel of Wadi Dawasir from the point where
it debouches into the desert from the Latwa strait. The
outer line of Tuwaiq lay to our right streaked with the bushy
courses of numerous freshets, whose mouths towards the
plain were choked with *Ghadha*-covered sand-ridges, one of
which, greater than the rest, is known as Qauz al Sha'diya
from the torrent-bed of that name which I had crossed
farther up in the midst of Tuwaiq during my journey of 1918.
A few drops of rain had fallen upon us as we prayed, and an
intermittent drizzle accompanied us on the last stage of the
day's journey across a gravel plain lightly sprinkled with
sand to the broad Farsha channel, in whose lightly wooded

bed we intended to pitch our last camp. It was a charming
spot when we saw it next morning, for the evening twilight
had passed into the gloom of night by the time we reached
the fringe of bushes. The wind whistled eerily about us as we
lay in the open, and the lightning flashed from angry clouds
that rolled their drums of muffled thunder. A march of
48 miles had wearied us in spite of the pleasant weather
conditions of the day, and the studied sullenness of Zayid
cast a gloom over our spirits just when we might have been
celebrating the last night of a great and successful adventure
with such merriment as the slender remnants of our stores
might permit. I made no attempt to join the party round
the coffee-fire, and Zayid withheld the invitation on which
I insisted, as indeed I had done throughout the march. So
I ate my dates alone with the usual pot of tea to wash them
down. The conditions were unfavourable to my customary
study of the stars, and my stock of paraffin had long since been
exhausted. There was nothing to do but get into bed, and
I had scarcely done that than the floodgates of heaven opened
to drench us with a heavy shower, which happily stopped
as suddenly as it had begun, though all through the night
there was an intermittent spitting that prevented continuous
slumber. Suwid called out to the four corners of the uni-
verse announcing our presence and identity in the time-
honoured fashion of the desert lest men of evil intent might
be prowling or lurking about in the cover of bushes and
darkness. A roar of laughter greeted the customary invitation to all and sundry to come and share our meal. Look ye,
oh people, he concluded, we are of the men of Ibn Sa'ud
marching on the king's business to Sulaiyil, and I am Suwid
of the Dimnan, son of Al Azma. Come unto us and welcome,
if you would share our fare. We have good things in plenty,
and coffee. The silence of the night closed upon us again,
broken only by the cud-chewing of the weary camels, which
had at last found fodder in plenty—*Markh* and *Hamdh* and
Ghadha—and had been allowed to wander about under guard
for an hour or so after we had unsaddled them.

I was woken by a rather belated call to the morning
prayer, and the twittering of birds among the bushes and

trees—*Samr* and *Sarh*—around us was pleasant to my ears after the unbroken silence of the great desert. We took things easily enough while the camels grazed again on the wet vegetation and the wind dried our sodden bedding and baggage. The stars had gone before my waking, and only the faintest outline remained of the triumphal arch. Jupiter and Regulus had sunk to rest and the great question had been answered. The thing had happened and never more would we march in the dark. Where there's a will, says a proverb of Arabia, there's a way, and every man wins what he wills.

Immediately after prayers and the usual coffee we sent off 'Abdullah ibn Ma'addi and Suwid in advance to announce our coming to the astonished Mayor and Corporation of Sulaiyil. And we did not forget to commission them to prepare a suitable dinner against our arrival. Our common craving was for lamb, a good fat lamb well stewed, after two and a half months with little meat—and then only camel and occasional hares, our share of the latter working out at about one and a half per head in 68 days. And, even more, we yearned for bread, which we had not tasted since leaving Hufuf, for Ibn Jiluwi's staff had omitted to include flour in our stores. So we looked forward to the flesh-pots of Sulaiyil as we started off in the wake of our messengers about 8 a.m. along the northern fringe of the Farsha channel. On our right across a flat plain, partly gravel and partly alluvial clay, the low cliff of northern Tuwaiq converged gradually on our course, which was set, very slightly to the north of west, on the narrow pass by which the Wadi emerges from its passage through the barrier. On the other side the gentler slopes of southern Tuwaiq converged from the south-east on the same point, while between the two the mile-wide scrub-jungle of the Farsha ran in a straight line slightly south of east to the southern shoulder of the Rammak dunes.

Everywhere the droppings of sheep announced that we were within hail of civilisation and I picked up a marble pestle from the sands, the lost property of a careless shepherd. The *Sarh* trees in full blossom were a delight after the treeless desert, standing 20 or 30 feet high, as also did the acacias

adorned with their charming yellow tassels. Birds sang or
twittered in their branches, and swallows swooped low along
the ground snapping up the insects that hummed gently
among the flowers of spring. It was indeed a charming
scene. And at last we saw a building of the sons of men, a
little round watchtower of the shepherds, on the edge of the
bushy channel beyond a clay bottom called Al Manqa, the
swamp. It was dry now, this swamp reputed to hold water
for months on end after rains, but the deep footprints of
wading cattle in the hard clay told a pleasant tale of other
times. We paused a moment to gaze upon the little tower,
15 feet high and circular, the first habitation of men we had
seen since leaving Jabrin.

Our journey was drawing to an end. We could see the
tamarisk clumps of Latwa in the gorge and there were
tamarisks in the Farsha bed, while we could make out ahead
the stone ruins on the outer slopes of Tuwaiq, which I had
seen 14 years before. Suddenly there was a movement in
the bushes afar off to our left front—perhaps cattle. But,
no! it was men moving stealthily in open order on a wide
front, moving as if to intercept us. We counted seven—there
might be more—and there was an instinctive grasping of the
rifles slung on the saddle-poles, the sound of ammunition
pushed home into the breeches for action. But we continued
our advance, unchecked, slowly, steadily, until it seemed—still
from afar—that the men ahead carried no weapons. Why!
said Salih, they are unarmed! Ay, said another, and 'tis
women they are, not men, but coming across our path—
wood-gatherers perhaps for the village fires, and doubtless
thinking we come to raid their folk. See! how they come to
bar our way. For such are the women of Najd! By this
time the nearest were near enough to hail. Peace be upon
you! we cried. And upon you be peace! they answered
shrilly, and hail, and welcome! We halted as the bevy of
ladies reached us, black-smocked and veiled with the black
muslin of their fashion. And greetings were exchanged
again while an old woman, with charming voice, took up the
rôle of spokesman, standing in advance of the rest. What is
the news? asked Zayid. All good, replied the old lady, but

welcome to you, and whence come ye ? We come as ye see,
replied Zayid, from the desert. We are 'returners,' returned
from our hunting. We have seen nought but good—no
pastures indeed but rains abundant. And saw ye tracks of
foes ? she asked. None, said Zayid ; but tell me, what of
your harvest ? and what the price of flour and dates among
your people ? Praise be to God, that has blessed us this
season, she replied ; you will get two measures [1] of fine flour
for the dollar, and dates at six weights or seven.[2] The other
women stood a little way back from their champion, open-
eyed and open-mouthed doubtless under their concealing
veils, but one of them, evidently the daughter of the charm-
ing-voiced old lady, had come a little forward to her mother's
elbow and had coyly contrived to disarrange her veil sufficiently to reveal a pair of sparkling eyes under a brow that
was perfection. Her charm met with the inevitable, though
silent, tribute of the weathered gallants, whom her mother
kept in conversation, and I noticed that the comparative
splendour of my accoutrements and the manifest superiority
of my steed had served to focus a lovely gaze in the right
direction. It was no time, however, for dalliance, and Zayid
and the old lady had soon exhausted the possibilities of such
polite conversation as was required by the circumstances of
our meeting. So we turned with heavy hearts from our first
glimpse of human beauty after weeks and months of barren
travail, but we counted it for luck that our first human encounter had been so charming. A Brimstone butterfly flitted
over the sea-green shrubs of *Harm* as if to challenge comparison, and we passed on through the bottle neck of the Latwa
valley, leaving the women to think of their wood-cutting and
other things. And I was back once more among the familiar
scenes of a distant, but unforgotten, past.

The stone-built ruins of the original settlement of Sulaiyil
still covered the gentle slope of Tuwaiq where it runs down
to the Wadi's edge. Its bastions and battlements still
crowned the ridge with their gaunt skeletons. But the valley
itself bore the scars and blisters of a long unmerciful drought,
which had fallen upon this country of the south a year or two

[1] *Sa'*.   [2] *Wazna*.

after my first visit and had endured without a break until now, when my second coming had been heralded by abundant rains. So again there was hope for the future to console the folk for the miseries of the past. The scattered palm-groves of 1918 were nowhere to be seen—the palms had perished and been cut down. Most of the score or more of wells had become derelict for the well-cattle had died off from starvation, and the impoverished cultivators had not been able to replace them. The scattered huts and granges of the tenant-workers had fallen into ruins. There was nothing but desolation, with occasional fields of standing corn where a few wells had been kept in commission by the richer owners. So we came to a bulge in the valley flanked on the north by the grim remains of Qasr Tari, and there we found wells at work for the irrigation of ripening crops—wheat and barley. Four men and a woman were straining at the ropes to lift the great water-skins to the level of the creaking wooden rollers, over which the water poured to the tank that fed the ducts.

A slave rose from the shade of a spreading tamarisk by one of the wells to greet us in the name of Sulaiyil's mayor. Welcome to you, he exclaimed, and welcome again! God give ye life and strength! But an hour since your messengers arrived among us, and I have come out at the bidding of the Amir, Farhan, to be at your service. His name was Majid, a man of cheerful countenance and pleasing words, and of fine stature withal. We dismounted to be greeted in turn with the kiss of peace. The camels were unloaded and driven to the well, where willing hands had soon filled the trough for their drinking. And then there was making and drinking of coffee and tea. The journey was over and the waterless desert had been crossed, probably for the first time in human history—375 miles or more between water and water. Yet the camels drank but sparingly. They were too thirsty.

CHAPTER V

EPILOGUE

A company come up out of the Empty Quarter, wherein is drought and famine!—ZAYID.

THE tale is ended—of the Empty Quarter. An hour's riding brought us in the early afternoon of March 14th to the palm-groves of Sulaiyil, where tents had been pitched against our coming at the corner of one of the hamlets of the oasis—Al Muhammad. Little had changed here in 14 years—the same long line of mud houses jutting out into the desert, the same red-smocked women at the village well, the same hordes of children with little or nothing to do, the same seemingly aimless and hopeless existence of the elders. Yet the passage of years had brought worse rather than better things. The drought had killed off the cattle and reduced the area under palms. The peace had closed the commercial avenues leading to the unblockaded Turkish marts of war-time Yaman. And the collapse of the Persian Gulf pearling industry under the weight of the world-wide economic depression had thrown the citizens of the desert oasis out of their strange but normal employment. Old 'Abdullah ibn Nadir, who had entertained me so hospitably in the rival hamlet of Al Hanaish, had been gathered to his fathers, and his son, Salim, reigned prosperously enough in his stead. Farhan al Ruwaiya still ruled as Amir in Al Muhammad, a charming man in his old age, fox-visaged, avaricious, but full of kindness to obliterate the less favourable impression left by his pardonable attitude in those days. And another of the great merchants of then came to crave alms, fallen from the pedestal of wealth to beg his bread, with a small boy to lead his blind footsteps to the sources of charity. Poverty was now widespread and I must have distributed the equivalent of farthings and half-

pence to at least 500 persons during the two days of my
sojourn—mostly starving children and women in the extremities of wretchedness. Yet the rains of the past weeks
had brought new hope to many who had resigned themselves
in hopeless despair to the will of God.

We sat down to a mid-day meal of mutton and sopped
bread and rice, eating our fill after empty days. And in the
evening we dined with Farhan—a similar meal, simple, well
cooked and full of nourishment. But our stomachs revolted
at such exuberance, and for some days we suffered the torments of the damned for no apparent reason but the taking of
good food in plenty into systems attuned to desert starvation.
It was said that the flocks of Sulaiyil graze largely on the
Sana, a violent purge well-known to the epicures of Mecca,
and it may be that their meat is seasoned with the physic.
Or, maybe, the chill that came with the cold winds and rain
that beat upon us these days had worked upon our unaccustomed surfeit to make us ill.

For ill indeed we were, all of us ! and the ides of March
dawned bleak and stormy on a company prostrated by the
vicious grip of the colic. In the intervals of pain and miserable inaction I ranged the gardens for butterflies and plants,
while a host of small boys brought me small birds caught in
their home-made snares. It was a long and weary way that
yet lay before us, and the time was short if we would reach
Mecca for the celebration of the pilgrimage. We could not
afford to dally and there was nothing to keep us at Sulaiyil
after our camels had rested a while and filled their bellies with
the desert plants by day and the rich lucerne spread before
their couches at night.

In the coming days and weeks we would revisit the settlements of Wadi Dawasir to find them as inhospitable and
unfriendly as before—but not openly hostile—under the
guidance of a bigoted prelate ; we would see the oases of the
great Wadi Bisha and cross the sister channels of Tathlith
and Ranya ; we would in due course trail wearily over the
vast lava-field of the Buqum, where they point out to this
day the routes of the advancing and retreating hordes of the
Abyssinian Abraha in the ' year of the Elephant ' ; and we

should see the latest of the great battle-fields of Arabia, strewn with the skulls and bones of the Sharifian army, caught and annihilated by the Wahhabis under the walls of Turaba. And at last we should reach Mecca on the ninetieth day after our setting forth from Hufuf.

The camels which had carried us across the desert would carry us through the pilgrimage. And then we would part for ever, myself and my companions, to remember the good and forget the evil of our strange association in an enterprise which had filled my dreams for 14 years and racked their nerves for as many weeks. To them and the great beasts that bore us—hungering and thirsting but uncomplaining—the credit of a great adventure. Mine the pleasure of telling the tale with heartfelt homage to the Arabian Caesar.

' Let a man be true in his intentions and his efforts to fulfil them, and the point is gained whether he succeed or not.'

THE END.

APPENDICES

A. METEORITES AND FULGURITES.

By Dr. L. J. Spencer, F.R.S.,
Mineral Department, British Museum.

1. METEORIC IRON AND SILICA-GLASS FROM THE METEORITE CRATERS OF WABAR.

The large piece of metal found near the craters at Wabar shows the concave surfaces characteristic of weathered meteoric iron. It is in part covered with rusty scale and is evidently only a remnant of a much larger mass. As received at the British Museum the mass weighed 25 pounds (11·4 kilograms). The shape is irregular with maximum dimensions in three directions at right angles of 10 × 6 × 5 inches. Some of the loose scale has been cleaned off, but on one side there is a thick mass of laminated scale with cemented sand grains. The scale is dark brown in colour and is magnetic. After the mass was photographed (fig. 14a) one end was sawn off with a hack-saw, and the two cut surfaces were filed flat and polished. On immersing the polished surface in a very dilute solution of nitric acid the internal crystalline structure of the mass was at once revealed, and the etching was stopped after two or three minutes with the result shown in fig. 14b. The beautiful patterns shown on the etched surface are known as Widmanstätten figures, and on this scale are to be seen only in meteoric irons. The structure consists of alternating bands of two alloys of iron and nickel, broader bands of kamacite being separated by very narrow bands of bright taenite. A third constituent occupying the angular interspaces is known as plessite, which also consists of iron and nickel but in different proportions. A few minute blebs of bronze-yellow troilite (iron sulphide, FeS) are embedded in the nickel-iron. According to their crystalline structure there are several types of meteoric iron ; the Wabar iron is to be classed as a ' medium octahedrite.' A complex system of very fine lines (' Neumann lines ') is shown on the bands of kamacite. These are slip bands probably produced by the shock when the meteorite struck the earth.

A detailed chemical analysis of the Wabar iron made by Mr.

365

M. H. Hey in the British Museum shows the presence of 92·00 per cent. of iron and 7·30 per cent. of nickel, with small amounts of cobalt, copper, and sulphur, and traces of platinum, chlorine, and carbon. The specific gravity is 7·66.[1]

In addition to this large piece of iron, Mr. Philby also collected six small pieces of iron and many fragments of completely rusted material with cemented sand grains. These again are also weathered remnants of larger masses. The largest fragment of metal weighs 33 grams (just over one ounce). One piece was sawn in two, polished, and etched to determine the internal structure. This was markedly different from that shown by the large mass. The structure is there but it does not come out so clearly, showing a fuzziness as if it had been partly obliterated. The narrow taenite bands are still clearly seen, but the kamacite is minutely granulated. This change in structure can be brought about artificially in meteoric irons by heating them to a temperature of about 850° C. There are indications of this granulation commencing in parts of the large Wabar mass, as shown in the photograph (fig. 14b).

Meteorites arriving from outer space presumably have a temperature of absolute zero (minus 273° C.). During their brief flight of a few seconds through the earth's atmosphere, when the surface is made incandescent by friction with the air, there is not time for the conduction of any appreciable amount of heat into the interior of the mass. When they are picked up immediately afterwards they are never more than just warm. Small masses of iron of a few pounds that have been actually seen to fall show the Widmanstätten structure sharply defined up to a very narrow zone on the exterior, indicating that the temperature could not have approached 850° C.

At Wabar conditions must have been very different and indeed exceptional. Here there must have been a shower of large masses of iron that excavated the group of craters, and direct evidence of the development of a very high temperature is supplied by the remarkable silica-glass collected by Mr. Philby. The cindery and slaggy masses scattered in quantity around the craters no doubt gave rise to the legend of the burnt city. They might equally well have suggested a volcano. But on examination it was found that this material is a nearly pure silica-glass, containing according to Mr. Hey's detailed analysis 92·88 per cent. of silica together with small amounts of alumina, iron oxides, lime, potash, etc. The specific gravity is 2·10, the refractive index 1·468, and the glass is optically isotropic.

[1] The full account of the Wabar meteorite will be published later in the *Mineralogical Magazine*.

This is the most abundant and remarkable occurrence of silica glass that has yet been discovered in nature. In addition to broken cindery masses up to 9 inches across there are large numbers of ' bombs ' of various shapes and sizes, ranging from 5 inches across to small ' black pearls.' These ' bombs ' are very light, being cellular and very full of bubbles. The bubbles are of all sizes, ranging from $2\frac{1}{2}$ to $\frac{1}{5000}$ inch. Many of these ' bombs ' consist inside of snow-white silica-glass resembling pumice, and coated outside with a thin skin of jet-black silica-glass. The black glass is almost free from bubbles and its surface is usually quite smooth and glossy, but is often beset with tiny pimples, also of black glass. Mr. Hey's analysis of this black glass shows rather less silica than that quoted above for the white glass, namely silica 87·45 per cent., much more iron (ferrous oxide 5·77 per cent. and ferric oxide 0·28 per cent.), and also a little nickel (NiO 0·35 per cent.).

These ' bombs ' were no doubt ejected from a pool of molten silica formed by the fusing of the clean desert sand at the spot where the meteorite struck the earth, and their highly cellular character was no doubt due to the partial vaporization of the silica. As they flew outwards through an atmosphere of silica, iron, and nickel vapours they became coated with the skin of black glass, and the tiny pimples perhaps represent dew-drops of silica condensed on their surface. At a slightly later interval of time the less pure sandstone (containing silica 92·06 per cent.) beneath the desert sand became involved, melting to a grey and bluish silica-glass in which are embedded angular fragments of the white glass already consolidated but not yet shot out from the crater, and giving rise to a kind of ' pudding stone ' (fig. 12b). This specimen shows a ropy surface of fused silica (fig. 12a) and seems to have been one of the ' bombs ' ejected slightly later.

Quartz melts at a temperature of about 1700° C. and at a still higher temperature in the electric arc it can be vaporized. A simple calculation shows that temperatures exceeding this order could be produced by the sudden impact of a large meteorite, such as a large mass of iron possessing a momentum that would receive relatively little check from the resistance of the air.

A mass of 100 tons ($2·24 \times 10^5$ lb.)[1] of iron travelling with a

[1] This is a moderate estimate. The Hoba meteorite in South-West Africa, now actually 60 tons, has partly rusted away and when it fell the weight was about 100 tons. A million tons has been assumed to be the weight of the meteorite which made the crater in Arizona ; a sphere of iron of this weight would have a diameter of 208 feet—small for a celestial body. The velocity might be up to 45 miles per second, and squaring this velocity much higher figures would result.

velocity of 25 miles (1.32×10^5 feet) per second possesses, according to the equation $e = \frac{1}{2}mv^2$, a kinetic energy measured by 1.95×10^{15} foot-pounds. If this mass is suddenly stopped the energy of motion will be transformed into heat and, according to Joule's mechanical equivalent of heat, would yield 2.51×10^{12} British thermal units—that is, sufficient to raise the temperature of 2.51×10^{12} pounds of water $1°$ F. But we are dealing with limited quantities of iron and quartz sand, the specific heats of which at higher temperatures have been determined as 0.22 and 0.25 respectively. Dividing this amount of heat between the 100 tons of iron and an equal mass of sand, the temperature developed would be of the order of $2.38 \times 10^{7°}$ F. or $13,000,000°$ C. Even with a velocity of only 10 miles per second the temperature would be about $200,000°$ C.

This result seems absurd, and no doubt many factors have been overlooked in this simple calculation. But what one puts into the mathematical machine, that one gets out. The heat developed would be more than sufficient to vaporize the whole mass ; but the shock was instantaneous and there would not be time for the conduction of heat to the centre of the mass of iron, before it, together with the surrounding ground, was shot out by the gases generated. Any moisture in the sand and underlying rocks would be instantly converted into steam, but probably the gases developed by the vaporization of iron and silica would be still more effective in producing a tremendous ' back-fire.'

The sharply developed Widmanstätten structure shown by the larger mass of the Wabar iron proves that this portion of the mass was not raised to a temperature above $850°$ C. The partial destruction of this structure and the development of a granular structure seen in the smaller piece does, however, indicate that such a temperature was here reached. It is clear that the pieces of iron that we have for examination are merely remnants of a much larger mass or masses. That some iron and silica were actually vaporized is proved by the structures shown by the ' bombs ' of silica-glass.

Fortunately such meteoritic falls with the formation of craters are of rare occurrence on the earth's surface, though it has been suggested that they have been more frequent on the moon. With the possible exception of the Siberian fall on June 30th, 1908, about which little is yet known, none has occurred within historic times. London would be completely wiped out by such a fall. In fact few examples of meteorite craters are yet known as topographical features of the earth's surface. Mr. Philby's observations and the examination of the material he collected at Wabar have thrown much light on the problem. The largest crater, three-quarters of a mile across and 570 feet deep, in Arizona, was first known in 1891 and has been the subject of much controversy. More conclusive evidence has been given from the group of craters discovered in 1931 near Henbury in Central Australia, but the Wabar occurrence with the wonderful development of silica-glass is the most conclusive of all.[1]

Another small piece of meteoric iron, much the size and shape of a small bean and weighing only 8 grams ($\frac{1}{4}$ oz.), was picked up on the sand at Naifa, about 110 miles south-by-east of Wabar. This fragment is perhaps part of the Wabar shower (in which case the giant meteor travelled from the south), or it may have been transported by the Arabs. In this connexion mention should be made of the ' Nejed ' meteoric iron, since in crystalline structure and chemical composition it is exactly like the Wabar iron. Two masses of this weighing 131 and 137 lb. came from Arabia in 1885 and 1893 but their history is obscure. They were said to have fallen during a thunderstorm in 1863. It seems very probable, however, that they had been transported from Wabar by the Arabs before that date. One of the masses is preserved in the British Museum collection of meteorites in the Natural History Museum at South Kensington.

At 'Ain Sala, Adraj, and Umm Tina, not very far from Naifa, Mr. Philby found in the desert several small and much-weathered fragments of meteoric stones. They merely look like ironstone concretions and were cleverly spotted by Mr. Campbell Smith amongst the large collection of rock specimens. In thin microsections they are seen to be of the same type as the meteoric stone found by Mr. Bertram Thomas in 1931 at Buwah in the same district, and described as the Suwahib meteorite.[2] These stones no doubt all belong to the same meteoritic shower, but are quite distinct from the Wabar shower of meteoric irons, there being no connexion between the two. The Arabian desert is evidently a good place for the preservation of meteorites fallen in ages past.

2. FULGURITES.

Silica-glass in another form, quite distinct from the more abundant material at Wabar, was collected in small amount at three other spots on the desert. These specimens have the shape of small tubes, very much like worm-casts in sand, and were noted

[1] An article, ' Meteorite Craters,' by L. J. Spencer appeared in *Nature* of May 28th, 1932 (pp. 781-784), a few days after Mr. Philby's collections were unpacked at the British Museum.

[2] ' A new meteoric stone from Suwahib, Arabia,' by W. Campbell Smith, *Mineralogical Magazine*, 1932, vol. 23, pp. 43-50.

2A

by Mr. Philby as ' accretions,' evidently without any knowledge
of their real nature.   They are fulgurites or lightning-tubes,
produced when discharges of lightning strike the ground, the
intense heat of the powerful spark fusing the quartz sand along
the path of the electric current.   The inside of such tubes of
silica-glass is always smooth and glazed, and the outside is rough
with adhering grains of partly fused sand.   The walls are usually
very thin and friable, and specimens can be collected only as
fragments.   Though roughly cylindrical, the tubes taper away
downwards and are sometimes branched.   When flattened they
often have thin flanges of fused material projecting from the sides
of the tube : these have been called ' winged fulgurites.'   The most
complete specimen in the Mineral Collection of the British Museum
is a portion 3 feet in length of a tube $1-1\frac{1}{2}$ inches in diameter, from
Maldonado, Uruguay ; and the longest, but made up of pieced
fragments, is nearly 16 feet in length, from near Dresden.   A
fulgurite in the sand-dunes at Drigg on the coast of Cumberland
was traced for 30 feet without reaching the end.   Specimens are
very rarely found and are not common in collections.

The specimens collected by Mr. Philby are fragments found
loose on the surface of the sand.   They were found in hollows
between the sand-dunes, and an interesting fact is that they are
taken by the Arabs as indications of the presence of water.   No
doubt the lightning would strike in the wetter and more conduct-
ing parts of the ground.

(1). From Bani Jallab (collected 9/2/32).—Narrow tubes $\frac{1}{2}$ cm.
in diameter, the longest fragment 7 cm. in length.   These are
cylindrical and straight and are remarkable in having very
thick walls, there being only a thread-like central cavity.   Nearly
the whole of the fulgurite here consists of a grey silica-glass full of
small bubbles.   This suggests that the lightning struck dry sand,
and that there was very little radial expansion of the tube caused
by the pressure of water-vapour.   One piece shows a division
into two branches.

(2). Bani Jafnan (18/2/32).—Fragments of irregular shape
with spine-like projections.   Here the walls are thin and the
central cavity large with inside glazing.   The largest fragment is
$3\frac{1}{2}$ cm. long with a flattened cross-section of about $1\frac{1}{2} \times \frac{1}{2}$ cm.

(3). Hibaka Qa'amiyat (24/2/32), about 40 miles west of
Shanna.—Broken fragments of flattened tubes with projecting
spines and wings.   The walls are thick but with a well-marked
central cavity, being intermediate between those in (1) and (2).
The largest fragment is 4 cm. long with a cross-section of about
2×1 cm.

B. GEOLOGICAL RESULTS.

1. MINERALOGY AND PETROLOGY.

By W. Campbell Smith, M.C., M.A.,
Mineral Department, British Museum.

(a). *Introductory.*

In addition to the meteorites and the remarkable materials associated with the formation of the meteorite craters, Mr. Philby brought back a very extensive geological collection. The meteorites have been described by Dr. L. J. Spencer, and the fossils and their bearing on the geological history of Arabia by Mr. L. R. Cox. The remaining specimens, rocks and minerals, afford further, though less precise, evidence of the geological structure of the country, and a wealth of material illustrating the peculiar conditions prevailing in dry desert regions.

It will be convenient to classify the material under the following headings :

Rocks outcropping at the surface ;
The gravel plains and the ' walking stones ';
The sands ;
Surface deposits.

(b). *Rocks outcropping at the surface.*

To the west of the escarpment of Jurassic rocks, described in the report on stratigraphy and palaeontology by Mr. L. R. Cox as forming the Tuwaiq plateau, Mr. Philby has found a great area of older rocks occupying the country west of a line running roughly from Duwadami (west of Riyadh) to the neighbourhood of Bisha and Tathlith (south-east of Mecca). Near Duwadami the rocks collected are mica-schists, serpentine, and granite. Along the course of the Wadi Dawasir from the eastern part of Jizl westwards, a great variety of rocks was encountered, as is shown by the following brief list of localities and specimens :

Jizl, eastern part -	- Altered volcanic ' ash,' and ashy sand-stone. Altered biotite-porphyry.
Jizl, western part	- Red altered rhyolite.
Abraq Majarib -	- Altered white rhyolite or felsite.
Shaib Malah -	- Red biotite-granite, vein-quartz, horn-blende-porphyry.
Bani Shauhata -	- Red graphic granite, vein-quartz, microdiorite.

Bani Hubai - -	White granite poor in biotite, pink aplite.
Mahmal, between Bani Hubai and 'Arq.	White biotite-granite.
Country east of Tathlith	? Epidiorite.
West of Tathlith - -	Microdiorite, red granite.
Khushaim Dhib - -	Red pegmatite, pink aplite, white biotite-granite.
Al Muta'arridhat - -	Altered basalt (? spilite), white hornblende-granite, epidote in vein-quartz.
Dahthami - - -	Red biotite-granite, altered dolerite.
Near Wadi Ranya -	Banded rhyolite.
Raudhat ibn Ghannam -	Red jasperized rhyolite.
Bir ibn Ghannam -	Pink aplite.
Plateau of Sha'ib al Dha'a.	Hornblende-biotite-granite, epidote in vein-quartz.
Wadi Kara - - -	Quartz-schist, and fine-grained gneiss.
Turaba - - -	Hornblende-schist, quartz-porphyry.

There is no evidence of the age of the older volcanic rocks in this part of the country or of the period of intrusion of the granites, but they are in a general way similar to the old volcanic igneous and metamorphic rocks from the Eastern Desert of Egypt on the other side of the Red Sea.

At present no rocks intermediate in age between these old igneous rocks and the fossiliferous Jurassic limestones of the Tuwaiq plateau have been discovered. The Cretaceous rocks are, like the Jurassic, pale cream-coloured limestones, but friable sandy beds occur in the same region and form the lowest beds exposed in the Buwaib pass. At Sulaiyil and Khashm Amur in Wadi Dawasir compact yellow limestones overlie yellow sandstones. They contain fragments of shells but none identifiable. A crystalline buff-coloured limestone was also found at Al Qaha.

Other compact cream-coloured limestones—but without fossils—were collected at Dakaka Barbak and Raudha Barbak (Summan), and between Al Jida and Shaukiya ridge (Hasa), also south of Hufuf, on the ridge between Khin and Jabrin, and at Qaliba and Maqainama, and at Wadi Dawasir. There is at present no evidence as to the age of these rocks.

At Umm al Nussi and Hafaïr, south of Jabrin, broken nodules of grey chalcedony were found, and drab-coloured flints were scattered about at Hafaïr and Dharbun. Both flints and chalcedony were probably derived from limestone beds.

The Miocene rocks are best represented in Jaub Anbak and at Nasla near Anbak. The fossiliferous beds are white clayey limestones or marls, the calcium carbonate being in a very fine state of division and probably chemically precipitated. Some of it is cemented with salt into a hard rock.

Above the fossiliferous stratum the beds consist of :

No. 1. Pink oölitic limestone with small shells and foraminifera.
No. 2. Brick-red very friable calcareous sandstone.
No. 3. Pink and white calcareous sandstone.

Beds very similar to Nos. 2 and 3 also occur at Jaub Ba'aij and at Al Kharza, associated in the last place with a pebbly conglomerate. At Qarn Abu Waïl near Sikak the rocks associated with the Miocene fossils are pale green sandy clay impregnated with salt, and a pink calcareous clay with the carbonate in an extremely fine state of division. A similar red clay comes from Judairat wells.

The white marls are similar to the material quarried for the manufacture of earthenware between Hufuf and Mubarraz. Quarries near Hufuf also show 10 or 12 feet of pale green and pink clays with fibrous gypsum and plates of selenite. No fossils were found in these beds. A similar greenish clay occurs on a ridge near 'Uyun.

Compact limestones found at various localities give good examples of the polish or desert varnish so often recorded in dry desert regions. The colour of this polished surface varies from buff or drab to brick red, but the most common colour is grey in various shades. In some of the grey fragments the polished surface is an actual skin—the ' Schutzrinde ' described by J. Walther.[1]

One of these limestones with a pale grey polish from Mamura contains foraminifera (*Alveolina*) and seems to be a pure limestone. Another, dull brown in colour, contains abundant minute angular quartz grains in a cryptocrystalline calcite cement. The grey ' Schutzrinde '[2] seems to form on limestones of more than one kind, but was not found on the limestone pebbles collected from the gravel plains. It occurs both on projecting parts of outcrops and on loose pieces. Some calcareous concretions are entirely coated with it.

Localities from which Mr. Philby brought examples are :

[1] Walther (Johannes).—*Das Gesetz der Wüstenbildung in Gegenwart und Vorzeit.* Leipzig, 1912, pp. 144-153.

[2] That the grey colour and polish are a surface effect is indicated by a specimen of a quite different yellow crystalline shelly limestone from Mulaiha near Khuthaiqan which lithologically resembles some of the Cretaceous limestones.

Mutaiwi, Qaliba, Maqainama, Bir Fadhil, Raqqat al Shalfa, Bir Mukassar ; also from Bani Jafnan, Mamura, Abu Muhairat, and Shuqqat al Hawaya, west of Abu Muhairat. At the last locality the ' varnish ' is not grey, but buff and brick red.

A rock of more than ordinary interest outcrops among the sands at Zuwaira and west of Abu Muhairat. At first sight it looks like an oölitic limestone consisting of spherical grains between $\frac{1}{2}$ and 1 millimetre in diameter. Closer inspection shows that quite 50 per cent. of the grains are of colourless quartz and the rest are rounded grains of limestone coated with a thin film of recently deposited calcium carbonate. The rock appears to be a consolidated quartz-limestone-sand like those found by Mr. Bertram Thomas[1] about Shanna. It is lightly cemented with a calcareous cement, which has also coated the detrital grains, giving them a dull surface.

In the same region very fine-grained friable quartz-sandstones with a very small amount of calcareous cement were found at Abu Muhairat, Abal Khadim, and Umm Tina. These are pale olive-buff or light buff in colour and must have a very low content of the iron oxides which give colour to the more recent sands. Slightly more coarse-grained sandstones of the same type, some free from any calcareous cement, occur at 'Ain Sala. They consist almost entirely of quartz, the grains of which are often as much as 1 millimetre in diameter and well rounded. It is noticeable that the smallest grains are angular or only slightly rounded. At a depth of 22 fathoms in a well at Bir Fadhil the sandstone contains small pebbles up to 2 or 3 millimetres in diameter.

Pure sandstones of this kind may have been the original rocks in which the meteorite craters of Wabar were found. The rocks surrounding the craters, described by Dr. Spencer in his note on the meteorites, are cream-coloured sandstones with a peculiar fritted appearance. Mr. Hey's analyses showed them to contain 92 per cent. silica. Under the microscope the quartz grains, about half a millimetre in average diameter, are seen to be shattered and traversed by unusually numerous fracture planes. With them, often forming a matrix, is a quantity of pure white opaque powdery mineral which has not at present been fully determined, but which is in all probability amorphous silica.

White chalky sandstones similar to those found by Major R. E. Cheesman at Jabal Ghanima, near Hufuf, are found to have a wide distribution. They consist of abundant small rounded quartz grains set in a hard opaque white calcareous cement.

---

[1] Bertram Thomas, *Arabia Felix*, 1932, p. 367.

They seem to be quite unfossiliferous except at one or two localities in Hawaya and Bani Zainan, where they contain casts of *Melanoides tuberculata*.

Mr. Philby first met with these on the western edge of Al Na'la, on the route to Hufuf, and they appear again in collections from Umm al Khisa, 'Uyun, and the Thuwair ridge. Here and at Al Kharza they form low ridges, thinly strewn at the last locality with pebbles from the gravels. Beyond Hufuf they appear on the ridge between Khin and Jabrin, forming hillocks at the southern edge of Summan and at intervals to as far south as Adraj, and at Hawaya, Bani Zainan, and Rumaila.

Cheesman found the same kind of rocks forming Jabal Jawamir and Jabal Jabrin al Wasti.

At Jabal Jawamir Cheesman found them underlain by white and pink sandstones cemented with salt. Mr. Philby found a pink compact sandstone (but with calcareous cement) beneath the white chalky sandstones at Al Kharza and probably in the same relation also at Jaub Ba'aij.

There is no certain evidence of the age of these chalky sandstones but they are almost certainly younger than the Miocene; they are probably even younger than the gravels which form the stony plains.

The presence in them at some localities of *Melanoides tuberculata* indicates deposition of the sands at those places in water, but it is possible that the cementing material has been derived from the gradual seeping up of solutions rich in calcium carbonate (and probably sulphate), as in the 'surface limestones' of parts of South Africa. That supplies of calcium salts are available is shown by the prevalence of surface deposits of gypsum and of calcareous concretions over much of the area occupied by the 'chalky' sandstones.

Some pebbly calcareous sandstones from Raqqat al Shalfa and the eastern edge of Sahma have a white calcareous matrix like that of the 'chalky' sandstones, and it may be that these too are surface deposits. Cheesman, however, found a rather similar rock underlying loose gravels in the Jafura desert.

True conglomerates with rounded water-worn pebbles are only found in the beds of the Wadi Sahba and Wadi Dawasir. In the latter they form knolls near Barzan, the conglomerates overlying sandstone. There they contain pebbles of sandstone as well as of quartz, granite, etc., and the matrix is sand, with a thin film of gypsum frequently surrounding the pebbles. The matrix of the Wadi Sahba conglomerate is much more calcareous and resembles that of the 'chalky' sandstones. A conglomerate from Wadi Ranya has all the appearance of a recently cemented gravel.

Freshwater sediments.—Probably the most recent sub-aqueous sediment encountered is a fine calcareous silt, light drab in colour, from Numaila and Shuqqat al Khalfat. At the latter locality it is associated with the freshwater shells (*Unio*) reported on by Mr. G. C. Robson. The silt consists of minute angular grains (0·14 mm.) of quartz and other minerals, and calcite dust. It would seem quite possible for such material to be blown during dust-storms into pools of standing water.

Volcanic rocks.—Mention will be made below of some fragments of basalt found on the surface of the desert about 'Uj and Umm al Hadid, many hundreds of miles from any known volcanic centre. The nearest extinct volcanoes seen by Mr. Philby were in the neighbourhood of Turaba (Harrat al Buqum and Harrat al Nawasif). The specimens collected at Abal Raiyat in this neigh-bourhood are volcanic ' bombs ' and pieces of basaltic scoria of the usual dull red colour, but from 'An (west of Turaba) comes also a specimen of red, weathered trachyte which shows affinities with some of the lavas of the Abyssinian region, which are mainly of Tertiary and more recent age. Further collecting of the com-pact unweathered lavas, especially trachytes, in this region would probably discover some very interesting material.

(c). *The gravel plains and ' swalking tones.'*

The great gravel plains traversed by Mr. Philby present the most varied assortment of beautiful pebbles. All being more or less polished by wind action, they show their brilliant colours and the characters of the stones to the best advantage.

These gravels were the subject of a short note in Appendix VII. to Major R. E. Cheesman's book *In Unknown Arabia* (Macmillan & Co., London, 1926). Cheesman found them extending from Harmaliya, in the Jafura desert, across the plain of (?) Saramid and (south of Wadi Sahba) to Jabal 'Aqula, 15 miles north of Jabrin. Bertram Thomas crossed them farther east, north of Banaiyan in the Jaub area and in northern Sanam. Mr. Philby encountered them first at Mutrib and Al Kharza, where they lightly cover the surface limestone, and records them con-tinuously from Zubara Mahmid to Hidbat al Budu'. A few pebbles were collected at 'Uj, and the gravels are followed again from Maqainama to Tuwairifa. A rather separated patch was found at Umm al Hadid and Ibrahima.

There is a further gravel plain away to the south-west, for Mr. Philby collected pebbles similar to those of the northern plains from Sahma, Abu Bahr, and Hidba Farsha.

The pebbles of these plains are the same as those recorded from Cheesman's collection : quartz, buff and yellow limestones with black mottlings, black and dark purple rhyolites, quartz porphyries, epidosites and epidotized volcanic tuffs.

The only types frequently collected by Philby, which are very rare in Cheesman's samples, are fine-grained red and white granites.[1]

In the discussion of the problem of the origin of the gravels encountered by Major Cheesman (*loc. cit.*, p. 423) it was stated that ' we have no knowledge of the original source of the pebbles.' That was the position in 1926 but Mr. Philby has succeeded in clearing up this question very satisfactorily.

He finds west of a line running roughly from Bisha and Tathlith (south-east of Mecca), to about Duwadami (west of Riyadh), a mass of old igneous and metamorphic rocks forming the backbone of the country. From the eastern part of Jizl to Turaba he found a variety of red and white granites, dark porphyries, brown, banded, and dark red rhyolites, and vein-quartz (often with epidote). These are types abundantly represented in the gravels, and there is no reason to look elsewhere for their source. One may definitely ascribe the gravels of the southern area (Sahma to Hidba Farsha) to these older igneous rocks outcropping farther west along the course of the Wadi Dawasir, and one may reasonably infer a western source for the extensive gravels of Jafura and Summan.

Evidence of the age of the gravels is very scanty. The suggestion made in the note on Major Cheesman's collection that they were Pliocene corresponding to those in the Baktiari series of 'Iraq was little more than a guess, but may be near the truth. From their position with relation to rocks of known age all we can say is that they are definitely post-Miocene. Their relation to the white chalky sandstone of Jabrin and Hufuf is not clear, but some of the evidence points to their being older than these rocks, which, as pointed out, may be a recent or sub-recent surface formation.

The vast extent of the gravels shows them to be something much more extensive than the deposits of such Wadis as Sahba and Dawasir, and they are clearly of earlier date than the erosion of the present Wadi beds.

The yellow and buff limestone pebbles in these gravel plains show to perfection the remarkable effects of etching by solutions, which takes place when the limestone pebbles are embedded in the moist sand below the surface. These ' Rillensteine ' or etched

---

[1] A piece of red granite, such as could have been derived from a large pebble, was found at Qasr Dahbash (Jabrin), and the fragment found by Cheesman in the well spoil-heap near Jabal Jawamir may be a chip of such a stone.

pebbles are well known wherever limestone pebbles occur in sandy deserts. The formation of the 'rills' was long supposed to be due to wind action, but it is now known to be a solution effect. The solution is well demonstrated in some of the limestones containing corals referred to above, the coral being left standing out in relief from the surrounding matrix. Wind action, producing a natural sand-blast, results in a smooth polishing and not grooving of the stones, and the formation of wind-faced stones, also known as 'ventifacts' or 'dreikante,' is well illustrated in all its stages by the limestones.

A common form has a long elliptical base with two gently sloping sides, both polished and meeting in a gently curving edge. Another form is very long and thin, pointed at both ends like a spindle. More abundant, however, are circular discs with a flat, slightly pitted and polished surface. These are derived from the cutting down of the flattish circular pebbles which are rather abundant in the gravels. According to Dr. A. Wade, who has made a careful study of wind-faced pebbles in Egypt, they represent the very last stage in the cutting down of the stones, the flat polished surface being almost level with the surface of the sand.

'Walking stones.'—The Arabs believe that some stones in the desert walk about, leaving a track in the sand. They attribute this remarkable power to the work of spirits. Major Cheesman's Marri guide traced him the pattern of the track in the sand, and his drawing of it resembles as much as anything a long and very curly tail, having in it several very irregular loops. He described the stones as round and about the size of a hen's egg, and he later produced an oval pebble of vein-quartz about $6 \times 5 \times 5$ cm. which he said was one of the kind that do walk.[1] Still Cheesman's party never saw one on the move or even at the end of its track, though the soldiers arranged one with a sufficiently good imitation of the track to take in his guide, who was delighted until he discovered the trick.

Mr. Philby brought back several of these 'walking stones.' The largest was 'found by two members of the party who first saw the tracks and then tracked it down' at Hibaka Qa'amiyat. This is a smooth cylindrical pebble of limestone about 12×6 cm. and weighs 670 grams. Another from Tuwairifa is a flattened 'dreikante,' roughly triangular, 4 cm. long, and weighs 26 grams. While the former could easily roll along, the latter could do nothing but crawl !

Of quite a different kind is a second 'walking-stone' from Tuwairifa. This is the half of a rounded piece of very vesicular black basaltic scoria weighing 18 grams, and 4 cm. in diameter.

[1] R. E. Cheesman, *In Unknown Arabia*, London, 1926, p. 236 and p. 283.

Yet another and larger piece of exactly similar basaltic scoria is from Bir Fadhil. It weighs 207 grams and measures roughly $9 \times 5 \times 5$ cm. It is not clear whether this was claimed as a ' walking stone ' or whether it is merely ' the kind that do walk,' but it is interesting to find in an earlier collection sent by Mr. Philby two pieces of reddish-brown basaltic scoria from Harra Kishb near Taïf (B.M., 1931, 430, 1) of which ' the tracks for about fifty yards were seen by H.H. Amir 'Abdullah.'

The explanation of how the belief in ' walking stones ' arose must be left to others, and to this problem may be added another. How do the fragments of basaltic scoria come to the desert ?

The Arabs say that pieces like the stone from Bir Fadhil are occasionally found on the surface of the sands. As we have seen, the party did find another one at Tuwairifa.

The identification of the stones as basaltic scoria was confirmed by means of a complete quantitative chemical analysis made by Mr. M. H. Hey. The composition agrees fairly well with some kinds of basaltic lavas (nepheline-basanite).

In addition to the two pieces of scoria, two other fragments of basalt were found, one at 'Uj and the other at Umm al Hadid, both far removed from the ' walking stones.' They are typical basalts : the former glassy, very vesicular and closely resembling the ' walking stone ' of Tuwairifa ; the other is a well-crystallized olivine-basalt, an angular fragment, somewhat vesicular, not at all water-worn but polished by wind action.

These two pieces of basalt and the ' walking stones ' of basaltic scoria were found at intervals along 150 miles of Mr. Philby's route. Although found in the district of the gravel plains, no others were found among the gravel pebbles and it is most unlikely that they are water-borne. The nearest volcanic area is in the neighbourhood of Turaba, east of Taïf, 600 miles away. There is no hint of any undiscovered volcano in the Rub' al Khali, and the basalts seem quite out of place in this part of the desert.[1] The only probable explanation seems to be that stones of this kind have been carried and dropped by passing Arabs, and some support for this idea may be found in the information given to Mr. Philby that the powder of such stones is used by the Badawin as a medicine for the eyes.

(d). The sands.

The sands of the Rub' al Khali are very uniform in character and call for little comment ; they consist almost entirely of quartz,

[1] Two other pieces of basalt were collected on an earlier trip at 'Ashaira near Taïf.

the grains of which are well rounded and seem to average about 0·7 mm. in diameter. Some sands contain a mixture of colourless and pale yellow-coloured quartz, and the general colour of the sands is pinkish buff. A bright orange sand from 'Ain Sala, consisting almost entirely of very well rounded millimetre grains of quartz, is an exception. Nearly every sample examined contained minute grains of limestone, the prevalence of which in these sands was first noticed in Mr. Bertram Thomas' collection. The limestone grains are both white and brown, and are usually among the finer constituents averaging 0·07 mm. in diameter. Sometimes, however, the sands include pellets of the white ' chalky ' sandstones, and of the drab or grey limestones which measure 2 or 3 millimetres across. The heavy minerals of the sands have not been determined, but the green glauconite noted in Mr. Bertram Thomas' specimens appears frequently as isolated grains. Rounded grains of felspar are frequently observed. From a mineralogical point of view the ' singing sand ' of Naifa presents no peculiar characters. It consists mainly of quartz as clean well rounded grains averaging 0·3 mm. in diameter, the largest reaching 0·7 mm. In addition to quartz there are small white and brown grains of limestone and occasional grains of felspar.

(e). Surface formations.

Calcium carbonate.—Calcareous concretions occur in various forms at most localities on Mr. Philby's route between 'Ain Sala and Hawaya. Outside these limits they were collected also at Raqqat al Shalfa, Tuwairifa, Umm al Hadid and Bani Zainan.

For the purpose of description one can divide them roughly into three kinds :

(1). Patches of extremely irregular shape probably formed in the sands by the seeping upwards of calcareous solutions. When the sand is carried away they remain as hard masses, often somewhat polished by the wind. Some take on a shiny grey coat or rind and then look like very cellular pieces of coke.

(2). Hard crusts formed on the surface of limestone or sand. The rock within, softened by weathering, may ultimately be carried away, leaving only the hollow calcareous crusts or flat platy fragments.

(3). Tubular concretions. These are often quite straight and reach about 1 cm. in diameter. Rarely they are curved like roots. Usually they are hollow. They have probably been formed round stems or roots of plants in the sand. They are not common in the collection but are represented by specimens from between Hadh abu Khashba and Hawaya.

Calcareous deposits on a more extensive scale evidently once occurred at 'Ain Sala. Here Mr. Philby collected a large number of roughly cylindrical pieces of tufa, each encasing a perfectly cylindrical smooth-walled tube. The tubes measure from 1–2 cm. in diameter and reach 15 cm. in length. They have quite smooth inside walls and are usually uniform in diameter from beginning to end. Some pieces of tufa contain more than one tube ; and in such cases the tubes are nearly parallel or very slightly diverging. The outer surfaces of the pieces of tufa, while approximately cylindrical, are uneven and very porous like typical calcareous tufa or travertine. Some are partly smoothed and a little polished by wind action.

For some time no clue could be obtained as to what had caused these tufa-cased tubes. Roots and plant stems were suggested, but the tubes seemed too smooth and too straight and uniform in diameter for these. The explanation was by a fortunate chance supplied by Colonel J. K. Robertson, who remembered having seen similar tubes in calcareous tufa from Trans-Jordan. At his suggestion a specimen has been kindly presented to the British Museum by Mr. J. E. G. Palmer. It consists of a stem of the reed *Arundo*, 14 mm. in diameter, completely encased for over 40 cm. of its length in a cylindrical casing of calcareous tufa, with a radiating structure. When pulled clear of the reed stem the inside of the tube is seen to be perfectly smooth and very uniform in diameter. At the nodes there are swellings in the outer surface of the tufa casing. When Mr. Philby's hollow cylinders are compared with this specimen, there is no possibility of doubting that they too are the casings of reed stems.

The specimen from Trans-Jordan was found by one of Messrs. Rendel, Palmer & Tritton's engineers in the bed of Wadi Zahar, a tributary of Wadi al 'Arab, on the eastern escarpment of the Jordan valley.

From this identification, and from the abundance of the hollow cylinders lying scattered about, one must conclude that a reed bed grew at 'Ain Sala at no very distant (geological) date. One may perhaps associate this reed bed with the period at which lived the fresh-water shells mentioned in Mr. Cox's report, for at one of the localities for these, namely Abu Muhairat, Mr. Philby collected also a single specimen of tufa showing the hole left by a reed stem. This is so far the only other record of these interesting relics of moister times.

Gypsum.—In the form of surface crusts gypsum seems to be widespread over parts of Mr. Philby's route. Fine-grained ' gypseous tufa ' was collected at Dharbun, 'Uj and Bir ibn Juhaiyim. At the first-named locality it overlies a pink sandstone. Farther south similar deposits appear in Bani Jafnan, Abu Khashba (exposed in a cliff), and along the route from Shanna to Abu Muhairat.

At a few localities the gypseous masses consist of aggregates of crystals of a very flat habit and roughly circular in plan. These were found in the cliff at Jaub Ba'aij, at Umm al Nussi and at the well of Hafaïr.

Tubular concretionary forms occur at many localities and are probably formed round plant roots or stems like those of calcite described above; in fact many of them do consist in part of calcium carbonate. The interior wall of these tubes is often lined with white powdery gypsum, like that which often coats the surface of the ' gypseous tufa.'

In addition to these surface ' tufas ' and concretions, Mr. Philby found at many localities crystals of gypsum filled with quartz grains which they have enclosed as they grew in the moist sand.[1] They are familiar to visitors to Touggourt in Algeria as ' desert roses,' the crystals being pinkish buff in colour, roughly hexagonal in outline and flat lenticular in cross section. Most of the Algerian specimens occur in groups and clusters, but those found by Mr. Philby at Judairat are single loose crystals about 8 cm. in diameter.

The crystals found at other localities are of a different shape. These are more like the common habit of gypsum crystals with the clinopinacoid (010) and the pyramids (111) well developed, but the prisms and orthodomes are represented only by cavernous rough hollows. Some of these exceed 10 cm. in length. Occasionally twin-crystals of the well-known swallow-tail habit are found. Smaller crystals are often better formed and have rough prism faces still preserved.

Crystals of these kinds were found at 'Ain Sala, Manifa, Ziqirt, Mamura, Turaiwa, and Bir ibn Suwailim.

The smaller crystals often occur in groups, pink or drab in colour. In these the sand is so thick, and projects from the surfaces to such an extent, that they appear to be built up wholly of quartz grains, and the gypsum which gives to the aggregate its form is almost undetected even by a lens. Sometimes the sand grains become too much for the gypsum and the underlying crystal-form is then quite obscured.

Gypsum in its other forms, clear colourless plates known as selenite and white compact alabaster, was found only in the clay quarries near Hufuf and (the alabaster) at Jaub Judairat and in

---

[1] In their manner of growth these resemble the sand-filled calcite crystals of Fontainebleau, which often contain from 60 to 80 per cent. of sand.

small pieces at Jaub Anbak. These occurrences are probably connected with the Miocene beds of these districts.

Limonite.—The ' iron pan ' so common in many sandy formations does not appear to be frequently found in the Rub' al Khali. Three specimens, supposed at first to represent rounded concretions of ' iron pan,' were found on close examination to be stony meteorites similar to the one found by Mr. Bertram Thomas at Buwah in Sawahib. They are the subject of a special note.[1]

Limonite with a highly polished surface was collected near Dhabba in 'Arma, and in the form of ' iron pan ' and ferruginous tubular concretions appears on the surface near Dughm in the Riyadh district.

2. STRATIGRAPHY AND PALAEONTOLOGY.

By L. R. Cox, M.A.,

Department of Geology, British Museum.

(a). The Jurassic Rocks of Jabal Tuwaiq.

Mr. Philby's previous journeys have shown that the Tuwaiq plateau, whose western edge forms a continuous escarpment, 500 to 800 feet in height, from Wadi Dawasir in the south to beyond Zilfi in the north—a distance of over 400 miles—is formed by Jurassic rocks. Immediately to the west, in the plain, there are extensive exposures of limestone of somewhat earlier age than the rocks of the escarpment, but so far these have yielded no fossils. Still farther west, as far as the igneous complex of western and south-western Najd, the older rocks are masked by vast spreads of gravel. A few fossils collected from three localities on the Tuwaiq plateau (Bakkain to the north-west of Riyadh, and 'Ashaira and Hamar about half-way between Riyadh and Wadi Dawasir) were described in 1921 by R. B. Newton,[2] who considered their age to be Sequanian or Kimmeridgian.

On his most recent journeys Mr. Philby has collected numerous specimens from the Tuwaiq Jurassic, largely from richly fossiliferous exposures in the neighbourhood of the Haisiya pass, to the N.W. of Riyadh, but also from the Sha'ib Markh district, 50 miles farther north, and, in the south, from Khashm Amur, where the Wadi Dawasir cuts through the Tuwaiq escarpment.

The Haisiya fossils are preserved in a brittle light yellow marly limestone and include ammonites, which enable their age to be determined definitely as Upper Callovian. The following are among the species from this locality.

[1] 'Meteoric stones from Suwahib, Arabia,' by W. Campbell Smith, *Mineralogical Magazine*, March, 1933, vol. 23.

[2] *Ann. Mag. Nat. Hist.*, 9th series, vol. vii., pp. 389-403.

AMMONOIDEA :
   Erymnoceras spp.

LAMELLIBRANCHIA :
   Parallelodon sp.,
   Mytilus jurensis Roemer,
   Mytilus (*Arcomytilus*) cf. *asper* (J. Sowerby),
   Mytilus (*Pharomytilus*) *plicatus* (J. Sowerby),
   Heligmus integer Douvillé,
   Lopha cf. *solitaria* (J. de C. Sowerby),
   Exogyra nana J. Sowerby,
   Chlamys cf. *fibrosa* (J. Sowerby),
   Chlamys n. sp.,
   Ceratomya excentrica (Roemer),
   Ceratomya cf. *paucilirata* (Blanford),
   Ceromyopsis cf. *helvetica* de Loriol,
   Ceromyopsis cf. *rostrata* Douvillé,
   Quenstedtia cf. *mactroides* (Agassiz),
   Homomya inornata (J. de C. Sowerby),
   Pholadomya carinata Goldfuss,
   Pholadomya aubryi Douvillé.

At Uwainidh, in the same neighbourhood, a well-preserved specimen of the lamellibranch *Lopha hastellata* (Schlotheim) was found. Specimens collected at Riyadh itself show that the town is underlain by Jurassic limestones similar to those of Haisiya.

The fossils from Sha'ib Markh consist mainly of casts of a large species of *Nerinea* (*N.* cf. *desvoidyi* d'Orbigny) preserved in a yellowish-brown sandstone, but also include *Homomya* cf. *inornata* (J. de C. Sowerby) and *Mactromya* (= *Unicardium*) cf. *globosa* Agassiz. It is interesting to note that the matrix of these specimens is identical with that of the specimens of the same species of *Nerinea* recorded from Bakkain in Newton's paper, and of the brachiopods from Hamar recorded as *Rhynchonella* cf. *subvariabilis* Davidson.

The Khashm Amur fossils occur partly in a sandstone somewhat lighter in colour than the *Nerinea* bed of Bakkain and Sha'ib Markh, and partly in a light-coloured marly limestone. They include the following species :

GASTROPODA :
   Nerinea cf. *desvoidyi* d'Orbigny.

LAMELLIBRANCHIA :
   Parallelodon sp.,
   Musculus n. sp.,

Mytilus (*Pharomytilus*) *plicatus* (J. Sowerby),
Heligmus cf. *asiaticus* Douvillé,
Mactromya cf. *globosa* Agassiz,
Ceratomya excentrica (Roemer),
Ceromyopsis cf. *helvetica* de Loriol,
Homomya inornata (J. de C. Sowerby),
Pholadomya aubryi Douvillé.

The above fossils include the three species found in the *Nerinea* bed of Sha'ib Markh ; hence their horizon appears to be the same. Several of the species in the list are also found in the Callovian of Somaliland ; it is therefore probable that these beds, like those at Haisiya, are of Callovian age.

To sum up, it may be seen that there is strong evidence for assigning a Callovian rather than a Sequanian-Kimmeridgian age to all the fossils yet collected from the Tuwaiq Jurassic. The well-characterised species *Lopha philbyi* Newton (unfortunately a synonym of *L. costellata* (Douvillé)), originally collected by Mr. Philby at Hamar, has not been found at other Tuwaiq localities, but is now known to be abundant in the Callovian (and perhaps also the Bathonian) of Somaliland, while in Sinai it marks a horizon considered by Douvillé to be Upper Bathonian. The Tuwaiq *Nerinea*, which is specifically distinct from—although closely related to—*N. desvoidyi*, a Corallian species, was also collected by Major H. S. Hazelgrove from near Naubat, in the Aden hinterland.[1] The age of the beds at Naubat is uncertain, although Callovian fossils have been reported from (?) Gol Rakab, in the hinterland of Shaqra, north-east of Aden.[2] Fossils from Dhala, some 50 miles north of Naubat, described by Newton and Crick (*loc. cit.*), are of Lower Kimmeridgian age. This fauna of higher horizon is characterised by *Parallelodon egertonianus* (Stoliczka), *Nucula cuneiformis* J. de C. Sowerby, and *Trochus arabiensis* Newton, which have not yet been found in the Tuwaiq district.

(b) The Upper Cretaceous Rocks of the 'Arma Plateau.

To the north and north-east of Riyadh, and some 30-40 miles east of the Tuwaiq escarpment, a parallel escarpment marks the western edge of the 'Arma plateau. At Khafs, about 60 miles north of Riyadh, this escarpment is about 200 feet in height, but it sinks in a southerly direction until it reaches the level of the gravelly plain of the western part of the Rub' al Khali desert.

[1] See Newton, *Ann. Mag. Nat. Hist.*, 8th series, vol. ii., 1908, p. 9.

[2] See Stefanini, Appendix to O. H. Little, *The Geography and Geology of Makalla (South Arabia)*, 1925, p. 194.

The 'Arma escarpment is formed by white and cream-coloured limestones which prove to be of Upper Cretaceous age. The most abundant fossil species, numerous specimens of which were collected by Mr. Philby at Khafs and at Masajiri, is the large plicated oyster, *Lopha dichotoma* (Bayle), a form found in the Senonian of Persia and many localities in northern Africa. Other fossils found at Khafs include, in addition to internal casts of several molluscan species, a specimen of the well-known Senonian lamellibranch *Roudairia drui* (Munier-Chalmas), indeterminate Rudists, a large discoidal Foraminifer probably belonging to the genus *Orbitoides*, and several well-preserved corals belonging to two species of the genus *Cyclolites* (*C. elliptica* Lamarck and *C. polymorpha* (Goldfuss)), both Senonian species ; hence there is every justification for assigning a Senonian age to the rocks of the 'Arma escarpment. Further work must decide whether any Cretaceous rocks of lower horizon occur immediately to the west.

(c) *Eocene Rocks*.

It is most probable that Eocene rocks occur somewhere between the 'Arma plateau and the Miocene met with south of the Gulf of Bahrain, and limestones at Hufuf may perhaps be referable to that formation. No fossils, however, were obtained. Dr. G. M. Lees found that the Qatar peninsula is formed of Eocene rocks, an observation confirmed by Mr. B. S. Thomas, who collected Eocene fossils when approaching Dauha from the south.

(d) *Miocene Rocks*.

At Qarn Abu Waïl, near Sikak, at the southern end of the Gulf of Bahrain, and in the neighbourhood of Jaub Anbak, some 30 miles to the south-west, collections were made from several exposures of richly fossiliferous beds which prove to be of Miocene age. These beds consist of soft white and pink marls with casts of numerous small shells and many well-preserved oyster shells belonging mainly to the species *Ostrea latimarginata* Vredenburg, although a few are referable to *O. hyotis* (Linné). The molluscan casts belong mainly to the species *Diplodonta* cf. *rotundata* (Montagu) and *Clementia papyracea* (Gray), but several other species, belonging to *Mytilus*, *Anomia*, *Chlamys*, *Anadara*, *Lucina*, *Cardium*, *Cypraea*, *Turritella*, and other genera, are present. Some specimens of *O. latimarginata* bear a scar indicating growth attached to a *Turritella* shell, as in a Persian Miocene specimen of the same species figured by Douglas.[1] A white or pink fora-

---

[1] *Contributions to Persian Palaeontology*, Part 1, 1927, pl. i., fig. 2.

APPENDICES

387

miniferal oölite occurs in association with these molluscan marls.
Beds of gypsum are also found, and have been quarried at Jabrin,
which appears to be situated near the south-western limit of the
Miocene gulf.

Both the presence of *O. latimarginata* and the general lithology
of the beds indicate their contemporaneity with the lower Fars
beds of Persia, which are of Burdigalian-Helvetian (*i.e.*, Lower to
Middle Miocene) age. Beds of the same age have recently been
found at Kuwait. At Jaub Anbak the fossiliferous beds are overlain by red sandstones which may also belong to the Miocene
series, although they could be equivalent to the Bakhtiyari beds
of Persia, which are Pliocene in age.

(e) *Pleistocene or Holocene.—Superficial Lacustrine or River
Deposits.*

Mr. Philby's discovery of superficial deposits with freshwater
shells at numerous localities in the heart of the desert is of great
interest, since they indicate that less arid conditions formerly
prevailed there. At Ziqirt the deposit consists of a fairly compact
calcareous rock, and at Hawaya of an equally compact but more
arenaceous rock ; in both of these rocks the shells (mainly
Melanoides tuberculata (Müller)) are represented only by their
external moulds. A soft calcareous surface rock, from Khillat
Hawaya, contains small *Planorbis* shells. At other localities,
notably Shuqqat al Khalfat and Abu Muhairat, the shells occur in
considerable quantities loose and in a good state of preservation.
As Mr. G. C. Robson and Major M. Connolly show in their
report, all of these shells appear to be referable to living
species ; hence there is unfortunately no evidence as to the
precise age of the deposits.

In conclusion it must be recorded that Mr. Philby's collection
of fossils has been generously presented by His Majesty the King
of the Hijaz, Najd and its Dependencies to the Geological Department of the British Museum (Natural History). It is hoped that
it will be possible to publish more detailed descriptions of the
fossils elsewhere. In drawing up the above report I must ac-
knowledge the help of Miss H. M. Muir-Wood, Dr. L. F. Spath,
and Dr. H. D. Thomas in determining respectively the brachiopods, ammonites, and corals.

3. FRESHWATER SHELLS.

Mr. G. C. Robson of the British Museum writes as follows :
Major M. Connolly has now concluded the examination of your
Arabian shells and I enclose his list of stations with the names of
the various forms found at each.

The fauna represented is a typical Syro-Mesopotamian assemblage containing some widely distributed forms (e.g. *Melanoides tuberculata*) which are not evidential. It has no special affinities with more remote faunas, *e.g.* with those of the Nile or North Africa. One would say in general that it is a representative sample of the general ' Near Eastern ' fauna.

It is quite apparent that a statistical analysis will not yield any profitable results because we do not know enough of the modern local fauna to say how significant any peculiarities observable in your forms may be. So far as we are concerned the fauna is undatable though it shows no significant deviations from the modern fauna.

One outstanding fact is the occurrence of the *Unio* which undoubtedly proves that there was a good and permanent water supply. *U. terminalis* is a LAKE form, at least in its modern distribution. The *Corbicula* is also evidential. It is said to be characteristically fluviatile and its presence indicates something more than marshes, ditches and small streams.

LIST OF ARABIAN SHELLS COLLECTED BY MR. PHILBY.

Locality.	*Species.*
1. Bir Fadhil - -	*Melanoides tuberculata* (Müll.).
	Corbicula crassula Mouss (?)[1].
2. Shuqqat al Khalfat	*Unio terminalis* Bgt.[2]
3. Numaila - -	*Unio* ,, ,,
	Bulinus truncatus (Aud.).
	Mel. tuberculata (Müll.).
4. Raqqat al Shalfa -	,, ,, ,, small.
	Corb. crassula Mouss. (?).
	Bul. truncatus (Aud.).
	Lymnaea lagotis Schrank (?)[3].
5. Tuwairifa - -	Fragments, possibly *Unio*.
6. 'Ain Sala - -	,, *Cypraea* sp.
	,, *Cardium leucostomum*.
7. Hadhat abu Khashba	*Mel. tuberculata* Müll., medium size.
	Lymnaea juv., probably *lagotis*.
	Mel. tuberculata Müll.

[1] None of these shells appear to be the large *C. fluminalis* Müll., of which the altitude is greater than the width ; all the series under notice are more broad than high, and it is questionable what name to apply to them, as there are so many, probably synonyms ; *crassula* Mouss. is one of the oldest, and probably =*syriaca* Locard and other later ones.

[2] All the *Unios* seem to fall within the limits of this variable species.

[3] Only a few immature shells, but all are apparently *lagotis*, the common Syrian form.

8. Abu Muhairat	-	*Unio terminalis* Bgt.

Mel. tuberculata, large and small.
Corb. crassula Mouss. (?).
Planorbis cf. *corneus* (Lin.).[1]

9. Abu Sabban -   -   *Mel. tuberculata*, smallish.
                Corb. crassula Mouss. (?).

10. Khillat Hawaya -   *Mel. tuberculata*, highly sculptured.

11. Kimida -   -   -   *Mel. tuberculata*, small.

12. Wadi Ranya -   -   *Planorbis* sp. (?), a deformed single specimen.

In various boxes (unlabelled but from Abu Muhairat) are the same shells over again, the most interesting being two or three good specimens of *Bulinus truncatus* and the best Lymnaeas, though small at that.

There is nothing from which to date the collection geologically, as all the species appear to be still existent in the Near East, but the presence of the Unionidae and, to a less extent, the Corbiculidae and *Lymnaea* proves the presence of a plentiful supply of fresh water, probably rivers or lakes, in the district where these species have occurred.

N.B.—The above remarks, kindly made at my request by Major Connolly (who identified the specimens) in collaboration with Mr. Robson, should be read as relating to the general importance of my collection of freshwater shells from the Rub' al Khali, and not as a final, authoritative contribution to the literature of the subject. The question of the full significance of these freshwater shells from the Arabian desert is still engaging the active consideration of the experts. It may be of interest to add here that all the flint implements found in association with these freshwater shells on the surface of a gravel-strewn alluvial soil are of Neolithic (or possibly later) provenance. No Palaeolithic flints were found by me anywhere in the Rub' al Khali.—H. St J. B. P.

[1] Most of the shells from Arabia are peculiarly deeply umbilicate for this widespread species, but it is extremely variable (*vide* Germain in Rec. Indian Museum, vol. xxi.) and, as it is recorded as of frequent occurrence in Asia Minor although not from Syria or Palestine, there is no reason to doubt its occurrence in Arabia.

C. OSTRICH EGGS.

REPORT ON SOME STRUTHIOUS EGG-SHELL FRAGMENTS,
COLLECTED BY MR. PHILBY ON HIS RECENT JOURNEY
ACROSS ARABIA.

By Percy R. Lowe, B.A., M.B.(Cantab.).

The struthious egg-shell fragments collected by Mr. Philby at
various localities on his journey across the Rub' al Khali resolve
themselves into two categories, *viz.* : (1) those which are definitely
recent and which, except for the loss of the very high superficial
polish of the ' skin,' have the colour and smooth appearance which
eggs of *Struthio syriacus*, the Syrian Ostrich, naturally possess ;
and (2) those which are fossilized or mineralized, and have been
stained various colours ranging from almost chocolate-brown,
with a shade of mauve in it, to a *café au lait* tint. Besides the
very distinctive coloration of the fossilized fragments there is a
very conspicuous bevelling of their edges from wind-swept sand
erosion.

This bevelling has taken place at the expense of the superficial
or outer surface, and in the case of the Shuqqat al Khalfat fragment extends inwards from the edge for a distance of four millimetres. In addition to this bevelled condition and the peculiar
staining, all the fossilized fragments also exhibit a very high sand-
polish. This is, if anything, most marked on the outer surface,
and the high glaze in almost every instance overlies a slightly
roughened, or excavated, surface. My colleague, Mr. Campbell
Smith, regards this latter as etching caused by the action of dew.

It is curious to note that the two series of definitely recent shell-
fragments belonging to category (1) were collected at Mahadir
Summan and Bani Ma'aridh respectively : that is to say, at the
beginning and towards the end of Mr. Philby's journey across the
Rub' al Khali.

All the shell-fragments collected in the middle stages were very
definitely more mineralized, deeply stained, and almost invariably
rendered thinner, sometimes very much thinner, by a longer exposure to sand erosion.

The recent fragments collected at Mahadir Summan were
thought to have belonged to one single egg, and it is interesting to
note that the Syrian Ostrich has not been seen (so Mr. Philby
understood from his escort) in this part of Arabia for forty or
fifty years. It seems to be practically certain that both the
recent and fossil series belonged to the same species of Ostrich
(*S. syriacus*), but it is suggested here that the fossilized series may

belong to an older horizon, possibly corresponding to a period coeval with the old land surface before its submergence by sand.

Psammornis—A Giant Struthious Bird.

A notable exception as regards specific distinction must be made, however, in regard to a fragment collected at Shuqqat al Khalfat. This had a thickness of 3·0 mm. as contrasted with the least worn of the recent shell-fragments which varied from 1·9 to 2·1 mm. In dealing with the relative thickness of egg-shells this represents a comparatively enormous difference, and there can be no doubt in my mind that it belonged to an egg which very greatly exceeded in size those of *S. syriacus*. As regards thickness it approaches typical fragments of *Psammornis rothschildi* (3·2 mm.), collected between Tuggourt and El Oued in Algeria by Rothschild and Hartert, and described by Andrews as belonging to a new genus of fossil Ostrich.

Microscopical examination of sections cut from the fragment found by Mr. Philby in Arabia agree in all particulars with similar sections cut from fragments of *Psammornis* egg-shells collected in Algeria. Moreover, the peculiar greyish-brown staining of the Arabian fragment corresponds exactly with a fragment found in Algeria. The only conclusion, therefore, at which I can arrive is that the very large struthious bird known as *Psammornis* also inhabited Arabia.

The Arabian egg-shell fragment was discovered by Mr. Philby in an old river bed in about Latitude 22° N. at a spot where fresh-water shells were found. Lord Rothschild informs me that the Algerian fragments were collected by him on an area of ground which had been recently denuded of sand hills by violent wind storms and on which some old wells had been discovered. They were found on the surface in the immediate vicinity of the wells.

This extension of the range of *Psammornis* is interesting in that it suggests that, during the period in which that genus flourished, there was a much more extensive land connection with Northern Africa than now exists ; while the fact that the *Psammornis* egg-shell fragment was found in association with freshwater *Mollusca* seems also to suggest that it was a member of a fauna which occupied the old land surface of Arabia before it was overwhelmed by desert conditions.

I have recently described[1] struthious egg-shell fragments collected in red Hipparion clay (Lower Pliocene) in Northern China of a species apparently belonging to the genus *Struthio*.

[1] *Palaeontologia Sinica*, 1931, vol. vi., fascicle 4, pp. 1-40, pts. 1-4, figs. 1-2.

From the same deposit I described the pelvis of an Ostrich to which I gave the name *Struthio wimani*. The egg-shell fragments of the Pliocene Ostrich, which was very considerably larger than the Recent Ostrich, averaged 2·6 mm. in thickness. Having been weathered out of clay they had undergone little or no erosion from atmospheric agents, whereas the Arabian egg-shell fragments were considerably sand worn ; so that we may surmise that the latter fragments were originally much more than 3·0 mm. in thickness ; from which I conclude that *Psammornis* must have been, at least, half as large again as the Recent Ostrich.[1]

I may add that the eggs of the Northern African Ostrich (*S. camelus*) range, according to my measurements, taken with a Vernier scale, from 1·8 mm. to 1·9 mm. in thickness.

[1] In a subsequent letter Dr. Lowe, in answer to enquiries from me, wrote as follows : (1). It is curious that you raise the question whether *Psammornis* might really belong to the *Aepyornis* (or ' Roc ') group—a fossil struthious genus confined so far to Madagascar—because I have already raised this question (Proc. Zool. Soc., 1928).

Lambrecht considers this hypothesis to be supported by the discovery of a fossil bone (the tarso-metatarsus of a three-toed Struthionid) in the Oligocene beds of the Fayum, to which he has given the name of *Stromeria fayumensis*.

There is, however, in the present state of our lack of knowledge always the question : What are the relations between *Psammornis* and the Pliocene *Struthio wimani* of China ? Therefore I should not like to commit myself definitely to the idea that *Psammornis* could be referred to the ' Roc.' It is an interesting speculation. Of course it is not definitely proved that the fabulous ' Roc ' or ' Ruc ' was founded on the huge Madagascan *Aepyornis*, but I believe there can be little doubt that it was so.

(2). Do Ostriches drink water ? I have no practical knowledge derived from observation, but I do know from Lynes' paper on the birds of North and Central Darfur (*Ibis*, 1925, p. 791) that you could have included birds in general with your Ostrich question.

Lynes says, ' In Northern and Central Darfur, for example, not one of the birds can possibly get any drinking water, dew included, all the year round except during the four, five or, at most, six rainy months.' Bates told me much the same as regards the Southern Sahara—no water, no dew, and clothes can be dried at night. I imagine then that an Ostrich could go for an indefinite time without drinking.

Aepyornis, by the way, in Madagascar could have got plenty of water, and there is a question as to at least one species whether it was not an inhabitant of the margins of lakes.

Newton in his *Dictionary of Birds* says, ' Though the Ostrich ordinarily inhabits the most arid districts, it needs water to drink and, moreover, it will frequently bathe.' But any bird will if it gets the chance.

D. 'SINGING SANDS.'

DR. VAUGHAN CORNISH has kindly supplied the following observations after a conversation on the subject with me :

About my idea that the big noise of sands in the desert may be due to reverberation upon a gliding plane within the dune, I send you this note to supply something that you can refer to at your convenience.

My idea of the mechanism—an idea to be tested locally—is that, as the surface sand grains on the loose, steep, lee slope of the dune roll down as the result of any slight disturbance, they engage and entrain those immediately beneath, and these in turn entrain those under them, the disturbance deepening ; and all the while the noises which the sand grains make increase, but have a confused character. At last, however, a definite plane is reached where the propagation downward of the disturbance ceases ; and that this under-surface should be definite and plane, or nearly plane, seems natural enough when one recalls the fact that sand which remains long under pressure acquires a considerable degree of fixity, without the presence of any cementing material.

The change from a confused noise to a steady roar which you noticed, I attribute, subject to some crucial test, to the passage of the superincumbent sand over this sloping floor. That such internal planes of gliding occur in the movement of soil of a clayey nature I know from my observations of the great landslides in the Culebra Cut of the Panama Canal. I even collected specimens of the surface of the gliding plane which were grooved and polished by the relative movement of the superincumbent material.

As regards the point which you mentioned, namely that you felt the sand below you sucking at your foot, and at your hand when plunged into it, at the time when these movements and noises were going on : an explanation occurred to me shortly after our conversation. In the paper which I mentioned to you by G. H. Darwin (Min. Proc. Inst., C.E., vol. lxxi. (1883), pp. 350-378, *On the Horizontal Thrust of a Mass of Sand*) it is stated that, before the sand slipped, the grains elbowed each other aside so as to assume a more open order than that in which they had been packed. If the same thing happened when the sand of the dune started sliding, the air of the interstices would be rarefied by expansion ; its pressure would no longer be equal to the superincumbent pressure of the atmosphere, and so the foot or hand immersed in the loose, upper layers would be pressed down by the atmosphere which was entering to fill the partial vacuum.

These are the ideas which have occurred to me from my recollection of work done a good many years ago ; but, remembering another writer besides Osborne Reynolds and G. H. Darwin, I looked up a paper by C. E. S. Phillips in Proc. Roy. Inst., vol. xix., p. 742 (Lecture, February 11th, 1910), the abstract of an experimental lecture which I attended. This not only contains the gist of Osborne Reynold's work on piling of sand grains, but some original experiments by Major Phillips, in which he obtained first a rattling sound and finally a distinct, musical note from the flow (with differential movement) of sand in a glass tube. He devised the experiment, I think, with a view to explaining the sounds of desert, as distinguished from sea-beach, sands. I had forgotten this at the time of our conversation, when your observations called up the memory of what I had seen on a large scale on the Panama Canal. Major Phillips' experiment has already tested and proved the idea that sand can emit a definite note when the grains flow upon a gliding plane ; I think that the observations which so many of us have made of this changed consistency of the sand at a certain depth, supplemented by the well-established fact of interior gliding planes in ordinary earth-slides as exemplified by those in the Culebra Cut, are a useful supplement to his experiment, in that they provide some account of the existence of such surfaces of separation under conditions of unrestricted flow free from the artificial restrictions of the small, glass tube. Please make any use you like of these notes. It would, at any rate, be worth while setting travellers to look out for the existence, or non-existence, of a plane of gliding in desert sands which roar.

E. MAMMALS OF THE RUB' AL KHALI.

(With acknowledgments to Captain J. G. DOLLMAN of the British Museum.)

(1) Bat : *Eptesicus* sp. 1 specimen from Shanna.

(2) Desert Fox : *Cynalopex* sp. 3 specimens from 'Ain Sala and Abal Khadim. These appear to be the same form as the one originally obtained by Bertram Thomas, and may need description. (Arabic names : *Tha'l, Tha'lab* and *Husni*.)

(3) Cat : *Felis ocreata*. 1 damaged skull from Umm al Qurun. (Arabic names : *Atfa'* or *Hirra*.)

(4) Hare : *Lepus*, probably *omanensis cheesmani*. 31 specimens from various localities in Jafura, Jiban and Rub' al Khali. (Arabic name : *Arnab*.)

(5) Jerboa : *Jaculus*. 4 specimens from Jafura and Jabrin. (Arabic name : *Jarbu'a*.)

(6) Gerbil : *Gerbillus*, probably *arduus*. 2 specimens. (Arabic name : *Fār*.)

(7) *Oryx leucoryx* (*beatrix*). 1 head, several pairs of horns, bones, etc. (Arabic name : *Wudhaihi*.)

(8) White Gazelle. Several pairs of horns. (Arabic name : *Rīm*.)

F. BIRDS OF THE RUB' AL KHALI.

By N. B. Kinnear,
Of the British Museum.

This small collection made by Mr. Philby is of considerable interest since it not only shows what birds inhabit the Rub' al Khali, but also the species which cross these inhospitable sands *en route* to their summer breeding quarters.

Certain of the specimens obtained, more especially those inhabiting the edge of the desert proper, are winter visitors from further north. It is of considerable interest to note that of these migratory species five have been obtained in the British Isles, though only as very rare stragglers.

(1) Arabian Stone Curlew (*Karwān*): *Burhinus œdicnemus astutus.* 2 specimens from Jaub Ba'aij and Salwa (January 11th). Others seen at 'Ain Sala and Khillat Hawaya. This bird is resident and not uncommon in Southern Arabia, extending into 'Iraq and Southern Persia.

(2) Macqueen's Bustard (*Hubāra*): *Chlamydotis undulata macqueenii.* 1 specimen from Hadida (Wabar) (February 4th). Others seen at frequent intervals in Rub' al Khali. Found from South Russia to Turkestan and Baluchistan. It migrates south in the winter to India and Arabia and occasionally wanders to Western Europe, having been observed in the British Isles on four occasions.

(3) Sparrow Hawk (*Shabbūt*): *Accipiter nisus nisus.* 1 specimen from Anbak (January 12th), where a pair was observed. This is the common Sparrow Hawk of the British Isles, Europe and parts of Siberia. It passes through Arabia on migration in spring and autumn.

(4) Scops Owl (*Qubaisa*): *Otus scops scops.* 1 specimen from Hidbat al Farsha (March 13th). A small owl was heard but not seen at Shanna (February 22nd). This little Scops Owl is widely distributed in Europe and Western Asia. It is a winter visitor to Arabia and Africa, as far south as Uganda. It is a rare wanderer to Great Britain.

(5) Eastern Desert Wheatear (*Umm Ghurair*): *Oenanthe deserti atrogularis.* Specimens from Maqainama, Tuwairifa and Sa'afij (January 24th to February 2nd), and frequently observed at many points during the journey. According to Major Cheesman this is the most plentiful Wheatear found in Jabrin during the winter. Colonel Meinertzhagen also recorded it as common at Aden. This Desert Wheatear nests in Central Asia and passes south in winter to N. Africa and India, many wintering in Arabia. Stragglers have occurred in Orkney and Kent.

(6) Arabian Pied Wheatear (*Bijri* or *Da'ja*) : *Oenanthe lugens lugentoides*. From Sulaiyil (March 15th). Previously recorded from Yaman, Aden Protectorate and Northern Somaliland.

(7) European Stonechat (*Busaiya*) : *Saxicola torquata rubicola*. From Sulaiyil (March 15th). The common European Stonechat is a winter visitor to Arabia, and also passes through on migration in spring and autumn.

(8) Desert Warbler (*Suwaiwala*) : *Sylvia nana nana*. Specimens from Sanam, Majari Ma'shiya, Bani Jallab, 'Ain Sala and Adraj (February 6th to 12th). Very frequently observed throughout Rub' al Khali. Major Cheesman remarks that this little Warbler was the commonest bird in Jabrin, and Mr. Philby's experience was the same. Indeed wherever bushes occurred in the desert, there were sure to be a pair or two of this Warbler about them. It inhabits the sandy deserts of S.W. Asia from Sinai to Sind.

(9) Black-headed Wagtail (*Sa'u*, female *Sa'wa*) : *Motacilla feldegg feldegg*. From Sulaiyil (March 15th). This bird breeds in S.E. Europe and E. Asia, and migrates through Arabia in spring and autumn, a certain number also wintering there. This Wagtail has occurred four times in England.

(10) White Wagtail (*'Aqaili* or *Mislik*) : *Motacilla alba* ? subsp. From Sulaiyil (March 15th). One specimen observed (?) at Sahma in waterless desert. The Sulaiyil specimen was too much damaged to make out for certain to which race of White Wagtail it belongs. As Cheesman and Meinertzhagen met with examples of *Motacilla alba dukhunensis*, the Indian White Wagtail, on passage, it very probably belongs to that race, which breeds in Siberia.

(11) Palestine Short-toed Lark (*Hamrā*) : *Calandrella brachydactyla hermonensis*. Specimens from Summan (near Maqainama) and Numaila (January 23rd to 29th). Others observed. This rufous form of the Short-toed Lark inhabits Palestine, and in N. Africa is found locally as far west as Morocco. Apparently it wanders in winter, as specimens have been found in the Sudan and Wyman Bury obtained two examples in the Yaman.

(12) Bifasciated Lark (*Umm Sālim*) : *Alaemon alaudipes doriae*. Specimens from Maqainama, Hawiya, Tuwairifa, Sa'afij and Sanam (January 25th to February 6th) ; and very commonly observed throughout the journey. The Bifasciated Lark is one of the few birds which inhabit the interior of the Rub' al Khali. Besides Arabia, this form inhabits Sind and Baluchistan.

(13) Desert Lark (*Hamrā*) : *Ammomanes cinctura*. 1 specimen from Jafura (January 14th). Another specimen comes from Khufaifiya in Najd (November 22nd, 1931). These Desert Larks do not agree with any specimens in the British Museum collection, and with further study may perhaps turn out to be a new race.

(14) Brown-necked Raven (*Ghurāb*) : *Corvus corax ruficollis.*
4 specimens from Jabrin, Numaila and Hadh Fāris (January 21st
to February 8th), and observed *passim.* The Brown-necked
Raven ranges from Western India to N. Africa and is widely distributed in Arabia, penetrating far into the deserts. As a rule it is
found in pairs and breeds early in the year. Cheesman took a nest
in the Jafura district on February 13th and Mr. Philby found
three young in a nest at Numaila on January 28th.

N.B.—In addition to the above-mentioned birds which are duly
authenticated by identification by Mr. N. B. Kinnear, the following may be noted as having been observed by me
(H. SʰJ. B. P.) :

(a) Eagle (*'Aqāb*) : probably the Abyssinian Tawny Eagle—
Aquila rapax raptor.

(b) Vulture (*Nasr*) : possibly the Egyptian Vulture—*Neophron
percnopterus.*

(c) A species of Hawk—? Harrier (*Abu Haqab*).

(d) Cream-coloured Courser (*Daraja* or *Darjalan*) : *Cursorius
cursor cursor* (identified from a specimen from near Riyadh and
apparently the same as the birds observed in the Rubʻ al Khali).

(e) Aucher's Shrike (*Srad* or *Suraiti*) : *Lanius excubitor aucheri.*
One seen at Shanna and apparently the same as a specimen shot
at Qaiʻiya in Najd.

(f) Hoopoe (*Hudhud*). One seen in Sanam (February 4th).

(g) Swallows (*Abu Khusaifān, Riqaiʻi*). Two seen on separate
occasions in the midst of Rubʻ al Khali on January 27th and
March 6th. Plentiful at Sulaiyil.

G. REPTILES.

(Identified and listed with notes by Mr. H. W. PARKER of the
British Museum.)

1. LIZARDS.

(a) Geckonidae.

(1) *Stenodactylus sthenodactylus* Licht. 5 specimens from
Dafina in Central Najd. This species has not been recorded from
Arabia proper, but only from Sinai, Palestine, Syria and North
Africa.

(2) *Alsophylax blandfordii* Strauch. 5 specimens from Rubʻ al
Khali. Has not been recorded before between the Hadhramaut
and Egypt.

(3) *Hemidactylus persicus* Anderson. 1 specimen from the
Hasa (?). As the name implies, this is a Persian species, extending

down to 'Iraq. The only true Arabian record is from Hufuf (Major Cheesman).

(4) *Ceramodactylus major* Parker. 2 specimens from Rub' al Khali.

(b) Agamidae.

(1) *Phrynocephalus maculatus* Anderson. 11 specimens from Rub' al Khali. This is a sand-dwelling form.

(2) *Phrynocephalus arabicus* Anderson. 33 specimens from Rub' al Khali. This is the stony-ground (gravel and steppe) analogue of the preceding species.

(3) *Agama jayakari* Anderson. 1 specimen from Rub' al Khali.

(c) Lacertidae.

(1) *Acanthodactylus cantoris* Günther. 5 specimens from Rub' al Khali. These are intermediate between the sub-species *arabicus* (Aden to Hadhramaut) and *blandfordi* (Persia). Bertram Thomas got the former race at Dhufar and the latter at Jaub al Izba (? 'Adhba), but none of his specimens showed any intermediate characters.

[N.B.—As my specimens all came from the Rub' al Khali between Jabrin and Shanna, the Great South Desert would seem to form a bridge between the two races.—H. St J. B. P.]

(2) *Acanthodactylus scutellatus audouini* Boulenger. 7 specimens from Rub' al Khali.

(3) *Acanthodactylus boskianus asper* Audouin. 1 specimen from Rub' al Khali.

(4) *Acanthodactylus* sp. n. (?). 1 ♂ from Rub' al Khali.

(5) *Eremias brevirostris* Blanf. 1 specimen from Rub' al Khali.

(6) *Eremias adramitana* Boulenger. 4 specimens from Rub' al Khali.

(d) Scincidae.

Scincus mitranus Anderson. Numerous specimens from Jafura and Rub' al Khali.

2. SNAKES.

(1) *Tarbophis güntheri* Anderson. 1 specimen from the Hijaz.

(2) *Psammophis schokari* Forsk. 1 young specimen from Qatarat (Rub' al Khali).

3. FROGS.

Rana ridibunda Pallas. 3 young specimens from the Hasa. Cheesman found this species at Hufuf but, naturally, it is not widely distributed in Arabia.

H. INSECTS.

1. BEETLES (COLEOPTERA) OF THE RUB' AL KHALI.

By K. G. BLAIR,
Of the British Museum.

THE beetles collected by Mr. Philby are naturally predominantly of desert type, by far the greater proportion of them belonging to the Tenebrionidae. For the most part these are rather large black species, some of which run in the sunshine while others conceal themselves by day.

The Tenebrionidae, which include 60 out of 67 specimens, are represented by 7 out of a total of 11 species, only one of which (*Mesostena puncticollis* Sol.) is at all widely distributed, being a common Egyptian and Arabian insect. Four species were not represented in the British Museum collection until collected recently by Mr. Bertram Thomas in the same region. Two of these four, *Tentyria thomasi* Blr. and *Pimelia arabica* Klug, supsp. *thomasi* Blr., were then described as new. The remaining two species, an *Apentanodes* and a *Rhytinota*, are apparently undescribed. There is also an extremely interesting larva that may be that of a *Sepidium* sp. Unlike most Tenebrionid larvæ it is clothed with long silky hairs and the legs are very strong, flattened, and with immense claws. It is evidently a mighty burrower, probably descending deep into the earth. The larvæ of the subfamily Sepidiinae appear to be completely unknown. The stout, cylindrical yellow larva, resembling a large wire-worm, would perhaps be turned out when digging for water.

Apart from Tenebrionidae, the most interesting beetle is the Dynastid, *Temnorrhynchus* sp., which may also prove to be undescribed.

A list of the beetles as so far provisionally identified is appended.[1]

(a) Tenebrionidae (Desert Beetles).

(1) *Apentanodes philbyi* sp. n. 1 specimen from 'Ain Sala.

(2) *Erodius octocostata* Peyer. *Passim* (45 specimens).

(3) *Erodius reichei* All. 2 specimens from Bani Jallab.

(4) *Tentyria thomasi* Blr. 9 specimens (Madara to Naifa).

(5) *Rhytinota deserticola* sp. n. 1 specimen from Tuwairifa.

(6) *Mesostena puncticollis* Sol. 8 specimens (Shanna and Naifa).

(7) *Pimelia arabica* Klug, subsp. *thomasi* Blr. 1 specimen from Marbakh abu Laila.

[1] For a detailed list of the Tenebrionidae captured by Mr. Philby, with descriptions of new species, see Blair, K. G., in *Ent. Mo. Mag.*, lxix. (1933), pp. 4-7.

(b) Buprestidae.

Psiloptera mimosae Klug. 1 specimen from Abu Khashba. A rather distinct form obtained also by Mr. Bertram Thomas.

(c) Dermestidae.

Dermestes frischi Klug. 1 specimen from 'Ain Sala. One of the ' bacon-beetles ' of almost cosmopolitan distribution. It feeds on dried carcases.

(d) Hybosoridae.

Hybosorus illigeri Rche. 1 specimen from Buraika. A species of wide distribution in S. Europe and Africa, and extending eastwards to India.

(e) Dynastidae.

Temnorrhynchus sp. 4 specimens from Bir Fadhil, Bani Jallab, Qa'amiyat and Hadh Hawaya.

2. BUGS (HEMIPTERA HETEROPTERA) OF THE RUB' AL KHALI.

By W. E. CHINA, M.A.,
Of the British Museum.

(a) Pentatomidae.

Chroantha ornatula H.S. 1 specimen from Numaila. Previously recorded from Arabia (Hadhramaut) by Theodore Bent. Also recorded from many countries of S. Europe, N. Africa and Asia between Spain and Turkestan.

(b) Cydnidae.

Amaurocoris orbicularis Jak. 1 specimen from Qa'amiyat. Recorded from Turkestan and Arabia (Bertram Thomas, 1930).

(c) Capsidae.

(1) *Laemocoris* sp. n. 1 specimen from 'Ain Sala. Allied to L. *zaruduyi* Reut. from Persia. This genus is distributed from Spain, Algeria, Egypt and Persia to Turkestan.

(2) *Tuponia pallida* Reut. Bani Zainan. This species is new to the British Museum collection. It was known only from Turkestan.

(d) Belostomatidae.

(1) *Hydrocyrius columbiae* Spin. (Giant Water Bug). From Hufuf. Previously recorded from the same locality by Cheesman. Also recorded from Masqat and from several African countries from Algeria to Abyssinia and Mozambique.

3. BUTTERFLIES AND MOTHS (LEPIDOPTERA) OF THE RUB' AL KHALI.

(With acknowledgments to Mr. N. D. RILEY, Keeper of the Entomological Department, British Museum.)

(a) Butterflies.

(1) *Apharitis gilletti* Riley (originally described from Somaliland but previously not taken in Arabia, where *A. acamas* Klug occurs in Syria, 'Iraq and Aden as well as in Sind and Egypt). 1 specimen from Khillat Adraj—about a score of others seen at many localities in district of Al Rimal.

(2) *Pyrameis Cardui*. 1 specimen seen near Naifa but not taken.

(b) Moths.

		Specimens.
Sphingidae	*Macroglossa stellatarum.* 1 seen at 'Ain Sala but not taken.	
Agrotinae	*Chloridae peltigera* Schiff.	1
,,	*Euxoa saracenica* Tams	1
Hadeninae	*Scotogramma trifolii* Roths	1
Erastranae	*Tarache hortensis* Swinh.	1
Catocalinae	*Leucanitis cabylaria* B. Haas	1
,,	*Anydrophila* ? sp. n. near *simiola* Pang.	1
Ophiderinae	*Anumeta stramineata* B. Haas	2
,,	,, ? sp. n. near *spatzyi* Roths	1
,,	,, ? sp. n. near *cestis* Menat	4
,,	,, ? sp. n. near *hilgerti* Christ.	49
,,	,, ? sp. n. near *spilota* Ersch.	64
,,	*Tathorhynchus exsiccata* Led.	2
Lasiocampidae	*Chilena* ? sp. n. near *geyri* Roths	1
Anerastünae	*Saluria* ? sp. n.	1
,,	,, ? sp. n.	2
Phycitinae	*Lardamia biformis* Roths	6
,,	*Heteregraphis* ? sp. n.	28
,,	,, ? sp. n. near *costabella*	1
,,	*Ancylosis* ? sp. n.	2
,,	*Ortholepis* ? sp. n.	1
Larentünae	*Eupithecia* ? sp. n.	1
,,	,, ? sp. n.	1
,,	,, ? sp. n.	1
Sterrhinae	*Evis* ? sp. n.	6

N.B.—It is worthy of note that, of the 180 moths listed above and representing 25 species, no fewer than 16 species, comprising 164 moths, cannot for the moment be referred to any known species. Further study may reduce the suspected number of new species but it is evident that the Rub' al Khali has developed a strikingly peculiar lepidopterous fauna.

4. FLIES (DIPTERA) OF THE RUB' AL KHALI.

(With acknowledgments to Miss AUBERTIN of the British Museum.)

(a) Calliphoridae.

(1) *Rhynchomyia callopsis* Loewe. 1 ♂.

(2) 3 ♂ of a creature, probably referable to the genus Araba, from Bani Zainan. Miss Aubertin says ' she has never seen anything like these before, and does not quite know what to make of them.'

(b) Tachinidae.

1 specimen of an unidentifiable Tachinid.

5. GRASSHOPPERS (ORTHOPTERA) OF THE RUB' AL KHALI.

(With acknowledgments to Mr. B. P. UVAROV of the British Museum.)

(a) Mantidae.

(1) *Eremiaphila laevifrons*, Uvar. A single adult from Shuqqat al Khalfat, and numerous indeterminable larvæ, perhaps of the same species, from six widely scattered localities. Originally described from Masqat.

(2) *Genus* ?, *probably new*, but only one immature specimen collected from Naifa.

(b) Acrididae.

(1) *Schistocerca gregaria*, Forsk. Desert Locust. Specimens from five localities in Al Rimal.

(2) *Platypterna pictipes*, Uvar. 1 specimen from Shuqqat al Khalfat. Described from Masqat and also taken by me at Jidda.

6. WASPS, BEES, ETC. (HYMENOPTERA) FROM THE RUB' AL KHALI, COLLECTED BY MR. PHILBY.

BY MR. HUGH SCOTT,
Of the British Museum.

So far as it is possible to draw conclusions from the material, these Hymenoptera are southern Palaearctic forms, with little or no Ethiopian or Oriental affinity. It is noteworthy that one widely spread species of ant is represented in the Rub' al Khali by a variety previously recorded from Syria (*i.e.* Palaearctic), but in the Qara Mts. by a subspecies widely distributed in Tropical Africa. This may indicate a certain line of division between the faunas of the southern coastal mountains of Arabia and the desert to the north of them. But as many of the species are represented by single or very few specimens, and can only be referred to their genera, without more precise determination, it is risky to generalise too much.

(a) *Ichneumonidae* (*Ophioninae*).

(1) *Ophion* sp. from Madara. 1 specimen.

(2) *Hemicospilus* sp. 4 specimens from 'Ain Sala, Hadh Faris and Hawaya. These do not agree with any named species in the British Museum.

(b) *Braconidae* (*Cheloninae*).

Phanerotoma sp. 1 from Madara.

(c) *Eumenidae*.

(Solitary true wasps.)

Odynerus sp. near *O. floricola* Sauss. 1 from 'Ain Sala.

(d) *Pompilidae* (*Psammocharidae*).

(Solitary fossorial wasps preying on spiders, with which they provision their nests.)

(1) *Platyderes* sp. 1 from Bani Jafnan.

(2) *Pompilus* sp. near *P. platyacanthus* Kohl. 1 from 'Ain Sala.

(e) *Scoliidae*.

(Solitary parasitic wasps. In cases where the habits of these insects are known they are parasitic on the larvæ of beetles of the Cockchafer type, but this may not apply to the genus referred to here.)

Iswara sp., possibly *I. chobauti* André, a species recorded from Baluchistan. 7 specimens (all males) from Bani Jallab, Wabar, Shanna, Naifa and Qa'amiyat. The males in this genus are fully winged and, presumably, good fliers ; the females are short-winged and probably quite unable to fly.

(f) *Bees*.

Megachile sp. (a small leaf-cutter bee). 1 specimen from Abal Khadim.

(g) *Ants*.

(1) *Camponotus* (*Tanaemyrmex*) *compressus* F., subsp. *thoracicus* F. From 'Ain Sala (1 soldier, 2 large workers, 1 small worker). Exactly the same subspecies was obtained by Bertram Thomas in the Qara mountains. Previously recorded from the deserts of Algeria and Tunisia.

(2) *Messor barbarus* L., subsp. *semirufus* André, var. *nigriceps* Santschi. 3 workers from Tuwairifa. This form of the species was previously recorded from Palestine. The form of *Messor barbarus* obtained by Bertram Thomas in the Qara mountains is different, and is distributed through Abyssinia, the Sudan and Tropical Africa.

(3) *Crematogaster (Sphaerocrema)* sp. 7 females from Bir Fadhil, Madara, Abu Khashba and Hawaya. This species, unfortunately indeterminable in the female sex alone, was also obtained by Bertram Thomas in the Rub' al Khali. The venation of the forewings is abnormal, the discoidal cell being absent ; and it may eventually prove necessary to create a separate subgenus or genus for this species.

(4) *Crematogaster (Acrocoelia) auberti* Emery, subsp. *jehovae* Forel. 2 workers from Bani Zainan. This subspecies was previously recorded from Palestine.

(h) *Termite.*

A single dilated individual of the winged caste from Bani Zainan—indeterminable without more material.

J. FLORA OF THE RUB' AL KHALI.

(With acknowledgments to Mr. J. RAMSBOTTOM, Keeper of the Botanical Department, British Museum.)

Arabic Name.	Scientific Name.
Abal -	- *Calligonum* sp.
Ādhir -	- {*Artemisia monosperma* Del. {*Artemisia scoparia* Waldst. and Kir.
Alqa -	- *Dipterygium glaucum* Decne.
Andab -	- *Cyperus conglomeratus* Rottb.
'Āqūl -	- {*Prosopis stephaniana* Kunth. {*Prosopis* sp.
Arfaj -	- {*Francoeuria crispa* Cuss. {*Rhanterium suaeveolens* Desf.
'Arrād -	-
Arta -	- *Calligonum comosum* L'Herit.
Birkan -	- *Fagonia glutinosa* Del.
Dhā'a -	- *Lasiutus hirsutus* (Forsk.) Boiss.
Dhānūn (Dhanūn or Idhnūn)	*Phelipaea lutea* Desf.
Dhumrān -	*Traganum mudatum* Del.
Duraima -	*Fagonia cretica* L. (also *Fagonia mollis* Del.)
Fānī -	-
Ghadhā -	- ? *Arthrocnemon fruticosum* Moq.
Ghāf -	- *Phragmites communis* Trin.
Hādh -	- *Cornulacea monacantha* Del.
Halam -	-
Hamdh -	- ? *Zygophyllum album.*
Harm -	-
Harmal -	- *Rhazya stricta* Decne.
Ithil -	- *Tamarix* sp. Cf. *T. articulata* Vahl.

Khīs (Khīsa) - Dwarf palm.
Kurraish -
Markh - -
Namas - - *Juncus maritimus* Lam.
Nussi - - *Aristida* sp.
Qarnua - - aff. *Erodium bryonifolium* Boiss.
Qasab - - *Graminea indet.*
Qataf - -

Ramrām - { *Heliotropium europaeum* var. *tenuiflorum* (Guss.) Boiss.
Heliotropium lignosum.
Heliotropium sp. aff. *hispidum* Forsk.
heliotropium sp.

Rimdh - -
Sabat - - *Aristida* sp.
Sa'dān - - *Neurada procumbens* L.
Salam - - { *Acacia asak* Willd.
Acacia flava Schweinf.
Samr - - { *Acacia laeta* R. Br. (pods).
Acacia tortilis Hayne (branch).
Sarh (Sarha) - *Maerua uniflora* Vahl.
Shinān - - ? *Seidlitzia rosmarinus* Bunge.
Suwwād - - ? *Suaeda vermiculata* Forsk.
Tarfa - - *Tamarix gallica* L.
Tarthūth - *Cynomorium coccineum.*
Thamām - - ? *Graminea* sp.
Thullaith - *Halapeplis perfoliata* (Forsk.) Bge.
Zahr - - *Tribulus macropterus* Boiss.

K. LIST OF LOCALITIES, HITHERTO NAMELESS, TO WHICH NAMES WERE ASSIGNED BY THE EXPEDITION.

(1) Raudhat al Rumh (in Summan, near Maqainama)—bronze arrow-head found here.

(2) Raqqat al Shalfa (in Al Rimal, north of Numaila)—flint implements found.

(3) Shuqqat abu Nahār (in Al Rimal, south of Numaila)—bushy pasture land.

(4) Bir Maqran (near Tuwairifa)—buried well in gravelly valley bed.

(5) Bir Mukassar (near western edge of Bani Mukassar tract)—buried well in gravel patch.

(6) Bir al Makhfi (west of 'Ain Sala)—exposed rock in sands and suspected buried well.

(7) Al Sailān (near 'Ain Sala)—exposed rocky patch, possibly site of forgotten well.

(8) Al Manīfa (near 'Ain Sala)—prominent rocky hillock in horseshoe hollow of sands.

(9) Bir Jafnān (at northern edge of Bani Jafnan tract)—(?) buried well.

(10) Umm al Qurūn (south of Bir Jafnan)—conspicuous exposure of white gypsum.

(11) Umm al Sahanain (south of Umm al Qurūn)—two flat circular exposures of gypsum.

(12) Umm Tīna (north of Shanna)—exposure of gritty alluvial soil with flint flakes and fragments of stony meteorite.

(13) Abu Muhairāt (at western edge of Al Qatarat)—large deposits of freshwater shells.

(14) Abu Sabbān (west of Abu Muhairāt)—deposits of freshwater shells.

(15) Wadi Hawāya (in Hadhat al Hawaya)—a series of four valley-like troughs with exposures of the rock-bottom.

(16) Bir Hawāya (in Khillat al Hawaya)—suspected buried well.

L. LAND ALTITUDES IN RUB' AL KHALI.

Note.—This list, prepared from my aneroid and hypsometer readings by the staff of the Royal Geographical Society, should be regarded as provisional.

+ = above sea-level   − = below sea-level   ? = estimated altitude

Altitude in feet.	Locality.	Remarks.
Sea-level.	'Ūqair.	on coast.
+425	Hufuf.	town.
+470	Qasr Dulaiqiya.	
+420	Bir Nabit.	
+250?	Ba'aij wells.	camp at +325.
Sea-level.	Salwa.	on coast.
+140	Qarn Abu Waïl.	top of isolated hill.
− 20	Sikak.	at foot of above.
+140	Abu Arzila well.	
− 5	Anbak.	bed of estuary.
+120	Judairat well.	
+225	Hafaïr ibn al Adham well.	
+450	Qadha well.	
+510	Wadi Sahba.	camp in channel.
+560	Surr al Ma'id.	in channel.
+415	Birkan well.	camp at +580?
+450	Khin village.	
+490	Jabrin (Umm al Ramād).	{ Major Cheesman's altitude for this locality +604.
+570	Qasr ibn Dahbash.	
+635	Hafaïr wells (Jabrin basin).	
+670	Dharbun summit.	foot of ridge +550?
+615	Qaliba well.	
+585	'Uj well.	
+680	Bir ibn Juhaiyim.	
+850	Maqainama well.	
+775	Bīr Fadhil.	
+855	Shuqqat al Khalfat.	shell deposit.
+800	Numaila well.	
+600	Tuwairifa well.	
+765	Wabar craters.	
+590	Faraja well.	
+680	Umm al Hadid well.	
+660	Ibrahima well.	
+785	Majari Tasrat valley.	camp.
+600	Majari Ma'shiya valley.	camp.
+790	Khillat Judair.	camp.

Altitude in feet.	*Locality.*	*Remarks.*
+730	'Uruq Bani Jallāb.	camp.
+525	'Ain Sala well.	
+510	Naifa well.	
+555	Ziqirt well.	
+925	Umm al Qurūn.	gypsum exposure.
+960	Umm al Tina.	exposure of bed-rock.
+925	Shanna well.	
+910	Bir ibn Suwailim.	
+930	Mamura well.	
+940	Zuwaira well.	
+960	Turaiwa well.	
+1080	Qatarat.	camp on sandy downs.
+980	Abu Muhairat.	shell deposit.
+1195	Hibaka Qa'amiyat.	camp on downs.
+1050	Abu Sabban.	shell deposit.
+1230	Abal Khadim.	camp on downs.
+1340	Khillat Hawaya.	camp on downs.
+1280	Hadhat Hawaya.	camp in depression.
+1450	Qasbat Hawaya.	camp on downs.
+1350	Khillat Hawaya.	camp on downs.
+1110	Khillat Adraj.	camp on downs.
+510	Naifa well.	see above.
+1110	Khillat Adraj.	camp on downs.
+1010	Bani Zainan.	camp on downs.
+1280	Hadhat Hawaya.	eastern edge.
+1085	Hadhat Hawaya.	western edge.
+1145	Sahma gravel plain.	true desert surface.
+1360	Bani Ma'aridh.	camp on downs.
+1345	Abu Bahr gravel plain.	eastern edge.
+1645	Abu Bahr gravel plain.	western edge.
+1870	Rumaila sand downs.	western edge.
+1900	Jiddat al Farsha.	camp on steppe.
+2125	Farsha channel.	camp.
+2135	Sulaiyil.	oasis.

N.B.—Where different altitudes are given for localities of a single name they refer to camps in different parts of the same region.

M. DIVISIONS OF MURRA TRIBE.

Section.	Chief Shaikh.	Sub-section.	Shaikhs and Notables.
A. Al Ghafrān. (600)	Hamad ibn Sālih ibn Jallāb.	1. Al 'Uwair.	Hamad ibn Sālih ibn Jallāb. Faraj al 'Uwair. Sālih ibn 'Ali al 'Uwair. 'Ali ibn Sālih al Jahmān. Muhammad ibn Humaiyid. Sālih ibn 'Ali Abū Laila. Hamad ibn Sultān ibn Hādi. Sa'id ibn al Uhaimir. Sālim ibn Sa'id al Dimāgh. Hamad ibn Muhammad ibn Suwailih.
		2. Āl Zāyid.	
		3. Al Burais.	
		4. Al Buqaih.	
		5. Al Bannā.	
		6. Al Nifl.	
		7. Al Shaiba.	
B. Al 'Adhba. (400)	Faisal ibn 'Abdullāh ibn 'Abdul Rahmān ibn Nuqaidān.	1. Al Mansūr.	Faisal ibn Nuqaidān. Sālim ibn Nuqaidān.
		2. Al Jufaish.	Jābir ibn Hamad ibn Barjis ibn Hanzāb.
		3. Al Fāris.	Hazzā' ibn Hazzā'. ? Fādhil (author of Bir Fādhil). ? —— ibn Huqai. ? —— ibn 'Afair.
		4. Al 'Afair.	Mit'ab ibn Sa'āq. ? —— ibn al Adham.
C. Al Buhaih. (500)	Mit'ab ibn Muhammad ibn Sa'āq (ibn Simra).	1. Al Simra.	

Section.	Chief Shaikh.	Sub-section.	Shaikhs and Notables.
C. Al Buhaih.—*Contd.*		2. Al Sunaid.	Muhammad ibn ʿAdaiya.
		3. Al Hasana.	Rāshid ibn Andaila (? Nudaila).
		4. Al Saʿīd.	Muhammad al Hutail.
		5. Āl Sālih ibn Dharfās.	Tālib al Muhanna.
		6. Al Hunaitim.	Mitʿab ibn Munakhkhas.
		7. Al Juhaish.	Suwīd ibn al Hawal.
		8. Al Buraid.	ʿAli al Madhūs.
		9. Al Suwaihit.	Jābir ibn Faraj (deceased).
		10. Al Zaqība.	(?) Muhammad ibn Luhaim.
		11. Al Rāshid.	Muhammad ibn Rāshid.
			ʿAli ibn (?) Sālih.
D. Al Jarrāba. (300)	Hamad ibn Nahhāb.	1. Al Jabrān.	Saʿīd ibn Fasl (dead).
			Jābir ibn Sālim ibn Fasl.
			Sālim ibn Fasl.
		2. Al Najm.	Muhammad al Haswān.
		3. Al Nābit.	Mubārak ibn Rāshid ibn Māʿyuf.
		4. Al Ghayāthīn.	Saʿīd ibn Saʿīd al Harair.
		5. Al Bazzām.	ʿAli ibn Khamīs.
E. Al Hutaila. (50)	Muhammad ibn Suwailih.	*No Sub-sections (?)*	Possibly same as Saʿīd sub-section of Al Buhaih.
F. Al Dimnān. (60)	Suwīd ibn Hādi al Azma.	1. Al Azma (?).	Suwīd al Azma.
			Sālim ibn Suwailim.
		2. Al Dhakma.	Muhammad ibn ʿAli al Dhakma.
		3. Al Khaiyārīn.	ʿAli ibn Nāshir.

Section.	Chief Shaikh.	Sub-section.	Shaikhs and Notables.
G. Al Jābir. (300)	Faisal ibn Hamad al Muradhdhaf.	1. Al Zuqaima.	Faisal al Muradhdhaf. ? 'Uwaida ibn Adhaimān. ? Āidh ibn Uzra. ? 'Ali ibn Juhaiyim. ? Sālih ibn Minya. ? Salih ibn —— ?
		2. Al Hādi ibn Hamad.	Dhaighām ibn Hajjāj. 'Ali abū Sāq.
		3. Al Ghadhwān.	Hamad ibn Nautān.
		4. Al Miqlin.	? Sa'ūd ibn Qurai. ? 'Ali ibn Dahbāsh. ? Hādi ibn Shadūk. ? Sālim ibn Jābir.
H. Al Fuhaida (Al Bishr?) (400)	Lāhūm ibn Shuraim.	1. Al Shafi'.	Lāhūm ibn Shuraim.
		2. Al Shāfi'.	'Ali ibn Jilmūd.
		3. Al 'Azib.	'Ali ibn Handhal.
		4. Al Numai'ān.	Sālih ibn Rashdān.
		5. Al Ghānim ibn Hādi.	Bajjāsh ibn Hamad.

N.B.—The figures in brackets under the name of each section are a rough estimate of the number of tents (i.e. families) comprising each according to my informants, 'Ali ibn Jahmān and Suwīd al Azma. Assuming an average of four persons per family the population of the Murra tribe would be 10,440 (say

10,000) souls for the 2610 tents claimed. This estimate is probably somewhat exaggerated and perhaps 5000 souls would be a nearer estimate of the total tribal strength. The sections are distributed geographically as follows :—

Ghafrān	Shanna neighbourhood and Al Khirān.
ʿAdhba	Jībān and neighbourhood down to Bīr Fādhil.
Buhaih	Jāfūra.
Jarrāba	Wabār and central part of Al Rimāl.
Hutaila	Hasā province (?).
Dimnān	Waterless desert from Maqainama to Najrān.
Jābir	Jabrīn and district.
Fuhaida	Hasā province (?)

INDEX

(N.B.—All long vowels only are marked.)

413

Leather, 115, 136, 137, 145, 169, 193, 227, 267, 278, 290, 292, 301
— butter-jug, 281
Lees, Dr. G. M., 123, 291
Libyan Desert, xx, 57, 99, 114, 140, 175, 326, 327, 329
Lice, 293
Lightning, 286, 287, 293, 295, 297, 306, 357
— -tubes, see Fulgurite
Limestone, 8, 62, 66, 111, 112, 121, 170, 213
Lion, Constellation of, xxii, 351, 352
Līwā, see Jiwā
Lizard, 62, 83, 102, 124, 144, 229, 244, 253, 255, 257, 259, 312, 317, 347, 354, 397, 398
—, Spiny-tailed, 352
Locust, 30, 38, 39, 49, 83, 113, 145, 183, 347, 402
— -lore, Badawīn, 38
London, 91, 171
Longitude, 196, 197, 202, 319
Lowe, Dr. P. R., 113, 390-392
Lucerne, 363
Luhaim, Muhammad ibn, 38
Luminosity of atmosphere, q.v.
Luwai, Khālid ibn, 74, 331
Luxor (= Al Iqsar), 163

M

Mā, Rijm al (cairn), 355
Ma'ābida (quarter of Mecca), 349
Ma'addī, 'Abdullāh ibn (chaplain of expedition), 8, 9, 11, 18, 50, 56, 62, 130, 135, 154, 184, 200, 202, 235, 263, 324, 358
Ma'āridh, Banī (sand-tract), 86, 318, 323, 332, 333, 334, 335, 336, 337
' Mabaq ' = Anbāk, q.v.
Madāïn Sālih, q.v.
Madāra (sand-region), 134
Madīna, xx, 50, 204
Madjūb, Hājj (Rohlfs' guide), 328
Magan (or Maganna), 119, 120, 121
Mahādīr Summān, q.v.
Mahāmil (desert), 127
Mahdār Hamda, q.v.
Mahmal (district in Najd), 127
Mahmīd, Zubāra (sand-ridge), 31
Mahra (tribe), 34
Ma'jaba (palms), 94
Majann (? ruins), 67, 79, 103, 120, 121

Majārī Ma'shīya, q.v.
— Tasrat, q.v.
Mājid (slave), 361
Majma'a (capital of Sudair), 5, 314
Makhfī, Bīr al (? well), 201
Makīka (dish of rice and Abal sprouts), 171, 196, 278
Makīnīya (rock-pools), 125, 348
Mālikī (school of Islām), 77
Mammals, 394
Māmūra (well), 244
Manāhīl (Manhālī) tribe, 11, 103, 196, 214, 226, 231
Manāsīr (tribe), 10, 28, 33, 34, 38, 48, 49, 52, 57, 58, 77, 78, 81, 130, 132, 171, 173, 189, 278, 310
—, Abal Sha'r group of, 57
—, Āl bū Mandhar group of, 10, 57
—, — — Rahma group of, 10, 57, 58
Mandhar, Āl bū, see Manāsīr
Mānī, al 'Abd ibn, 58
—, Rāshid al 'Abd ibn, 49, 57, 58, 63
—, Rāshid ibn, 58
Manīfa (hillock near 'Ain Sala), 202
— (ridge in Jafūra), 24
Manjūr, al (well and sand-region), 183
Manjūrat al Hādī, q.v.
Manna, 116
Manqā, al (dry swamp), 359
Mantids, 30, 37, 62, 71, 133, 170, 172, 320, 338, 402
Mantle (Bisht), 249, 255, 285, 303, 316, 329
Map (Mapping, etc.), xxii, xxiii, 40, 47, 62, 71, 73, 88, 89, 91, 92, 129, 137, 140, 158, 160, 164, 168, 174, 197, 201, 211, 244, 298, 317
Maqainama (well), 6, 74, 85, 103, 109-126, 127, 134, 137, 139, 143, 146, 148, 163, 192, 228, 236, 264, 294, 319, 330, 331, 336, 346, 348
— (well in N. Hasā), 119
—, Ramla (sand-region), 131, 133
Maqarr al Suqūr, q.v.
Maqran, Bīr, 147
—, Wādī, 140, 147, 148, 228
' Maradvath ' = Muradhdhaf, q.v.
Marbakh (pasture-land), 35, 344
— abū Laila, q.v.
— al Sa'qa, q.v.
Marshad, 'Ain ibn (spring), 97
Ma'rūf the Cobbler, see Arabian Nights

INDEX

433

185, 186, 187, 188, 189, 191,
196, 197, 201, 203, 209, 211,
215, 216, 219, 220, 221, 222,
225, 230, 231, 233, 235, 243,
245, 254, 255, 256, 257, 264,
265, 266, 271, 273, 274, 275,
277, 281, 282, 285, 289, 292,
294, 297, 302, 305, 309, 312,
313, 314, 325, 326, 329, 330,
333, 339, 340, 341, 342, 344,
349, 353, 354, 355, 357, 359,
360, 362
Zāyid (subsection of Ghafrān), 59, 145

Zibda (wells), 71, 72
Zilfī, 244
Zinc ointment, 75
Ziqirt (wells), 104, 186, 194, 196,
201, 203, 207, 209, 210, 211,
212, 214, 217, 229, 236, 246
— (= gens d'armes), 214
—, Hamrān (dune-ranges), 209, 212
—, Hawāïr al (depression), 214
Zones, Plant, 131, 258, 259, 271,
280
Zubāra Mahmīd, q.v.
Zuwaira (well), 244, 245, 246